HORROR

HORROR
ANOTHER 100 BEST BOOKS

EDITED BY
Stephen Jones and Kim Newman

WITH A FOREWORD BY
Peter Straub

CARROLL & GRAF PUBLISHERS
NEW YORK

HORROR: *Another 100 Best Books*
Copyright © Stephen Jones and Kim Newman, 2005.

Published by
Carroll & Graf
An Imprint of Avalon Publishing Group Incorporated
245 West 17th Street • 11th Floor
New York, NY 10011-5300

All rights reserved. No part of this book may be reproduced in whole or in part without written permission from the publisher, except by reviewers who may quote brief excerpts in connection with a review in a newspaper, magazine, or electronic publication; nor may any part of this book be reproduced, stored in a retrieval system, or transmitted in any form or by any means electronic, mechanical, photocopying, recording, or other, without written permission from the publisher.

Library of Congress Cataloging-in-Publication Data is available.

ISBN: 0-7867-1577-4

9 8 7 6 5 4 3 2 1

Designed by India Amos, Neuwirth & Associates

Printed in the United States of America

CONTENTS

Foreword by PETER STRAUB • xiii

Introduction: It Seemed Like a Simple Idea at the Time...
by STEPHEN JONES and KIM NEWMAN • xvii

1 **Robert Silverberg** on *The Revenger's Tragedy*
by CYRIL TOURNEUR [1607] • 1

2 **Chelsea Quinn Yarbro** on *Pikovaia Dama/The Queen of Spades*
by ALEKSANDR PUSHKIN [1834] • 5

3 **Elizabeth Hand** on *A Christmas Carol*
by CHARLES DICKENS [1843] • 9

4 **Doug Bradley** on *Jane Eyre*
by CHARLOTTE BRONTË [1847] • 14

5 **Jay Lake** on *Rekopiz Znaleziony w Saragossie/
The Manuscript Found in Saragossa*
by JAN, COUNT POTOCKI [1847] • 20

6 **K. W. Jeter** on *New Grub Street*
by GEORGE GISSING [1891] • 24

7 **David J. Skal** on *The Picture of Dorian Gray*
by OSCAR WILDE [1891] • 29

8 **Les Edwards** on *The War of the Worlds*
by H. G. WELLS [1898] • 34

9 **Tony Richards** on *The Hound of the Baskervilles*
by SIR ARTHUR CONAN DOYLE [1902] • 39

10 **Rick Hautala** on *The Boats of the "Glen Carrig"*
by WILLIAM HOPE HODGSON [1907] • 43

CONTENTS

11 **Jean-Marc Lofficier and Randy Lofficier** on *Le fantôme de l'Opéra/The Phantom of the Opera*
by GASTON LEROUX [1911] • 47

12 **Tim Lucas** on *Fantômas*
by PIERRE SOUVESTRE and MARCEL ALLAIN [1911] • 50

13 **Christopher Wicking** on *The Case of Charles Dexter Ward*
by H. P. LOVECRAFT [1927–28] • 55

14 **Barbara Roden and Christopher Roden** on *They Return at Evening*
by H. R. WAKEFIELD [1928] • 60

15 **Sydney J. Bounds** on *Creep, Shadow!*
by A. MERRITT [1934] • 64

16 **Chaz Brenchley** on *The Trail of Fu Manchu*
by SAX ROHMER [1934] • 69

17 **Stephen Volk** on *The Devil Rides Out*
by DENNIS WHEATLEY [1934] • 73

18 **Gahan Wilson** on *The Haunted Omnibus*
ed. ALEXANDER LAING [1937] • 78

19 **Robert Weinberg** on *The Edge of Running Water*
by WILLIAM SLOANE [1939] • 82

20 **T. M. Wright** on *L'Étranger/The Stranger*
by ALBERT CAMUS [1942] • 86

21 **David A. Sutton** on *Sleep No More: Twenty Masterpieces of Horror for the Connoisseur*
ed. AUGUST DERLETH [1944] • 90

22 **Storm Constantine** on *Lost Worlds*
by CLARK ASHTON SMITH [1944] • 95

23 **Stefan Dziemianowicz** on *Jumbee and Other Uncanny Tales*
by HENRY S. WHITEHEAD [1944] • 99

24 **Gwyneth Jones** on *Great Tales of Terror and the Supernatural*
ed. HERBERT A. WISE and PHYLLIS FRASER [1944] • 104

CONTENTS

25 Joel Lane on *The Opener of the Way*
by ROBERT BLOCH [1945] • 108

26 Christopher Fowler on *Gormenghast*
by MERVYN PEAKE [1946–50] • 113

27 Gary Gianni on *Carnacki the Ghost-Finder*
by WILLIAM HOPE HODGSON [1947] • 117

28 Randy Broecker on *Darker Than You Think*
by JACK WILLIAMSON [1948] • 121

29 Tanith Lee on *Tales of Horror and the Supernatural*
by ARTHUR MACHEN [1949] • 125

30 Lucius Shepard on *Nineteen Eighty-four*
by GEORGE ORWELL [1949] • 130

31 David Bischoff on *House of Flesh*
by BRUNO FISCHER [1950] • 136

32 Anne Billson on *Fancies and Goodnights*
by JOHN COLLIER [1951] • 141

33 Nancy A. Collins on *The Killer Inside Me*
by JIM THOMPSON [1952] • 145

34 Laurence Staig on *The Third Ghost Book*
ed. LADY CYNTHIA ASQUITH [1955] • 149

35 Andy Duncan on *The Body Snatchers*
by JACK FINNEY [1955] • 153

36 John Gordon on *The Talented Mr. Ripley*
by PATRICIA HIGHSMITH [1955] • 157

37 Norman Partridge on *The Hunger and Other Stories*
by CHARLES BEAUMONT [1957] • 161

38 Robert Irwin on *The Blind Owl*
by SADEGH HEDAYAT [1957] • 166

39 Mark Morris on *The Midwich Cuckoos*
by JOHN WYNDHAM [1957] • 169

CONTENTS

40 **Howard Waldrop** on *A Scent of New-Mown Hay*
by JOHN BLACKBURN [1958] • 173

41 **Ed Gorman** on *A Stir of Echoes*
by RICHARD MATHESON [1958] • 178

42 **Muriel Gray** on *The Weirdstone of Brinsingamen*
by ALAN GARNER [1960] • 181

43 **Terry Dowling** on *Tales of Terror*
ed. CHARLES HIGHAM [1961] • 185

44 **Peter Atkins** on *Some of Your Blood*
by THEODORE STURGEON [1961] • 189

45 **Jack Womack** on *We Have Always Lived in the Castle*
by SHIRLEY JACKSON [1962] • 193

46 **Darrell Schweitzer** on *The Case Against Satan*
by RAY RUSSELL [1962] • 197

47 **Peter Crowther** on *Something Wicked This Way Comes*
by RAY BRADBURY [1963] • 200

48 **Ian MacLeod** on *The Collector*
by JOHN FOWLES [1963] • 204

49 **Glen Hirshberg** on *Who Fears the Devil?*
by MANLY WADE WELLMAN [1963] • 208

50 **Simon Clark** on *A Wrinkle in the Skin*
by JOHN CHRISTOPHER [1965] • 212

51 **Nancy Holder** on *Rosemary's Baby*
by IRA LEVIN [1967] • 215

52 **Ellen Datlow** on *The* Playboy *Book of Horror and the Supernatural*
Selected by THE EDITORS OF PLAYBOY [1967] • 219

53 **Terry Lamsley** on *Pages from Cold Point*
by PAUL BOWLES [1968] • 224

54 **John Farris** on *Outer Dark*
by CORMAC MCCARTHY [1968] • 228

CONTENTS

55 Stephen Baxter on *The Book of Skulls*
by ROBERT SILVERBERG [1971] • 231

56 Elizabeth Massie on *Harvest Home*
by THOMAS TRYON [1973] • 235

57 P. N. Elrod on *The Night Stalker*
by JEFF RICE [1973] • 239

58 Michael Swanwick on *Blood Sport*
by ROBERT F. JONES [1974] • 243

59 Nicholas Royle on *Nightshade*
by DEREK MARLOWE [1975] • 246

60 Roz Kaveney on *Peace*
by GENE WOLFE [1975] • 250

61 David Drake on *The Year of the Sex Olympics: Three TV Plays*
by NIGEL KNEALE [1976] • 253

62 Marc Laidlaw on *Our Lady of Darkness*
by FRITZ LEIBER [1977] • 257

63 Paul McAuley on *The Cement Garden*
by IAN McEWAN [1978] • 260

64 Jo Fletcher on *Darkness Weaves With Many Shades*
by KARL EDWARD WAGNER [1978] • 264

65 Sir Christopher Frayling on *The Bloody Chamber and Other Stories*
by ANGELA CARTER [1979] • 269

66 Thomas Ligotti on *Sweeney Todd*
by STEPHEN SONDHEIM and HUGH WHEELER [1979] • 274

67 D. F. Lewis on *The Collected Stories of Elizabeth Bowen*
by ELIZABETH BOWEN [1980] • 278

68 Christopher Golden on *Dark Forces: New Stories of Suspense and Supernatural Horror*
ed. KIRBY McCAULEY [1980] • 282

CONTENTS

69 **John Burke** on *Tales from the Nightside*
by CHARLES L. GRANT [1981] • 286

70 **Yvonne Navarro** on *They Thirst*
by ROBERT R. McCAMMON [1981] • 290

71 **Poppy Z. Brite** on *The Face That Must Die*
by RAMSEY CAMPBELL [1983] • 294

72 **David Stuart Davies** on *The Woman in Black*
by SUSAN HILL [1983] • 298

73 **Michael Marshall Smith** on *Pet Sematary*
by STEPHEN KING [1983] • 301

74 **Anthony Timpone** on *Clive Barker's Books of Blood Volumes One, Two, and Three*
by CLIVE BARKER [1984] • 306

75 **Nancy Kilpatrick** on *Perfume: The Story of a Murderer*
by PATRICK SÜSKIND [1986] • 310

76 **Bill Sheehan** on *Finishing Touches*
by THOMAS TESSIER [1986] • 314

77 **Kelly Link** on *Strange Toys*
by PATRICIA GEARY [1987] • 317

78 **Allen Koszowski** on *The Dark Descent*
ed. DAVID G. HARTWELL [1987] • 321

79 **Graham Joyce** on *Misery*
by STEPHEN KING [1987] • 325

80 **Frank M. Robinson** on *The Silence of the Lambs*
by THOMAS HARRIS [1988] • 329

81 **Mark Chadbourn** on *Prime Evil*
ed. DOUGLAS E. WINTER [1988] • 334

82 **Jay Russell** on *By Bizarre Hands: Stories by Joe R. Lansdale*
by JOE R. LANSDALE [1989] • 338

83 **Peter H. Cannon** on *The Grotesque*
by PATRICK McGRATH [1989] • 342

CONTENTS

84 **David Morrell** on *Carrion Comfort*
by DAN SIMMONS [1989] • 345

85 **Stephen R. Bissette** on *From Hell*
by ALAN MOORE and EDDIE CAMPBELL
[1989–99] • 349

86 **David McGillivray** on *American Psycho*
by BRET EASTON ELLIS [1991] • 354

87 **Brian Hodge** on *Lost Souls*
by POPPY Z. BRITE [1992] • 358

88 **China Miéville** on *The Course of the Heart*
by M. JOHN HARRISON [1992] • 362

89 **Adam Simon** on *Flicker*
by THEODORE ROSZAK [1992] • 366

90 **Paul Di Filippo** on *X, Y*
by MICHAEL BLUMLEIN [1993] • 371

91 **Caitlín R. Kiernan** on *Skin*
by KATHE KOJA [1993] • 375

92 **Tananarive Due** on *Throat Sprockets: A Novel of Erotic Obsession*
by TIM LUCAS [1994] • 378

93 **Simon R. Green** on *The Off Season: A Victorian Sequel*
by JACK CADY [1995] • 382

94 **S. T. Joshi** on *The Nightmare Factory*
by THOMAS LIGOTTI [1996] • 385

95 **Roberta Lannes** on *A Sight for Sore Eyes*
by RUTH RENDELL [1998] • 389

96 **Michael Shea** on *Reprisal*
by MITCHELL SMITH [1999] • 393

97 **John Pelan** on *A Haunting Beauty*
by SIR CHARLES BIRKIN [2000] • 397

98 **Jeff VanderMeer** on *House of Leaves*
by MARK Z. DANIELEWSKI [2000] • 401

CONTENTS

99 Richard A. Lupoff on *Feesters in the Lake & Other Stories*
by BOB LEMAN [2002] • 406

100 Tim Lebbon on *More Tomorrow & Other Stories*
by MICHAEL MARSHALL SMITH [2003] • 411

Lists of Recommended Reading • 415

    Appendix I: *Horror: 100 Best Books* • 415

    Appendix II: Further Reading • 419

Selected Webliography • 438

About the Editors • 445

Index to the Books, Authors, and Contributors • 447

Acknowledgments • 453

FOREWORD

Peter Straub

EVER SAVVY, ALSO incredibly well informed, Stephen Jones and Kim Newman have chosen to bring out this companion volume to their 1988 collection *Horror: 100 Best Books*, at what seems to me exactly the right time, which is to say the moment at which a sophisticated contemporary reader might well come to the startling recognition that the one hundred most significant, most interesting books in the sprawling, multiform, definition-shedding field of horror might well be substantially different from any such list compiled nearly twenty years ago. Things have changed, in my opinion radically and entirely for the better.

That horror now should be a different kind of animal than it was in, say, 1975, to pick the year of *'Salem's Lot* and my substantially less successful first effort at writing a horror novel, *Julia*, might seem inevitable. Over the past thirty years, general fiction itself mutated and evolved, as the generation dominated by Bellow, Roth, and Updike gradually gave way to writers such as Jonathan Lethem and Michael Chabon. The culture changed, and so did tastes in literature, a matter already in evidence by the late 1980s. But it's an odd and telling fact that while general literature shifted away from the 1970s Bellow-Updike axis to a Thomas Pynchon–influenced model, then yet again around the time of the new millennium, horror writing pretty much stuck to its guns from the mid-1970s to the late '90s, which is the reason it began to seem pretty tired. Witches, vampires, haunted houses, and serial killers chased each other round and round the tree until they met the fate of the tigers in *Little Black Sambo*—they turned to butterfat. It was as though everyone noticed except the writers—especially, alas, those who, while replicating the old formulas in largely self-published chapbooks, supposed themselves to be innovators. (Douglas Winter got so fed up with this lazy spiral that in a speech at the World Horror Convention in 1994, he told everyone that horror didn't actually exist, at least not in the way they thought of it. Using a phrase particular to the demolition industry, he recommended that the assembled conventioneers "make some sky.")

As the contributors to this book demonstrate, sky has been made, in abundance. During the late 1990s, this wonderful thing happened—it became clear that a number of emerging writers had figured out how to extend, ignore, or transform horror's (and dark fantasy's) supposed boundaries. By doing so, they were treating it as what at its best it had aspired to be all along, a kind of literature distinguished from other kinds chiefly by an angle of vision that, while resisting most culturally determined forms of denial, celebrated the grotesque, the eccentric, the marginal, and the magical. This point of view respected the hard facts of loss, pain, emotional extremity, and grief; mainly, I think, it honored the capacity of vivid, liberated imagination to discover unexpected and often unsettling truths. Among these writers—most of whom are included here—were Poppy Z. Brite, Dan Chaon, Peter Crowther, Terry Dowling, Tananarive Due, Jeffrey Ford, Christopher Fowler, Elizabeth Hand, Glenn Hirshberg, Graham Joyce, Caitlín R. Kiernan, Tim Lebbon, Thomas Ligotti, Kelly Link, Christopher Rowe, Michael Marshall Smith, Rosalind Palermo Stevenson, Jeff VanderMeer, and Conrad Williams. The non-fiction writers Stefan Dziemianowicz and Bill Sheehan, both of whom appear in this volume, provided intelligent and supportive commentary on the exciting developments, as did almost everyone who contributed reviews and essays to Dziemianowicz's luxuriantly thoughtful journal *Necrofile* (1991–98, RIP).

Readers of a conservative bent—inherent conservatism being one of the qualities critics reflexively attribute to horror—generally respond with a shudder of distaste to my concept of the genre (or nongenre) as the essentially boundaryless product of a particular interpretive stance, but here I was tutored by my own experience, and I want to explain how it happened. Between 1988 and 1994 I published three novels that concentrated on childhood trauma, the profound shadow of the Vietnam war, emotional extremity, grief, buried crimes, and buried feelings. There was nothing supernatural in these books; and although they dealt with multiple murders, they did not actually feel like mystery novels—they were more like what I thought mystery novels *should* be. If asked to categorize them, I would have called them thrillers, with the unspoken proviso that these thrillers (1) were not housebroken and (2) read better if read twice. Initially to my dismay, later to my satisfaction, just about every reviewer of these books used his or her first sentence to describe them as horror novels.

Instead of responding freshly to the objects of their attention, these reviewers listened to tapes already installed in their heads; what a surprise! Yet the knee-jerk genre assignment did not otherwise affect their responses to the books, which received almost universally appreciative reviews. For the most part, my earliest readers saw what was going on in these books and understood my concerns. Which meant, I began dimly to grasp, that they had no problem with giving horror an extremely generous and wide-ranging brief. If reviewers could do that without even bothering to think about it, how could I not follow their lead and internalize a definition that felt so comfortable as to be tailor-made?

Then, as if to prove the point, came "The Specialist's Hat" (Link), *The Tooth Fairy* (Joyce), *Mortal Love* (Hand), "Notes on the Writing of Horror: A Story" (Ligotti), and a host of other, startlingly original fictions that seemed to emerge from an utterly free and unconfined imaginative space. If I were one of the people in this book, I'd have a lot of trouble trying to make my selection. It's wonderful, this sense of amplitude, of a rich bounty.

—PETER STRAUB
New York City
April 2005

INTRODUCTION:
IT SEEMED LIKE A SIMPLE IDEA AT THE TIME...

AND THAT TIME was 1988.

Actually, that was when *Horror: 100 Best Books* was published. The simple idea came as many as two years earlier, and it was initially a lot more simple. A small British publisher (Xanadu Publications) was issuing a series of *100 Best Books* books, and had recruited experts such as H. R. F. Keating, David Pringle, and Michael Moorcock (with James Cawthorn) to cover, respectively, crime, science fiction, and fantasy.

Their format was that the expert would select the top hundred titles himself, and write miniessays about why they made the grade. When we—Stephen Jones and Kim Newman—first pitched ourselves for the project, we thought we'd do exactly that kind of job: making lists, arguing about them, trading off entries, and writing the book ourselves. We even made a tentative list, which we showed to a few other writers and experts who, to a man (well, to Les Daniels), complained that their *own* books weren't on it.

Then, independently, we both had a different idea. This is actually how it happened: Steve said to Kim (in a Mexican restaurant just off London's Charing Cross Road), "I know how we should do this book." Kim said, "We should get a hundred writers to do individual essays on books they pick." Steve said, "How did you know I was going to say that?" And Kim said, "Because I was going to say that, too."

So, after a great deal of commissioning, collating, and other business too tedious to go into, the book came out in 1988 from Xanadu in the United Kingdom and Carroll & Graf in the United States. There was even a high-priced (for the time) limited edition with signatures of most of the then-living authors (and facsimiles of the dead ones),

INTRODUCTION

copies of which are still available if you want to sell one of your relatives on the organ transplant black market to get hold of one.

Horror: 100 Best Books (note no "*The*") has been through several slightly revised editions from various publishers, won an award (the Bram Stoker Award, from the Horror Writers Association), came out in a Tenth Anniversary Edition in 1998, and has even been imitated a couple of times—by Maxim Jakubowski's *100 Great Detectives* and Mark Morris's *Cinema Macabre* (which has a mere fifty contributors). We don't actually hold ourselves responsible for the plethora of "100 Best" clips-and-talking-heads documentaries on television, though we have appeared in them from time to time.

Since 1988, list-making and pantheon-building have become something of a mania, though in a spirit that is quite antithetical to our intent: most "100 Best" books/films/CD Roms/Internet chatroom screeds are dictatorial, in effect saying, "These are the things you should pay attention to and you can ignore the rest." Often, they serve as substitutes for independent thought and set in stone critical picks that need to be argued with—any "100 Best Films" listing that excludes *The Ghost Goes Gear* is worthless in our books.

And don't talk to us about listings that set aside notions of quality and pick out not the "best" but the "best-selling," "top-grossing," or "most profitable" of anything. Or—most pernicious of all—those assembled after random surveys about as reliable as an election in Zimbabwe to come up with lists of "favorite" films or books voted for by folks who haven't read or seen anything that came out more than five years ago and haven't even bothered with anything interesting that came out recently.

We hope that you'll listen to our contributors, maybe even argue with their choices, and then come up with your own list. The point is to do all the reading that makes you qualified to compile such a list, not to rush out and collect all the titles on anyone else's list and feel that your mission in life is over.

Compiling the first *Horror: 100 Best Books* in 1988 made us read titles we'd never considered before; and this time around, we were still making discoveries, not only of recent material but also of vintage

INTRODUCTION

work. If not for K. W. Jeter, for instance, that Penguin paperback of *New Grub Street* might have remained unopened on Kim's shelves for another fifteen years, which is how long it had been there since he bought it. Now George Gissing's book makes his *favorite novels of all time* list—not just for the horrific moment where the down-and-out novelist is forced to move into the most humiliating address in London, which in the 1880s was the street where Kim now lives!

One of the advantages of our format, as opposed to the single-author "100 Best," is that we can go back to the well. Having set out a definitive list of the "100 Best Anything," an expert can hardly do a sequel called "The 100 Next Best . . ." However, nearly two decades on, we can easily find another hundred contributors and solicit another hundred essay topics.

When we set out to do this follow-up book, we expected many would-be contributors to look at the contents of the first volume—which we had to send out as a list of books they *couldn't* choose—and cry off because everything they might want to write about had already been taken. In practice this complaint never came up. Our distinguished contributors last time around might have knocked off *Dracula, Frankenstein, I Am Legend, The Shining,* and M. R. James, but they left out *The Picture of Dorian Gray, The Phantom of the Opera, Our Lady of Darkness, Misery,* and John Collier. As our own recommended further reading list indicates, important titles down through the centuries have still slipped through our contributors' net.

Horror has changed a lot since 1988. It has ceased to be a publishers' category, making hard times for some of our subjects and contributors, but it has also become more entwined with the mainstream of popular culture. Trends have come or gone and lingered or burned out—"literary experiment," "young adult," "splatterpunk" (hah!), "extreme horror" (i.e., misogynist crap), "dark suspense," "hard crime," "quiet horror," "vampire romance," "terror soap," "new weird," blockbusters from market leaders, books associational with television hits such as *The X Files* or *Buffy the Vampire Slayer.*

Of course, horror is about what we're afraid of, and we're afraid of different things these days: back then, we were terrified of nuclear

INTRODUCTION

war between the superpowers, the plague of AIDS, or that the iron rule of Margaret Thatcher and Reagan-Bush (I) would extend forever. Now we are terrified of devastating terrorist attacks, the plagues of SARS or mutant flu, or that the iron rule of Tony Blair and Bush (II) will extend forever.

We've grown older, which brings its own fresh horrors every year—the deaths of parents and friends (and far too many contributors to *Horror: 100 Best Books*); interesting new medical conditions; catching ourselves saying and doing things older people said and did that we once swore we wouldn't ("In our day, we had songs with proper lyrics and tunes you could hum such as 'Anarchy in the U.K.'"); losing patience when we notice younger people saying and doing things we used to and now wonder why we weren't clouted for them. At least no one has run us over with a camper van yet.

Though we hope to be thought-provoking and even scary—criticism *can* be scary, as any author knows—this is also a book of celebration. Everyone here has earned their place, whether they are writing about or written upon; some are so long dead we're not even sure who they were, such as the author of *The Revenger's Tragedy,* while others have barely brushed the shell out of their hair, but all number among the selected, the deservedly acclaimed "Best."

Once again we hope that this volume will appeal to both the relative newcomer and the veteran aficionado. As with the earlier volume, it was a logistical nightmare to compile—although the invention of e-mail made a huge difference to our deadlines and mailing costs.

However, having apparently learned nothing since 1988, at the time of writing we are actually considering a limited edition of this book signed by all the contributors, and we are already compiling a list of those we might approach for a third volume in another decade or two...

—STEPHEN JONES and KIM NEWMAN
London, England
May 2005

This volume is dedicated to the memory of those contributors to Horror: 100 Best Books *who are no longer among us:*

John Blackburn
Robert Bloch
Hugh B. Cave
R. Chetwynd-Hayes
Frances Garfield
George Hay
Michael McDowell
Milton Subotsky
Karl Edward Wagner
Donald A. Wollheim

HORROR

1 [1607]

ROBERT SILVERBERG on

The Revenger's Tragedy
by CYRIL TOURNEUR

In the standard edition of The Plays of Cyril Tourneur *(1978), editor G. Parfitt acknowledges that Thomas Middleton (1580–1627) has at least as strong a claim as Tourneur (1575?–1626) to be regarded as author of* The Revenger's Tragedy *and that "unless new evidence emerges... the play has to be regarded as anonymous." Bluntly titled with a main character whose name gives away the game, this is one of the great Jacobean revenge tragedies and offers both an especially impressive body count and an array of perverse and/or criminal activities. Alex Cox's 2002 film (titled without the apostrophe), which opts to credit Middleton, uses Liverpudlian locations and has a ferocious performance from Christopher Eccleston as Vindice. Tourneur's other works include* The Atheist's Tragedy *(1611) and an elegy on the death of Prince Henry (1613); he died in Ireland after accompanying Sir Edward Cecil on an unsuccessful raid against Spanish treasure ships. Middleton, who probably contributed passages to Shakespeare's* Macbeth *and* Timon of Athens, *is best known for* The Changeling *(1622).*

HORROR IN PLAIN view was a Shakespearean specialty. The blinding of Gloucester in *King Lear*, the smothering of the blameless Desdemona, and the mutilations perpetrated in *Titus Andronicus* come quickly to mind. But in the Jacobean era a striking band of lesser figures created plays that went far beyond Shakespeare in reaching for a tone of grandguignolesque frenzy: Webster's *The White Devil*, Kyd's *The Spanish Tragedy,* Marston's *The Malcontent,* and many more. It was the mysterious Cyril Tourneur, though, who most nearly crystallized the flamboyant sensibility of his times. In *The Revenger's Tragedy* of 1607, the earlier and greater of his two known plays, he refined the drama of grisliness to an extraordinary degree.

Little is known of Tourneur. He is a shadowy figure who dodges in and out of the official records of his time under several names. His early life is virtually a blank to us; we have scattered documentation of his literary career, which lasted only (as far as we know) about a decade, and some sketchy information about his later years. We aren't even sure he wrote *The Revenger's Tragedy*. (Some recent scholars have attributed the play to another fire-and-brimstone seventeenth-century playwright, Thomas Middleton. The evidence in favor of Middleton is just about as convincing as that for Tourneur, and vice versa; since there seems to be no way to arrive at the truth, I prefer to stick with the long-standing attribution to Tourneur.)

Nobody looks upon Tourneur as one of the great originals of the Elizabethan theater. He took materials already in the common domain, borrowing a plot device here, a character type there, even the structure of an entire scene, and, by infusing them with peculiar fire of his own, gave unique life to his work.

We can hear echoes of *Hamlet*, for example, in the parallels between the two mothers, Gertrude and Graziana. Both sons have a quasi-sexual interest in their mothers, and Vindice, like his predecessor, eventually forces his morally flexible mother to reconsider the evils of her ways and leads her to repentance. (Tourneur's Graziana is forced to it by her sons at dagger's point, a typical Tourneur touch.) Hamlet and Vindice both have major scenes involving skulls, too, although, as we will see in a moment, they are rather different in purpose. And the setting of Tourneur's play is the dark, feverish, steamy fantasy Italy, savage and corrupt and amoral, rife with rape and murder and treachery, of a host of more familiar Elizabethan plays.

Derivative though Tourneur may be, though, his vision of evil is so intense that his *Revenger's Tragedy* reaches an almost sublime level of ghastliness. Looking down detachedly on his cast of bloody-minded characters and yet passionately involved, he writes of decay and lust and villainy with a ferocious gusto, a cosmic humor; his play is, as it were, a comedy of terrors.

The first line of the text provides the memorable stage direction that tells us what we are in store for: "Enter Vindice, holding a skull." The skull is that of his beloved Gloriana, poisoned by the duke of this unnamed Italian principality when she refused his sexual advances. For Hamlet, the skull of Yorick touches off an extended philosophical meditation on the transience of human existence; but for Vindice, Gloriana's skull is the instrument of his terrible revenge, and we will see it again at the center of the action in the third act's remarkable scene of over-the-top vengeance, when it serves as the strangest of all literary murder weapons.

The play focuses narrowly on one man and one action alone. Tourneur bathes his Vindice—the name itself means "revenger"—in a beam of white light that reveals that there is *nothing else* in the play, no hidden corners; we do not feel, as with Ben Jonson, that we are looking at a captured segment of a bustling, sprawling world. The confines of Vindice's world are the limits of the play; nothing else exists. He has but one goal—destruction of "the nest of dukes" who have done him such injury—and the play sweeps along at a furious pace toward that goal. In this he is unlike Hamlet, whose greatness as a literary figure lies in his ambivalence, his perpetual self-questioning, which bubbles out into the texture of the play most notably in the soliloquies. Vindice has moments of soliloquy, too—indeed, the play opens with quite an astonishing one—but never a moment of Hamlet-like inner despair. He does reflect on the action in which he is bound, such as the moment when he is called on to tempt his mother and prostitute his chaste sister for the sake of his scheme, and he shows a bit of sorrow at this necessary treachery. But generally he moves swiftly along on his murderous project, never pausing to wonder whether he'd be happier calling the whole thing off.

The verse moves swiftly, too, and every few pages reaches one of those frenzied climaxes that epitomize the whole play, as in this famous passage of Act Two, when Vindice seeks to embroil his sister in his plan:

> Oh think upon the pleasure of the palace,
> Secured ease and state; the stirring meats,
> Ready to move out of the dishes, that e'en now quicken
>   when they're eaten,
> Banquets abroad by torch-light, musics, sports,
> Bare-headed vassals, that had ne'er the fortune
> To keep on their own hats, but let horns wear 'em,
> Nine coaches waiting—hurry, hurry, hurry!

This choppy, irregular verse, which at one point breaks the confines of pentameter completely and explodes into an unmetrical, overlong line, brings the scene of temptation to a breathless peak. And the play moves right along through the remaining acts, in which murder piles upon murder until Vindice has achieved (and, indeed, overachieved) his task. The ceaseless sardonic fury of *The Revenger's Tragedy*, the cool moral ambiguity, the sense of an irresistible stream rushing away to flow over some towering precipice's edge—these are things no other dramatist of the era managed with the same overwhelming effect.

With the passionate conviction of a youthful writer, Tourneur tells a story that must have been close to his own feelings. The death of Vindice at the climax of his revenge is the ultimate triumph, not the punishment meted out by an angry god. His defiant final speech ("We die after a nest of dukes—adieu") is not the outcry of a tortured man, but the ringing words of one who has done a splendid job of bloodletting and is greatly pleased with his work.

In *The Revenger's Tragedy* the strange mind of Cyril Tourneur was free to revel in the lust and gore that so evidently delighted it, and produced the richest work of horror of the Elizabethan stage.

ROBERT SILVERBERG (b. 1935) published his first short story, "Gorgon Planet," in *Nebula Science Fiction* in 1954. The following year he became a professional author and has written more than a thousand short stories and countless novels (many under a bewildering array of pseudonyms) in all genres. Among just some of his best-known books are *Thorns, Son of Man, Dying Inside, Lord Valentine's Castle,* and *Majipoor Chronicles.* He was also the editor of the *New Dimensions* anthology series, *Men and Machines, Great Short Novels of Science Fiction,* and the two *Legends* fantasy anthologies. *Phases of the Moon: Stories from Six Decades* was a recent retrospective collection from Subterranean Press. Silverberg has won five Hugo Awards, five Nebula Awards, and has been designated a Grand Master by the SFWA. His 1972 novel *The Book of Skulls* has been purchased by Paramount for filming (and is discussed in this present volume by Stephen Baxter), while *The Positronic Man,* which he wrote in collaboration with Isaac Asimov, was adapted into the Chris Columbus movie *The Bicentennial Man* starring Robin Williams.

2

[1834]

CHELSEA QUINN YARBRO on

Pikovaia Dama/The Queen of Spades
by ALEKSANDR PUSHKIN

"Pikovaia Dama," by Aleksandr Pushkin (1799–1837), is one of the most anthologised of all ghost stories (e.g., in Charles Higham's Tales of Terror, 1960—Terry Dowling's choice in this volume—and Robert Aickman's The 4th Fontana Book of Great Ghost Stories, 1967). A German officer in St. Petersburg seeks the secret of the three cards that will ensure a winning streak at faro and pesters an ancient countess *to death only to learn the secret from her specter and suffer madness and punishment when he tries to make his fortune with the trick. In 1890 Tchaikovsky turned the tale into an opera, and it is often done on stage, screen, and radio. Thorold Dickinson's* The Queen of Spades *(1949), with Anton Walbrook and Edith Evans, is a faithful, impressive film version. Other film/television adaptations (*Pikovaia Dama, Pique dame, La dama di picche*) came in 1910 (German and Russian), 1913 (Italian and American), 1916 (Russian), 1921 (Hungarian), 1927 (French, German), 1937 (French), 1954 (American short and an* Inner Sanctum *TV episode), 1960 (Russian, from the opera), 1965 (French), 1982 (Russian), and 1999 (a record of Placido Domingo's star turn in the Tchaikovsky). To save our readers the trouble of damning themselves, we can reveal that "the secret of winning at cards" is to play, in succession, a three, a seven, and an ace. Be especially careful not to play a queen instead of the ace, for ruin lies that way.*

ABOUT THE TIME I was starting grade school, the family's next-door neighbor was a retired teacher—Miss Patterson—who had been a high school teacher for forty years. She was very much of a type you sometimes see in Depression-era films: quiet, self-contained, a bit autocratic, and rigorously bookish. In retrospect, I realize she was hungry for students when she first asked me if I wanted to read any of her books. Since my mother often boasted of my reading prowess— I had started reading early—I was selected for Miss Patterson's attention, and I am exceedingly grateful to her for it.

She had kept a great many of her schoolbooks, among them a series done in the 1930s for secondary students as part of the WPA programs to put printers, binders, and writers/translators back to work. These were local products, or so Miss Patterson believed, distributed to Bay Area schools in 1937 or 1938, roughly ten years before I encountered them. They were called *Great Stories from Other Lands*. The books were fairly short—between thirty thousand to forty thousand words—and aside from retellings of classic myths, excerpts from *Don Quixote,* a collection of Balzac's short stories, a pair of novelettes by Goethe, and a book on the fables of South

America, there was a translation of Aleksandr Pushkin's great story of compulsion and madness *Pikovaia Dama/The Queen of Spades*, and that was the one that caught my fancy. I just loved it. Even then I had a taste for the macabre.

The book itself was utilitarian in design, with heavy boards and simple black lettering on gray-green cloth. It had two illustrations: the frontispiece was a Lynn Ward-style woodblock of a young man with insane eyes holding up three cards. The second illustration showed a very grand old woman wearing out-of-date clothing and a plethora of jewels, clasping her hand to her throat, her face a horrified rictus. From the first time I saw it, I beseeched (as only a six-year-old can beseech) Miss Patterson to "help" me read it—which meant she was to fill in all the words I didn't know yet.

What a great story *Pikovaia Dama* was for me then! Poor Hermann, caught up in the glamour of gambling, killing the countess for the secret, and being betrayed by it. The story spirals in on itself hypnotically, and even now it can hook me. Then, it was so much better than Nancy Drew mysteries and similar fare that was usually offered to me, I couldn't understand why my classmates didn't share my enthusiasm. I read it every chance I got until fourth grade. I still do, in various translations, every decade or so, and I listen to the opera based on it about every year.

There is an odd little coincidence between this story and my own work: the countess learned the secret of the winning hand of cards from le Comte de Saint-Germain when she was in Paris as a girl. That story marks, as far as I can remember, my first interest in that most intriguing gentleman.

When I was approached about this project, I tried to find a copy of that particular 1930s edition of the book on the Internet, but without success: those WPA projects did not tend to remain in the system once they reached a certain stage of dilapidation. In addition, a lot of Russian literature disappeared from school shelves in the 1950s during the McCarthy era, and I suspect *Pikovaia Dama*, if it didn't disappear from hard use, may have been one of the casualties. I did find another edition of the story published in London in 1928 by Blackamore Press.

It has vellum-backed cloth boards, and was a limited edition of three hundred and ten copies, two hundred and fifty of which are on Rives vellum; it is fully illustrated in color—much grander than the old schoolbook I knew, and fiendishly expensive.

I wish now I had asked Miss Patterson to give it to me, for it would have a prized place in my library, but I didn't. She died in 1951, and her estate went to a niece. Miss Patterson's books were packed up with the rest of her things, and I have no notion what happened to them. If you had asked me then if I would still miss that book more than half a century later, I wouldn't have believed it—but I do.

CHELSEA QUINN YARBRO (b. 1942) was born in Berkeley, California, where she lives with three autocratic cats. A professional writer and tarot reader for more than thirty-five years, she has sold more than seventy books and more than eighty works of short fiction and essays. Her first story was published in 1969 in *If* magazine, and she became a full-time writer the following year. Her novels include the werewolf volumes *The Godforsaken* and *Beastnights*; the quasi-fictional occult series *Messages from Michael, More Messages from Michael, Michael's People,* and *Michael for the Millennium;* the "Brides of Dracula" trilogy; the "Mycroft Homes" series with Bill Fawcett (as "Quinn Fawcett"); and the movie novelizations *Dead & Buried* and *Nomads.* The author is best known for her series of historical horror novels featuring the Byronic vampire Saint-Germain, loosely inspired by the real-life eighteenth-century French count of the same name. The first book in the cycle, *Hôtel Transylvania: A Novel of Forbidden Love,* appeared in 1978, and has been followed by a number of sequels, including *The Palace, Blood Games, Path of the Eclipse, Tempting Fate, Out of the House of Life, Darker Jewels, Better in the Dark, Mansions of Darkness, Writ in Blood, Blood Roses, Communion Blood, Come Twilight, A Feast in Exile, Night Blooming, Midnight Harvest, Dark of* *the Sun,* and *State of Grace.* A spin-off sequence featuring Saint-Germain's lover Atta Olivia Clemens comprises *A Flame in Byzantium, Crusader's Torch,* and *A Candle for D'Artagnan,* while her short fiction has been collected in *Cautionary Tales, The Saint-Germain Chronicles, Signs & Portents, The Vampire Stories of Chelsea Quinn Yarbro,* and *Apprehensions and Other Delusions.* In 2003 the World Horror Association presented her with its Grand Master Award.

3 [1843]

ELIZABETH HAND on

A Christmas Carol
by CHARLES DICKENS

Originally published as A Christmas Carol in Prose Being a Ghost Story of Christmas, *Charles Dickens's (1812–70) brief novel was an immediate sensation in 1843, prompting the author to deliver further holiday-themed moral bogey tales in successive years:* The Chimes: A Goblin Story of Some Bells That Rang an Old Year Out and a New Year In *(1844),* The Cricket on the Hearth: A Fairy Tale of Home *(1845), and* The Haunted Man and the Ghost's Bargain: A Fancy for Christmas *(1848). These were first collected in one volume,* Christmas Books, *in 1852. A* Christmas Carol *has been adapted for many media, almost as often under the title* Scrooge, *and may well be the most-adapted single novel of all time, certainly rivaling franchises such as* Dracula, Sherlock Holmes, *and* Tarzan. *No author since Shakespeare introduced so many characters to popular culture than Dickens, and the miserly Ebenezer Scrooge is his most lasting creation, constantly invoked in everyday speech, newspaper cartoons, even sermons (Joseph D. Cusumano's* Transforming Scrooge: Dickens' Blueprint for a Spiritual Awakening, *1996) and popular science (Robert Gilmore's* Scrooge's Cryptic Carol: Visions of Energy, Time, and Quantum Nature, *1996). It is probable that if* A Christmas Carol *had not been written, Christmas would not be celebrated now in any manner we would recognize. Among many, many modernized or parodic versions are* Mickey's Christmas Carol *(1983),* Blackadder's Christmas Carol *(1988),* Scrooged *(1988), and* Ms. Scrooge *(1987), and the book has influenced such Christmas fables as the film* It's a Wonderful Life *(1947). Bruce Bueno de Mesquita reassessed the facts to make Dickens and Tiny Tim the villains in* The Trial of Ebenezer Scrooge *(2001), while Anne Moore and Marvin Kaye delivered straighter sequels in* A Christmas Carol 2: The Wedding of Ebenezer Scrooge *and* The Last Christmas of Ebenezer Scrooge *(both 2003). Paul Davis's* The Lives and Times of Ebenezer Scrooge *(1990) is an exhaustive, though now sadly outdated, listing of adaptations and spin-offs. Simon Callow's* Dickens' Christmas: A Victorian Celebration *(2003) is an anthology including* A Christmas Carol *and many other writings and illustrations that demonstrate its influence.*

Has THERE EVER been a more successful ghost story than *A Christmas Carol*? Written in a white heat between early October and November 1843, Dickens's completed manuscript appeared in book form a few days before Christmas. By January 6, 1844—Twelfth Night—the first pirate texts hit the streets, and by February multiple stage versions were vying for London audiences. Since then, the cascade of adaptations—in text, film, stage, television, radio, advertising, musical, animation, greeting cards, ballet, and modern dance—has never ceased pouring from Dickens's short novel, one of the Ur-texts of contemporary horror.

Even if you've never actually read Dickens's little book—just over a hundred pages long—you've almost certainly absorbed the story of a coldhearted, solitary man haunted and ultimately saved by ghosts. Is there anyone who wouldn't recognize some version of Ebeneezer Scrooge? He is the middle-aged "man of business," a successful broker on the London Exchange, holed up in his underheated office on a frigid Christmas Eve, his underpaid clerk shivering over an account book.

Stooped and wretched as he is, Scrooge's long shadow falls upon most of us in the industrialized world. He is one of the earliest existentialist figures in modern fiction, held accountable for his own history by four spirits—the ghosts of Jacob Marley, of Christmas Past, Present, and Yet to Come—who visit him on Christmas Eve. Scrooge's subsequent spiritual reclamation may be kick-started by the visions shown him by the first two ghosts, but there's little doubt that it's the terrifying, silent ghost of Christmas Yet to Come who seals the deal by showing Scrooge his own headstone in an abandoned churchyard. The simplicity of the ghost's gesture—it points wordlessly at the neglected grave—underscores the *horror vacui* that has enveloped Scrooge as the Ghosts show him the wasteland he's made of his life.

Unlike his American contemporary, Edgar Allan Poe, Dickens builds his sense of horror through character and not effect. The walls of Scrooge's haunted house are composed not of rotting timbers and crumbling stone, but of memory. Scrooge is literally haunted by himself. His refusal to engage with his fellow man has exiled him from his own humanity; his refusal to enter into either sacred or profane time—the former exemplified by the Christmas season, the latter by any human commerce not strictly of an economic nature—condemns him to the void.

It's a very modern terror, and a secular one. There are obvious Christian underpinnings to Dickens's text; yet its elements (Tiny Tim's "God Bless us, every one!" notwithstanding) are more aligned with the revels and cycles of the older, pagan year than they are to any contemporary fundamentalist Christianity.

Dickens wrote *A Christmas Carol* in part as reaction to the first report of the Children's Employment Commission, issued early in 1842, as well as in anguished response to the increasing industrialization of the English countryside, a process that undermined the nation's agricultural economic base, thus eradicating much of its folk culture. The most memorable vision shown Scrooge by the ghost of Christmas Past is the sight of the ebullient young Ebeneezer at his employer Fezziwig's annual Christmas party. It's a scene reminiscent of the idealized English Christmas invented by Washington Irving in the "Bracebridge Hall" stories in *The Sketch-Book of Geoffrey Crayon, Gent* (1819–20); and its terrible poignancy, for both Scrooge and the reader, comes from knowing that past is irrevocably lost.

The loss is more than Scrooge can bear. Gazing upon the ghost "burning high and bright," with a face "in which in some strange way there were fragments of all the faces it had shown him," he extinguishes its light.

The second spirit, the ghost of Christmas Present, is very much a benign lord of misrule; "a jolly Giant, glorious to see," who sits upon a throne heaped with every kind of holiday fare and carries a torch like a horn of plenty. He takes Scrooge upon a festal tour across the face of the Earth (and beneath it), "a long night, if it were only a night," wherein the exuberant giant leaves some of his essence at each place they visit, "in misery's every refuge, where vain man in his little brief authority had not made fast the door, and barred the Spirit out . . ."

But the ghost's goodwill ages him. "My life upon this globe, is very brief . . . It ends to-night," he tells Scrooge. Then, in a terrible revelation, the ghost shows Scrooge the ravaged creatures that haunt *him*:

> From the foldings of its robe, it brought two children; wretched, abject, frightful, hideous, miserable. They knelt down at its feet, and clung upon the outside of its garment. . . . No change, no degradation, no perversion of humanity, in any grade, through all the mysteries of wonderful creation, has monsters half so horrible and dread.

The children are human Ignorance and Want; they cling, vampire-like, to the Ghost but can only be destroyed or reclaimed by human intervention. Scrooge recoils; the ghost disappears with his demonic stepchildren, leaving the terrified man to face his final, mute companion, the specter pointing to Scrooge's own neglected grave.

The story could end there. Because, of course, that's where it really *will* end, for all of us. But what kind of Christmas story would *that* be? T. S. Eliot remarked that humanity can't bear too much reality; and so Scrooge is redeemed. What's more, he redeems himself. (Any overt Christian influence is dismissed in just four words, describing the reformed Scrooge's very busy Christmas Day: "He went to church.")

The "man of business" takes his dead partner's exhortation to heart. Scrooge makes mankind his business. Not by preaching temperance, or abstemiousness, or the virtues of isolation; but through fiscal generosity and expansiveness of spirit—neither of which have yet rid us of those two terrible children who cringe in the shadows of Plenty. Scrooge may be reformed, but his ghosts are with us still.

> **ELIZABETH HAND** (b. 1957) was born in California and grew up in Yonkers and Pound Ridge, New York. She received a B.A. in cultural anthropology and playwriting from Catholic University of America in Washington, D.C., where she lived from 1975 until 1988, when she moved to the coast of Maine and bought a three-hundred-square-foot lakefront cottage with no running water or indoor plumbing. Her acclaimed novels include *Winterlong, Aestival Tide, Icarus Descending, Waking the Moon, Glimmering, Black Light,* and *Mortal Love,* along with numerous film novelizations and media tie-ins. Hand's short fiction has been collected in *Last Summer at Mars Hill* and *Bibliomancy,* while with her friend Paul Witcover, she created and wrote the influential 1990s postpunk DC Comics series *Anima.* Her work has received two World Fantasy Awards, two International Horror Guild Awards, the Nebula Award, the James M. Tiptree Jr. Award, and the Mythopeoic Society Award, as well as an Individual Artist's Fellowship in Literature from the Maine Arts

Commission and the National Endowment for the Arts. Hand is a longtime contributor of reviews and essays to the *Washington Post*, among many other magazines and newspapers, including the *Village Voice* and *The Magazine of Fantasy & Science Fiction*. She has two teenage children and is currently working on a novel, *Generation Loss*.

4

[1847]

DOUG BRADLEY on

Jane Eyre
by CHARLOTTE BRONTË

The Brontë sisters all cloaked themselves in male pseudonyms when their novels were first published—Charlotte (1816–55) called herself "Currer Bell." A template for many, many Gothic romances—perhaps most notably Daphne du Maurier's Rebecca *(1938)—*Jane Eyre *brings its put-upon heroine to an isolated old dark house where she is both attracted to and repulsed by an ambiguous but saturnine man and uncovers his deadly, tragic secret. As in many later stories, mysteries and horrors are resolved with a conflagration. It has been adapted for the stage, film, radio, and television dozens of times—the version that terrified young Master Bradley was a BBC-TV serial from 1963 with Ann Bell and Richard Leech. Films were made in 1910, 1914 (two of them), 1915 (as* The Castle of Thornfield*), 1918 (as* Woman and Wife*), 1921, 1926 (as* Die Waise von Lowood*), 1934 (with Virginia Bruce and Colin Clive), 1944 (with Joan Fontaine and Orson Welles), and 1996 (with Charlotte Gainsbourg and William Hurt). The first*

TV version was made in 1949 (on Studio One, *with Mary Malone and Charlton Heston), and subsequent one-off or serial versions came in 1955 (from Brazil), 1961, 1970 (with Susannah York and George C. Scott), 1983 (with Zelah Clarke and Timothy Dalton), and 1997 (with Samantha Morton and Ciarán Hinds). Val Lewton claimed that* I Walked With a Zombie *(1943) was a transposition of* Jane Eyre *to the voodoo-haunted West Indies. This connection was developed by Jean Rhys in an outstanding prequel,* Wide Sargasso Sea *(1966)—which tells the story of how Bertha Rochester came to be mad; it was filmed in 1993 with Karina Lombard and Nathaniel Parker. Charlotte has been played on screen by Olivia de Havilland (*Devotion, *1946), Vickery Turner (*The Brontës of Haworth, *1973), Julie Harris (*Brontë, *1983) and Amanda Root (*London, *2004).*

Tucked away amid the apparently innocuous surroundings of the BBC's Sunday tea-time Classic Serial back in the 1960s was an adaptation that, in my house at least, kept the bedroom lights and the nightmares burning for weeks: Charlotte Brontë's *Jane Eyre.* Nor was the novel a disappointment to me when I came to read it some years later. It is Gothic horror of the first water.

Something, it seems, was stirring in the collective unconscious of the early Victorian gentlewoman. Less than thirty years separate *Jane Eyre* from Mary Shelley's *Frankenstein,* while, just across the kitchen table from Charlotte, her sister Emily was at work on *Wuthering Heights,* and Anne was busying herself with *Agnes Grey* (all three Brontë novels were published in the same year: 1847). Like Shelley's, Charlotte's life was haunted by tragedy: between 1821 and 1825, her mother and two sisters died. Within two years of the publication of their books, Emily, Anne, and her brother Branwell were dead. Charlotte enjoyed a measure of success and fame, forging friendships with literary figures such as Thackeray and Mrs. Gaskell. She married in 1854 but died nine months later, three weeks short of her thirty-ninth birthday.

The tone is set in the opening pages. The orphaned, ten-year-old Jane reads Bewick's *History of British Birds,* but it is not pictures of chaffinches and robins she is entranced (and scared) by, but images of "death-white realms," a "solitary churchyard," and a "black, horned thing seated aloof on a rock, surveying a distant crowd surrounding a gallows." It sounds more like something from Goya's *Horrors of War* than an ornithological handbook.

Jane's reverie is broken by the arrival of the Reed children, mocking and teasing her. Jane responds with fury. Now an adult—Mrs. Reed, her aunt and guardian—intervenes, but this is not a rational adult voice: rather the mother succeeds in topping the children's cruelty, declaring, "Take her away to the red room, and lock her in there."

The red room is a place of blood and death: always gloomy and always cold, dominated by the furniture: " a bed supported on massive pillars of mahogany hung with curtains of deep-red damask . . . like a tabernacle." Charlotte introduces a shocking note of titillation and bondage to the brutality as the two female servants who take Jane, kicking and screaming, to the room, decide they need to restrain her. One of them removes her garters to tie the child to a chair. Jane sits in the room as daylight fades into darkness, imagining the possibility of the ghost of Mr. Reed, who died in the room, appearing. When she gives way to her fears, the servants release her from the room, but Mrs. Reed orders her to be locked up again and Jane is finally removed in the morning, unconscious and in a state of nervous collapse.

Jane is now sent to Lowood school. Enter Mr. Brocklehurst, representing the twin pillars of religious idealism and education. Good news? Not a bit of it. Jane sees him as "a black pillar . . . [a] straight, narrow, sable-clad shape . . . the grim face at the top . . . like a carved mask." His methods are closer to concentration camp than school. Lowood stands as a sister academy to Dickens's Dotheboys Hall in *Nicholas Nickleby*, the regime built around long hours, joyless learning, a starvation diet, ritual humiliation, and extreme cruelty of punishment ("she quietly, and without being told, unloosed her pinafore, and the teacher instantly and sharply inflicted on her neck a dozen strokes with the bunch of twigs").

It is the darkest and most brutal start imaginable, and a brilliant evocation of the helpless, sensitive child trapped in a loveless, uncaring world. We have reached the end of the seventh chapter, and barely a civil word has passed between two human beings. And all of this is merely the appetizer. The main course has yet to be served.

Jane finds employment at Thornfield Hall with responsibility for Adèle, Mr. Rochester's ward. Is it a case of out of the low wood, into the thorn field? It doesn't seem so. Everything about Jane's new home seems agreeable. Until she takes a tour of the house: "While I paced softly, the last sound I expected to hear in so still a region, a laugh, struck my ear. It was a curious laugh; distinct, formal, mirthless."

This is, of course, the first appearance of Mrs. Rochester, the crazy Creole first wife of Mr. Rochester, whom he keeps shut up in one room at Thornfield: a creature of the night who has learned to steal the keys to her prison and wander around the house while everyone sleeps. To this day I cannot stand at the bottom of a flight of stairs leading up to an attic door without thinking of her. She is the witch in the cupboard, the madwoman in the attic. (This is a triumph of imagination over fact, by the way, as she is not actually described as being in an attic in the book.) Psychologically I suppose we might expect our monsters to live in the basement, but she's in good company: think "Mrs. Bates" in *Psycho*, think the first arrival of Pazuzu in Regan's house in *The Exorcist*.

As Jane and Rochester's relationship develops, Mrs. Rochester's nighttime excursions grow more frequent and more frightening. Jane is disturbed by "a demoniac laugh—low, suppressed and deep—uttered, as it seemed, at the very key-hole of my chamber door." She tries to burn Rochester alive in his bed. A visitor to the house is physically attacked ("she sucked the blood; she said she'd drain my heart").

Things reach a climax the night before Jane and Rochester are to be married. Jane wakes from sleep troubled by dreams presaging disaster to find Mrs. Rochester in her room, examining her wedding dress, wearing her veil, peering into her face. Brontë now removes any doubt as to whether she knows the genre she's working in as Jane describes the encounter to Rochester:

"[Her face was] ... purple: the lips were swelled and dark; the brow furrowed; the black eyebrows raised over the blood-shot eyes. Shall I tell you of what it reminded me?"

"You may."

"Of the foul German spectre—the Vampyre."

The wedding collapses as Mrs. Rochester's identity is revealed and Rochester is exposed as a bigamist. Jane flees, and Mrs. R. later burns Thornfield to the ground, killing herself and blinding her husband in the process. Jane is taken in by the Rivers siblings, St. John, Mary, and Diana, but rejects their evangelical piety and the offer of life as a missionary's wife (rejecting the Baptist, the Virgin, and a Roman goddess: how bold a symbolic gesture was that for the 1840s?), and, hearing Rochester's voice calling to her in the night, flees back to her wounded hero and, reader, she marries him.

In his preface to the current (2003) Penguin Classics edition, Professor Michael Mason suggests that *Jane Eyre* is the most widely read novel of all time, having achieved an estimated readership of more than ten million. It is no accident. The sheer intensity of the writing (it seems Charlotte habitually wrote with her eyes closed to shut out the real world and sharpen the clarity of the imagined thought), allied to the boldness and deep richness of the themes (abandonment and loss; cruelty, fear, and madness; love thwarted and regained; damnation, redemption, and salvation), make it without doubt one of the greatest novels of all time and one I would unhesitatingly recommend should be sitting on the shelves of any self-respecting horror library.

DOUG BRADLEY (b. 1954) was born in Liverpool and now lives in London with his wife and two children. It was while he was studying at Quarry Bank High School that he first met and worked with Clive Barker. After moving to London in 1977, Bradley cofounded the Dog Company (a small-scale touring theater company) with Barker and worked as the company's leading actor over the next five years, playing roles as diverse as the Devil, Dr. Frankenstein, and a cartoon rabbit not very loosely based on Bugs Bunny. In 1986 Barker invited his old school friend to play the iconic leader of the demonic Cenobites—today known around the world as "Pinhead"—in the film *Hellraiser*. The film's success led to the actor starring in a string of sequels: *Hellbound: Hellraiser II, Hellraiser III: Hell on Earth, Hellraiser: Bloodline, Hellraiser: Inferno, Hellraiser: Hellseeker, Hellraiser: Deader,* and *Hellraiser: Hellworld*. Bradley teamed up with Barker again in 1990, appearing as Lylesberg in *Nightbreed*. His other genre film credits include *Proteus, Killer Tongue* (*La Lengua asesina*), the CGI *Dominator* (which he also executive-produced), *Prophecy: Uprising,* and such shorts as *Driven, On Edge,* and *Red Lines,* based on stories by Christopher Fowler. Bradley has been heard as Barlow the vampire in *Stephen King's 'Salem's Lot* on BBC Radio, and since 2002 has been performing his one-man show, *An Evening With Death,* a compendium of writings on the subject from Shakespeare to Barker. Bradley's book *Sacred Monsters* (aka *Behind the Mask of the Horror Actor*) compares his own experience of playing Pinhead with that of other horror actors. It is based on the illustrated lecture *The Man in the Mask,* which he has performed at the National Film Theatre in London, the 1997 World Fantasy Convention, and the 2000 British Fantasy Convention, among other venues. Inducted into Fangoria's Hall of Fame in 1989, he is a regular guest at conventions on both sides of the Atlantic. In 1996 he won the Best Actor Award at the Fantafestival in Rome for his performance in *Hellraiser: Bloodline,* and he received a Career Achievement Award at the 25th anniversary Fantasporto festival.

5

[1847]

JAY LAKE on

Rekopiz Znaleziony w Saragossie/
The Manuscript Found in Saragossa
by JAN, COUNT POTOCKI

Jan, Count Potocki (1761–1815), a Polish soldier and traveler, was influenced by the Arabian Nights tales when he put together this monumental, labyrinthine novel, which, in its full version, covers stories told over sixty-six nights. Potocki, who wrote in French, apparently began work on the book in 1797, and privately published it in installments throughout the rest of his life. When he killed himself, the book was apparently left unfinished—but nobody really knows. Among many variant editions of various portions of the whole of the work are Manuscrit trouvé a Saragosse *(1804),* Avadoro, Histoire Espagnole *(1813),* Les Dix Jours d'Alphonse van Worden *(1814), and the six-volume Polish* Rekopiz Znaleziony w Saragossie *(1847). Elizabeth Abbott translated segments of the work into English as* The Saragossa Manuscript: A Collection of Weird Tales *(1960) and* The New Decameron: Further Tales from the Saragossa Manuscript *(1966). A scholarly edition of the complete* Manuscrit trouvé a Saragosse *appeared in French (1989), and was translated into English by Ian Maclean as* The Manuscript Found in Saragossa *(1995). Polish director Wojciech Has adapted the book into an epic-length film,* Rekopiz Znaleziony w Saragossie *(1965), with Zbigniev Cybulski as van Worden, while a single segment became a French television series,* La Duchesse d'Avila *(1973).*

*T*HE MANUSCRIPT FOUND in *Saragossa* is a novel both Gothic and picaresque, its history as strange as its contents. Nominally a travelogue of one Alphonse van Worden, a Walloon officer entering

Spanish service in 1739, the book alleges to have been composed from a manuscript found hidden in Saragossa in 1809 by a French officer after that city's siege. It is in fact a complicated, multilayered book entangling more than a dozen major story lines in tales framed within tales framed within tales. Imagine a sort of inverted *Canterbury Tales*, with van Worden traveling among and between the storytellers rather than awaiting them at the Tabard Inn.

Potocki employs many of the standbys of modern horror and conspiracy literature—Cabbalists and other secret magicians, shape-changers, the walking dead, hidden religious conspiracies, and a maze of cryptic confusion worthy of any modern best seller. The storytelling structure echoes many recent literary tropes in its sliding frames and shifting perspectives, while the details of sexual and violent encounters are startling in their frank depiction. Even the language, at least in the generally available translation by Ian Maclean, is surprisingly contemporary.

The details of the book's history are, if anything, more curious than the contents. Jan Count Potocki was a Polish nobleman and polymath of the late eighteenth century who traveled widely, as far as Cairo and Urga. He served in various militaries, was one of the first people to ride in a hot-air balloon, and managed various literary endeavors as writer, publisher, and even librarian. *The Manuscript Found in Saragossa* was composed in French, rather than Potocki's native Polish, and published in fits and starts over a number of years before and after his death. The original French text was lost, and only a Polish translation survived into the modern era, though sufficient French fragments exist as a guide to retranslation from Polish to French, and from there to English.

In short, when I first read this, I thought I was being put on by a modern writer, that Potocki's authorship was simply one more frame around the story. However, the story's rhythm does drag on a bit, which is what finally convinced me that this was a genuine text of its era—that and the substantial body of scholarship surrounding the book. But the plot elements are amazing. Near the very beginning of the book we are treated to the story of Pacheco the Demoniac, which manages to include incest (both intergenerational and transgenerational), necrophilia, hauntings, walking corpses, sex changes/bodily transformations, and the icy grip of Spanish etiquette in the space of four pages.

What greater grist for the mill of dark imagining? Brooding, sexually charged bloodlust, postmodern weirdness, and one of the strangest publishing histories since Gutenberg first whittled an illuminated capital for his Bible.

Inasmuch as it has a plot, *The Manuscript Found in Saragossa* recounts the sixty-six days of van Worden's journey across Andalusia, dueling with bandits, arguing with innkeepers, and alternately pursuing and being pursued by the Great Sheik of the Gomelez, the Old Man of the Mountain, a powerful and enigmatic figure who could give Kaiser Sose a run for his money. Other characters, most notably the Gypsy chief and Ahasuerus the Wandering Jew, make repeated appearances as well to alternately aid and bedevil the honor-stricken young officer.

But the fun of this book is not in the putative story line, but rather in the wrenching spirals of the narrative, and the bizarre contortions through which Potocki puts his vast cast of characters. He explores tropes of horror and dark fantasy, using both narrative technique and plot elements that, like *Tristram Shandy*, feel more than a century ahead of their time. The sheer walleyed lunacy of the book is inspired, the curious story line is intriguing, and under other circumstances, *The Manuscript Found in Saragossa* could well have launched an entire literary tradition the way its Chaucerian predecessor did. As it stands, the book is a response to the Age of Reason, much like our own pop culture obsessions with horror, magic, and religious themes. Potocki, a widely traveled intellectual, chose to dive into the darkest places within the pages of his masterwork.

Whether the reader is interested in the roots of genre literature as they rise from the Gothic novel tradition, looking for obscure inspiration for modern storytelling, or simply chasing cheap thrills, this book has it all.

JAY LAKE (b. 1964) was primarily raised in Taiwan and Nigeria. His father was an officer in the U. S. Foreign Service. During his adult life, Lake has lived in Texas and Oregon, pursuing a career in advertising and marketing while raising his child and developing his writing career. He published his first story in 2001; since then he has embarked on a rapidly burgeoning career as both an author and a short fiction editor. Winner of the John W. Campbell Award for Best New Writer, and a Hugo and World Fantasy Award nominee, his "New Wave" and "New Weird"-inspired short fiction has been collected in *Greetings from Lake Wu, Green Grow the Rushes-Oh, Dogs in the Moonlight,* and *American Sorrows.* He has edited the anthologies *All-Star Zeppelin Adventure Stories* (with David Moles), *Exquisite Corpuscle* (with Frank Wu), *Spicy Slipstream Stories* (with Nick Mamatas), *TEL : Stories,* and five volumes of *Polyphony* (with Deborah Layne), all for Wheatland Press. Another anthology is *44 Clowns,* (coedited with Mike Brotherton), while *Rocket Science* is a forthcoming novel from Fairwood Press.

6 [1891]

K.W. JETER on

New Grub Street
by GEORGE GISSING

An account of the lives and troubles of the Victorian literary business, New Grub Street catches exactly the circumstances of the times but also contains a great deal of material that is all too true a century later. George Gissing (1857–1903) was an academic who lost his position upon being convicted of theft, traveled in America, and made a career as a novelist. The book is populated by representatives of the various type of literary effort but chiefly contrasts the unhappy fate of the serious novelist Edwin Reardon with the success of the shallow journalist Jasper Milvain. Gissing is honest enough to own up to Reardon's weaknesses as a man and an artist, giving the novel a sense of unflinching self-analysis amid its potent chronicle of financial and social desperation. Tony Ramsay scripted a three-part "Classic Serial" adaptation for BBC Radio 4 in 2002.

IT SAYS A great deal about writers that the novel widely considered to be the best ever written about writers and the writing life—at least in the English language—is at its heart a horror novel.

George Gissing certainly lived the life of a writer, or more particularly, the life of a writer as most writers know it. Other than a brief period of critical lionization and relative financial security at the end of his life (born in 1857, Gissing wrote most of his novels in the period from 1886 to 1897), his was the existence of a hack writer, scribbling furiously for pennies, a typically Victorian/Edwardian demon of literary industry that modern writers, coddled by their labor-saving word processors, can barely dream of emulating.

(Given Gissing's starving early days, it's ironic that acceptance into the upper strata of the British lit biz might have killed him off: sick in bed at St. Jean Pied de Port in southwestern France, he was secretively—and against doctor's orders—fed "beef tea" by his recently acquired friend and admirer H. G. Wells. In this case, Wells didn't know better than everyone else, as he always thought he did; Gissing's fever spiked and he was dead within hours. One has visions of Wells humming a distracted tune and furtively pushing the dirty bowl and spoon under the deathbed with his foot while the doctor examined the deceased's body.)

In fairness, of course, it wasn't just the economics of a hack writer's life, grueling as those were and continue to be, that made Gissing's life miserable. He was as given to willing degradation and self-destruction as many other writers, though in his case it was not through the usual solvent alcohol (still popular today!), but by means of his involvement with the opposite sex. He threw away a promising academic career for the sake of a prostitute, with whom he continued to torture himself—including disastrous marriage—for a good part of his subsequent life. Of course, writers other than Gissing have done the same, if differing in the details; at a conference in Poitiers, I had a slight biographical disagreement with another writer whom I much admire, my friend Norman Spinrad, when he referred to the effect of drugs on the life of Philip K. Dick. "Norman," I said, "marrying the wrong women screwed Phil up more than drugs *ever* did." (A plug here for Tom Dardis's excellent—and sobering—study *The Thirsty Muse: Alcohol and the American Writer* (1989), which makes the point that Hemingway and Fitzgerald did themselves in through both vices—drink and, to paraphrase Nelson Algren's advice to a young man, sleeping with people whose problems were worse than their own.)

Economics and sex cross preordained paths in *New Grub Street*. Before the protagonist Edwin Reardon's "becoming practical" about his writing career, he attempts a rapprochement with the wife who had expected better financial results from him. It doesn't work, to the surprise of none of his friends, who observe his downward arc with mixed *Schadenfreude* and presentiment of their own destinies. For Reardon, Gissing's lacerating self-portrait, practicality is achieved at last through suicide.

When it comes to money itself, Gissing is very likely the bleakest writer of his time. His early novel *Demos* (1886) brutally depicts the kind of economy generally described as "Dickensian" (though Gissing makes Dickens's depictions of poverty seem positively cheery by contrast), to the reconstruction of which the once most powerful economy the world has ever seen is now busily dedicating its foolish energies. (*Ave atque vale*, the United States calls out to the world, as it slides beneath the waters of its own self-created Third World.) One would be correct to imagine, just from the title, that Gissing's 1889 novel *The Nether World* is even grimmer. But bad as it gets, penury isn't the true horror in *New Grub Street*, considered by George Orwell, among others, to be Gissing's masterpiece. There the horror is the wasting, at whatever wages, of one's only God-given life.

Midway through *New Grub Street*, the second-generation literary drudge Marian Yule drags herself to her most dreaded haunt, the domed reading room of the British Museum:

> The days darkened. Through November rains and fogs Marian went her usual way to the Museum, and toiled there among the other toilers. Perhaps once a week she allowed herself to stray about the alleys of the Reading-room, scanning furtively those who sat at the desks. . . .
>
> One day at the end of the month she sat with books open before her, but by no effort could fix her attention upon them. It was gloomy, and one could scarcely see to read; a taste of fog grew perceptible in the warm, headachy air. . . . She kept asking herself what was the use and purpose of such a life as she was condemned to lead. When already there was more good literature in the world than any mortal could cope with in his lifetime, here was she exhausting herself in the manufacture of printed stuff which no one even pretended to be more than

a commodity for the day's market. What unspeakable folly! To write—was not that the joy and the privilege of one who had an urgent message for the world? . . .

The fog grew thicker; she looked up at the windows beneath the dome and saw that they were a dusky yellow. Then her eye discerned an official walking along the upper gallery, and in pursuance of her grotesque humour, her mocking misery, she likened him to a black, lost soul, doomed to wander in an eternity of vain research along endless shelves. Or again, the readers who sat here at these radiating lines of desks, what were they but hapless flies caught in a huge web, its nucleus the great circle of the Catalogue? Darker, darker. From the towering wall of volumes seemed to emanate visible motes, intensifying the obscurity; in a moment the book-lined circumference of the room would be but a featureless prison-limit.

"An urgent message for the world"—that shows how much of a disappointed idealist Gissing was at heart. If writers limited themselves to *that,* the bookstore shelves would be stripped of nearly all those pretty, glossy bundles that have become, in America now and increasingly elsewhere, ornaments to the coffee-drinking experience. More often than not, the only urgent message from the scrabblers is, "The rent's due," and from the megasuccessful, "I'm afraid to shut up, for if I should, what am I?"

Darker, darker—the motto Gissing carved over his writing desk. And yet, and yet . . .

> Sometimes the three hours' labour of a morning resulted in half-a-dozen lines, corrected into illegibility. His brain would not work; he could not recall the simplest synonyms; intolerable faults of composition drove him mad. He would write a sentence beginning thus: "She took a book with a look of—;" or thus: "A revision of this decision would have made him an object of derision—"

After that harrowing—and accurate—description of writer's block, Gissing depicts his doomed hero staggering to the finish line:

> The last volume was written in fourteen days. In this achievement Reardon rose almost to heroic pitch, for he had much to contend with beyond the mere labour of composition.... And before the end of the fortnight it was necessary to think of raising another small sum of money; he took his watch to the pawnbroker's ... and sold a few more books. All this notwithstanding, here was the novel at length finished. When he had written "The End," he lay back, closed his eyes, and let time pass in blankness for a quarter of an hour.

The writer's usual indulgence of self-pity—Gissing could certainly manage that in full measure. But there is something heroic, however meanly so, in the futile efforts he describes. In darkness, light—that would not have been seen otherwise. They scribble on, not even knowing if they have a message for the world. Perhaps it's not for them to judge. Let those who read, however many left, do that.

K. (KEVIN) W. (WAYNE) JETER (b. 1950) was born in Los Angeles and started reading science fiction and suspense novels at an early age. While others in class were reading the "acknowledged" classics, Jeter wrote his book reports on novels by authors such as Philip K. Dick and Robert Sheckley. He attended college at Cal State Fullerton in the late 1960s and early '70s, graduating with a degree in sociology. He completed his first novel, *Dr. Adder*, in 1972. Soon afterward he met Tim Powers and another budding writer, James Blaylock. When one of Jeter's professors showed the manuscript of *Dr. Adder* to Philip K. Dick, the author liked it but suspected that Jeter was actually a government agent. Consequently they broke off personal contact until 1976. Jeter went on to write such SF novels as *Seeklight, The Dreamfields, Glass*

Hammer, Death Arms, Farewell Horizontal, Madlands, and *Noir,* plus the Victorian fantasies *Morlock Night* and *Infernal Devices.* He is also the author of the highly original horror novels *Soul Eater, Dark Seeker, Mantis, In the Land of the Dead, The Night Man,* and *Wolf Flow.* These days Jeter is better known for his media tie-ins and novelizations, including two *Alien Nation* and two *Star Trek: Deep Space Nine* books, a *Star Wars* trilogy ("The Bounty Hunter Wars"), and three sequels to Dick's *Blade Runner* and the "director's cut" of the film.

7

[1891]

DAVID J. SKAL on

The Picture of Dorian Gray
by OSCAR WILDE

In 1889, J. M. Stoddart, the American agent for Lippincott's Magazine, visited London and took Arthur Conan Doyle and Oscar Wilde (1854–1900) to dinner. He solicited from them The Sign of [the] Four, the second Sherlock Holmes novel, and The Picture of Dorian Gray. Wilde's novel was published first in an 1890 issue, in its entirety rather than as a serial, and slightly revised for its appearance as a book a year later. Though some critics were properly scandalized by the tone, others felt that the story delivered a sermon-like moral in which Dorian is punished for his superficiality, prompting an infuriated Wilde to write a preface designed to prevent such a reading ("those who find ugly meanings in beautiful things are corrupt without being *charming—this is a fault"). He was much cheered when the British bookselling chain W. H. Smith refused to carry* Dorian Gray. *Some of Wilde's witticisms are lifted for the intertitles of the John Barrymore movie* Dr. Jekyll and Mr. Hyde *(1920), but there have been many faithful screen adaptations, most notably Albert Lewin's 1945 film with Hurd Hatfield as Dorian, George Sanders as Sir Henry, and Angela Lansbury as Dorian's first love victim. Other film and television Dorians include: Valdemar Psilander (the Danish* Dorian Gray's Portræt, *1910); Wallace Reid (1913); Harris Gordon (1915); Varvara Yanova (who played the male part in drag in the Russian* Portret Doriana Greja, *1915); Henry Victor (1916); Bernd Aldor (*Das Bildnis Dorian Gray, *1916); Norbert Dán (the Hungarian* Az Élet Királya, *1918, with Bela Lugosi as Sir Henry); John Fraser (1961, a year after he had played Lord Alfred Douglas, the probable real-life inspiration for the character, in* The Trials of Oscar Wilde*). Also, Helmut Berger (*The Secret of Dorian Gray, *1970); Shane Briant (1973); Peter Firth (1976, a TV version of John Osbourne's stage adaptation); Patrice Alexsandre (*Le Portrait de Dorian Gray, *1977); Belinda Bauer as a female Dorian (*The Sins of Dorian Gray, *1983); Veruschka von Lehndorff (*Dorian Gray im Spiegel der Boulevardpresse/The Image of Dorian Gray in the Yellow Press, *1984). Also,* Ethan Erickson *(Dorian, 2001); Josh Duhamel (2002); Stuart Townsend (beside the point in* The League of Extraordinary Gentlemen, *2003); David Gallagher (2005); and Ryan Philippe (*Dorian Gray, *2005). Skits and variants, with unaging videotape or home movies, include* Phantom of the Paradise *(1975),* Take Off *(1978),* Dinner With a Vampire *(1988), and* Portrait of the Soul *(1999). "Amarantha Knight" (Nancy Kilpatrick) added explicit sex in a renovelization,* The Darker Passions: The Picture of Dorian Gray *(1995), and there have, of course, been gay and straight porno movies based on the story—Jesus Franco's* Das Bildnis der Doriana Gray *(1976),* Dorian Gay *(1981),* Portrait of Dorian *(1992), and* The Seven Deadly Sins: Gluttony *(aka* The Porno Picture of Dorian Gray, *2003).*

ON ITS SURFACE, Oscar Wilde's *The Picture of Dorian Gray* seems to be a supernatural morality tale set in the art world of

Victorian London, but it also has close affinities to the mad-science genre trail-blazed by Mary Shelley's *Frankenstein* (1819), Robert Louis Stevenson's *The Strange Case of Dr. Jekyll and Mr. Hyde* (1886), and H. G. Wells's *The Island of Dr. Moreau* (1896). All share the theme of presumptuous overreaching and the production of monsters. All are informed by the Faust mythos. All embody strange, secularized creation myths. Dangerous, forbidden knowledge and experience run rampant, providing the kind of chills the reading public has never been able to resist.

Wilde's only novel, *Dorian Gray* revolves around a privileged young man of unusual physical beauty, who, entranced by his own full-length portrait in oil, entertains a fatal reverie of immortality:

> How sad it is! I shall grow old, and horrible, and dreadful. But this picture will remain always young. It will never be older than this particular day of June. . . . If it were only the other way! If it were I who was to be always young, and the picture that was to grow old! For that—for that—I would give everything! Yes, there is nothing in the whole world I would not give! I would give my soul for that!

Some unnamed force grants Dorian's wish, with disastrous complications. He is not only frozen in age, but in soul and conscience as well. At the prodding of a cynical mentor, the epigram-spouting epicurian Sir Henry Wotton (the book's closest approximation of Mephistopheles, and a clear stand-in for Wilde himself), he descends into a Victorian underworld of sensation for its own sake. For the most part, Dorian's sensual sins go tantalizingly undescribed, but a homoerotic miasma hovers over the proceedings. Older men loll about his house, exchanging bitchy repartee. The artist who painted the canvas is clearly infatuated with Dorian, if not pathologically obsessed. The portrait begins to show steady signs of his corruption, and Dorian locks it up in his childhood playroom, where it eventually assumes the appearance of a debauched satyr. He murders his portraitist and drives two others (including a smitten actress, whose major function in the novel seems to be providing a "beard" for Wilde's sexually ambiguous antihero) to suicide. When he finally attacks the cursed painting with a knife, Dorian himself dies, a shriveled nightmare, his portrait restored to its original beauty.

Dorian Gray was immediately attacked by critics, who had reason to suspect that Wilde was using his story to flaunt the subject of homosexuality in blatant literary euphemism. The *London Daily Chronicle*'s assessment was among the most scathing:

> It is a tale spawned from the leprous literature of the French Décadents—a poisonous book, the atmosphere of which is heavy with the mephitic odours or moral and spiritual putrefaction—a gloating study of the mental and physical corruption of a fair, fresh and golden youth, which might be horrible and fascinating but for its effeminate frivolity, its studied insincerity, its theatrical cynicism, its tawdry mysticism, its flippant philosophisings, and the contaminating trail of garish vulgarity.

Dorian Gray itself has outlived such charges, but for Wilde, the scandal over the book was just the beginning of another, personal horror story whose ending he could not control—his trial and imprisonment for acts of "gross indeceny" in 1895 and the total destruction of his personal and professional lives. He died, impoverished and in exile, in 1900.

Although his reputation temporarily suffered, his plays banished from the British stage, his name banished from polite society, Wilde has since risen from the grave to have the last laugh. *The Picture of Dorian Gray* is now universally regarded as a major Victorian novel, and has been adapted for the stage, film, and television more than a dozen times, with no end in sight. One can easily imagine a futuristic update on the story, replacing the studio-created painting with a laboratory-created clone.

Dorian Gray can be analyzed on any number of levels, but much of the novel's power comes from Wilde's superimposition of a primitive conceit on a hypercivilized world, a time-honored horror tradition.

Dorian's magic portrait has its origins in ancient fears of soul-stealing mirrors, reflections, and doppelgängers, all of which persist today in such modern guises as identity theft anxiety; extreme cosmetic makeovers (arguably driven by the fear of mirrors); and, of course, human cloning.

As a story of supernatural energy transference, *Dorian Gray* is also linked closely to the vampire genre, which frequently employs the eternal youth gambit and difficulties with reflections. In his working notes for *Dracula* (1897), Bram Stoker took possible inspiration from *Dorian Gray* in an art-world subplot, later dropped, wherein we would have learned that the master vampire could not be photographed (only an X-rayish skeleton would appear) or painted (the image would always look like someone else). Wilde was the first suitor of Stoker's wife, the former Florence Balcombe, a legendary beauty who (it has been said) preserved her legend simply by refusing to be photographed or painted after age forty. Perhaps Dorian Gray should have opted for a similar strategy. It would certainly have saved him a lot of trouble.

> **DAVID J. SKAL** (b. 1952) was born in Garfield Heights, Ohio, and now makes his permanent home in Glendale, California. His interest in horror, fantasy, and science fiction began at an early age. A graduate of Ohio University, Athens, and an alumnus of the Clarion Writer's Workshop, where his teachers included Damon Knight, Harlan Ellison, and Samuel Delany, he began a career as a science fiction writer, contributing short stories to science fiction magazines and original anthologies. He published three novels during the 1980s that combined elements of science fiction and horror: *Scavengers, When We Were Good,* and *Antibodies.* His first non-fiction work, *Hollywood Gothic: The Tangled Web of Dracula from Novel to Stage to Screen* (1990, revised 2004), was nominated for a Hugo Award and was followed by *The Monster Show: A Cultural History of Horror.* His subsequent meticulously researched studies include *V is for Vampire, Dracula: The Ultimate Illustrated Edition*

of the World-Famous Vampire Play, Dark Carnival: The Secret World of Tod Browning (with Elias Savada), *Dracula: A Norton Critical Edition* (with Nina Auerbach), *Screams of Reason: Mad Science and Modern Culture, Vampires: Encounters With the Undead, Death Makes a Holiday: A Cultural History of Halloween, Citizen Clone: The Morphing of America,* and *Claude Rains: An Actor's Voice* (with Jessica Rains). Skal has also written, produced, and directed a dozen original DVD documentaries on Universal Studios' classic horror and science fiction films, a behind-the-scenes chronicle of the Academy Award-winning film *Gods and Monsters,* and scripted segments on classic horror icons for the television series *Biography.* He was recently appointed Lansdowne Visiting Scholar at the University of Victoria in British Columbia, teaching a multimedia course based on his books.

8 [1898]

LES EDWARDS on

The War of the Worlds
by **H. G. WELLS**

In 1897, Pearson's Magazine *in the United Kingdom and* Cosmopolitan *in the United States serialized* The War of the Worlds *by Herbert George Wells (1866–1945); it was published in book form a year later. Though it draws on a tradition of "future war" stories popular in the late nineteenth century (in the wake of George Chesney's "The

Battle of Dorking," 1871), this was the first story of an invasion from outer space, and stands at the head of a whole genre of SF/horror in which aliens arrive on Earth with hostile, aggressive intentions. Even before book publication, and to Wells's sputtering fury, American magazines plagiarized the work: the New York Journal *and the* Boston Post *ran versions in which their own cities were devastated by Martians rather than Wells's London. Garrett P. Serviss wrote* Edison's Conquest of Mars *(1898), a sequel to the New York version, in which the real-life inventor mounts a retaliatory strike against the red vermin. Many hands have provided sequels, spin-offs, or revisions: compare Manly Wade Wellman and Wade Wellman's* Sherlock Holmes's War of the Worlds *(1975), Christopher Priest's* The Space Machine *(1976), George H. Smith's* The Second War of the Worlds *(1976), and the contributors to Kevin J. Anderson's anthology* War of the Worlds: Global Dispatches *(1996). The War of the Worlds has spun off the famous Orson Welles Mercury Theater of the Air radio adaptation (1938), the Byron Haskin-directed George Pal film (1953), a concept album by musician Jeff Wayne (1978), a TV series (1988–90) notion ally sequelizing the 1953 film, and the Tom Cruise-starring Steven Spielberg movie (2005). In comics, Marvel's futuristic* War of the Worlds *sequel (centering on anti-Martian rebel Killraven, once bizarrely partnered with Spider-Man) commenced in* Amazing Adventures #18 *(1973); DC's tardy response was* Superman: War of the Worlds *(1999), pitting the Man of Steel against the Welles version of the invasion. The second volume of Alan Moore and Kevin O'Neill's* The League of Extraordinary Gentlemen *(2003) offers more teamups but returns to Wells's time period.*

I WONDER IF IT'S possible for a book to be too famous. Certainly, anyone with a passing acquaintance with the literature of the fantastic will know of H. G. Wells's *The War of the Worlds*. Any history of science fiction will refer to it as one of the precursors of modern SF, usually pointing out—with some gravity—that the term had not yet been invented when Wells was writing, and perhaps suggesting that he is to blame for the creation of the entire genre.

I expect, too, that many people will be aware of Orson Welles's use of the story to scare a large number of Americans with a realistic radio broadcast; and, of course, we must not forget George Pal's rollicking 1953 movie with those splendid manta-shaped Martian war machines. It's part of our culture, part of our collective experience—so much so that when I first went to the local grammar school, at age twelve, it was on the list of "recommended reading" given to all first-year pupils. That must mean that it is real literature then. So, like those other seminal novels *Dracula* and *Frankenstein*, cornerstones of the horror genre, almost everyone knows *The War of the Worlds*, and even if they have not gone so far as to actually read it, they will know the story and have an opinion about it. It's an invasion story, with Martians. Oh, and there are those tripod things. But as with *Dracula* and *Frankenstein*, it seems to me that the common perception of Wells's book has drifted some way from the original, and I want to argue that there is something deeper to it than heat rays and black smoke that merits its inclusion in any list of scary stories.

It's easy enough to be seduced by the SF trappings of the story, and perhaps it was Wells's intention to dazzle us with glittering machines and ultratechnology before revealing the dark heart of the tale. Indeed, as a ten-year-old casually picking up my mother's library book, that is just what drew me in. "Across the gulf of Space," the stunning opening gives us the Martian view of Earth and paints a picture of a decayed and wasted Martian civilization, drawing its resources together to fling a desperate invasion toward us. The author goes to some length to depict mankind's unsuspecting ignorance and "infinite complacency" as "intellects vast, cool and unsympathetic... slowly and surely drew their plans against us."

From this lofty view we are then plunged into the initially mundane and comfortable life of the story's narrator, who is to lead us through subsequent events. Wells's narrative rushes onward from this point with the same inexorable ruthlessness as the Martian war machines. The invaders come to Earth—somewhat inelegantly, it must be said—and the main concern of the unaware citizens is that there might be men in the strange cylinders. Wells has already played a writer's trick on us. We know what's inside and that it's not friendly, in the same way that in a horror movie, we know that going down into the cellar is a bad idea. When the Martians appear, we are given a detailed description of the full horror of their appearance so that the narrator is "overcome with disgust and dread." It is not long before the famous heat ray makes its appearance, and the final outcome seems inevitable. In the headlong race toward the end of Book One, Wells treats us to some stirring adventures and narrow escapes culminating in the splendid battle with the battleship *Thunder Child*.

The *Thunder Child*, culmination of man's technology and power and a symbol of his conceit, is wiped from the face of the Earth in a blast of fire and vapor. While she dies valiantly, cutting down a Martian in her last rush, it is clear now that the Martians cannot be stopped.

So far it's a rattling good story. Add a flaky scientist (Jeff Goldblum, of course) or a muscular, cigar-chomping commando type ready to "kick Martian butt," and Hollywood beckons. However, Wells is by no means finished with us, and it seems to me that the second book, *Earth Under the Martians*, is somewhat overlooked. It is here that the real horror lies.

Wells has rather allowed us to assume that the Martians have come because the resources of their own planet are exhausted. He has simply neglected to mention the most important resource of all. Trapped with an insane curate by the debris from a falling Martian cylinder, the narrator is able to observe the Martians at close quarters, and now he discovers their true nature. We have already seen that the Martians have been capturing people and keeping them in cages. Our hero watches in horror as a Martian, clasping a struggling figure in a metallic embrace, begins its hideous meal. The Martians have come, not just to take our world, to destroy our civilization. They have come to eat us, draining the blood from their victims with hoots of gastronomic glee.

Isn't it one of our darkest, most atavistic fears? Doesn't the dread permeate even the earliest stories we hear?

"Why, Grandma, what big teeth you have!"

"My dear, all the better to *eat* you with."

It was certainly this that gave my ten-year-old self a reluctance to turn out the light. That reawoke those fears I thought I'd left behind—of the shadowy, shifting forms of bedroom furniture, and of what lurked under the bed, waiting its chance.

Man is finally saved by the merest chance; but before the book ends, we are given a view of Earth under Martian rule—where men are herded and farmed, fattened and bred, and even those who are free are consumed by the one vital and overwhelming impulse: to avoid being eaten. For all the "rout of civilization" and the "massacre of mankind," the zap of the heat ray and the creeping black smoke, in the end, like the best of horror writers, Wells has tapped into one of our most deep-seated fears. In our darkest moments and in our most hidden thoughts we know it.

We are prey.

LES EDWARDS (b. 1949) studied at the Hornsey College of Art from 1968 to 1972. On leaving he began to work as a freelance illustrator and swiftly established himself as a stalwart of the U.K. illustration scene. In a career spanning thirty years, he has painted a great number of covers, for such series as *The Mayflower Books of Black Magic*, *The Fontana Books of Horror*, *The Star Books of Horror*, *The Reign of Terror* series for Corgi Books, *The Year's Best Horror Stories* for DAW Books, and *The Mammoth Book of Best New Horror* for Carroll & Graf. He has also created covers for works by Graham Masterton, Guy N. Smith, Theodore Sturgeon, Les Daniels, August Derleth, R. Chetwynd-Hayes, Brian Lumley, Ramsey Campbell, and Stephen King. His cover for the 1988 Ace paperback edition of Wells's *The War of the Worlds* was reused on the Bantam Classic edition in 2003. He has created two graphic novels based on the works of Clive Barker and painted a number of movie posters, including Barker's

Nightbreed and John Carpenter's *The Thing*. Some of his early work is collected in *Blood & Iron* (1989), and he has recently been producing the covers for Anne McCaffrey's "Pern" series, novels by Mary Gentle, and illustrations for some of Terry Pratchett's stories. Under the pseudonym "Edward Miller" he has begun working in a different style, painting covers for books by China Miéville, Mark Morris, Steve Erikson, Simon Clark, and Tim Lebbon, and the new "Not at Night" series from PS Publishing. In 1995 Edwards was Artist Guest of Honour at the World Science Fiction Convention, where he painted another version of Wells's Martian invaders for the souvenir book cover. He has won Best Artist in the British Fantasy Awards on five occasions, and has been nominated in that category every year since 1994. He has twice been nominated for the World Fantasy Award for Best Artist, and in 2004 he was nominated for a Chesley Award for his painting *The Snow Witch*.

9

[1902]

TONY RICHARDS on

The Hound of the Baskervilles
by SIR ARTHUR CONAN DOYLE

Tiring of Sherlock Holmes, Sir Arthur Conan Doyle (1859–1930) had his famous sleuth tumble fatally over the Reichenbach Falls locked in combat with his nemesis Moriarty in "The Final Problem" (1893). Almost immediately Doyle was pressured by readers, editors, and publishers to bring Holmes back from the dead; he held out for the better part of a decade. Eventually, Holmes turned up alive in The Empty House *(1903), but before that Doyle produced a "posthumous reminiscence" that remains the best known of the Holmes stories.* The Hound of the Baskervilles *first appeared in* The Strand Magazine *from August 1901 to April 1902, and was issued as a novel by Newnes in the United Kingdom and McClure, Phillips in the United States as soon as the serialization was finished. It is the most-filmed and -televised of all the canon; oddly, the first film version—the Danish* Den Graa Dame *(1903)—switched the phantom hound for a female ghost, but all subsequent adaptations have gone with the glowing-eyed dog. A 1914 German* Der Hund von Baskerville *was so successful that it inspired a series of sequels in which the novel's villain returns to plague Holmes again. The best-known (and best) versions came from Sidney Lanfield in 1939 (with Basil Rathbone) and Terence Fisher in 1959 (with Peter Cushing); others to star in* Hound *include Eille Norwood, Carlyle Blackwell, Cushing (again), Stewart Granger, Peter Cook, Ian Richardson, Vasilly Livanov, Jeremy Brett, and Richard Roxburgh. Among many Holmes pastiches are a few that pick up plot threads from* Baskervilles: *Richard L. Boyer's* The Giant Rat of Sumatra *(1976) and Michael Hardwick's* The Revenge of the Hound *(1987); the 1937 film* Silver Blaze, *with Arthur Wontner as Holmes, turns the well-remembered horse-racing story into a sequel to* Hound *and was released in America as* Murder at the Baskervilles. *Doyle's original* Hound *manuscript was broken up in 1902 when publisher McClure, Phillips supplied American booksellers with individual sheets for window display. A single leaf from the beginning of chapter 12, headed "Death on the Moor," was sold at auction in New York in November 2004 for $78,000. The largest single collection of* Hound *manuscript pages resides in the Berg Collection of the New York Public Library.*

SHARING ITS PODIUM with Dickens's *A Christmas Carol*; Burroughs' first *Tarzan* novel; and, much later, Ira Levin's *The Stepford Wives,* this is undoubtedly one of the best-known pieces of fiction in the world. It is certainly the most famous of Conan Doyle's tales, with numerous film and television adaptations, and it is arguable that the entire series of Sherlock Holmes stories would never have enjoyed the shelf life they have without its inclusion. But why? What is it about a rather short Edwardian detective novel, centered around of all things a spooky dog, that has captured the public's imagination in such an enduring fashion?

To begin with, it is a ferociously readable book. In his 1974 afterword, John Fowles guesses that the title of chapter 3 must be the least read chapter title in all literature, simply because chapter 2 ends with the words "they were the footprints of a gigantic hound!" The helpless reader is catapulted onward in this way throughout the telling of the tale. Yet there must be more to the phenomenon than that.

Sherlock Holmes first appeared in 1887 in *A Study in Scarlet,* and with him was born a cultural template the like of which previously had not been seen—one for the industrial and scientific age. We'd had wise men in our literature and folklore long before the "great detective." What we had not had was such a creature of pure intellect. Holmes relies upon it the way the rest of us rely on our pulse. We all know about his idiosyncrasies—the violin, the pipe, the cocaine habit. They are there to fill in a void because, essentially, Holmes has very little human side at all, or what there is, Conan Doyle keeps mysterious. He is a detached being, a puzzle-solving machine, setting the precedent in our culture for characters so diverse as Mr. Spock from *Star Trek* and, more recently, *CSI*'s Gil Grissom. In the prizefight that is existence, Holmes occupies the blue corner, representing logic, depth of knowledge, and pure reason.

In the red? The answer to that is, in some Holmes stories, Moriarty. But Moriarty is long gone by the twentieth century. This leaves his corner open, to be occupied by . . . what exactly?

Dr. Watson, our narrator, describes his first glimpse of the Baskerville estate in this way: "There rose in the distance a grey, melancholy hill, with a strange jagged summit, dim and vague in the distance, like some fantastic landscape in a dream." And there we have it, that classic archetype from horror lore, the "bad place." Sherlock Holmes is not up against any faceless master criminal this time. He is up against a direct opposite of logic: superstitious cant. He's engaged in the battle of his life . . . and seems to know it.

Fowles has already examined the role of the "ghost dog" in British folklore, and I'll not discuss that here. The hound is purely emblematic of the terrain it inhabits. Under Conan Doyle's pen, Dartmoor—upon which the rather gloomy Baskerville Hall stands—is a place of curling mists and depthless shadow, of bracken and crags. A landscape across which escaped convicts roam unchecked. The birthplace of our deepest primal fears, in fact.

Some of it is hyperbole. Fowles, again, has observed that there is no marsh on the moor deep enough to swallow a man. But that is not the point. Conan Doyle's Dartmoor actually *makes* us want to believe in a vast spectral hound with glowing eyes—it touches an ancient nerve in us, one that puts aside all reason in favor of bestial panic.

Watson, apparently, goes to the place on his own, leaving Holmes behind in London. And yet, halfway through the book, the sleuth turns up. He has traveled down independently, and been camping out on Dartmoor for the past few nights to take a look at what is going on. Partly this is reason facing superstition head on, a cool intellect convincing itself there is nothing in the dark to be afraid of. But rarely in a Sherlock Holmes story has the great detective been so hands-on in his method of investigation. Perhaps he recognizes the enormity of the task.

In the end, reason shines through, intellect prevails. The whole business is revealed as a man-made sham. At this point Holmes promptly retreats to his more civilized life in the metropolis. Could it be he senses he has won the battle, but not nearly the war? Like Dartmoor, our fears are still out there, however much our logic struggles to deny them. There will be more "hounds."

TONY RICHARDS (b. 1956) is the author of four horror novels: the Bram Stoker Award-nominated *The Harvest Bride, Night Feast, Postcards from Terri,* and *Ghost Dance.* Widely traveled, he often uses the places he has visited as settings for his work. His short fiction has appeared in *The*

Magazine of Fantasy & Science Fiction, Weird Tales, The 3rd Alternative, Alfred Hitchcock's Mystery Magazine, 12th Armanda Ghost Book, The Fontana Book of Great Horror Stories, The Pan Book of Horror Stories, Dark Terrors 6, and *Gathering the Bones,* and he shows up regularly in the pages of *Cemetery Dance* magazine. He was a major contributor to the 1985 *Science Fiction Film Source Book,* and he has reviewed for publications ranging from *Ad Astra* to *Prism* and *Horror Quarterly.* Though he has held down a variety of different jobs, he is currently working as a full-time freelance writer, and lives in North London with his wife.

10 [1907]

RICK HAUTALA on

The Boats of the "Glen Carrig"
by WILLIAM HOPE HODGSON

Though many of the writers who were most inspired by him could charitably be described as bookish weeds, William Hope Hodgson (1877–1918) lived an action-packed, muscular life. He was a lieutenant in the merchant marine (though not very happily), established a prototype system of body-building (the School of Physical Culture), and served in the Royal Field Artillery throughout World War I (he was wounded, recuperated, and returned to the front; he died at Ypres in the last year of the war). The Boats of the "Glen Carrig," like The Ghost Pirates *(1909)* and the stories collected in Deep Waters *(1967),* draws on the lore of the sea, and spreads out its tendrils to influence the fishy horror fantasies of H. P. Lovecraft and Dennis Wheatley (whose Uncharted Seas, *1938*, *is practically a remake*). Terry Pratchett wrote about Hodgson's The House on the Borderland *(1908) in* Horror: 100 Best Books, *and Gary Gianni has an essay on Hodgson's collection* Carnacki: The Ghost-Finder *(1947) later in this volume.*

Talk about *in medias res.* With absolutely no preamble, the reader is dropped into a lifeboat lost somewhere "in the unknown seas to the Southward." The *Glen Carrig* has foundered and gone under, and after five days adrift, the survivors sight land. This island, apparently, is not on any of their charts. The narrator gives it the name, "The Land of Lonesomeness," and they set ashore to explore an island where the deformed trees are monstrosities, and eerie wailings fill the night.

I first read William Hope Hodgson's masterpiece when I was in my early twenties, when the book was reprinted as part of Ballantine Books' "Adult Fantasy Series." Following the success of J. R. R. Tolkien's *The Lord of the Rings* in paperback, series editor Lin Carter unearthed fantasy treasures for a greedy reading public, yours truly included. It was a more innocent time. We could never have imagined computer CGI effects that would rival our own imaginations and—finally—bring Tolkien's trilogy to the movie screen. Even the name of the publishing series—"Adult Fantasy"—has taken on entirely different connotations. But I'll never forget the delightful frisson, the deep sense of fear and dread this book gave me. One of my clearest memories—from life or literature—is how I felt upon reading the opening chapters of *The Boats of the "Glen Carrig."*

"The Land of Lonesomeness" . . . ?

I'll say! Before the survivors leave the island, they discover evidence of previous castaways and learn what may be . . . I emphasize *may* be . . . the source of the wailing they hear after dark. They never know for sure.

And that, to me, is the sheer beauty and power of William Hope Hodgson's novel. His characters encounter all manner of horrors in their struggle to survive: screaming trees with distorted faces trapped inside them ... gigantic, bloated toadstools with the texture and consistency of corpse flesh ... gigantic crabs and ravenous "devil fish" that kill with a swiftness and rapacity neither the characters nor the reader can comprehend ... a vast continent of floating seaweed that hides hideous terrors, until they surface at night to wreak havoc on the survivors. And throughout it all, Hodgson maintains a remarkable balance. He never *explains* what these horrors are. He tells his tale and leaves the reader as much in the dark as the characters, who accept what they encounter at face value.

Because *The Boats of the "Glen Carrig"* was Hodgson's first novel (and, unfortunately, his life and literary career were cut tragically short by World War I), the writing is not what you would call splendid. It is, in fact, downright clunky, with punctuation that will make you cringe, and syntax and sentence structure even more horrid than the creatures in his story. Some of the plot devices are either predictable or else challenge the reader's credulity past the breaking point.

But the sheer power and drive of Hodgson's imagination and storytelling, the ineffable mystery of supernatural forces never flag. Anyone who has read Hodgson's work might be inclined to choose either *The House on the Borderland* or his masterpiece *The Night Land* to classify as "great," but I'm sticking with my choice. *The Boats of the "Glen Carrig"* was the first novel (after a steady diet of Alfred Hitchcock anthologies and *Twilight Zone* collections) that showed me what a sustained piece of supernatural fiction can and should do. In some ways I feel as though I was much younger than twenty-one when I first read the book. It awakened within me a sense of wonder and mystery and dread of the "unknown" that remains with me today and that I try to inject into my own writing.

Many people have not heard of, much less read, William Hope Hodgson. Lin Carter did fantastic fiction a wonderful service by reissuing paperback editions of forgotten classics such as *The Boats of the "Glen Carrig."* Without him, this marvelous book would have sunk, as her namesake did, to the depths and never been seen again. Hodgson's work is now available online, and I urge everyone to seek it out it, read it, and let yourself be plunked down into the middle of a vast ocean where horrors and monstrosities abound because, like the ancient maps warned, "Here there be dragons."

RICK HAUTALA (b. 1949) was born and raised in Rockport, Massachusetts. A graduate of the University of Maine in Orono with a M.A. in English literature, Hautala lives in southern Maine with author Holly Newstein. Writing under his own name as well as the pseudonym "A. J. Matthews," he has published more than thirty novels and more than sixty short stories that have appeared in a variety of national and international anthologies and magazines. He is the author of the million-copy best seller *Nightstone*, as well as *Winter Wake, Dead Voices, Little Brothers,* and *Cold Whisper*. His most recent books under his own name include *Bedbugs* and *The Mountain King*. As "A. J. Matthews" he has published *The White Room, Looking Glass,* and *Follow*. He and artist Glenn Chadbourne are putting together two collections, *Occasional Demons* (short stories) and *Four Octobers* (novellas), for Cemetery Dance Publications. A fourth "Body of Evidence" teen thriller, *Last Breath* (cowritten with Christopher Golden), was published in 2004 and was followed by *Throat Culture*. He is currently working on *The Singing Sands*, the first in a young adult series titled "Mockingbird Bay."

11 [1911]

JEAN-MARC LOFFICIER and RANDY LOFFICIER on

Le fantôme de l'Opéra/The Phantom of the Opera
by GASTON LEROUX

In 1896, one of the counterweights holding up the chandelier (not the chandelier itself) fell onto the audience during a performance at Charles Garnier's Paris Opéra. Gaston Leroux, creator of the boy reporter sleuth Rouletabille and the magician detective Cheri-Bibi, drew on urban legends connected with the Paris Opéra for his novel Le fantôme de l'Opéra. *Film rights to the novel were secured by Universal Pictures, which starred Lon Chaney in a troubled 1926 production (issued in several variant versions) remembered for the actor's skull face and sequences of wonderful, surreal melodrama. Illustrated photoplay editions of the Chaney movie were published by Grosset & Dunlap (United States) and The Reader's Library (United Kingdom). Many subsequent adaptations, including the 1986 Andrew Lloyd Webber musical, have scrambled elements of the original—an unmasking, the catacombs, the chandelier—but invented their own stories. Film and television phantoms include Claude Rains (1943), Herbert Lom (1963), Maximilian Schell (1983), Robert Englund (1989), Charles Dance (1989), Julian Sands (1998) and Gerard Butler (2004); onstage, various versions have been vehicles for Edward Petherbridge, Peter Straker, and Michael Crawford. Looser adaptations include the rock-themed* Phantom of the Paradise *and the likes of* Phantom of the Ritz *and* Eric's Revenge: The Phantom of the Mall. *Susan Kay's novel* Phantom *(1990) retells Leroux's story very imaginatively, providing a full biography of Erik. A new translation of the Leroux story has been prepared by Jean-Marc and Randy Lofficier.*

Almost twenty-six years ago my wife and writing partner, Randy, set out to teach herself French. She started out with reading magazines, specifically *Elle*, which in France is a weekly. She mostly read the ads, because they were the easiest things to understand. But after several months of application, she finally began to realize that she could read the articles as well. She then moved on to comics, a natural choice in our household.

Then, one day, she felt that she had mastered enough of the language to tackle something meatier: a novel.

Why did she choose *The Phantom of the Opera* as her first novel? To be honest, neither of us can remember today. Perhaps because it was there. Perhaps it was because she thought she knew it from having seen the various film adaptations. However, it doesn't really matter, because tackle it she did.

The first thing that astonished her was how modern the prose read. It didn't feel like a book that had been written almost a hundred years earlier. The second thing that grabbed her was that the story was far more than what the various films had shown. As she explained, there was a depth to Erik's character that was totally lacking in anything she had seen previously. The truly monstrous nature of his being, as reflected in the horror of his face, was brutally chilling.

The hero, Raoul, was quite a wimp, and Christine was foolish and naïve. But Erik was evil and devious, totally convinced of the righteousness of his actions. As one learns about him through the Persian's narrative, one feels that one could believe he had truly existed.

We both recognized that like E. L. Doctorow after him, Leroux had ably blended fact and fiction in a way that increased the reality of the horror. It was hard to realize that none of what was described in the book had actually happened. Also, because the author was a journalist, the language is crisp and punchy, not flowery. Those elements combined to make it a gripping read that drew Randy in (as it had done to me years earlier) without giving her a moment's pause.

And perhaps that is what made *The Phantom of the Opera* truly horrific, the feeling that one was reading about possibly real events. One could see the rat catcher and his herd of vermin as they ran beneath the streets of Paris. One wants to see the vast lake where Erik lived. We were both fascinated by the city that was the Paris Opéra.

How was it possible that a chandelier had not fallen during a major performance, injuring dozens of people? Was the opera filled with secret doorways and passages? We truly wanted to believe that it was.

Randy was doubly shocked when she eventually saw the version of *Phantom* available in English. All the power of the language was missing, and it had become turgid and heavy. Of course, it was also clear that the various adaptations of the book onto film had missed the essential core of Erik. He was not a tragic hero, but instead a true villainous monster. His soul was even more corrupt than his flesh. Totally ignored is the fact that because his exterior was hideous from birth, he was rejected as a human being by everyone he met, including his parents. The innate cruelty of mankind was as responsible for his later actions as he was himself. By pretending that, like Quasimodo, his perverted exterior hid a heart of gold, the unpalatable truth is never exposed: Erik has no heart. It was crushed into a small, hard stone before he ever left childhood.

We know that for most people, *The Phantom of the Opera* is a story of doomed romantic love. But for Randy and I it will always remain a powerful tale of fear and brutality. Randy has read it several times over the years and she never fails to come to the final pages without a sense of true horror having touched her once again.

JEAN-MARC LOFFICIER (b. 1954) and **RANDY LOFFICIER** (b. 1953) are a prolific husband and wife team of writers, editors, and translators. Jean-Marc was born in Toulon, France, and Randy was born in Philadelphia. These days they make their home in the Languedoc region of the south of France, while still running a business in Los Angeles. Their book credits include *Les Maîtres de L'Insolite* and *Les Maîtres de la Science-Fiction*, *Robonocchio*, *Shadowmen* and *Shadowmen 2*, *Arsène Lupin vs. Sherlock Holmes: The Hollow Needle*, *Doc Ardan: City of Gold and Lepers*, a young adult novelization of Disney's *Basil The Great Mouse Detective,* and such reference works as *English through Comics, Science Fiction Filmmaking in the 1980s, Into the Twilight Zone: The Rod Serling Programme Guide, The Dreamweavers, French Science Fiction Fantasy Horror & Pulp Fiction,* and *Pocket Essential Tintin,* along with several video and *Doctor Who* guides. They have written scripts for a number television shows, including episodes of the animated *Duck Tales* and *The Real Ghostbusters,* plus the live-action special *ALF's Halloween* and an episode of *Cheers.* Winners of the 1990 Inkpot Award for Outstanding Achievement in Comic Arts and also various Eisner and Harvey Awards, the Lofficiers have scripted and translated numerous comic books, including issues of *Dr. Strange, Clive Barker's Hellraiser, H. P. Lovecraft's Cthulhu, Cadillacs & Dinosaurs, The Dracula-Frankenstein War, Batman: Nosferatu, Alone in the Dark, Witchblade: Phenix,* and *Witchblade: Blood Oath.*

12 [1911]

TIM LUCAS on

Fantômas
by PIERRE SOUVESTRE and MARCEL ALLAIN

Fantômas, *which would have been called* Fantômus *if publisher Arthème Feyard had been able to read Pierre Souvestre's handwriting, was the first in a rapid run of novels, each self-contained but picking*

12 : SOUVESTRE AND ALLAIN

up plot threads like a serial, which recount the struggle between the dogged Paris flic Inspector Juve and the shadowy archcriminal Fantômas, invariably involving the heroic Fandor, his girlfriend Hélène, and Fantômas's lover Lady Beltham. In 1913, filmmaker Louis Feuillade delivered the Fantômas *movie serial, with René Navarre as Fantômas and Edmond Bréon as Juve. This made the character even more famous, in France and abroad, and essentially founded the cinema of adventure, mystery, espionage, escape, and action. The character has been revived in film many times—there was an American* Fantomas *(1920) with Edward Roseman, a French remake with Jean Galland (1932), the Belgian* Monsieur Fantômas *(1937), a 1947 version with Simone Signoret as Hélène, and a trio of 1960s efforts with Jean Marais as Fantômas and Fandor (and many other disguises). The criminal's last major media appearance was a French TV series, directed by Claude Chabrol and Jean Louis Buñuel, with Helmut Berger as the shadowman and Gayle Hunnicutt as Lady Beltham. Fantômas lingers in popular culture—even* The Pink Panther *(1964) parodies Juve and Fantômas as Inspector Clouseau and the Phantom.*

*F*ANTÔMAS EXPLODED IN the heart of pre–World War I France like a bomb flung from an opera gloved hand. It was the first of thirty-two novels of terror written by Souvestre (1874–1914) and Allain (1885–1969), all paperback originals published monthly between February 1911 and September 1913. Each volume carried the distinctive "Fantômas" logo and a chilling cover painting by Gino Starace—a severed hand clutching a roulette wheel, a nurse screaming in a room splashed with blood, a man disposing of someone's head from a hatbox—establishing their paternal ties to the American crime pulps of the 1930s and '40s. Unlike the eighty-page "novels" promised on the covers of *The Shadow,* each new Fantômas novel was as thick as cake—actually Dickensian in its accumulation of character and incident—and the French public reached for their pocket knives to cut its signatures with ravenous appetite.

For some reason, the Fantômas novels have been absorbed into the genre of mystery and detection rather than into the horror genre, where they truly belong. As Geoffrey O'Brien observed, "Fantômas is not a puzzle, but an intoxicant." The Starace painting on the cover of *Fantômas* shows the title character—"The Genius of Crime" (a phrase that Sax Rohmer would appropriate for his Dr. Fu Manchu)—in tie and tails with a black mask and glinting dagger, straddling the whole of Paris. Larger than life, he is seemingly beyond arrest, a Reign of Terror incarnate, but Inspector Juve refuses to accept this. Fantômas may seem a fantastic enlargement of earlier French literary figures such as Rocambôle and Arsène Lupin—those archetypes of "the gentleman thief"—yet the book's true villain of the piece turns out to be a very clever and tangible murderer named Gurn, whom Juve merely *suspects* of being Fantômas. What elevates *Fantômas* to greatness, in my estimation, is that nowhere do Souvestre and Allain explicitly confirm or deny Juve's suspicions.

As the book opens, Juve summons Fantômas into being by speaking his name aloud:

> "Fantômas!"
> "What did you say?"
> "I said: Fantômas!"
> "And what does that mean?"
> "Nothing . . . everything!"
> "But what is it?"
> "No one . . . and yet, yes, it is someone!"
> "And what does this someone do?"
> "Spreads terror!"

Did Fantômas exist before this moment?

Remarkably, everything we learn about this archcriminal originates with Juve, who holds Fantômas personally accountable for all that thwarts or vexes him. If crime lends meaning to the life of a policeman, might Fantômas be the inverse projection of a detective with a gargantuan ego? Lending credence to this interpretation is that Juve's own colleagues scoff at his belief in this mythical Fantômas. However, as the book continues, as we repeatedly encounter characters on both sides inhabiting different disguises Juve's paranoia slowly infects us. The more colorfully a new incidental character is described, the more heavily the stage makeup is troweled on, so to speak, the more we delight in sussing out whether they are in fact Fantômas, Juve, or the very person they claim to be.

One begins to suspect that Juve himself is Fantômas. In the course of his quixotic investigation, Juve shows himself an equal master of disguise, and when he aids and abets Charles Rambert—a young man wanted for the murder of the novel's first victim—Juve reveals himself as someone who places his personal needs and instincts above the requirements of law. Sensing a kindred spirit in this innocent fugitive, he bestows on him the new identity of "Jérôme Fandor," an alias chosen because it "sounds something like Fantômas." Thus Juve unwittingly confesses a sense of enchantment with his foe, a dichotomy reflected elsewhere in the character of Lady Beltham, the lover and chief accomplice of Fantômas who is also the widow of a man he murdered.

In *Juve contre Fantômas* (aka *The Exploits of Juve*, 1916; revised as *The Silent Executioner*, 1987), the authors persist in teasing us with the question of whether Fantômas truly exists—until the final chapter. In a perfunctory finale (at least as represented by the English translation), a figure in black is explicitly identified as Fantômas. The mystery ends, but what arises in its place is one of the most seminal characters in the annals of horror fiction, comparable to Bram Stoker's Dracula in the sheer number and variety of its offspring. Notable examples include Sax Rohmer's Fu Manchu, Angela and Luciana Giussani's Diabolik, Grant Morrison's Fantomex, and that quirky Australian imitation of Clarence W. Martin, Ubique—the Scientific Bushranger.

The end of the first Fantômas cycle coincided with the onset of World War I. Pierre Souvestre—the series' prime mover—died in 1914 at age forty, less than one year into his military service. Marcel Allain revived the character in 1925 with a series of thirty-four sixteen-page magazine stories, later collected in five additional books. (A few more followed.) Though Allain's works aren't the equal of those he wrote with Souvestre, all five were translated for the English market—which can be said of only a paltry seven titles from the classic run. Of those seven, *Le Mort qui Tue* (aka *Messengers of Evil*, 1917) is outstanding, with Fantômas committing murders while wearing the skin of a dead man's hands for gloves, and *L'Agent Secret* (aka *A Nest of Spies*, 1917) is arguably the smoking gun behind Fritz Lang's *Spione* (1928), James Bond, and all the spy entertainment we enjoy to this day.

Fantômas exists in a few different English translations. The earliest, published in 1915 and credited to Jules Verne's translator Cranstoun Metcalfe, is the preferred and most complete text. The uncredited William Morrow translation (1986) is expurgated and rather too modernistic in flavor. There also exists a Mayflower Dell (United Kingdom) paperback original, published in 1966 under the bizarre title *A Mad Woman's Plot*. This lively, somewhat condensed translation was the work of Raymond Rudorff, who also translated Ornella Volta's study *The Vampire* (1970) and whose own books include *Studies in Ferocity: A Book of Human Monsters* (1969) and *The Dracula Legend* (1972).

TIM LUCAS (b. 1956) was born in Cincinnati, Ohio, where he and his wife, Donna, co-edit *Video Watchdog*, described as "The Perfectionist's Guide to Fantastic Video." Founded in 1990, the now-monthly periodical has won two Rondo Awards for Best Magazine. The author of the novels *Throat Sprockets* and *The Book of Renfield: A Gospel of Dracula*, Lucas has written and/or edited a dozen volumes of Signet Books/Video Times' *Your Video Guide* series. His other non-fiction works include *The Video Watchdog Book* and the in-depth study *Mario Bava: All the Colors of the Dark*. A respected contributor to such reference books and magazines as *Eyeball Companion*, *The BFI Companion to Horror*, *Fangoria's Best Horror Films*, *The Shape of Rage: The Films of David Cronenberg*, *Modern Critical Views: Anthony Burgess*, *Sight and Sound*, *Film Comment*, *Cahiers du Cinéma*, *Cinefex*, *Fangoria*, *Gorezone*, *The Dark Side*, *American Cinematographer*, *Spin*, and *Heavy Metal*, he has also written liner notes and recorded audio commentaries for more than thirty DVD releases.

13 [1927–28]

CHRISTOPHER WICKING on

The Case of Charles Dexter Ward
by H. P. LOVECRAFT

Howard Phillips Lovecraft (1890–1937) did not place "The Case of Charles Dexter Ward" during his lifetime. In 1941, August Derleth and Donald Wandrei had the forty-eight-thousand-word short novel professionally retyped from the author's handwritten manuscript. An abridged version of the tale appeared under the blurb "The Last of the Lovecrafts" over two issues of Weird Tales *in May and July 1941, and the unexpurgated version was published in Arkham House's second bumper collection of Lovecraft stories,* Beyond the Wall of Sleep *(1943). It has occasionally been reprinted as a stand-alone volume (from Panther in the United Kingdom in 1963, for instance) but is more often included in collections of Lovecraft's work. Needing a film to go with the title of Edgar Allan Poe's poem "The Haunted Palace," Roger Corman had Charles Beaumont adapt* Charles Dexter Ward *as a 1963 vehicle for Vincent Price, with sinister support from Lon Chaney Jr. (and, allegedly, additional dialogue from Francis Ford Coppola). Director Dan O'Bannon tried again in 1992, reconfiguring the Lovecraft plot as a private-eye mystery with Chris Sarandon as Ward and his evil ancestor Curwen for the little-seen* The Resurrected.

"SINISTER, SEETHING HORROR strictly for the iron-nerved addict..." and "From the pits of unspeakable horror came the evil of another time, to devour his soul."

Such are the blurbs on the cover of the May 1963 Panther paperback of *The Case of Charles Dexter Ward*. There is no mention of Lovecraft as such, apart from his byline. That's the edition I would have first read at about that time, and only once since, its pages yellowing and brittle with the passage of time.

In 1963 I was working as an assistant film editor (including on Orson Welles's *Chimes at Midnight*), and later that year I'd be doing interviews with the likes of Roger Corman and Jacques Tourneur for the French magazines *Positif* and *Midi-Minuit Fantastique*.

Did I know that Corman had made the yet-to-be-released *The Haunted Palace*, based on the book? Is that why I read it? Or was Lovecraft in the air anyway?

Whatever, it struck me back then like an absolute thunderbolt, I suppose because it touches on something that fascinates me—the notion that there's more to this world than we're as yet aware, that we're perhaps connected umbilically to other planets and civilizations (past/present/future?). Otherwise, why the urge since the dawning to take to the skies? Why, of course, to go home!

Early in 1964, when I interviewed Corman ("that typewriter you hear in the other room is Charles B. Griffith, working on a rewrite of our adaptation of *The Gold Bug*"), he was contrite about the "unhappy circumstances" that led to "Edgar Allan Poe's" *The Haunted Palace* being "treachery" to Lovecraft (Poe's stories having pretty much run dry for the production company AIP, apart from "Murders in the Rue Morgue" and "The Gold Bug").

I had no idea what he meant, of course, until the film finally came out. Treachery indeed, and tragedy insofar as I couldn't imagine a true adaptation now being made. But at least a seam of material had now been opened up for AIP in other Lovecraft stories, so perhaps there might be hope for something more authentic to come along.

In the next few years I continued as a correspondent for various French, American, and English magazines, visiting the sets of Tourneur's *City under the Sea* and Daniel Haller's *Monster of Terror* (from Lovecraft's "Colour out of Space"), among others, while my screenwriting activities began to bear fruit until, in a mystical irony, I found myself doing rewrites on *The Gold Bug* (four years after Charles B. Griffith) as well as *The Oblong Box* for Michael

Reeves and, yes, AIP, which subsequently put me on the payroll as the Blue-Eyed Boy.

Monster of Terror (aka *Die, Monster, Die!*) turned out to be pretty tacky, yet AIP continued to adapt Lovecraft, and Dan Haller had followed it up with a version of "The Dunwich Horror," which was not yet released in Britain when AIP's English honcho, Louis M. "Deke" Heyward, called me in for a meeting. Did I think I could get any more mileage out of *The Case of Charles Dexter Ward*?

Did I, hell!!! Excitement and enthusiasm flooded back. I'd have been ready to start right away. But Deke said, "Read the book again. Take a look at our other Lovecraft adaptations." I said I didn't need to. "But you haven't seen *The Dunwich Horror* yet. I'll book a screening room and you can run them all."

So he did. And I did. Read the book again and got even more excited. But made the mistake of sitting down in the screening room. *The Haunted Palace, Monster of Terror,* and now *The Dunwich Horror.* Each, from a Lovecraft perspective, more atrocious than the last. My heart sank. Four and a half hours of treachery and tragedy. This is all they really wanted. A contemporary adaptation of *Charles Dexter Ward* with all the weird touches and new ideas I could bring to it would be far more expensive than an AIP budget would stand, and be so radical anyway that I was sure I'd never get it through.

Believe it or not, I didn't try. I never went back.

So, all these years later, would *Charles Dexter Ward* still be my favorite horror novel? In fact it doesn't seem to be regarded as a novel these days, rather as a long short story. Now Lovecraft gets more than a byline on the covers. Now he's "The 20th-century horror story's dark and baroque prince" (Stephen King).

The Case of Charles Dexter Ward turns out to be even more remarkable than I (only dimly) remembered it. Divided into five seductively headed chapters ("A Result and a Prologue," "An Antecedent and a Horror," "A Search and an Evocation," "A Mutation and a Madness," and "A Nightmare and a Cataclysm"), it's a stylistic *tour de force*, opening daringly with the disappearance from "a private hospital for the insane" of the twenty-six-year-old Ward himself.

Though then proceeding to tell its two separate but interconnected past-tense stories through a third-person narrator, it manages to make them as grippingly spellbinding as if they were happening "now," or told first person.

In a nutshell, the initially unworldly Ward, with his antiquarian interests, learns of a mysterious ancestor, Joseph Curwen, who has been virtually written out of history. In tracking back into this past life, Ward becomes subsumed by Curwen (there's a tip of the hat to Wilde's *The Picture of Dorian Gray*, which Lovecraft much admired). His quest, via "ye essential saltes," becomes awesomely otherworldly, embracing "some vast and revolting menace, of a scope and depth too profound and intangible for more than shadowy comprehension."

Yet, for all such cosmically convoluted concepts (and prose), Lovecraft intelligently earths his vast visions in the mundane, the better to make us believe them. Just as *Dracula* was up to date in 1897, *Charles Dexter Ward* is set very firmly in the then present, with its references to Prohibition and the Curwen portrait installed "above a cleverly realistic electric log."

I was especially drawn to the story's concept of "ye essential saltes" (as apparently is the Finnish rock band His Infernal Majesty). Some three decades before Crick and Watson discovered DNA, it seemed to me that Lovecraft had essentially postulated some similar "building blocks" of life (or at least rebirth), an early, magical, grotesque, and messy form of cloning.

The emotional and narrative centerpiece is the long section where Dr. Willett, "Ward's family physician," whose knowledge of his patient and investigation into his behavior provide the narrative spine, gets to go to the Curwen house, and down to the catacombs where the unholy work has been carried out. ("Devil take ye! Those cursed things have been howling down there for a hundred and fifty-seven years gone!")

And delightfully, even in this terrifying section the classicist Lovecraft keeps contemporary references alive and allows himself a sideswipe at the same time. The frightened Dr. Willett repeats the

Lord's Prayer to himself, "eventually trailing off into a mnemonic hodge-podge like the modernistic 'Waste Land' of Mr. T. S. Eliot."

CHRISTOPHER WICKING (b. 1943) is the internationally celebrated British screenwriter of such classic cult movies as *The Oblong Box, Scream and Scream Again, Cry of the Banshee, Murders in the Rue Morgue, Blood from the Mummy's Tomb, Demons of the Mind,* and *To the Devil a Daughter.* Originally a critic, Wicking collaborated with such studios as Hammer and American International Pictures on a run of unconventional, and structurally daring horror films during the late 1960s and '70s. His other screen credits from this period include *Venom, Medusa,* and *Dream Demon,* although such potentially interesting Hammer projects as *Nessie, Vampirella,* and *Kali Devil Bride of Dracula* remained unfilmed. Nowadays Wicking divides his time between screenwriting/script consultancy and, via his Dublin-based company Midnight Movies Ltd., is developing various film and television projects. Recent writing assignments have included *Powers,* a children's *X Files* for BBC-TV; *The Judge's House,* a pilot episode for the fantasy series *Shiver;* an adaptation of Peter Ackroyd's novel *Hawksmoor;* and the original horror screenplay *Needles.*

14 [1928]

BARBARA RODEN and CHRISTOPHER RODEN on

They Return at Evening
by H. R. WAKEFIELD

H. (Herbert) R. (Russell) Wakefield's first collection of supernatural tales, They Return at Evening, *was published by Philip Allan in 1928 and reprinted by Barbara and Christopher Roden's Ash-Tree Press in 1995. Among the stories in the volume are such classics as* "Professor Pownall's Oversight"; "He Cometh and He Passeth By!"; "The Seventeenth Hole at Duncaster"; *and the volume's most famous tale, the chilling* "The Red Lodge," *about a house that drives a succession of owners and tenants to madness and/or death. Although he produced well-received work in other genres—notably mystery stories and true crime studies—Wakefield (1888–1964) is best remembered for his ghost stories, and he returned to the form throughout his life, in the collections* Old Man's Beard *(aka* Others Who Returned, *1929),* Imagine a Man in a Box *(1931),* Ghost Stories *(1932),* A Ghostly Company *(1935),* The Clock Strikes Twelve *(1940, expanded 1946), and* Strayers from Sheol *(1961). In later years Wakefield's career was kept alive by editor August Derleth, who used his stories in original anthologies and published the author's final two collections under the Arkham House imprint. Wakefield has rarely been adapted to other media, though his* "The Triumph of Death" *(1949) became an episode of the 1968 BBC-TV series* Late Night Horror, *starring Claire Bloom.*

PITY POOR H. R. Wakefield, who through an accident of timing saw his first collection of ghost stories, *They Return at Evening*, published in the same year as E. F. Benson's *Spook Stories* and midway between M. R. James's *A Warning to the Curious* (1925) and *Collected Ghost Stories* (1931).

This has led to his being conveniently, if unfairly and erroneously, labeled a "Jamesian" writer of ghostly tales; and while he was not averse to using certain conventions of that genre when it suited him (notably, in his first collection, in the excellent "The Seventeenth Hole at Duncaster"), those approaching *They Return* looking for stories written to a Jamesian formula are apt to be disappointed.

Modern readers are also inclined to be put off by the accusations of misogyny and sadism that have—not unjustly—been leveled at Wakefield, even though similar criticism has not harmed the critical standing of (to take one example) E. F. Benson. M. R. James wrote in 1929 that "H. R. Wakefield, in *They Return at Evening* (a good title) gives us a mixed bag, from which I should remove one or two that leave a nasty taste. Among the residue are some admirable pieces, very inventive." This, from James, amounts to high praise, but that "nasty taste" tag has unfortunately lingered in the memory longer than has his accolade.

John Betjeman was more unequivocal: "M. R. James is the greatest writer of the ghost story. Henry James, Sheridan Le Fanu and H. R. Wakefield are equal seconds," he wrote in 1972, and looked at objectively one can only nod one's head at Betjeman's judgment in including Wakefield with these other names. Le Fanu, M. R. James, and Henry James all helped, at various times and in various ways, to transform the ghost story, to show how a genre that was in danger of becoming formulaic and stale could be altered to fit a changing world with new standards, expectations, and perceptions.

Unlike many of his contemporaries, who were content to ring changes on well-worn themes and conventions, Wakefield was never afraid to change with the times, combining the elegance and structure of the classic ghost story with a more modern, complex approach.

This tendency is demonstrated in several of the tales in *They Return at Evening,* such as "Professor Pownall's Oversight," which on first glance seems to be nothing more than a conventional tale of supernatural revenge. However, in the final three pages Wakefield manages brilliantly to pull the rug out from under the feet of the reader, first by suggesting that the entire story to that point has been the mere fabrication of a madman, and then indicating that it may be something much more terrifying. In typical Wakefield fashion, the story then ends, leaving the reader to decide for himself or herself what has happened. As in many of his stories, tension builds steadily throughout, to reach a sudden and horrifying crescendo that quickly ends the tale, the author resolutely declining to cross every *t* and dot every *i*.

He plays much the same trick in "The Third Coach," in which a supposedly hardened criminal and con man is revealed to be a mild-mannered clergyman suffering from delusions; or is he? The story ends with a note of black humor that typifies Wakefield's style but that leaves the reader going over the story again from a completely different angle.

"He Cometh and He Passeth By!" pays slight homage to James's "Casting the Runes," in that both concern a dabbler in the black arts who revenges himself by means of a piece of paper passed on to his victim that presages violent death, but for the most part Wakefield's plots were his own. (In an interesting twist, L. T. C. Rolt acknowledged that he consciously modeled his own story "New Corner," about a haunted racetrack, on Wakefield's golfing ghost story "The Seventeenth Hole at Duncaster," one of the finest tales in *They Return*.)

Unlike many other ghost story writers of the time, who agreed with James that supernatural tales should be set slightly in the past, Wakefield set the majority of his stories in the (then) present day, with references to radio, films, current celebrities, and fast cars littering the tales. He did, however, agree with the dictum that a writer should write about what he knows; hence "And He Shall Sing . . ." is set in the world of publishing, a world that Wakefield, who was an editor and publisher, knew intimately.

Writers also feature prominently (and not always flatteringly) in his stories; in *They Return at Evening* the profession is represented by Mr. James Partridge in "A Peg on Which to Hang—," who is described as "a writer by habit and inclination, though being the fruit of honest but rich parents, he is not in the paralysing position of having to rely on his pen, ink, and paper for his means of subsistence."

Wakefield used an incident from his own life in what is almost certainly his most famous story, and the cornerstone of *They Return at Evening*, "The Red Lodge." In 1917 he stayed at a house that had an evil reputation, and while there the author found himself "oppressed by a fear without a name," which caused night after night of insomnia. He discovered that different people were affected by the house in different ways, and that five such people had committed suicide over the previous thirty years. It claimed another life the year after Wakefield stayed there. He considered the house a death trap, and it was transformed into the superficially charming, but utterly malignant, Red Lodge, whose "Permanent Occupants" are presumably still there at the end of the tale, awaiting the next hapless tenant, the renting of haunted houses not yet being, as one character points out, a criminal offense.

They Return at Evening would be a key collection if only for "The Red Lodge"; but taken as a whole, the volume assumes a place at the very head of books of supernatural fiction. It ranks with *Ghost Stories of an Antiquary* as one of the most assured and polished debuts in all of supernatural literature, and in it H. R. Wakefield boldly lays claim to being one of the most important writers of the weird tale, bridging the gap between the classic style of an earlier age and the more modern approach of writers in the post-World War II era.

After reading the volume, one has to agree with critic H. C. Harwood, who wrote (in a 1928 review of *They Return at Evening*), "Sheer devilry, Mr. Wakefield. Many thanks."

BARBARA RODEN (b. 1963) and **CHRISTOPHER RODEN** (b. 1948) founded Ash Tree Press, which specializes in supernatural fiction, in 1994. Since then, the Press has published more than a hundred titles and won a World Fantasy Award and a Special Award of the Trustees of the Horror Writers Association. Barbara Roden was born in Vancouver, British Columbia, Canada. She read her first grown-up collection of ghost stories, which included Wakefield's "The Red Lodge," at age nine and was hooked on the genre from that moment. After joining the Ghost Story Society in 1990, she began editing its newsletter in 1993 and took over editing its journal, *All Hallows*, the following year. In 2004 the title won the International Horror Guild Award for Best Periodical. Christopher Roden was born in Stourbridge, West Midlands, England. He founded the Arthur Conan Doyle Society in 1989 and in 1992 edited two volumes of *The Oxford Sherlock Holmes* for Oxford University Press. Between them they have edited and/or introduced a number of collections of supernatural fiction, including the World Fantasy Award-nominated anthology *Shadows and Silence* and the Bram Stoker Award-nominated *Acquainted With the Night*.

15 [1934]

SYDNEY J. BOUNDS on

Creep, Shadow!
by A. MERRITT

In ancient Ys, Alan Caranac destroys Dahut, a seductive and evil witch. In a modern reincarnation, Alan again fights Dahut when she sends the shadow of one of her victims to drive Alan's friend Dick Ralston to suicide. Dahut is joined by the sorcerer De Keradel, and together they sacrifice paupers to an ancient god, the Gatherer, in exchange for absolute power. Alan risks his life to destroy Dahut again. Abraham

15 : MERRITT

Merritt (1884–1943), known for his fantasy novels (The Moon Pool, 1919; The Ship of Ishtar, 1926), dipped a toe into horror with the Sax Rohmer-influenced Seven Footprints to Satan (1928, filmed 1929). He made a more sustained essay in the pulp supernatural with Burn, Witch, Burn! (1933, filmed by Tod Browning as The Devil Doll, 1936), which is not to be confused with the American title of the British film Night of the Eagle (1962), an adaptation of Fritz Leiber's novel Conjure Wife (1943). Burn, Witch, Burn! introduces the characters of psychiatrist/occult detective Dr. Austin Lowell and underworld tough guy adventurer McCann, who pitch in again in Creep, Shadow! to help Alan Caranac against De Keradel, leftover lover of the earlier novel's villainess Madame Mandelip (who became a male transvestite played by Lionel Barrymore in the film). First published in hardcover by Doubleday in 1934, it appeared as Creep, Shadow, Creep! from Methuen in the United Kingdom the following year. The title formation refers to a rash of similarly styled songs of the 1920s and '30s ("Laugh Clown, Laugh," "Sing, Baby, Sing") but survives in pop culture only in Merritt's horror-inflected mode (Die, Monster, Die!, 1965; Scream, Blacula, Scream!, 1973). The book retained the altered title when reprinted "complete and unexpurgated" as Issue No. 11 of Murder Mystery Monthly ("a $2.00 Mystery for 25c") in 1943, but was back to the original when it became the first story in the premier issue of the pulp A. Merritt's Fantasy Magazine (December, 1949). Though Creep, Shadow! is influenced in its reincarnated love-hate story by H. Rider Haggard's She (1887), the Breton legend of Ys came to Merritt via Robert W. Chambers' "The Demoiselle d'Ys" (1895). Another familiar version is Edouard Lalo's opera Le Roi d'Ys (1888).

THE FIRST PUBLICATION of this novel was as a seven-part serial in the American pulp magazine *Argosy Weekly*, which had the subtitle "Action Stories of Every Variety." The story copped the cover for the first installment, dated September 8, 1934. Each installment was headed by a black-and-white illustration.

Because *Creep, Shadow!*, like other Merritt novels, started life as a serial, it has the built-in advantage of a series of cliff-hangers.

On the contents page of the magazine a blurb reads, "Modern science against ancient and evil sorcery." The blurb to the first installment reads, "Four men commit suicide—without apparent reason! Is the supernatural responsible? Do sorcerers hold sway today?"

A case could be made that Merritt's fantasy was a forerunner of the kind of story published in *Unknown Worlds;* it seems likely that John W. Campbell Jr., the editor, was familiar with this story when he started his fantasy magazine.

Abraham Merritt worked as a newspaper reporter and assistant to the editor on the staff of *American Weekly,* the supplement for the papers owned by William Randolph Hearst. *Creep, Shadow!* was his last novel; he stopped writing fiction when he was promoted to editor.

Merritt was regarded as a master of fantasy in pre-Tolkien days. So how does he qualify for a horror selection?

"Horror" is a commercial category, and an odd one out. "Crime," "romance," "science fiction," and "Western" are labels indicating the type of story; but horror is an emotion and specifies what readers must feel if the story is to be successful. It is possible to write a short story featuring this one dominant emotion; with a novel, the most we can hope for are individual scenes that arouse horror during the course of the book.

Are there scenes of horror in *Creep, Shadow!*? Consider some of the ingredients: witchcraft, a land of shadows, an elder god who demands human sacrifice. Here is a quote to give you a taste:

> They had substance, these shadow hounds of Dahut. Tenuous, misty—but material. I dropped my gun and fought with bare hands. From the dogs came a strange and numbing cold. They tore at my throat with red eyes burning into mine, and it was as though the cold poured into me through their fangs. I was weakening. It was growing harder to breathe. The numbness of the cold had my arms and hands so that now I could only feebly struggle against the black cobwebs. I dropped to my knees, gasping for breath.

Writing in the first person was then a favorite method of authors striving for credibility with fantastic material.

In his young days, Merritt wrote poetry, and this colored his early work; the style of his late novels was influenced by his journalism and was less flamboyant.

In this story, Chicago-style gangsters with tommy guns fight on the side of good against evil; and the hero, after climbing down the outside of a tower block to escape from Dahut, enters another apartment, where he joins a poker game to win clothes so he can get home.

Although billed as a sequel to *Burn, Witch, Burn!* (1933), it is not necessary to have read the earlier novel to enjoy this one.

A final quote:

> My foot struck against a black and oval bowl. Not all black—there were stains along its sides, and inside was a viscous scum.
>
> The bowl of sacrifice!
>
> Abruptly the fog lifted . . . and there was the dream . . . if dream it had been. I recoiled from it. If it had been no dream, then I was doubly and trebly damned. If I had not beaten in the breasts of the sacrifices with my own hands, I had not lifted a finger to save them.

If you want a story with plenty of meat on the bone, try *Creep, Shadow!*

SYDNEY J. (JAMES) BOUNDS (b. 1920) was born in Brighton, Sussex, England. In 1937 he joined the Science Fiction Association, where he met Arthur C. Clarke, William F. Temple, and John Christopher (Sam Youd). During World War II, Bounds helped found a SF fan group, the Cosmos Club, and his early short stories appeared in the club's fanzine, *Cosmic Cuts*. His first professional sale, to publisher Gerald G. Swan, was a macabre tale involving a locked-room murder where the killer was a poltergeist. Although the story never appeared, by the late 1940s Bounds had begun contributing "spicy" stories to the monthly magazines produced by Utopia Press. He was soon writing hardboiled gangster novels for John Spencer under various pseudonyms, and became a regular contributor to such SF magazines as *Futuristic Science Stories, Tales of Tomorrow, Worlds of Fantasy, New Worlds Science Fiction, Science Fantasy, Authentic Science Fiction, Nebula Science Fiction, Other Worlds Science Stories,* and *Fantastic Universe.* When the science fiction magazine markets started to dry up in the 1960s, he became a prolific and reliable contributor to such anthology series as *New Writings in SF, The Fontana Book of Great Ghost Stories, The Fontana Book of Great Horror Stories,* the *Armada Monster Book,* and the *Armada Ghost Book.* His short fiction also turned up in *Tales of Terror from Outer Space, Gaslight Tales of Terror,* and *Frighteners.* One of his best-known stories, "The Circus," was scripted by George A. Romero for a 1986 episode of the syndicated television series *Tales from the Darkside.* In 2002 Cosmos Books issued the first ever collections of the author's work as two volumes of *The Best of Sydney J. Bounds: Strange Portrait and Other Stories* and *The Wayward Ship and Other Stories,* which were both edited by Philip Harbottle. More recently, Bounds's stories have appeared in *Keep Out the Night, The Mammoth Book of Vampires, The Mammoth Book of New Terror,* and *Great Ghost Stories,* and he is a regular contributor to Harbottle's *Fantasy Adventures* series published by Wildside Press.

16 [1934]

CHAZ BRENCHLEY on

The Trail of Fu Manchu
by SAX ROHMER

Dr. Fu-Manchu, "yellow peril incarnate," first appeared in "The Zayat Kiss" (Pearson's Magazine, 1913), which "Sax Rohmer" (Arthur Henry Ward, aka A. Sarsfield Ward, 1883–1959) followed with further serial-like shockers, assembled into The Mystery of Dr. Fu-Manchu (aka The Insidious Dr. Fu-Manchu, 1913). The series continued with The Devil Doctor (aka The Return of Dr. Fu-Manchu, 1916) and The Si-Fan Mysteries (aka The Hand of Dr. Fu-Manchu, 1917), then took a pause—though Rohmer has the Devil Doctor make an unbilled cameo in The Golden Scorpion (1919)—and resumed (after some hyphen-dropping) with Daughter of Fu Manchu (1929). The master fiend's threat to the world continued through The Mask of Fu Manchu (1932), Fu Manchu's Bride (aka The Bride of Fu Manchu, 1933), The Trail of Fu Manchu (1934; the first edition includes a final chapter dropped from most reprints), President Fu Manchu (1936), The Drums of Fu Manchu (1939), The Island of Fu Manchu (1941), and The Shadow of Fu Manchu (1948), before another hiatus broken at the last by Re-Enter Fu Manchu (1957) and Emperor Fu Manchu (1959). Initially a staunch enemy of the British Eastern Empire and, by extension, all Caucasians, Fu Manchu eventually clashed with Nazis and Communists, and it was suggested that the near-immortal villain might have been an Egyptian pharaoh rather than a Chinese mandarin. The Wrath of Fu Manchu (1973) consists of previously uncollected stories. There have been pastiches (Richard Jaccoma's Yellow Peril, 1978) and authorized sequels (Cay Van Ash's Sherlock Holmes-meets-Fu Manchu Ten Years Beyond Baker Street, 1984; and Fu Manchu solo The Fires of Fu Manchu, 1987). The *villain has kept a high profile in movies (played by Harry Agar Lyons, Warner Oland, Boris Karloff, Henry Brandon, Christopher Lee, Peter Sellers, and Paul Naschy); television (played by John Carradine in a 1952 pilot, and Glenn Gordon in a 1955–56 series* The Adventures of Fu Manchu*); and radio (Rohmer himself took part in a 1931 serial). In comics, Fu Manchu was in* Detective Comics *before the debut of Batman, was extensively revised as the father of Marvel's archetypal martial arts hero in* The Hands of Shang-Chi, Master of Kung Fu, *and appeared (without actually being named) in a feud with Professor Moriarty in Alan Moore and Kevin O'Neill's* The League of Extraordinary Gentlemen. *One of the great figures of twentieth-century popular culture, albeit potentially offensive to most of the world's population, Fu Manchu has given his name to a mustache, an orchid, a virus, an orange-and-lemon sweet (Trebor's "Fu Man Chews"), and some novelty records (Guy Lombardo's "Fu Manchu, Why Don't You Behave?," 1935; the Rockin' Ramrods' "Don't Fool with Fu Manchu," 1965, and Big Bad John's "Funky Fu Manchu," 1995). The Fu Manchu who appears in Mexican movies was an English stage magician named David Bamberg, who appropriated the name for his act.*

B ASICALLY WE'RE LOOKING at chickens and eggs here, unanswerable questions. Was it my discovering Fu Manchu at a tender age that inspired my fascination with the East, or was it that love of all things Oriental that led me, *inter alia,* to Fu Manchu? And did the books lead me to the movies, or was that, too, the other way around?

Logic insists that the orientalism must have come first, because that has internal family roots; my mother was born in Rangoon, and grew up in Kuala Lumpur and Singapore. I've always envied her that childhood at that time (eightysome years ago, since you ask). But she's never really talked about it, she's never done anything to inspire or to feed my interest, and it's not a heritable characteristic. When I fell for that whole "Romance of the East" creation, I found it or created it for myself. Maybe I did find the seeds of it in Fu Manchu. I don't know, I don't remember; I was very young.

The same caveat applies to the other question. Again logic wants to stick its oar in, to suggest that I must have seen the films first; they were much more prominent than the books when I was a child in the 1960s. But we didn't go to the movies much, and we didn't have a television at all until I was seven or eight. That was about the time my elder brother got his adult library ticket. I read all his book choices as well as my own, and that's certainly where I first came across Sax Rohmer. Whether that was before or after I first saw Boris Karloff or Christopher Lee is impossible of resolution, as is whether I had asked my brother to look out for the name.

That name, of course, is as fake as his creation. Arthur Sarsfield Ward knew no more of the expatriate Chinese community than he did of the Anglo-Saxon from which he allegedly compiled his pseudonym—just enough to sound authoritative to the vast mass of his readers who knew less than he did. This, of course, is the ideal position for the fiction writer, to have enough details at hand to lend a token credibility without being encumbered by too much inhibiting fact. The Fu Manchu books didn't introduce the notion of the "yellow peril"; the yellow press had done that already. Sax Rohmer wasn't even the first to play with it in fiction, any more than he was the first to feature a clean-shaven, clean-cut ex-colonial hero. He's working with types here, with that happy blend of cliché and prejudice that personifies pulp fiction. That doesn't matter; it's not a criticism. The point about types is that they are built on a compilation of observable traits in established classes of people. Nayland Smith—Sax Rohmer's hero and Fu Manchu's would-be nemesis—is a tall, lean, tanned, educated imperial with profound moral convictions and an overriding sense of duty, of mission, almost of destiny. That passes for a good description of my grandfather also, who was exactly that kind of empire-builder, albeit a soldier rather than a colonial officer.

If Nayland Smith comes from Central Casting, though, Fu Manchu himself comes from another place, where imagination outreaches its source material by a distance. He is the creation that justifies the series, that sets it apart from its pulp contemporaries and still gives it life after nearly a century in print, as well as defining its place in the canon of horror fiction. To those who oppose him, Fu Manchu is the devil doctor, the fiend made flesh. Everything about him is exaggerated, one step beyond the norm we call human: he's preternaturally tall, intelligent, cruel, ambitious, inventive, evil.

The Trail of Fu Manchu is emblematic of the whole series of thirteen novels, not breaching the established formula but doing its work as well as any and better than some. It also has the advantage of belonging to another brief sequence, those books that open in a London fog: from Dickens's *Bleak House* to Margery Allingham's *The Tiger in the Smoke*, it's the same fog and it does the same job, wreathing its stories in an atmosphere of doubt and disarray. Here the fog serves Fu Manchu so well, we wonder if he hasn't somehow summoned it up; it isn't until the air clears some days later that the forces of virtue start to make headway against him.

But remember this, Fu Manchu is the devil incarnate; he can be frustrated but never defeated. He is functionally immortal, living far beyond the normal span of man and surviving whatever cataclysmic blow his enemies may wreak against him. Coming back to the matter of chickens and eggs, he is strange-flavored chicken and thousand-year eggs; I have cooked and eaten both, and the world will hear from him again, even if I have to write the damn' thing myself.

CHAZ (CHARLES RICHARD) BRENCHLEY (b. 1959) was born in Oxford, England, and was inspired to become a fantasy writer after meeting J. R. R. Tolkien at age twelve. He briefly attended St. Andrews University before leaving in 1977 to become a full-time writer. After contributing hundreds of mostly anonymous stories to teenage romance and women's magazines and children's comics, he published the romance novel *Time Again* under the pseudonym "Carol Trent" in 1983. His first accredited book was the crime novel *The Samaritan* (1988), followed by *The Refuge*, *The Garden*, and *Mall Time*. As "Daniel Fox" he contributed stories to the *Dark Voices: The Pan Book of Horror* anthology series, and *The Mammoth Book of Frankenstein*. Before he could develop the pseudonym further, the horror novel *Paradise* (1994) was published under his own name. *Dead of Light, Dispossession*, the British Fantasy Award-winning *Light Errant*, and *Shelter* followed. Brenchley's books often reveal a moral conscience found lacking in much mainstream horror fiction. His "Outremer" fantasy series is set during the Crusades in Palestine, and titles published to date include *Tower of the King's Daughter, Feast of the King's Shadow*, and *Hand of the King's Evil*. He is also the author of three children's books: *The Thunder Sings, The Fishing Stone*, and *The Dragon in the Ice*, while *Blood Waters* is a collection of short stories.

17

[1934]

STEPHEN VOLK on

The Devil Rides Out
by DENNIS WHEATLEY

The Duc de Richleau, Dennis Wheatley's aristocratic savant hero, made his print debut in The Forbidden Territory *(1933), in which the duc and Jewish friend Simon Aron rescue Rex Van Ryn from a godless, oppressive, sinister culture—the Soviet Union. The Devil Rides Out is a sequel in which Rex is the sidekick and Simon the abductee, and the forces of Bolshevism are replaced by the equally dangerous powers of Darkness. The first of Wheatley's occult-themed books (which were a small but significant part of his large output),* The Devil Rides Out *is one of many novels and stories from authors as diverse as W. Somerset Maugham, Anthony Powell, Robert Irwin, Will Self, and Ira Levin to draw inspiration from the public and private career of self-described black magician Aleister Crowley. It was filmed by Hammer in 1967, with Christopher Lee as an authoritative duc. It is a mark of Wheatley's status as a best seller in Britain but a marginal name elsewhere that his title was kept for U.K. release but replaced by* The Devil's Bride *abroad, allegedly because U.S. distributors though the "Rides Out" made it sound like a Western. The duc, Rex, Simon and their fourth Musketeer, Richard Eaton, first meet in a conventional murder mystery,* Three Inquisitive People, *which the author wrote before the other books but did not publish until 1940. Though later exploits of the foursome—*Strange Conflict *(1941) and* Gateway to Hell *(1970)—returned to the world of black magic, the adventurers also continued to tackle more mundane international intrigue in* The Golden Spaniard *(1938),* Codeword—Golden Fleece *(1946),* The Second Seal *(1950),* The Prisoner in the Mask *(1957),* Vendetta in Spain *(1961), and* Dangerous Inheritance *(1965).*

NOWADAYS, ASTONISHINGLY, Dennis Wheatley (1897–1977) is almost unknown to the general public. Yet in the 1960s, when I was growing up, his name was synonymous with horror—to the extent that when I wrote a spooky story as a composition at age thirteen, my teacher wrote at the end: "You obviously want to be the next Dennis Wheatley!!" Well, yes, frankly—I did.

So why is Wheatley now so absent from present-day horror consciousness, given merely one scant paragraph in *The Penguin Encyclopaedia of Horror and the Supernatural*? (Joyce Carol Oates is given seven.)

His style might be labored, but look at Lovecraft. There might be racism, but look at Poe. If the accusation is true that Wheatley's works are spoiled by a terrible snobbery, perhaps he is cursed by the class-conscious era he lived in, when the British Empire still held sway. In a way, is it surprising that his "black magic" books are about the threat to civilized society of paganism; the clash of moral decay and decent "English" values?

The great thing about *The Devil Rides Out* is that the characters, like their author, take Satanism seriously. Upon finding a black cock and white hen at Simon's house, the avuncular duke tells the boy: "I'd rather see you dead than monkeying with black magic!" We know immediately what's at stake: a young man's soul. The theme, *Exorcist*-like, is the corruption of the young. And we are off to a heart-pounding start.

Simon is being initiated into a world of black magic, but so are we. Every piece of arcane lore the duke delivers sucks us in deeper. The more he tells us to beware, the more intoxicated we get by the allure of evil. Clearly the duke and Rex (i.e., King) represent a chivalric aristocracy dedicated to protect us, while Simon, the "English Jew," is a symbolic disciple—but to which side?

If you can forgive phrases such as "It's beastly cold up here" and "I see Simon has taken to the Cliquot again," there are chilling wonders here: Mocata's black servant's astral body with eyes like burning coals; Tanith's drive to the sabbat on Salisbury Plain; the stunning appearance of the Goat of Mendes, and the banquet of bestiality—rightly described as "Goya come to life."

Then when the action shifts to Cardinal's Folly and the good old family unit of Richard and Marie Lou Eaton (what could be more English than *that* surname?), what becomes at stake is the virgin child Fleur, not to mention the possibility of unleashing the Four Horsemen of the Apocalypse. Tarot cards, numerology, Egyptology, alchemy, hypnosis, the Quabalah, even lucky horseshoes are all thrown into the heady mix.

And the final battle within the "astral fortress" of the pentacle drawn on the floor, when Damien (sic) Mocata sends a succession of malefic forces to find a crack in our heroes' psychic armor, culminating in the slug-like Saiitii manifestation and the stomping hoofbeats of the Angel of Death, must be one of the most terrifying *tours de force* in all horror literature. Though the story then coasts for a couple of chapters, the author delivers a final coup de grâce with a twist worthy, surely, of a master.

It was Wheatley's unique talent to depict the world of the unseen and its occult rules as prosaically as, to me, O-Level maths—and a lot more exciting. Doubtless it was his ability to make the unbelievable (some might say absurd) totally real that made him the world's best-selling purveyor of supernatural fiction.

It was not surprising that this modern mystery play, this wild allegorical chess game between the powers of light and darkness, attracted Hammer Films. Happily, its director was to be Terence Fisher, whose "solemn, almost pedantic style" of "bourgeois splendor" versus "decay and death," according to David Pirie's *Heritage of Horror*, perfectly suited the material. It also had the benefit of a tight, magisterial screenplay by Richard Matheson. Notably, the possessory credit "Dennis Wheatley's" appeared above the title on the posters—testimony to his standing in the public consciousness in 1967.

Ironically, without *The Devil Rides Out* there may have been no *Rosemary's Baby*, no *Omen*, no *Wicker Man*, but it was probably *The Exorcist* and Stephen King that did for Wheatley by relocating horror in America's backyard and bedroom. Sadly, even British readers preferred America's backyard to an era they didn't recognize anymore, which is a shame. Dennis Wheatley is ripe for rediscovery. But the climate is different today, and perhaps the Christian right, who deplore even *Harry Potter*, would burn Wheatley's books at the drop of a pointed hat.

> **STEPHEN VOLK** (b. 1954) was born and brought up in Pontypridd, South Wales. After taking postgraduate film and TV studies at Bristol University, his first produced feature film script was for *Gothic* (1986), Ken Russell's idiosyncratic retelling of the events that led to Mary Shelley writing *Frankenstein*. He followed it with scripts for

The Kiss (1988), *The Guardian* (1990), *Superstition* (2001), and *Octane* (2003), and is currently working on a feature adaptation of John Masefield's children's fantasy *The Box of Delights* and a script for BBC Films, *The Interpretation of Ghosts*. His short film *The Deadness of Dad* (1997) won BAFTA Best Short and Best Short Film awards at the Galway Film Festival and Celtic Film Festival. Volk's "live" television play for Halloween, *Ghostwatch* (1992), managed successfully to pull off the difficult mock documentary form six years before *The Blair Witch Project* and caused questions to be raised in Parliament. It also has the dubious distinction of being later cited in the *British Medical Journal* as the first TV program to cause post-traumatic stress disorder in children. The writer's subsequent credits for the small screen have included two episodes of the BBC anthology series *Ghosts* ("I'll Be Watching You" and "Massage") and an episode of the TV show *Shockers* ("Cyclops"), while *Afterlife* is a new drama series combining psychology and the supernatural. Volk's other credits include *Answering Spirits*, a 1992 theatrical play about spiritualism; he novelized his screenplay for *Gothic*, and his short fiction has been published in *Samhain, All Hallows, Crimewave* and the anthologies *Midnight Never Comes, Shadows and Silence, Acquainted With the Night, Hideous Progeny, Poe's Progeny, Postscripts 3*, and *Best British Mysteries 2005*. He is currently working on his "first" novel.

18 [1937]

GAHAN WILSON on

The Haunted Omnibus
Edited by by ALEXANDER LAING

Originally published as The Haunted Omnibus *by Farrar & Rinehart in 1937, this bumper anthology edited by Alexander Laing (1903–76) was reissued as* Great Ghost Stories of the World *by Blue Ribbon Books in 1941. Featuring sixty illustrations by artist and wood engraver Lynd Ward (1905–85), the book contains twenty-seven stories, including such classics as "The Yellow Wallpaper" by Charlotte Perkins Gilman, "The Screaming Skull" by F. Marion Crawford, "The Horla" by Guy de Maupassant, "An Occurrence at Owl Creek Bridge" by Ambrose Bierce, "The Ghost-Ship" by Richard Middleton and "William Wilson" by Edgar Allan Poe, along with tales by A. E. Coppard, O. Henry, Saki, Lafcadio Hearn, May Sinclair, Michael Arlen, and others. Robert Bloch wrote on Alexander Laing's 1934 novel* The Cadaver of Gideon Wyck *(also illustrated by Ward) in* Horror: 100 Best Books. *Laing was also a poet (*The Sea Witch, *1933), historian of the sea (*Clipper Ship Men, *1944), and historical novelist (*Jonathan Eagle, *1955). His other genre novel is* The Motives of Thomas Holtz, Being the Weird Tale of the Ironville Virus *(1936), which—like* Gideon Wyck—*is an early entry in the "medical Gothic" sub-genre later popularized by Robin Cook.*

AMONG THE WAYS the world has changed since I was a creepy little kid is that it has become a slightly easier place for creepy little kids. For one thing, adults nowadays feel that they must first pretend to try and "understand" creepy little kids before they scold them; and for another, it is much easier and certainly far more respectable for creepy little kids to read creepy books.

18 : LAING

When I was a creepy little kid the creepy stuff we liked was mostly published in what were called pulp magazines, which were printed in oily ink on badly made paper that contained little bits of tree bark, and if you put your nose up close to them they smelled like vacant city lots.

The covers of these magazines had embarrassing titles printed in bright red and featured gaudy paintings of largely undressed women being menaced by space aliens or mad scientists or other kinds of drooling, perverted beings, and sometimes it seemed as if they had been expressly designed to enrage, or at least seriously offend, parents and other grown-ups starting with the grumpy old men who ran the cigar stores where all the pulps were sold.

For quite a while I thought cigar stores were the only place where creepy stories could be found, but then I discovered it was possible to buy old pulps in creepy secondhand bookstores, and it was in one of those places where I had the great good fortune to come across a very used book bound in green with big yellow letters reading *Great Ghost Stories of the World* printed on its spine.

I will never forget my growing astonishment as I scanned its astoundingly varied table of contents and had my first glimpse of its wonderful illustrations. It slowly began to dawn on me that up until now I had only begun, had just barely started, my exploration into creepiness. In my innocence I thought I'd plunged deeply into its continent, and now I realized I'd only been dawdling at its coastline.

Its editor, Alexander Laing, was a poet and writer of novels. Most of the latter were seafaring sagas, but he did write a grim and spooky little thriller about evil medical doings in a New England college of surgery intriguingly called *The Cadaver of Gideon Wyck*, which I read on account of his doing the book under discussion and because good old Bob Bloch spoke of it with ghoulish affection. I enjoyed it. So far as I know, *Great Ghost Stories* is his only anthology of others' work, which makes the skillfulness of its assembly all the more impressive.

Lynd Ward was probably one of America's greatest and most inventive illustrators, and I freely admit I never recovered from the impact of his work in this book. He is probably best known for *God's Man*, an astonishing visual narrative that is composed entirely of a series of stirring and sometimes highly disturbing woodcuts. He did a number of other works in the same vein, most notably *Mad Man's Drum* and *Song without Words*. His illustrations for others' books are legendary and include *Frankenstein, Faust,* and truly spectacular color lithographs for *Beowulf,* bless its heart. It is therefore hardly to be wondered that his drawings for *Great Ghost Stories* blew me away.

That title, by the way, is entirely inaccurate, as Laing by no means confined himself to spooks, though he includes some of the very best ever caught on paper, and the sole reason he printed only one of M. R. James's titles was because the publishers managing that author's estate (talk about really rotten timing!) had only just brought out a complete collection of that great man's work.

The unghostly stories in the collection cover a rich and heady multitude of genres, ranging from insane murderers (such as W. F. Harvey's "August Heat" and Robert Louis Stevenson's "Markheim"), to mythic entities responsible for such as Lovecraft (Algernon Blackwood's "The Wendigo" and Arthur Machen's "The White People"), to flat-out monstrosities (W. F. Harvey's "The Beast with Five Fingers" and one of the abovementioned M. R. James's best nonghost stories, "The Treasure of Abbot Thomas"). But that's just for starters.

Laing not only managed to include most of the best and most literate writers of more or less contemporary creepiness, he also subtly yet dramatically enlarged the reader's horizon (very much including my own young horizon) by sneaking in quotes and excerpts from such ancient and impressive historical sources as *The Panchatantra Sutra,* Pliny the Younger, and "The Second Kalandar's Tale" from *The Arabian Nights,* not to mention numerous intriguingly eerie bits from Shakespeare, John Aubrey, Milton, Ibsen, John Donne, and Sir Thomas Browne.

I still have the book, it's beside me as I type, much more used than when I first came across it, and it's still got the nameplate I bought for it. The plate shows a small mouse looking at a big book lit by a candle. I remember trying to tell myself that the mouse was really a frightening rat and much bigger than he seemed, and pretending that the perfectly innocent-looking book somehow resembled a wizard's dark grimoire, which it doesn't. But it was the creepiest nameplate the store had since, as I said at the beginning, things were far more difficult for creepy kids than they are now.

Going over the book for the purposes of writing this article, I find I am now able to discern new gold in its wonderful stories and greater richness in its magnificent illustrations. I was not wrong to love it. I am not wrong to love it now.

GAHAN WILSON (b. 1935) believes he was helped to get off to a good start in the horror business by being born dead. He was saved from this condition only because the family doctor intervened by bursting into the operating room and repeatedly plunging him first into a bowl of hot water and then into another filled with ice until he'd bullied the infant into living. Wilson spent his boyhood years in Evanston, Illinois, which was (and likely still is) littered with huge mansions sheltering rich eccentrics who tend to go mad in all sorts of interesting ways. After graduating from the prestigious Chicago Art Institute, he eventually succeeded in persuading highly dubious magazine editors to buy his macabre cartoons. Some of his earliest artwork appeared in the final issues of the original run of *Weird Tales*, although nowadays his work is mostly seen in *Playboy* and the *New Yorker*. His cartoons have been collected in a number of volumes, including *Gahan Wilson's Graveside Manner, Is Nothing Sacred?, The Weird World of Gahan Wilson, Still Weird, Even Weirder, Gahan Wilson's Gravedigger's Party, Gahan Wilson's Monster Party,* and *The Best of Gahan Wilson*. His short stories have appeared in magazines and anthologies and were collected in *The Cleft and Other Odd Tales*, and he has edited the anthologies *Gahan Wilson's Favorite Tales of Horror* and *The First World Fantasy Awards*. Along with a number of children's books and two peculiar mystery novels, he has also illustrated the graphic works *The Raven and Other Poems* by Edgar Allan Poe, *The Devil's Dictionary and Other Works* by Ambrose Bierce, and *Gahan Wilson's Big Book of Freaks*. He has presently extended his activities into movies and television and feels the best so far among those so far accomplished is the animated short *Gahan Wilson's Diner*, and an animated special for Showtime Networks entitled *Gahan Wilson's Kid*.

19 [1939]

ROBERT WEINBERG on

The Edge of Running Water
by WILLIAM SLOANE

William Milligan Sloane III (1906–74) spent most of his life as an academic publisher, at such respected houses as Funk & Wagnall's and Rutgers University Press, but had two brief spells of activity as a genre writer. In 1931 he wrote two plays, Back Home: A Ghost Play in One Act *and* Runner in the Snow: A Play of the Supernatural in One Act *(based on a werewolf anecdote by W. B. Seabrook). Toward the end of the decade he produced two novels,* To Walk the Night *(1937) and* The Edge of Running Water, *reissued in 1964 in an omnibus titled* The Rim of Morning. *Like Abraham Merritt's* Burn, Witch, Burn! *(1933, filmed as* The Devil Doll, *1936) and Fritz Leiber's* Conjure Wife *(1943, filmed as* Weird Woman, *1944),* The Edge of Running Water *sold to Hollywood at a time when most horror movies were based on Victorian properties or original scripts. Purchased by Columbia Pictures to add to a run of Boris Karloff mad science quickies, the 1942 film (meaninglessly retitled* The Devil Commands*) was entrusted to ambitious tyro director Edward Dmytryk, who brought more imagination to the project than Nick Grinde had to earlier films in the series and prompted Karloff to one of his more involved "deranged doctor" performances.*

Locating the great horror novels of the first half of the twentieth century is a difficult task for scholars because horror, as a separate genre, did not exist. Stories and novels were called horrifying or gruesome in reviews, but no reviewer categorized them as "horror." Instead, such works were considered to be "supernaturals" if they had a supernatural element, or "mysteries" if the supernatural element was unimportant or entirely missing from the story. Stylized horror novels were often labeled "Gothics." Disturbing short work by people such as James, Lovecraft, Blackwood, Bradbury, and many others were called "ghost stories." It wasn't until the 1950s when the H-word—horror—overwhelmed American comic books that the label started appearing on novels and short stories that were more than ghost stories and different than conventional mysteries. The public finally realized that some books could only be called horror.

Thus a majority of the finest horror fiction published from 1930 to 1950 in the United States, and to a lesser degree in England, was labeled as "fiction" or "mystery," when neither title did the book much justice. Being cross-genre efforts, such books had a difficult time finding a home, and the number of supernatural novels published from 1930 to 1950 dropped enormously, since publishers had no easy way of categorizing these hard-to-define novels. Those books that made it into print walked a thin tightrope among mystery, mainstream, and the supernatural. Perhaps the most successful book of its kind was *The Edge of Running Water* by William Sloane, published in 1939.

Sloane's novel was a slow-moving story that encompassed three days in an isolated house on the tip of the Kannebec River in Maine. The narrator of the novel, Dr. Richard Sayles, a psychologist, is sent a letter by an old friend, Dr. Julian Blair. Blair wants Sayles to come to visit and help him with an experiment he's been working on for five years. When Sayles reaches the isolated town, he soon learns that Dr. Blair is considered by most of the townspeople to be a maniac. Moreover, they think his experiment involves some sort of heat ray.

At the Blair house, Sayles mets Anne, the sister of the woman Blair had married years ago and who had later died. Anne has matured into a young woman, and within a short time Sayles falls in love with her. Also at the house is Mrs. Walters, a heavyset, very bossy woman who claims to be a medium as well as Dr. Blair's assistant.

Exactly as Sayles fears, Blair is unable to accept the death of his wife, and he has spent the past five years of his life assembling a machine to communicate with the dead. Unfortunately, while the machine does open a doorway between our universe and something else, communication is not possible. A murder mystery tangles up the situation with the townspeople and, in the end, Blair and most of his futuristic technology are swept into the darkness of the other universe, destroying any possibility of his device working.

Unlike a majority of modern horror novels, *The Edge of Running Water* is a deliberately paced, subtle novel. It is a story of growing tension, of the fears of ordinary people having to deal with something beyond their perception. There is no gore in the book, and the only murder is totally accidental. The horror of the novel comes from the perception of changed reality. In his laboratory, Dr. Blair has built a model of a séance, complete with seven figures made of copper wire, holding hands around a table. Flooding these figures with electrical impulses based on certain brain waves, Blair duplicates the moment of contact in a séance. He succeeds in opening a black doorway to another space-time, but he never succeeds in learning if that dimension is the home of the dead. The chills at the climactic scene of the novel are as intense and real as any modern horror novel and are grounded in everyday reality. After closing the book, the reader is left with a feeling "with the right equipment, that experiment could be done here tonight." For any horror novel to achieve that level of believability ranks it among the best novels of the supernatural ever written. *The Edge of Running Water* takes the reader to the edge of reality and makes it clear that the door outside is very close.

ROBERT WEINBERG (b. 1946) is one of the foremost authorities on weird fiction pulp magazines. His first professionally published story, "Destroyer," appeared in *If* in May 1969. Since then he has been the author of sixteen novels, including *The Devil's Auction, The Black Lodge, The Dead Man's Kiss,* and *The Armageddon Box*. He also wrote two popular trilogies for White Wolf Books, "The Masquerade of the Red Death" and "The Horizon War," while his short fiction is collected in *Dial Your Dreams*. In collaboration with Stefan Dziemianowicz and Martin H. Greenberg, he is the co-editor of such popular anthologies as *Between Time and Terror,* the World Fantasy Award-nominated *Famous Fantastic Mysteries, Girls' Night Out,* the Bram Stoker Award-winning *Horrors! 365 Scary Stories, Lovecraft's Legacy, Mistresses of the Dark, The Mists from Beyond, Nursery Crimes, To Sleep Perchance to Dream . . . Nightmare, Rivals of Weird Tales, Weird Tales: 32 Unearthed Terrors, Virtuous Vampires, Weird Vampire Tales, 100 Fiendish Little Frightmares, 100 Hilarious Little Howlers, 100 Tiny Tales of Terror, 100 Twisted Little Tales of Torment, 100 Vicious Little Vampire Stories, 100 Little Weird Tales, 100 Wicked Little Witch Stories,* and many others. His ten non-fiction books include *The Annotated Guide to Robert E. Howard, The Weird Tales Story, A Biographical Dictionary of SF/Fantasy Artists,* and *Horror of the 20th Century: An Illustrated History*. Weinberg is also the co-author of *The Science of Superheroes* and its sequel,

The Science of Supervillains, which separate the real science from the pseudoscience in comic books. He and co-author Lois H. Gresh recently finished work on their third pop-culture study, *The Science of James Bond.* Working for Marvel comics, Weinberg scripted the popular *X-Men* spin-off series *Cable,* and chronicled the adventures of his female supernatural detective, Sydney Taine, in the four-issue *Nightside* miniseries. He also scripted *Vampire: The Machievelli Conundrum* for Moonstone Comics. Weinberg is the recipient of two World Fantasy Awards, two Society of Technical Communications Awards, and two Bram Stoker Awards. He is also perhaps the only fantasy writer to serve as grand marshal of a rodeo parade.

20 [1942]

T. M. WRIGHT on

L'Étranger/The Stranger
by ALBERT CAMUS

The Algerian-born French writer Albert Camus (1913–60) was a close associate of Jean-Paul Sartre in the French Resistance during the Nazi occupation, but argued philosophically with the other writer, refusing to be labeled an existentialist (which hasn't prevented many critics from lumping him in with the famous movement). L'Étranger, which informs such essays in hardboiled psychosis as Jim Thompson's The Killer Inside Me *(1952),* is narrated by Meursault, who refuses to *"play the game" by pretending to beliefs or feelings he does not have and gives a cold account of his mother's death, a casual affair, and a murder. Italian director Lucino Visconti filmed* The Stranger *as* Lo Straniero *(1967), with Marcello Mastroianni oddly cast as Meursault; the Turkish writer-director Zeki Demirkurbuz made a looser adaptation,* Yazgi *(2001). Camus's other major works include the essay "Le Mythe de Sisyphe" ("The Myth of Sisyphus," 1942), the play* Caligula *(1944), and the novel* La Peste *(*The Plague, *1947), which all envision an absurd, random, horrifically violent universe. Camus was awarded a Nobel Prize for literature in 1957.*

THE CHORUS TO The Cure's 1978 hit "Killing an Arab," inspired by *The Stranger,* has the first-person narrator telling us that he's both alive, and dead, and that he's " . . . a stranger/killing an Arab."

At its core, horror fiction is about being in the mortal grip of forces we cannot understand, control, or define. Sometimes those forces are external. Sometimes they aren't. Sometimes they originate deep within us.

I first read *The Stranger* in one quick gulp when I was twelve years old; it scared the adolescent hell out of me. It is the oddly low-key but wrenching story, set in Algiers, of a young man named Meursault, who, in an instant of strangely passive compulsion, shoots an Arab man lying on a beach:

> I knew that I had shattered the harmony of the day, the exceptional silence of a beach where I'd been happy. Then I fired four more times at the motionless body where the bullets lodged without leaving a trace. And it was like knocking four quick times on the door of unhappiness.

The story's pervasive aura of claustrophobic and soul-shattering doom fascinated me, gave me lingering nightmares, made me feel small. I loved that fascination, of course, and I even loved the nightmares (they became a kind of alternate, terrible reality, which—

because, even then, I was a writer of dark fantasy and horror—also fascinated and consumed me). But because I had so identified with the novel's main character, I hated feeling small and alone and under the control of forces I didn't understand. At the same time, I was intrigued by the idea that I was a "stranger" to *myself*, although the idea, even then (perhaps especially then) that I didn't know myself nearly as well as I thought I did was one I found awfully compelling.

It is an idea that has driven many pieces of fiction, in and out of the horror genre. It was not, however, solely what drove Meursault, the protagonist in *The Stranger*. Inevitably what drove him was his own implacable and fatally resigned honesty about himself.

Meursault is not Count Dracula, nor a werewolf, nor one of the living dead (at least in the classic sense we have come to think of these creatures), nor one of a million wraiths babbling incessantly in empty houses. He does not strike terror in the hearts of men. He does not seek out hapless, innocent victims that he may live forever. In the novel he is dangerous, in his compulsions, to only two individuals: the Arab man lying on a beach, and himself.

Modern vernacular might characterize Meursault as a "slacker." He's clearly all but spiritually and intellectually dead; at best, he has distanced himself from the flow of life and, for that matter, from caring much about anything at all, in the small French community where his mother has recently died. Her death, however, is not nearly the tragedy, for Meursault, that the society in which he lives wants—indeed, *needs*—it to be.

As Camus said in his preface to a 1955 edition of *The Stranger*, Meursault "is foreign to the society in which he lives; he wanders, on the fringe, in the suburbs of a private, solitary, sensual life. And this is why some readers have been tempted to look upon him as a piece of social wreckage." But, Camus continues, Meursault is doomed not because he's a "piece of social wreckage" but because he, very simply, "cannot lie," cannot even embellish or exaggerate, as we all do to ensure that our daily dealings with others run smoothly.

Did this make him feel "small and alone and under the control of forces *he* didn't understand"? Did this make him feel that he was a *stranger* to himself? And, if so, was he the unwitting author of his own doom, like so many tragic characters in any genre, not just horror?

Meursault acts, in the novel, almost like someone being swept away on a tsunami. But he does not flail about and scream for help: he goes with the flow, lets the tsunami (the expectations of others—his few friends, his lawyer, the prosecutor, the judge—and his knowledge and expectations of himself) sweep him toward the inevitable because, very simply, he has no choice.

And he is, apparently, quite *aware* that he has no choice. Like so many in the genre of horror, he cannot pretend to be what he is not, even if it will save his life (similar, perhaps, to the vampire and the werewolf and, indeed, very similar to the living dead). His actions, or lack of action, in his own defense are driven not by hopelessness, which requires a resigned kind of negative energy, or despair, which needs something meaningful to be despairing *about,* but by an oddly passive compulsion to simply be what he *is*—a man whose life has been driven by forces within himself and, as well, external to him that he cannot—indeed, *does not want to*—control.

And that lack of control, on any level, puts us quickly in a world of nightmare that is at once grotesque, mystifying, and heartbreakingly, frustratingly recognizable. Even stranger, and more grotesque, when we become a part of that world, we, like Meursault, grow to welcome our own death.

> For everything to be consummated, for me to feel less alone, I had only to wish that there be a large crowd of spectators the day of my execution and that they greet me with cries of hate.

T. (TERRANCE) M. (MICHAEL) WRIGHT (b. 1947) has been writing fiction professionally since the late 1970s. Following the publication of *The Intelligent Man's Guide to Flying Saucers* (1968), he began turning out a series of popular and highly commercial horror novels with such titles as the World Fantasy Award-nominated *Strange Seed, Nursery Tale, The Playground, The Woman Next Door, Carlisle Street, The Children of the Island, A Manhattan Ghost Story, The Changing* (as "F. W. Armstrong"), *The People of the Dark, The Waiting Room, The Devouring* (another "F. W. Armstrong"), *The Island, The Place, The School, Boundaries, The Last Vampire, Little Boy Lost, Goodlow's Ghosts, Sleepeasy* and *The Ascending*. More recent titles include *Laughing Man, The House on Orchid Street,* the Bram Stoker Award-nominated *Cold House,* and *The Eyes of the Carp,* while *Bone Soup* contains a new novel, short fiction, poetry, and art.

21 [1944]

DAVID A. SUTTON on

Sleep No More:
Twenty Masterpieces of Horror for the Connoisseur
Edited by AUGUST DERLETH

Sleep No More: Twenty Masterpieces for the Connoisseur *was the first of three linked anthologies edited by August W. (William) Derleth (1909–71), published in hardcover by New York imprint Rinehart; it was followed by* Who Knocks? Twenty Masterpieces of the Spectral for the Connoisseur *(1946) and* The Night Side: Masterpieces of the Strange & Terrible *(1947). All three books were profusely illustrated by regional artist Lee Brown Coye (1907–81) in his finest scratchboard*

21 : DERLETH

style, and drew heavily on Weird Tales, *the British supernatural tradition, and authors Derleth was developing through his Arkham House list. Published in an inflated edition of 14,500 copies (the subsequent volumes merited runs less than half that size),* Sleep No More *was "sponsored" by Arkham and promoted by Derleth in his imprint's stock lists. The abridged U.K. edition that first fell into the trembling hands of young David Sutton appealed to an even more discerning connoisseur, by shrinking from twenty to twelve masterpieces. Omitted were "Johnson Looked Back" by Thomas Burke, "Thus I Refute Beelzy" by John Collier, "The Two Black Bottles" by Wilfred Blanch Talman, "The Cane" by Carl Jacobi, "The Kennel" by Maurice Level, "Midnight Express" by Alfred Noyes, "A Gentleman from Prague" by Stephen Grendon, and "The Rats in the Walls" by H. P. Lovecraft. It is especially odd that Panther should drop Lovecraft (Derleth's mentor) and "Grendon" (Derleth himself). Though credited as a reprint from* Weird Tales, *"A Gentleman from Prague" did not appear in the magazine until the November 1944 issue, and received its probable first publication in the anthology. Peter Haining wrote about Derleth's 1947 anthology* The Sleeping and the Dead *in* Horror: 100 Best Books.

During the 1940s, while he was hard at work establishing Arkham House as the premier publisher of weird fiction, August Derleth put together several reprint anthologies. Their evocative titles, which Derleth cleverly quoted from Shakespeare, include *The Sleeping and the Dead, The Unquiet Grave, The Night Side,* and *Night's Yawning Peal.* My copy of *Sleep No More* is a Panther paperback from 1964, its cover illustration a luminous green disembodied hand crawling across a carpet (from "The Return of the Sorcerer").

In that year I was starting out as a fan of horror, SF, and fantasy fiction, and these Derleth anthologies showcased—and were my first introduction to—the mix of classic English ghost and horror writers and those from the American pulp tradition. *Sleep No More* was the first such anthology I bought (and also the first in this reprint series that Derleth edited).

It was an influential volume that set me off on a lifelong love of horror fiction, which led, some four years later (during which time my education in the genre was fortified by the reading of many tomes of a similar disposition), to my starting my fantasy review fanzine, *Shadow*. At the time paperback anthologies were an excellent source of material, and easier and cheaper to come by than scarce hardcover collections or copies of *Weird Tales* and other pulps.

M. P. Shiel, one of a number of British authors whom Derleth would later reprint in Arkham House editions, is represented by the fantastic "The House of Sounds." Of the four writers from the British side of the Atlantic to be included in this anthology, Shiel's was the story that had the most haunting affect on me and was the first work of his I had read. The author's lavish prose and the evocative plot, set in a sepulchral brass and copper mansion chained over a thunderous cataract on a small island off Shetland, still resonates its aura of strangeness and phantasmagoria down the years.

In "The Occupant of the Room," set in the Swiss Alps, Algernon Blackwood builds up his tale of psychological horror to a feverish pitch of sustained terror that is not in any way diminished by the expected revelation at the end. "Count Magnus" is from M. R. James's first collection of ghost stories and concerns the eponymous violent alchemist and the researcher who delves too far. The story is typical of James's themes and of his style of dropping in detail upon detail to unsettle the reader. Finally there is H. R. Wakefield's "He Cometh and He Passeth By," a celebrated story that has as its protagonist an evil seducer, drug user, and Satanist.

The most memorable of the remaining eight stories is Clark Ashton Smith's "The Return of the Sorcerer." Imagine the frisson I felt as I read the tale in 1964, with its mention of *The Necronomicon* and the obvious association with H. P. Lovecraft's Cthulhu Mythos. Smith's exuberant prose extrudes the last ounce of horror from this story of rival Satanists. In the concluding paragraphs Smith moves the horror "off-stage," seen as shadows cast by lamplight through a doorway, but nevertheless the images are as potent as the gruesome denouement that quickly follows.

21 : DERLETH

Among the other stories is "'The Yellow Sign,'" an eerie tale, one of a series of loosely connected stories that Robert W. Chambers wrote concerning a strange book, *The King in Yellow*. An artist falls in love with his model, but they are doomed by the presence of the book; a strange clasp of black onyx; and a vile, corpse-like church warden. Chambers started out as a painter, and some of the unease in this tale comes from his ability to describe the artist at work. The other American writers in this book provide a snapshot of the pulp tradition, with the sweeping prose of Robert E. Howard in "The Black Stone" and Frank Belknap Long's tightly drawn "The Black Druid," both again exploring forbidden occult books. A tale about premature burial told by village elders, I would later learn that Hazel Heald's "The Horror in the Burying Ground" was one of H. P. Lovecraft's revisions and virtually all his own work. Set in the Minnesota hills, in "The Hand of the O'Mecca" Howard Wandrei creates a peculiar and evocative werewolf yarn that comes across like a fairy tale. And Henry S. Whitehead uses his firsthand experience of voodoo and the West Indies to craft the unsettling "Cassius." Robert Bloch's "The Mannikin" touches on a similar theme in a way and is a gruesome blend of Lovecraftian references, witches' familiars, deformity, and horrific possession.

Sleep No More advertises itself as "Horror for the Connoisseur," and so it felt reading it that first time. Though a slender book, it gave me my first taste of James, Shiel, Blackwood, Smith, and Howard—writers I would turn to again and again as my interest in the genre expanded. I didn't know anything about August Derleth at the time, but very soon wised up to America's foremost horror anthologist and publisher. I remain indebted to him for his genre introduction to this anonymous reader and for his invitation to . . . sleep no more!

> **DAVID A. (AMBROSE) SUTTON** (b. 1947) was recognized for his devotion to and achievement in the genre over many years with the British Fantasy Society's "Special Award" in 1994. He has also received the World Fantasy

Award, the International Horror Guild Award, and twelve British Fantasy Awards since 1978. From producing his own small press magazine, *Shadow Fantasy Literature Review*, and extensive editorial and administrative jobs for the British Fantasy Society and British Fantasy Conventions during the 1970s, he has also been involved in editing and publishing a number of small press publications, including the multiple-award-winning *Fantasy Tales* magazine, *Dark Horizons*, and *Fantasy Media*. More recently he compiled *Voices from Shadow*, a small non-fiction anthology celebrating the twentieth anniversary of his first genre magazine, and an anthology of new ghost and horror tales, *Phantoms of Venice*. Earlier fiction anthologies under his editorship include *New Writings in Horror & the Supernatural* (two volumes); *The Satyr's Head & Other Tales of Terror;* and, jointly edited with Stephen Jones, *The Best Horror from Fantasy Tales, The Anthology of Fantasy and the Supernatural, Dark Voices: The Pan Book of Horror Stories* (five volumes), and the acclaimed *Dark Terrors* series (six volumes) from Gollancz. His short stories have appeared in a number of periodicals and anthologies, including *Skeleton Crew, Best New Horror 2, 7, Final Shadows, Cold Fear, Taste of Fear, The Mammoth Book of Zombies, The Mammoth Book of Werewolves, The New Lovecraft Circle, Shadows Over Innsmouth, The Merlin Chronicles,* and *Beneath the Ground*. He lives in Birmingham, England, from where he regularly rambles through the surrounding hills, woodland, countryside, and mud. When not poring over Ordnance Survey maps, he is working on a batch of new short stories that he intends to combine with some of his best previously published work to form his first collection of horror tales, *Clinically Dead & Other Tales of the Supernatural*.

22 [1944]

STORM CONSTANTINE on

Lost Worlds
by **CLARK ASHTON SMITH**

Published in 1944 by August Derleth's small press Arkham House, Lost Worlds *was the third collection of stories by Californian author, poet, and artist Clark Ashton Smith (1893–1961), following the self-published* The Double Shadow and Other Fantasies *(1933) and a previous Arkham volume* Out of Space and Time *(1942), which Harlan Ellison wrote on in* Horror: 100 Best Books. *Personally selected by the author,* Lost Worlds *contains twenty-three stories, all but seven reprinted from the pulp magazine* Weird Tales. *The stories are "The Tale of Satampra Zeiros," "The Door to Saturn," "The Seven Geases," "The Coming of the White Worm," "The Last Incantation," "A Voyage to Sfanomoë," "The Death of Malygris," "The Holiness of Azédarac," "The Beast of Averoigne," "The Empire of the Necromancers," "The Isle of the Torturers," "Necromany in Naat," "Xeethra," "The Maze of Maal Dweb," "The Flower-Women," "The Demon of the Flower," "The Plutonian Drug," "The Planet of the Dead," "The Gorgon," "The Letter from Mohaun Los," "The Light from Beyond," "The Haunters from Beyond," and "The Treader of the Dust." The first edition, limited to 2,043 copies, uses a jacket photograph by E. Burt Trimpey of four of Smith's outré sculptures; Panther Books issued a two-volume paperback edition in the United Kingdom in 1974, presenting Smith's lost worlds in sections headed "Zothique, Averoigne and others" and "Atlantis, Hyperborea, Xiccarph and others." Arkham published a further four collections of Smith's fiction and three volumes of poetry. His work has subsequently been reprinted in various permutations and editions, most recently* The Emperor of Dreams: The Lost Worlds of Clark Ashton Smith

(2002), edited by Stephen Jones for the Gollancz "Fantasy Masterworks" series. In 2005 Night Shade Books announced a major republishing program of the complete Smith.

ONE OF THE reasons I fell in love with Clark Ashton Smith's work as a young teenager was his colorful use of language. As a fledgling writer I was impressed by arcane and unusual words, and reading Smith's baroque stories was like being drip-fed word honey, perhaps laced with some exotic and narcotic alcohol. I came to Smith via H. P. Lovecraft, and those great old Panther paperbacks from the 1970s, when the whole school of *Weird Tales*-spinners all came back into print in the United Kingdom. Lovecraft hardly reined himself in on the convoluted sentences, but Smith blazed on to greater excesses. And the things he described . . .

The lost worlds included in this collection imply a feverish imagination to say the least. Some could best be termed fantasy, others science fiction, but all are set in vivid and uncanny landscapes, some on the edge of destruction beneath the light of dying suns, peopled by arrogant warrior-kings and conniving magicians. They are also horror stories in the literal sense. Most of the tales describe dooms of various grotesque sorts, although there are a couple of tales that are reminiscent of Jack Vance in their somewhat humorous tone. In fact, I think Vance's "Dying Earth" stories probably owe more than a nod to Mr. Smith.

Returning to the stories after a long time away provided an interesting new perspective. They come across as slightly camp now, but still with the power to captivate. I might be smiling more than gasping nowadays, but the insanely opulent prose is still a treat. The lost worlds in question include "Xiccarph" (another planet) and forgotten realms of our own world, "Hyperborea," "Atlantis," "Averoigne," and "Zothique." To round off the collection there are also some stories under the heading "Others," which are random exotic corners of Smith's imagination.

Like Lovecraft, Smith invented a mythos, since most of his worlds are tentatively connected and their upper (and lower) realms are populated by gods and demigods of horrific attributes. The Cthulhu Mythos became a bona fide magical system espoused by chaos magicians in the late twentieth century, and it would be interesting to see Smith's mythos undergo the same process. Lovecraft, who had no belief in the occult, would have been disgusted if he knew what would happen to his material, but I think Clark Ashton Smith would have been more sympathetic, if not pleased.

There's a subtle difference in his stories to those of Lovecraft, which implies that on some level he's in awe of his creations rather than simply repulsed by them. If the god Zhothaqquah and his fellows aren't worse than Cthulhu's crew, they're on a level. Bat-like, slobbering, slavering, shuffling . . . multiple appendages appearing loathsomely from bloated amorphous shapes . . . you get the picture. Aphrodite they are not.

I identified with the outsider in Smith and can remember the huge impact a particular paragraph from "The Planet of the Dead" had on me when I was about fourteen. I just have to quote some of it:

> For Melchoir was one of those who are born with an immedicable distaste for all that is present or near at hand; one of those who have drunk too lightly of oblivion and have not wholly forgotten the transcendent glories of other aeons. . . . The earth is too narrow for such, and the compass of mortal time is too brief; and paucity and barrenness are everywhere; and in all places their lot is a neverending weariness.

Yes! I thought as I read that, heart swelling. I was the weird kid at school who was into weird things. I wanted to live in ancient Greece or Egypt. In Smith I found a mentor. His worlds were like those vanished aeons, and I could immerse myself in his violet prose and just be . . . somewhere else. The fact that most of the stories were so doom-laden and grim also appealed to the angry teen in me.

There are no kindly wizards in the *Lost Worlds*, but a horde of necromancers, sorcerers, torturers, and dark priests of the most perverse kind. They inhabit surreal and immense mansions and palaces, waited upon by peculiar familiars and automata. In the darkness they scheme the annihilation of their rivals. They breed strange and deadly flowers or decant poisons. They appear dead, sitting immobile as liches on obsidian thrones, but then exact horrible revenges on those who come to loot their silent, dust-wreathed halls. The gods of these stories are similarly without benign aspects. They are like the demons of Tibetan lore, kept at bay by clever magicians but eager to inflict monstrous torment upon their worshipers whenever the opportunity presents itself. The kings are mostly tyrants, and there are few female characters other than the occasional limpid maiden who's the beloved of a story's protagonist and who gets kidnapped or worse by passing torturers or a lustful wizard.

This could all come across, of course, as distasteful to modern sensibilities, but there is such a strong sense of "otherness" in Smith's stories that whatever occurs in those worlds seems, if not acceptable, then natural and faithful to the environment. It's almost as if he wrote while under the influence of a mind-altering drug, and was merely recounting things he was seeing rather than making it all up.

I still have a story I wrote myself when I was in thrall to Smith's worlds. It's really cute in its woe and angst, its rotting towers, its endless Wastes (capitalization of Terrible Deserts and Awful Crags de rigueur, of course), its revenant serpent people enslaved by a curse and so on. Smith was a great inspiration to me until I went on to find writers like Michael Moorcock, Jack Vance, and Tanith Lee, whose use of language was, while equally enthralling, much more suitable to modern writing. Still, I'll always have an affection for the abominable monstrosities of the Lost Worlds. Zothique and its contemporaries are still bizarre and barely frequented places, and tourism has not defiled them. Ideal for the discerning traveler.

STORM CONSTANTINE (b. 1956) lives in the British Midlands with her husband and a number of cats. Her novels and stories span the genres of science fiction, fantasy, and horror, and she has also written non-fiction titles on the Egyptian zodiac, Ancient Egyptian feline goddesses (with

Eloise Coquio), and esoteric psychology (with Deborah Benstead). Her novels include the "Wraeththu" trilogy (*The Enchantments of Flesh and Spirit, The Bewitchments of Love and Hate,* and *The Fulfilments of Fate and Desire*), *The Monstrous Regiment, Hermetech, Aleph, Burying the Shadow, Sign for the Sacred, Calenture, Stalking Tender Prey, Scenting Hallowed Blood, Stealing Sacred Fire, Thin Air, The Thorn Boy, Silverheart* (with Michael Moorcock), The "Magravandias Chroncles" (*Sea Dragon Heir, The Crown of Silence,* and *The Way of Light*), and the "Wraeththu Chronicles" (*The Wraiths of Will and Pleasure, The Shades of Time and Memory,* and *The Ghosts of Blood and Innocence*). *The Hienama* is a novella of the Wraeththu Mythos, and her short fiction is collected in *Three Heralds of the Storm, The Oracle Lips,* and *The Thorn Boy and Other Dreams of Dark Desire. The Grimoire of Deharan Magick: Kaimana: The Rite and Rituals of the Wraeththu* is published by the author's own imprint, Immanion Press.

23 [1944]

STEFAN DZIEMIANOWICZ on

Jumbee and Other Uncanny Tales
by HENRY S. WHITEHEAD

Jumbee and Other Uncanny Tales *was published by Arkham House in an edition of 1,559 copies. The volume collected fourteen tales of horror and the supernatural by the American-born Dr. Henry St. Clair*

Whitehead (1882–1932), an Episcopal minister who was one of the most highly regarded writers for the pulp magazine Weird Tales *during the 1920s and '30s. The collection was assembled posthumously by August Derleth and is the first of two volumes of Whitehead's fiction from the Arkham imprint, which also published his* West India Lights *in 1946. All of the book's stories previously appeared in pulp fiction magazines between 1926 and 1932, with the lion's share appearing in* Weird Tales. *All but one of the stories are set in the West Indies, where Whitehead had been appointed acting archdeacon to the Virgin Islands. The book's contents consist of "Jumbee," "Cassius," "Black Tancrede," "The Shadows," "Sweet Grass," "The Black Beast," "Seven Turns in a Hangman's Rope," "The Tree-Man," "Passing of a God," "Mrs. Lorriquer," "Hill Drums," "The Projection of Armand Dubois," "The Lips," and "The Fireplace." The jacket art was by Frank Wakefield, and the book was reprinted in the United Kingdom in the 1970s by Neville Spearman.*

IN THE 1920S and '30s the world was much bigger than it is today, and travel was more difficult and dear. People who wanted to escape to foreign lands and exotic locales often did so by way of their favorite pulp fiction magazines. *Weird Tales*, the leading weird fiction pulp, offered its armchair travelers transport to marvelous realms far off the beaten paths of most periodicals, and the Reverend Henry S. Whitehead was one of its top tour guides.

Whitehead was an Episcopal minister with an unusually worldly outlook. He had held a number of jobs before his ordination in 1913, and had been contributing fiction to a wide variety of pulps for nearly a decade. With his first sale to *Weird Tales* in 1924 he seems to have found a perfect fit for his literary interests. Virtually everything he wrote thereafter until his death in 1932 was supernatural fiction, and the bulk of it went to *Weird Tales*, where it consistently ranked as high in reader approval as the fiction of H. P. Lovecraft (with whom he corresponded), Clark Ashton Smith, and Robert E. Howard.

There had been nothing terribly distinguished about Whitehead's fiction, weird or otherwise, until the publication of "Jumbee" in 1926.

The story is a plotless account of folk beliefs and customs relating to the West Indian islands, but the narrator delivers it with the convincing nonchalance of one who knows and accepts ideas that require more than a little willing suspension of disbelief. The West Indies had been serving as fodder for pulp adventures long before Whitehead wrote his tale, but there was an understandable difference in his treatment. Whereas most other pulpsmiths built their island stories from bits and pieces of local color picked up secondhand and glued together with imagination, Whitehead wrote from direct experience: He had been appointed acting archdeacon of the Virgin Islands in 1921 and was a regular visitor to them until his death. Fiction set in a magic land where the occult is an inextricable part of the culture was simply Whitehead writing what he knew.

Whitehead must have realized he'd struck a mother lode of raw ore for weird fiction in what he absorbed from his island travels because he mined it for nearly two dozen stories, or just about everything he wrote from that point on. All but one of the fourteen stories collected in *Jumbee and Other Uncanny Tales*, his first collection, is set in Haiti or the Virgin Islands. To read these stories is to enter into a mystic realm whose bedrock is a rich and resonant mythology of mysterious gods, extraordinary supernatural beings, and sacred customs and rituals. The history of the islands abounds with vivid accounts of piracy and adventures of Dutch, French, Danish, Spanish, and English explorers, and Whitehead wove it seamlessly into his stories to enrich their atmosphere and root the supernatural in a tangible reality. Stereotypes of the natives and their culture were inevitable, but Whitehead refrained from cliché depictions of superstitious primitives who instinctively practiced black magic. He wrote with genuine sympathy for the islanders and presented them as spiritually healthier in their willingness to accommodate marvels that rigidly rational European settlers could not. Though they have their moments of horror, ultimately Whitehead's works are tales of the "uncanny" that evoke wonder as much as terror.

Most of the stories are narrated by the character Gerald Canevin, a traveling writer whom Whitehead modeled on himself. Canevin's inquisitiveness leads him down unusual byways, and his accounts of what he observes read like a Baedeker to the secret mysteries of island life. "Black Tancrede" begins with a pithy history of the slave trade before launching into the legend of an executed slave whose amputated hand still scuttles around the plantation where it was lopped off, seeking to avenge its owner's death. In "Cassius," scientific men discover that a half-glimpsed creature they dismiss as an island rodent is actually the magically animated body of an unborn twin that was surgically removed from a local. "Sweet Grass" condenses attitudes toward race relations and the taboo of miscegenation into a tale of a white settler's bewitchment by an island girl. Canevin is unsettled by much of what he sees, but he knows when to share his awe with the reader. In "The Tree-Man," he discusses *obi,* or the practice of herb magic, as background for a haunting story of an islander revered as the spiritual twin of a sacred island tree. And in "Passing of a God," his revelation that a tumorous growth on an island settler is slowly manifesting a benign *vodu* god the man once channeled is as close as popular fiction comes to describing a religious epiphany.

A second collection of Whitehead's tales, *West India Lights,* came out two years later, and its contents perfectly complement those of *Jumbee.* The stories are as vivid and colorful as when they were first written, and the echoes of the otherworldly that reverberate through them will persuade even the most jaded reader of supernatural horror fiction that the West Indies are, as Whitehead writes, "a land of the imagination."

> **STEFAN DZIEMIANOWICZ** (b. 1957) has spent most of his life in the New York/New Jersey area. Influenced by old television shows such as *The Twilight Zone* and *The Outer Limits,* and by parents who were both avid readers, he discovered the work of Ray Bradbury at an early age. After moving on to H. P. Lovecraft, he began reviewing books for *Crypt of Chthulhu* and *Fantasy Review.* One of the genre's busiest and most perceptive editors and critics, he is the

author of *Bloody Mary and Other Tales for a Dark Night*, *The Core of Ramsey Campbell: A Bibliography & Reader's Guide* (with Ramsey Campbell and S. T. Joshi), and *The Annotated Guide to Unknown and Unknown Worlds*. He has compiled a number of single-author collections, by such writers as Robert Bloch, Ralph Adams Cram, Jane Rice, Gerald Biss, A. Merritt, Andrew Caldecott, W. C. Morrow, Bram Stoker, Louisa May Alcott, and Charles Dickens. An editor of the British Fantasy Award- and International Horror Guild Award-winning critical magazine *Necrofile: The Review of Horror Fiction* (1991–99, with S. T. Joshi and Michael A. Morrison), he recently put together the three-volume *World Encyclopedia of Supernatural Fiction for Greenwood Press* with S. T. Joshi. Dziemianowicz has also edited or co-edited more than thirty anthologies, usually in collaboration with Robert Weinberg and Martin H. Greenberg. These include *Weird Tales: 32 Unearthed Terrors*, *Rivals of Weird Tales*, the World Fantasy Award-nominated *Famous Fantastic Mysteries*, *Weird Vampire Tales*, *A Taste for Blood*, *To Sleep, Perchance to Dream: Nightmares*, *100 Ghastly Little Ghost Stories*, *The Mists from Beyond*, *Sea Cursed*, *100 Creepy Little Creature Stories*, *100 Wild Little Weird Tales*, *100 Vicious Little Vampire Stories*, *100 Wicked Little Witch Stories*, *Between Time and Terror*, *100 Astounding Little Alien Stories*, *100 Tiny Tales of Terror*, *Virtuous Vampires*, *Rivals of Dracula*, *100 Fiendish Little Frightmares*, *Girls Night Out*, *Mistresses of the Dark*, the Bram Stoker Award-winning *Horrors! 365 Scary Stories*, *100 Twisted Little Tales of Torment*, *100 Hilarious Little Howlers*, and *Crafty Cat Crimes: 100 Tiny Cat Tale Mysteries*. He is a regular contributor to a number of genre magazines, *Publishers Weekly*, and numerous encyclopedia and reference projects.

24 [1944]

GWYNETH JONES on

Great Tales of Terror and the Supernatural
Edited by **HERBERT A. WISE** and **PHYLLIS FRASER**

First published as a 1,100-page hardcover by Random House's prestigious Modern Library imprint, Great Tales of Terror and the Supernatural *is split into two sections, "Tales of Terror" and "Tales of the Supernatural," with the stories arranged chronologically according to the authors' dates of birth. The "Terror" section contains twenty stories, by Honoré de Balzac, Edgar Allan Poe (two), Wilkie Collins, Ambrose Bierce, Thomas Hardy, W. W. Jacobs, H. G. Wells (two), "Saki" (H. H. Munro), Alexander Woollcott, Conrad Aiken, Dorothy L. Sayers, Richard Connell, Carl Stephenson, Michael Arlen, William Faulkner, Ernest Hemingway, John Collier, and Geoffrey Household. The "Supernatural" selection is more traditional, with thirty-two tales, from Edward Bulwer-Lytton, Nathaniel Hawthorne, Charles Collins and Charles Dickens, Joseph Sheridan Le Fanu, Fitz-James O'Brien, Henry James, Guy de Maupassant (two), F. Marion Crawford, O. Henry, M. R. James (two), Edith Wharton, W. W. Jacobs (again), Arthur Machen, Robert Hichens, Rudyard Kipling (two), Edward Lucas White, E. F. Benson (two), Algernon Blackwood (two), "Saki" (again), Oliver Onions, Walter de la Mare, A. E. Coppard, E. M. Forster, Richard Middleton, "Isak Dinesen" (Karen Blixen), and H. P. Lovecraft (two). The editors contribute a historical Introduction and detailed author notes and admit that: "Only in the case of* The Turn of the Screw *by Henry James have we consciously left out a classic we would have liked to include. Our only reason is its length—it is really a complete short novel, and would have taken up more space than we could spare." Weirdly, James Agate said exactly the same thing in his foreword to the 1934 collection* A Century of Thrillers: From Poe to Arlen. *Co-compiler Phyllis Fraser (Cerf Wagner) (b. 1911) was married to Bennet Cerf, the founder of Random House; Hollywood actress Ginger Rogers was her cousin, and she had played bit parts (mostly uncredited) in 1930s films such as* Vivacious Lady, The Black Room *(with Boris Karloff), and* Fighting Youth. *Less is known about Herbert A. Wise (1890–1961), who should not be confused with the British TV director (*I, Claudius*) or the credited director of* Castle of the Living Dead *(actually, Luciano Ricci).*

I WAS TEN YEARS old when I bought a massive volume of ghost stories at a rummage sale. I think it cost me sixpence. My mother was horrified. She'd brought her children up to be rational beings: science fiction was entirely acceptable; ghosts, ghoulies, and things that go bump in the night, definitely not! But she didn't take it away. My mother and father never forbade me to read anything (though occasionally they'd implore me to wait until I was old enough to appreciate what I was reading).

I didn't know I'd got hold of perhaps the greatest anthology of weird tales of all time, but the stories made a huge impact. I was impressed to the point of wake-up-screaming by "The Rats in the Walls" and "The Dunwich Horror" (H. P. Lovecraft), "The Haunters and the Haunted," or "The House and the Brain" (Edward Bulwer-Lytton) and "The Screaming Skull" (F. Marion Crawford). Oh, that pit, that squirming abyss deep under the old country house, where the dreadful shepherd tends his blobby, white-fleshed, naked livestock.... The unwise experiment of spending a night in that house "situated on the north side of Oxford Street, in a dull but respectable thoroughfare." Or the peevish, defensive tone of the madman who relates the tale of the skull in the cupboard. Not to mention that intensely horrible face made of crumpled linen. Nobody who has read M. R. James's "Oh, Whistle, and I'll Come to You, My Lad" at a young age will ever sleep easy with an extra, empty bed in the room.

It took me longer to realize that I was marked for life by the disquiet of J. Sheridan Le Fanu's "Green Tea"; by Professor Guildea's nauseating admirer in "How Love Came to Professor Guildea" (Robert Hichens); by the hinting, shying-away, circling around, Chinese-boxes narrative of Arthur Machen's "The Great God Pan"; by the invisible creatures of "What Was It?" (Fitz-James O'Brien); and by "The Horla" (Guy de Maupassant), or by the bowl of primroses delivered to a very sick boy in Walter de la Mare's "Out of the Deep."

I don't much go for pretty ghost stories, so I was less interested in Rudyard Kipling's gentle "They," but I liked "The Ghost Ship" (Richard Middleton) for the sarcasm, and I loved the shape-shifting falcon in Karen Blixen's "The Sailor Boy's Tale." For years I ignored most of the "Tales of Terror" section; if there was nothing spooky going on, how was my skin going to crawl? I still agree with the editors: "The literature of the tale of pure terror is comparatively limited. Good supernatural stories are far more plentiful." But children delight in sheer bloody-mindedness, so I relished "Leningen versus the Ants" (Carl Stephenson) and Richard Connell's "The Most Dangerous Game"; and when I realized what had happened at the punch line (I didn't get it at first) I considered "The Facts in the Case of M. Valdemar" (Edgar Allan Poe) very fine.

Most of the books I loved when I was a child had been handed to me with shining recommendations: from my sister, my parents; the librarian. Either that, or they'd been deemed necessary for my education. I loved *Great Tales of Terror and the Supernatural* because I had found it, and discovered for myself that it was vitally important to me.

I don't know why I'm drawn to supernatural horror—just lucky, I guess—but four decades later I still love this book, because I'm experienced enough to know that the stories are not only seminal (*Great Tales* material is buried at the heart of modern horror, and coils its mycorrhizoid tendrils everywhere) but also ingeniously, intuitively constructed. A writer's algorithm for creating terror in the reader lies here. You can read them for spine-tingling pleasure today; and you can read them and learn. You may examine the autobiography of Arthur Machen and suspect that his demonic visions of the unthinkable are child-sex trade in fancy dress; you may spot a barely disguised account of the moral and social consequence of untreated syphilis in

Edward Lucas White's grisly "Lukundoo." The causes of horror don't change much from age to age: we fear death, we fear the unforgivable crimes society denies. But the abyssal dimension, the stripping away of rational and material defenses, remains valid.

The horrific side of my writing owes everything to this anthology. You can read on my "Ann Halam" Web page how the newspaper "ghost" in *The Fearman,* the book that won me the Children of the Night Award for 1995, is a steal from "Oh, Whistle, and I'll Come to You, My Lad," *especially the way it moves;* and how the occult mechanism in the house on Roman Road is sampled from "The Haunters and the Haunted" (the most haunted house in London also features in *Band of Gypsys).* Arthur Machen's "The Great God Pan" and Lovecraft's "The Rats in the Walls" can both be traced in the circling, shuddering, Chinese boxes narrative of *Phoenix Café,* and M. Valdemar's fate recurs in *Castles Made of Sand.* Most of all I take my lesson from Sheridan Le Fanu, whose "Green Tea" doctrine you can find quoted by a character in *Castles Made of Sand* (the Gwyneth Jones novel with the most overt horror content so far).

There are circumstances when the internal and the external world may change places. The horrors of the abyss inside may enter the world we fondly regard as material, and a safe refuge from nightmare. Maybe that's a parable, a rich metaphor. Maybe it's the truth of a world to come.

Great Tales of Terror and the Supernatural is a very masterly collection. I could wish there were more stories by women: Charlotte Perkins Gilman's "The Yellow Wallpaper" should be in here, and May Sinclair's "Where Their Fire Is Not Quenched"; women more expert in the hidden literature could name many more. But this is the canon: work with it, add to it, transform it to your taste. If you care about weird tales, you need to know this old book. Let the ancient sorceries touch you.

GWYNETH JONES (b. 1952) was born in Manchester, England. She took an undergraduate degree in History of Ideas at the University of Sussex, which gave her a taste for scientific revolutions and societies in phase transition, which still echoes in her work. She's written more than twenty novels for teenagers, including several ghost and horror stories, mostly using the pseudonym "Ann Halam." These include *King Death's Garden, The Haunting of Jessica Raven, The Powerhouse, Crying in the Dark, Don't Open Your Eyes, Dr. Franklin's Island,* and *The Fearman,* which won the Dracula Society's Children of the Night Award in 1995. She also writes highly regarded science fiction and fantasy for adults, including the *Aleutian Trilogy* and the *Bold as Love* sequence. *Bold as Love,* the first in this series, won the Arthur C. Clarke Award in 2002. Her short story output is not prolific, but her horror fiction has appeared in several anthologies, including *The Mammoth Book of Best New Horror, The Architecture of Fear, Dark Terrors 5,* and *The Mammoth Book of Vampire Stories by Women.* She doesn't believe in ghosts but is afraid of them, and she always pays close attention to her nightmares.

25 [1945]

JOEL LANE on

The Opener of the Way
by ROBERT BLOCH

The Opener of the Way was the first book publication of the prolific Robert Bloch (1917–94). Produced by August Derleth's pioneering small press imprint Arkham House in an edition of two thousand copies, it collects twenty-one stories from Weird Tales *and other pulp magazines. These include the classic vampire story* "The Cloak" *(from* Unknown*) and* "Waxworks," *both adapted by the author for the Amicus anthology movie* The House That Dripped Blood *(1970). Other stories, such as* "Yours Truly, Jack the Ripper," "Return to the Sabbath," *and* "Beetles" *have been adapted frequently for radio and television shows including* Stay Tuned for Terror, Thriller, The Alfred Hitchcock Hour, *and* Tales from the Darkside. *The book has rarely been republished in a single volume, though several paperbacks have repackaged the Arkham material. Two U.K. collections called* The House of the Hatchet *(Tandem, 1965, and Granada, 1976) have overlapping but not identical contents; most of the stories from the Tandem* House *turn up in the companion volume to the Granada* House *titled* The Opener of the Way. *The late Hugh B. Cave wrote on Bloch's most famous work,* Psycho *(1959), in* Horror: 100 Best Books, *while Bloch himself contributed an essay on* The Cadaver of Gideon Wyck *by Alexander Laing (1934).*

ROBERT BLOCH WAS one of the all-time masters of horror fiction. He's best known for his psychological thrillers—*Psycho, The Scarf, Firebug,* and others—which, due to his background in supernatural horror and his innate pessimism, are chilling portraits of psychosis and despair. Bloch's engaging prose style and his fondness for black humor have misled some readers into imagining he is not fully serious. If you think that, you're not paying attention. The carefully timed shifts of awareness and stabs of unease in Bloch's writing reveal a worldview in which there are no reassurances. Life's a nightmare and then you die . . . if you're that lucky.

The key to Bloch's fiction is the interplay of external and internal forces, creating a world of paranoia in which neither the narrator nor the outside world can be relied on. Bloch honed his writing techniques in the 1930s and '40s, writing supernatural horror stories for *Weird Tales* and other pulp magazines. And despite the excellence of his 1950s novels, my favorite of his books is the debut collection he published with Arkham House in 1945: *The Opener of the Way*.

Why? Partly because his meteoric development from faux-Gothic pastiche to sour, elliptical portraits of urban damnation is so rapid it takes your breath away. But more importantly, because this book *rocks*. Buying and devouring the Neville Spearman edition seven years ago helped me get through a difficult time. I also have the two U. K. paperback collections derived from *Opener*, but my copies are frayed and desiccated in a manner reminiscent of Bloch's tale "The Eyes of the Mummy." In fact, I suspect something has gnawed them.

In a brief introduction, Bloch attributes his ideas to a secret collaborator, a "Mr. Hyde," who makes up in dark conviction what he may lack in good taste. Reading the stories—awkward and derivative though a few of them are—you never doubt for a minute that this is a writer who means business. His first published story, "The Feast in the Abbey" (1935), is pure nightmare: the story of a traveler lost in a forest in France at night, trying to reach his brother's home in the village but instead finding a gray and somber abbey where some kind of celebration is in progress. Bloch packs this potentially clichéd tale with a raging darkness, a brooding atmosphere of dread, that builds up to a resonant conclusion. When this story appeared, Bloch was seventeen.

Thereafter he fell under the influence of his friend and mentor H. P. Lovecraft. Six of Bloch's efforts in this vein are included here, and they show two things. One is that Bloch, from the outset, had a profoundly individual sense of ironic pessimism. The other is that Bloch was not content to replicate Lovecraftian settings or narrative structures. Rather, he focused on themes that appealed to him—such as the lore of ancient Egypt—and hammered out his own blacker-than-black pulp fever dreams, with a handful of dried Lovecraft stirred in for flavoring. "The Faceless God" (1936) has a criminal European explorer pursued and destroyed by the immemorial shadow of Nyarlathotep, the Lord of the Desert. Bloch writes as if in a trance: "Presently the figure struggled to its feet and glanced furtively over its shoulder.... And all the while the shadow lurked just a step behind." Better still, "The Eyes of the Mummy" (1938) portrays the survival of ancient Egyptian magic; its ending is a *tour de force* of creeping, dust-choked horror.

Two fine stories from 1938 show Bloch in transition from the pulp-Gothic mode to the landscape and language of modern America. "Return to the Sabbath" describes a European supernatural darkness invading the artificial shadows of a Hollywood horror movie. Its poetic bleakness is implicitly a lament for a depth and intensity of creative imagination rendered obsolete by commercial imperatives. "Slave of the Flames" uses the character of a pyromaniac to link the burning of Chicago in 1871 with the destruction of ancient Rome. Grim as these tales are, they have an element of mysterious poignancy that makes them particularly memorable.

Three more stories give us the new Bloch, the wisecracking cynic with a troubled heart. In "House of the Hatchet" (1940) we follow a bickering, ill-matched couple into a possibly bogus "haunted house" set up as a roadside attraction. The ensuing narrative is both ghostly and violent; yet its keynote is the icy silence of human self-interest. "Yours Truly, Jack the Ripper" (1943)—which Cornell Woolrich, another master of psychological horror, numbered among his favorite crime stories of all time—explores the idea that the Ripper might have been carrying out human sacrifices and thereby prolonging his life span. Bloch's sharp characterization and iron control of timing make this tale a classic of weird suspense. Finally, "One Way to Mars" (1945) is a sardonic parable about a drunken gangster's encounter with destiny. Is it spoiling the ending to tell you that his destiny is not redemption? Nope. We're talking Robert Bloch here.

Though most of his later fiction was nonsupernatural, Bloch never lightened up—except when he was telling a joke, and not always then. He wrote bleak, unsettling crime stories and dark, accusing science fiction. In 1978 he returned to his early stamping ground with the superb Lovecraftian novel *Strange Eons*. He remained a leading figure in the genre for more than half a century. By all accounts he was a profoundly likable man who had channeled all his bitterness into his work. And that's quite some bitterness, though his love of language and his pleasure in storytelling help to take the edge off his anger at human stupidity.

JOEL LANE (b. 1963) was born and lives in Birmingham, England, where he works as a freelance editor and writer. His tales of urban angst and doomed relationships have appeared in various magazines and anthologies over the past twenty years, and he was a prime member of the "miserabilist" movement within British horror during the 1990s. Influences on his writing include Robert Aickman, Ramsey Campbell, M. John Harrison, Cornell Woolrich, and Jean Genet. A collection of his short stories, *The Earth Wire*, was published by Egerton Press in 1993 and won a British Fantasy Award. Another collection, *The Lost District and Other Stories*, recently appeared from Night Shade Books. His essays on the weird fiction genre have appeared in *Foundation, Wormwood,* and elsewhere. Lane is the author of two novels, *From Blue to Black* and *The Blue Mask,* and two collections of poems, *The Edge of the Screen* and *Trouble in the Heartland.* He edited an anthology of subterranean horror stories, *Beneath the Ground,* for Alchemy Press, and he and Steve Bishop's anthology of crime and suspense stories *Birmingham Noir* was published by Tindal Street Press. Lane is currently working on his third novel, *Midnight Blue.*

26 [1946–50]

CHRISTOPHER FOWLER on

Gormenghast
by **MERVYN PEAKE**

*Active as a poet of light and serious verse, an illustrator (many editions use Peake's own sketches as cover images), a commercial playwright (*The Wit to Woo, *1957), a children's author (*Captain Slaughterboard Drops Anchor, *1939), and a radio scriptwriter, Mervyn Peake (1911–68) is nevertheless best remembered for the first volumes,* Titus Groan *(1946) and* Gormenghast *(1950), of the "Gormenghast Trilogy." The canon extends to* Titus Alone *(1959), a shorter book not completed to its author's satisfaction, and was certainly intended to continue into other works (a fragment exists of a fourth novel, to have been called* Titus Awakes*). The world of* Gormenghast *harks back to the castle-centered gothics of Anne Radcliffe and the scheming villains of Shakespeare, but might have been informed by the China-born Peake's knowledge of Peking's "Forbidden City," while the murderous social envy of Steerpike looks forward to* Kind Hearts and Coronets *or* Room at the Top *as much as it evokes Richard III. Peake adapted* Titus Groan *as a BBC radio drama in 1956; rights to the saga were acquired by Sting, who starred as Steerpike in a later radio dramatization but was never able to produce or star in a movie, contenting himself with a version of Patrick McGrath's Peake homage* The Grotesque *(1995). In 2000 BBC-TV mounted a lavish, somewhat cold three-part serial with Jonathan Rhys-Meyers as Steerpike and an array of British eccentrics including Christopher Lee, Ian Richardson, Richard Griffiths, Stephen Fry, Fiona Shaw, and Spike Milligan among the inhabitants of the rambling household.*

The *GORMENGHAST* TRILOGY is the twentieth century's thrilling peak of Gothic horror. A mountain analogy is appropriate, for it presents the reader with a demanding challenge, and scaling the book's heights requires concentration and stamina. It is not a fantasy, for there are only human elements here. Nor is it a trilogy; the first book, *Titus Groan,* is an immense prelude. The second, *Gormenghast,* is the great pulsing gut of the story. The last, *Titus Alone,* would be a landmark novel in anyone else's career, but is disastrous and dismissable in the context of the whole. It's argued that sickness robbed Peake of his imaginative power, but there are extraordinary passages in *Titus Alone*. Rather, the great Gothic fable was played out in the first two volumes and reaches an entirely satisfactory conclusion, making the last part redundant.

To my mind, *Gormenghast* deserves the spot occupied by *The Lord of the Rings;* it's certainly more bravely written—but herein lies the problem. Peake's style is not to everyone's taste. He is a densely descriptive writer, one of the greatest the world has ever known, and every sentence carries the weight of his subject. The first two volumes reach more than a thousand pages, but within them lives a vast moldering world unlike anything that has gone before.

I used to believe it was important to experience these books with time and youth on your side. I read them at fifteen, and they have haunted me ever since, but my father read them at seventy, and they had the same effect. What is the origin of their power, and why do they remain so underappreciated?

Gormenghast is a place, a vast, crumbling castle sinking under the weight of its history and traditions, a gloomy labyrinth of corridors and chambers so knuckle-scrapingly real you feel trapped inside them. It is a fractured mirror of England, static in time and smothered by centuries of conservatism, suffocating in meaningless rituals, and it is doomed to disappear from the moment that the youthful kitchen underling Steerpike climbs from a window to view his home from the outside.

Steerpike has no warmth or love for his place of birth but senses the power that surrounds him and grows ambitious. Crossing the vast flagstone roof, he lucks upon the bedroom of the castle's sulky time-biding first daughter, Fuschia, and senses that the family is vulnerable. From this point, his course is set. The empire is in fact ripe for collapse; Titus Groan, the seventy-seventh earl of Gormenghast, is the last of his line. Steerpike can only rise to the top by destroying the past, and sets about doing so with gusto. He has the great library burned down, sending Fuschia's father, Lord Sepulchrave, mad. He corrupts from within, making himself so indispensable to twin sisters Cora and Clarice that they rely on him to bring them food, and he allows them to starve to death in stifling darkness. He is the unseen force that turns the family against itself, spreading evil and collapsing the castle's power structure, but as a true anarchist, has nothing with which to replace the system. Steerpike is filled with the righteous anger of chaos, but he is also a coward, operating only behind the scenes.

The irony is that one man understands what is happening; Flay, the royal family's creaking, faithful servant, is the first to sense the truth about Steerpike, and pays for this knowledge by being banished from the kingdom. Now as much of an outsider as the lowliest peasant, only he can reveal the machinations behind Gormenghast's collapse. Toward the end of the second novel the castle floods, and as the family is forced to climb ever upward, Steerpike, now insane, visits sudden death on the inhabitants armed with a catapult full of stones. Before we reach this point, though, the ill-equipped Flay, now our unlikely hero, must fight the revolting, swine-toothed cook Swelter, "the pendulous horror," in the Hall of Spiders.

Death stalks these pages, death of tradition and the end of all things, as well as human destruction. The first volume was published just after World War II, and images of horror spike the text. The cat thrown at Steerpike's face rips a crimson wedge from his cheek. A dead animal skull is fixed to the chief librarian's spine. Rotting flower water is tossed in Steerpike's eyes. Insanity stalks the corridors of power, wailing like the starving near-corpses of Cora and Clarice. It's deeply peculiar, then, to encounter a very funny and lengthy romance, between Professor Bellgrove and the angular, humorless Irma, right in the center of the action—yet this is true to the essence of Gothic horror, for dark laughter is the only possible survival response to such a doom-laden catalog of events.

Why does *Gormenghast* remain outside the pantheon of classic horror? Perhaps it is too "literary," too descriptive, too unwieldy. Perhaps there is too little hope for the world here. As Peake puts it, "a spider stirs, and darkness winds between the characters." Certainly a passing knowledge of *Hamlet* is useful to the book's appreciation, for it feels like a perverse inversion of Shakespeare's tragedy. And like that woeful tale of destruction, it deserves to be revered, its heart-rending language and images remembered as long as there are books left to read.

CHRISTOPHER FOWLER (b. 1953) was born in Greenwich, South London. He is a director of the Soho movie marketing company the Creative Partnership, producing television and radio scripts, documentaries, trailers, and promotional shorts. He spends the remainder of his time writing short stories and novels of dark urban horror, usually filled with anxiety and satire and a blackly humorous twist. After publishing two non-fiction guides in the mid-1980s, *How to Impersonate Famous People* and *The Ultimate Party Book,* he turned to novels with *Roofworld, Rune, Red Bride, Darkest Day, Spanky, Psychoville, Disturbia, Soho Black, Calabash, Breathe,* and *Plastic.* He is currently writing the Bryant & May novels, six volumes of dark crime. The first, *Full Dark House,* was published in 2004 and won the British Fantasy Society's August Derleth Award for Best Novel. It has so far been followed by *The Water Room* and *Seventy-seven Clocks.* A contributor to the tail end of *The Pan Book of Horror Stories* series, his tales "Wageslaves" and "American Waitress" also both won British Fantasy Awards, and his short fiction is collected in *City Jitters, City Jitters 2, The Bureau of Lost Souls, Sharper Knives, Flesh Wounds, Personal Demons, Uncut, The Devil in Me,* and *Demonized* (which includes his hundredth published story). He also scripted the 1997 graphic novel *Menz Insana*, illustrated by John Bolton; reviews for *The Independent on Sunday* newspaper, and contributes a regular column about movies to *The 3rd Alternative*. Most of Fowler's novels are in various stages of development as movies, while his story "The Master Builder" was filmed by CBS-TV as *Through the Eyes of a Killer* (1992), starring Tippi Hedren. *Left Hand Drive*, based on his first short story, won Best Film in the 1993 British Short Film Festival.

27

[1947]

GARY GIANNI on

Carnacki the Ghost-Finder
by WILLIAM HOPE HODGSON

William Hope Hodgson (1877–1918) introduced occult detective Carnacki in "The Gateway of the Monster" (The Idler, January 1910). "The House Among the Laurels," "The Whistling Room," "The Horse of the Invisible," and "The Searcher of the End House" followed monthly until May; "The Thing Invisible" was scheduled to appear in the June issue but was pulled and eventually turned up in the New Magazine in January, 1912. Carnacki, the Ghost Finder, and a Poem *(1910), an abridged collection, appeared in the United States for copyright reasons.* Carnacki the Ghost-Finder *(Eveleigh Nash, 1913), collects all six stories, in slightly rewritten form. After Hodgson's death, a further three stories were discovered.* "The Haunted 'Jarvee,'" *revised by Hodgson's wife in 1919, saw publication a decade later in* Premier Magazine

(March 1929). Thanks to August Derleth, "The Hog" appeared in Weird Tales (January 1947), and all eight stories, along with the previously unpublished "The Find" (the only Carnacki case that does not involve even the apparent supernatural), were included in the 1947 Carnacki the Ghost-Finder, published under Arkham House's sister imprint Mycroft & Moran. "The Hog" and "The Find" were edited and somewhat revised by Derleth. This edition was reprinted in the United Kingdom in 1972 by Tom Stacey (and in paperback by Tandem). More recently all nine stories were reprinted in The House on the Borderland and Other Mysterious Places (2004) volume 2 of Night Shade Books' Collected Fiction of William Hope Hodgson set, edited by Jeremy Lassen. The character features in pastiche stories by A. F. (Chico) Kidd and Rick Kennett; four are collected in chapbook 472 Cheyne Walk: Carnacki: The Untold Stories (1992); and a further eight are added to the expanded Ash-Tree Press edition (2002). Donald Pleasence was very well cast as Carnacki in "The Horse of the Invisible," an episode of The Rivals of Sherlock Holmes (1971)—the television series based on Sir Hugh Greene's best-selling anthologies of Victorian and Edwardian detective fiction that reintroduced Carnacki and many other semi-forgotten sleuths to the public.

I WAS AMONG THE guests dismissed into a cold winter's evening after Carnacki related his experiences in the whistling room. With the odor of pipe and brandy still lingering in my nostrils, I made my way along the embankment, mulling over his strange narrative. I wondered if such things were possible. The detective's explanation concerning a giant pair of menacing lips materializing in the floor of an ancient bedchamber seemed terrifyingly plausible under the circumstances.

After all, Carnacki is never the sort given to exaggeration. He is sober-minded and resolute in his need to make us understand the danger associated with each of his cases involving paranormal activity.

It is chiefly that stern countenance that led to his reputation as being "something of a butt" with the fellows at the club. His references to the fourteenth-century manuscripts and warnings to clients foolhardy enough to step beyond the protective barrier of his electric vacuum-tubed pentacle provoke a barrage of big titters on many occasions. "I never did and never will allow myself to be blinded by a little cheap laughter," Carnacki proclaimed to me, and it is precisely that no-nonsense bearing I admire in the man. "If that's the case, his stories must be true," I murmured under a frigid breath.

I drew my scarf closer when suddenly I realized that the biting cold emanated from within my bones rather than from the air around me. Perhaps I had a touch of the creep. This was Carnacki's way of describing a physical pain in the spine resulting from the strain a ghostly fright sets up in the human nervous system. Lord knows he suffered his share of the creeps. He was almost killed in the case known as "The Gateway of the Monster" and his very soul was threatened when he confronted "The Hog"—fighting a monstrosity capable of reducing men to grunting, piggish abhorrences was beyond the ken of his colleagues in the consulting detective business. Only one who had witnessed such abominations could accurately describe the cosmic horror:

> I saw it, pale and huge through the swaying, whirling funnel of a cloud—a monstrous pallid snout rising out of that unknowable abyss. It rose higher, like a huge pale mound. Through a thinning of the cloud curtain I saw one small eye . . . I shall never see a pig's eye again without feeling something of what I felt then. A pig's eye with a sort of hell-light of vile understanding shining at the back of it.

The idea of hordes of swine flying around in storm clouds peering malevolently down upon their victims gave new meaning to the old expression "in a pig's eye."

The saying, which I heard frequently as a boy, was popular with an uncle of mine, who in an odd way reminded me of Carnacki. I remember a Christmas long ago when Uncle Lawrence surprised me with a gift of a Ouija board. I was equally surprised several days later when he returned to exchange it with a different gift. "Perhaps it's best not to meddle with such things," he explained nonchalantly. In its place I received a magic trick bag that made eggs disappear. Soon thereafter I discovered that an inverted drinking glass on a highly polished table worked just a well as any manufactured Ouija board. "In either case," warned my uncle, "when you mess around with it, you invite the devil into your home." The Carnackian resemblance was even more pronounced when Uncle Lawrence's visit would culminate in an after-dinner family ghost story.

In our house these stories were considered gospel, officially sanctioned anecdotes handed down throughout the years by family members, collected by my uncle, and retold in a fashion the family never grew tired of. He was a wonderful storyteller, with the ability to throw his voice lending an unearthly drama to the proceeding in our dining room. We all agreed he could have made a living onstage, although I seem to recall he was popular in the annual talent show at the insurance company where he worked.

A melancholy air now replaced my chill.

Those were magic evenings, listening to stories that mesmerized us and brought us closer together. But the years grind relentlessly, on, and somehow the impressions we thought were indelible become fainter—harder to conjure up.

Fortunately I find the spirit recaptured in the rosy glow of firelight whenever I visit Carnacki's Place. That author fellow who's always among the listeners—what's his name? Dodgson . . . Hodgson? He should commit Carnacki's stories to paper, record them so we can hold them in our hands. I'll suggest it to him at our next gathering.

Satisfied, I arrived at my front door, put the key in the lock, and hurried inside.

GARY GIANNI (b. 1954) was born and lives in Chicago, Illinois. He is an illustrator whose work has appeared in numerous books, comics, and newspapers. He has received the Eisner Award and the Spectrum Award for his work, and six years of his career were devoted to illustrating the stories of Robert E. Howard, featuring Conan, Solomon Kane, and Bran Mak Morn for publisher Wandering Star. Aside from writing and drawing his own comic book titled *Corpus Monstrum*, Gianni has produced artwork for such works as *Another Chance to Get It Right* by Andrew Vachss, *The Lost Adventure* by Joe R. Landsdale and Edgar Rice Burroughs, *Tom Strong* by Alan Moore, *The Slab* by Harlan Ellison, *Moby Dick* by Herman Melville, *Kidnapped* by Robert Louis Stevenson, *Twenty Thousand Leagues under the Sea* by Jules Verne, *The Last Pin* by Donald Wandrei, *Gateway of the Monster* by William Hope Hodgson, and *The Stories of O. Henry*. He has also illustrated "Thurnley Abbey" by Perceval Landon for *The Dark Horse Book of Hauntings*, "Mother of Toads" by Clark Ashton Smith for *The Dark Horse Book of Witchcraft*, and "Old Garfield's Heart" by Robert E. Howard for *The Dark Horse Book of the Dead*. In 2004 Gianni took over drawing the syndicated newspaper adventure strip *Prince Valiant* from John Cullen Murphy.

28 [1948]

RANDY BROECKER on

Darker Than You Think
by JACK WILLIAMSON

Jack Williamson (b. 1908) originally placed a forty-thousand-word "complete novel" of Darker Than You Think *with John W. Campbell's legendary pulp magazine* Unknown, *which published it in the December 1940 issue. Williamson expanded the text for the book version, published by Fantasy Press in 1948 in an edition illustrated by famed science fiction artist Edd Cartier. Described by critic Douglas E. Winter as "a werewolf novel that is not truly a werewolf novel," the story involves newspaper reporter Will Barbee, who discovers that his seductive rival, April Bell, is actually a flame-haired witch-woman, part of a lycanthropic cult awaiting the coming of the legendary "Child of Night." Plagued by feral dreams and with his friends dying one by one, Barbee finds himself drawn into a supernatural war waged against mankind by a semihuman race of prehistoric shape shifters. In 1976 the novel was republished in the United Kingdom by Sphere Books as part of "The Dennis Wheatley Library of the Occult," and it was reissued in the United States by Tor Books in 1999, with heading illustrations by David G. Klein. Jack Williamson wrote about Robert Louis Stevenson's* Dr. Jekyll and Mr. Hyde *in* Horror: 100 Best Books.

THE WOMAN IS naked and riding on the back of a huge prehistoric pterosaur, flying through a darkened sky filled with other, vague, animal shapes.

The year was 1976. I was in Uncle Hugo's Science Fiction Bookstore in Minneapolis when I spotted this particular paperback cover. It was a British Sphere Books edition, part of the "Dennis Wheatley Library of the Occult" series, and I knew the scene quite well that the cover painting beautifully depicted.

The artist I felt sure was Alan Lee, today best known for illustrating the works of J. R. R. Tolkien and his involvement with the recent *Lord of the Rings* films. During the 1970s, however, Lee did some wonderfully atmospheric covers for British paperback series, including *The Fontana Book of Great Ghost Stories*, among others. In those days, though, cover artists often went uncredited; this was no exception.

What was exceptional was this: Here was what I believed to be the work of a favorite artist of mine, on the cover of a novel that was an all-time favorite—*Darker Than You Think*, by Jack Williamson. Needless to say, I bought it.

Those already familiar with the novel or Williamson's work do not need any more cajoling by me to justify their inclusion in any kind of "best" literary assemblage (it should have been in the first *Horror: 100 Best Books*), but since I've told you more about Alan Lee so far, please bear with me and I'll try to get to the point without overstaying my welcome.

The image of that girl on the flying saurian (her name is April Bell, by the way) has been fluttering around in my mind ever since I first encountered her in the early 1960s. She also pulls a Lady Godiva on the back of a saber-tooth tiger, and I can't begin to tell you the wonders those scenes did for this adolescent. These creatures and others—wolves figuring prominently among them—are results of transformations in what is probably the most unique and original take written on an age-old subject and horror staple: lycanthropy. Shape shifting through witchcraft, but with a scientific spin on it.

Unique as it is, at the time I first read it, it was already more than twenty years old, having initially been written for that classic and revered home to so many great (and not-so great) writers of yore—the pulps. There were giants in those days, and Jack Williamson is one of them.

The operative word here is "is," as in "he is still writing some sixty-five years later." Celebrated for his science fiction, Williamson also wrote horror stories and fantasy adventures.

In *Darker Than You Think,* Williamson set down the notion that the blood of modern Homo sapiens carries a taint of evil, or Homo lycanthropus strain, as a result of the mating of witch folk and human females during witches' Sabbaths ages ago. This ancient race of witch folk are the basis of the various "were-beast" legends throughout the world.

This inherited gene strain varies in individuals, more recessive in some than in others, with many being unaware of their ancestry. Others conceal this evil nature, living among us and waiting for their "Black Messiah," a foretold "Child of Night," born with more abilities than any other, to come forward and lead them. Alcoholic newspaper reporter Will Barbee becomes caught up in the middle of a struggle between good and the stirrings of something darker awakening within him.

By combining *noir* and horror/fantasy elements with a pseudo-scientific approach, Williamson has crafted a brilliant piece of writing that succeeds not only within the pulp market that it was originally written for but, like a shape-shifter itself, has proven today to be that most elusive of beasts, an original and influential classic.

In the end it all comes down to that wonderful were-dactyl transformation, which brings us in a roundabout way back to that uncredited Alan Lee cover.

When we were introduced some years later I asked the artist about it and in 1989 I bought the original painting from him. Not a day since has gone by that I don't gaze upon the lovely April Bell, riding on her "Child of Night" toward a new world of gods and, well, monsters. And I blame it all on Jack Williamson. Thanks to him, it's darker than you think. And later.

RANDY BROECKER (b. 1951) was born and lives in Chicago. Having an older brother who, when not hitting him in the back of the head with a rolled-up newspaper, would bring home and share pulps and EC comics was a great help in shaping him into the monster and art-loving illustrator he is today. When his brother's friend, Rich Hauser, published *Spa-Fon* in the 1960s, Broecker's first published art appeared in that highly revered EC fanzine. Many years later, a meeting with publisher Donald M. Grant at the second World Fantasy Convention eventually led in 1979 to *The Black Wolf* and Broecker's first hardcover illustrations. Since then his artwork has appeared in books published by Cemetery Dance, Underwood-Miller, Highland Press, Robinson Publishing, Carroll & Graf, Pumpkin Books, Fedogan and Bremer, American Fantasy, Sarob Press, PS Publishing, and other imprints on both sides of the Atlantic. He was Artist Guest of Honor at the

2002 World Horror Convention and is the author of the World Fantasy Award-nominated study *Fantasy of the Twentieth Century: An Illustrated History* from Collector's Press, which also formed part of a three-in-one omnibus titled *Art of Imagination: 20th-Century Visions of Science Fiction, Horror, and Fantasy.*

29 [1949]

TANITH LEE on

Tales of Horror and the Supernatural
by ARTHUR MACHEN

Originally published by the Richards Press, Tales of Horror and the Supernatural *stands as a useful "best of" Machen. Overlapping but not identical with the contents of* The House of Souls *(1906), which T. E. D. Klein wrote on in* Horror: 100 Best Books, *the collection includes two-thirds of Machen's volume of linked novellas,* The Three Imposters *(1895), the short novel originally published as* The Terror: A Fantasy *(1917), and most of Machen's other important short fiction. Born Arthur Llewellyn Jones, Arthur Machen (1863–1947) worked as clerk, teacher, actor, and journalist while concocting stories of horror and dark fantasy firmly rooted in the myths and legends of his native Wales. "The Bowmen" is comparatively slight, but remains his most famous story because it inspired an early "urban legend." A patriotic anecdote about the ghostly appearance of King Henry's archers at the Battle of Mons, it was published in the* Evening News *in 1914 and accepted as fact by many readers—inspiring a number of reported sightings of "the Angel of Mons" at the front. In 1975,* Tales of Horror and the Supernatural *was split into two paperback volumes by Panther, featuring distinctive cover paintings by Bruce Pennington.*

DON WOLLHEIM, THE former esteemed editor and chief of DAW Books, and then my publisher, introduced me to this volume of stories in the late 1970s. Don said he thought I had some similar preoccupations as Arthur Machen appeared to. I did and do.

Machen was a contemporary of that other great genius of the inescapable horror, M. R. James. But where their heroes and their sometimes (only initially) cozy frameworks now and then concur, Machen is more fluid in his strongly evoked depiction of hopeless psychological dread. The frequently scholarly characters each writer uses are generally driven to their truly awful fates by the lure of the fabulous unknown.

Yet in the case of Machen, whether found in lyrical recurrent landscapes or the streets of London, events rest on a basic premise, which is that this world—this apparent reality—lies precariously adjacent to others run on different lines. They are usually terrible, occasionally too beautiful to be borne. They are hells, or the memory of a lost Eden, though neither have very much to do with essentially religious concepts. Only an opaque curtain, or veil, conceals these parallel realities. And while most of us live in happy ignorance this side of it, others seek to lift, the barrier or tear it away.

"The Great God Pan," one of Machen's more famous novellas, begins with a series of separated chapters, rather like loosely linked short stories in themselves. Each has one central sinister event. The novella then gradually draws itself together until the last chapter commences with a jolt most writers would be proud of springing. Dr. Raymond, with a "perfectly simple" operation on the *brain* of his innocent female ward, means to enlighten. But this successful attempt to peer beneath the veil beings endarkenment instead. Madness; hints of chilling, repulsive acts; and a medley of ritualized deaths result.

As in several other Machen stories, a "thinking" man is the

instigator. But the lethal conduit is a woman. Something Dionysian as well as Panish pervades the tale, but Dionysian at its most savage (see Euripides' *Bacchae*) a power improperly understood and wrongly unleashed.

But "The Great God Pan" is not alone in tackling this dark beyond the veil. In "The Novel of the White Powder," an unforeseen pharmaceutical reaction lets out a demon of the id or soul. A doting sister watches in helpless fright and despair the deterioration of her beloved brother into something "as formless as my fear, the symbol and presence of all evil." Seldom has any writer of horror topped the sense of claustrophobic oppression and dread in this tale.

In "The White People," however, unease results mostly from the main character's pleasant familiarity with the unveiled unseen. She—and Machen, I would say, write most convincingly here as a very young girl—notes, with evident complacence in her "green book" all the weirdness she is coming to delight in. We can only look on—unnerved spectators. The story "The Inmost Light" also engages with ideas of connection with unveiled forces. In this instance, again *something* is enticed through, something seemingly exquisite—but it takes payment in kind. Once more a woman is the channel. Machen employs an occasionally repeated image: the unexpected glimpse in at a window, which itself seems almost a cipher for glimpsing beyond the Veil. Here an entirely everyday scene among redbrick villas suddenly gives way on such a sight that: "I knew I had looked into another world . . . and seen hell open before me."

Conversely, in the lyrical, mystic story "The Great Return," Machen conjures the other face of the hidden coin. It is a beauty, power, and glory that stun, but bring healing rather than harm, while in "The Happy Children" both the supernatural and the horrors of *this* world are gilded by a firm hope of joy. "N," though, takes a more pragmatic look at the chance of a parallel paradise.

Carefully structured around the history and nostalgia of an ever-altering London, Machen seems to tap the feeling many of us may get, that half-remembered streets and other places sometimes run away as we approach, relocating somewhere slightly different, to confuse us. The magnificence of this finely controlled tale is all in its contrasts. But the premise once more is definite: "The universe, originally fluid and the servant of his (Mankind's) spirit, became solid and crashed down upon him overwhelming him beneath its weight and its *dead* masse." (My own italics.) Has the parable of the Fall, or the apparently intractable cement of the "real" world, ever been better analogized?

This work seems to have sympathies with H. G. Wells's "The Door in the Wall," and even with Ruth Rendell's wonderfully written departure, "The Green Road to Quephanda." It also finishes with surely a pair of the most disturbing paragraphs in the canon of literary horror. Or, come to that, of existentialism.

Throughout this fascinating collection, Machen produces constant surprises. "The Shining Pyramid," "Out of the Earth," and "The Novel of the Black Seal" contend with Faery and the Celtic legends. But what waits under *these* hills is far from either loveliness or enchantment. Yet in "The Bowmen" (a story that the *other* story, "Out of the Earth," indicates caused the truthful Machen public opprobrium), a patriotic myth is skillfully constructed. Then again, in "The Children of the Pool" Machen perpetrates a marvelous trick, leading us it seems into a straightforward and nightmarish horror yarn, only to confound us with something even blacker and more unsettling. "The Bright Boy" too, has a canny twist: dispatched to tutor the charming and clever little boy of the title, Joseph Last uncovers an unspeakable family secret. The story's denouement resolves with grim logic, and what might be called an obscene commonplace.

The entire shining volume concludes with its best tale. "The Terror" is indeed terrifying, but also one of the most cleverly plotted stories I have ever read, in or out of the genre.

Set in a quiet, rural Welsh community in 1915, it is a kind of short "detective" novel dealing in utter fear. All the clues are there, plus several red herrings, but the mounting miasma of an elusive yet inescapable, faceless and doubtless supernatural enemy, soon encloses the reader like a fog.

The start of the story involves, perhaps for contemporary tastes, rather a long preface. But it should be read, maybe, with contemporary notions of conspiracy theory in mind. It bears anyway on the following events, which soon come thick and fast.

A host of peculiar, singularly nasty, and unreasonable deaths occur—falls over rocks and into quarries by persons well used to the paths, inexplicable bludgeonings, drownings and asphyxiations of men, women, and children. These are presently categorized as murders, but who—or *what*—is responsible?

In the climate of World War I, information is governmentally suppressed—but everything is *suspected,* from enemy action to scientific "rays." Meanwhile, the terror spreads across the whole of Britain. Munitions factories are left standing by mysterious explosions that see three hundred dead carried out at a time, in *closed coffins.* Ships unmanned save by human bones founder on the coasts; clouds of what may be poison gas, lit with inner lights, float over the countryside; and feral panic begins to spread through both the human and the animal populations.

The final chapters, which outline the horrifying "siege" of Treff Loyne Farm, are a piece of sustained genius on their own. And the ultimate decoding of the terror proves dismayingly legitimate. Machen ends his story with an indictment of *this* world no less damning now for being couched in the elegant moral phrases of its past. Properly adapted, what a movie this would make!

TANITH LEE (b. 1947) began writing at age nine and became a full-time writer in 1975, when DAW Books published her novel *The Birthgrave.* Since then she has written and published about sixty novels, nine collections, and more than two hundred short stories. She also had four radio plays broadcast during the late 1970s and early '80s, and scripted two episodes of the cult BBC-TV series *Blakes 7.* She has twice won the World Fantasy Award for short fiction and was awarded the British Fantasy Society's

August Derleth Award in 1980 for her novel *Death's Master*. In 1998 she was short-listed for the Guardian Award for Children's Fiction for her novel *Law of the Wolf Tower*, the first volume in the *Claidi Journal* series. Tor Books has published *White as Snow*, the author's twisted retelling of the Snow White story, while Overlook Press has issued *A Bed of Earth* and *Venus Preserved*, the third and fourth volumes, respectively, in the *Secret Books of Paradys* series. More recent titles include *Cast a Bright Shadow, Here in Cold Hell,* and *No Flame but Mine*, comprising the Lionwolf Trilogy, while *Piratica* and its sequel *Piratica 2: Return to Parrot Island* are novels for older children about the exploits of a female pirate. *Metallic Love* is a sequel to her novel *The Silver Metal Lover* for Bantam Books, and rights to the 1981 original have been sold to Miramax Film Corp. Under the pseudonym "Esther Garber" she has also published a number of novels in the *Abstract Lesbian Fiction* series from Egerton House Publishing.

30 [1949]

LUCIUS SHEPARD on

Nineteen Eighty-Four
by GEORGE ORWELL

In 1948, Eric Blair (1903–50), who used the pseudonym "George Orwell," transposed the numerals on the calendar to come up with the title and the setting of this key twentieth-century dystopia. Orwell acknowledged *his debt to the Russian Yevgeny Zamiatin's* We *(1924) and obviously intends a contrast with the utopias of H. G. Wells and Aldous Huxley's more fantastical* Brave New World *(1932). In imagining Air Strip One, a totalitarian state that crushes the spirit of potential rebel Winston Smith, Orwell chiefly used Stalin's U.S.S.R. as a model, though he stirs in elements of Nazi Germany and even Britain under the wartime rule of another Winston (the Ministry of Truth is a caricature of the BBC, for whom Orwell worked during the war). The book's despairing, angry grimness is political in nature but has personal causes, too: the author was gravely ill during the writing. While working on the novel on the island of Jura, he was diagnosed with the tuberculosis that would kill him within a year. Though the book title is* Nineteen Eighty-Four, *most film and television adaptations have gone with* 1984. *It was first dramatized for television in 1953 on the American anthology series* Studio One, *with Eddie Albert as Smith. Better remembered is a 1954 BBC production, scripted by Nigel Kneale, produced (i.e., directed) by Rudolph Cartier and starring Peter Cushing. Kneale's script was remade in 1965, with David Buck. Edmond O'Brien played Smith in Michael Anderson's disappointing 1956 film, and John Hurt takes the role in a film by Michael Radford that plays up the ironic resonance of making 1984 in 1984. Anthony Burgess's* 1985 *(1978) combines an essay on the Orwell with a new-minted dystopia, while David Bowie's album* Diamond Dogs *(1974) partially adapts the novel, taking the motto of Winston Smith and his rebel lover, Julia ("We Are the Dead") as a song title. A facsimile edition of the original typescript was published in—yes!—1984.*

THE FAMOUS OPENING line of *Nineteen Eighty-Four* ("It was a bright cold day in April, and the clocks were striking thirteen.") generates an impression of sharpness and precision, of an environment subject to impersonal control, and serves as a doorway leading to a place that poses the opposite of that impression—a world of varicose ulcers and grit in the wind, smelling of "boiled cabbage and old rag mats," a world from which we do not emerge until Winston Smith, George Orwell's protagonist, is taken to meet his fate at the Ministry of Love, an edifice of glittering white porcelain and sterile light. Between these two poles we are immersed in a gray, murky, bitter milieu that bears a striking resemblance to our own. True, our colors are less muted, the governing authority somewhat less restrictive, the people less terrified, though our populace is nonetheless controlled by the machineries of fear, by threats against the various forms of their security, whether financial or mortal, fraudulent or real; but privacy is a dwindling commodity, the proles swill beer and watch television. . . . The basics are the same. History is being rewritten, truth has become utterly flexible, and we indulge in Two-Minute Hates, albeit with different demons, Osama and Saddam currently standing in for Goldstein. Give our culture a nudge or two, a couple of 9/11s more, and we are there.

I first read *Nineteen Eighty-Four* when I was fourteen, at the beginning of the Kennedy administration, and I felt instinctively that it was true . . . or rather that it had the potential to be true. Coming of age, as I did, in the days of the Cold War, I gleaned from the book a promise of eternal distant strife and that the gray terminals of the Soviet Union would stretch out across the intervening sea to neuter us with jolts of debasing energy. At the time I believed that the drab Soviet cities were the precursors of an all-consuming drabness, but I came to realize with the passage of years that every society carries these potentials. I am certain Orwell knew this as well, that he was not merely spinning an anti-Soviet cautionary tale. Every system, no matter its high ethics, how noble its goals, nurtures within itself the seeds of an oligarchy more controlling than that from which it sprang.

Nineteen Eighty-Four is probably the most claustrophobic novel ever written. Winston's very thoughts are subjects of observance. He works in a tiny cubicle and lives in a tiny room, both under the scrutiny of viewscreens, through which the government spies on his intimate moments. The haven he finds from all this is a no more than a slightly larger room and, when at last he is captured and punished for his thoughtcrime, he initially feels relief in being conveyed to the

Ministry of Love; with its cleanliness and spacious holding cells, its somewhat comforting sterility.

It is also a novel of dread. Winston knows from the outset, from the moment he realizes that he can no longer live within the abhorrent limitations of his culture and begins keeping a diary, that he will inevitably be caught and tortured and executed. That he is numb to the likelihood of personal extinction should, again, be familiar to us, for we are equally numb to the dread potentials of our own culture; we have been inoculated against them by the televised repetitions of a thousand mantras that promise us security. We have become so immunized against reality that a man onscreen—Big Brother in one of his many guises—holding a roll of duct tape and pointing to a color chart seems to the majority of our population soothing, a sturdy armor against terrorism. At night, walking around in my neighborhood, seeing the faint glow and flicker of a television set in every house I pass, I understand that it is only a short leap between television and viewscreen.

I cannot imagine what it would be like to come upon *Nineteen Eighty-Four* for the first time during the early years of this new century. Would a reader, assuming that his or her mind is capable of illumination, be shocked to discover how prescient Orwell was? Would he or she be alarmed by the resonances of the novel to see that Orwell's grim future dystopia was a foreshadowing of our own near future, or would they merely shrug, toss the book aside, and cast about for a lighter, more upbeat form of entertainment? And what would they think about Room 101, the room in the Ministry of Love in which the ultimate invasion of his psyche occurs and he is persuaded to think whatever his tormentors want him to think, no matter how absurd or wrong? (It's not really an academic question when one considers that the current attorney general of the United States is an avowed proponent of torture.) I suspect that they might view Room 101 in terms of the terrorist threat and say to themselves, "Well, of course the government has to have that option available to deal with these people."

The politics of *Nineteen Eighty-Four* fascinates us, holding up a slightly distorted mirror to our world, and the reason that we do not recoil from the prospect it presents, the imminent subversion and destruction of the democratic state, is that we believe events have gone beyond our ability to forestall them (at least we take refuge in that belief), or else we pretend it's not happening. There was a slogan during the 2004 U.S. presidential election that referenced the United States' "successes" in Iraq and Afghanistan: FREEDOM IS SPREADING ACROSS THE WORLD LIKE A GOLDEN SUNRISE. When one takes even a cursory glance at this particular golden sunrise, it becomes evident that the statement makes every bit as much sense as WAR IS PEACE, yet fifty-nine million Americans were coerced into believing it. And it would be naïve to think that Europeans or Latin Americans or Asians are less prone to manipulation. Yet the horrific effect of *Nineteen Eighty-Four* does not arise merely from our recognition of its author's prescience; it echoes Kafka and Conrad in its evocation of an infection at the heart of the world that corrupts every clean thing and permeates every orderly system. Winston's collapse before the terrors of Room 101 is as much a result of human inevitability as it is of political violence, and restates in visceral terms Mr. Kurtz's "The horror, the horror."

Reading the book now, revisiting familiar passages, tracking Winston Smith along his tedious daily circuit, I'm astonished to recognize how many of its terms have acquired the status of catchphrases, and equally astonished to note how many of them have a faintly humorous connotation (Big Brother, for example, has been appropriated for the name of a cloddish reality show, one in which cameras spy on a group of people closeted in a house). The book has insinuated itself so thoroughly into the culture, it's as if it were a self-fulfilling prophecy that has worked a gray magic on our world. And that is the power of *Nineteen Eighty-Four*: it portrays an obscenely repressive future that strikes us as virtually normal, that we ignore because of its familiarity, yet lurks at the edges of the believable, waiting its time.

LUCIUS [TAYLOR] SHEPARD (b. 1947) was born in Lynchburg, Virginia, and grew up in Florida. After leaving home at age fifteen, he traveled widely in the Third World and is currently writing a non-fiction book on Central America. His first professional sale was the novelette *The Taylorsville Reconstruction* to Terry Carr's anthology *Universe 13* (1983). Widely regarded as one of the finest writers in the science fiction, fantasy, and horror fields, he has been compared to Graham Greene and Ward Just, and his multigenre fiction has earned him the Hugo Award, Nebula Award, World Fantasy Award, Theodore Sturgeon Award, John W. Campbell Award, Locus Award, and the International Horror Writers Guild Award, among others. His debut novel *Green Eyes* (1984) involved science fiction, voodoo, and zombies, and he followed it with *Life during Wartime, Kalimantan, The Scalehunter's Beautiful Daughter, The Father of Stones,* the vampire novel *The Golden, The Last Time, Valentine, Louisiana Breakdown, Floater, Liar's House,* and *Two Trains Running.* His exotic short fiction has been collected in the Arkham House volume *The Jaguar Hunter, Nantucket Slayrides: Three Short Novels* (with Robert Frazier), *The Ends of the Earth, Sports & Music, Beast of the Heartland* (aka *Barnacle Bill the Spacer and Other Stories*) and *Night Visions 11* (which also includes work by Kim Newman and Tim Lebbon). Shepard's most recent books are *Trujillo and Other Stories,* a collection from PS Publishing, and the novel *A Handbook of American Prayer.* Forthcoming are the novel *Softspoken* and *Weapons of Mass Seduction,* a collection of film reviews and essays. Another fiction collection also is due from PS.

31

[1950]

DAVID BISCHOFF on

House of Flesh
by BRUNO FISCHER

In the early 1950s, Harry, a star player for a professional Manhattan basketball team, heads north to cool his heels for the summer at a woodsy upstate town. After a grueling season, too much alpha-male boozing, and a marriage gone south, his coach tells him it's time for a little rest and relaxation. But stay away from the women. However, the women can't stay away from Harry. In his Our Town *retreat, he meets and dates Doris Day look-alike Polly Wellman. Harry finds her just as resistible as his bombshell ex-wife, who visits to park a dog, Max, with Harry during a trip. But there's also this creepy old house and the sinister hulking veterinarian, Dr. Doane, rumored to have fed his first wife to his pack of savage dogs; and above all there is Lela, Dr. Doane's second wife, a smoldering* noir *babe. Harry falls into temptation's trap—and discovers hell doesn't have to have pitchforks and brimstone to be hot and full of an inescapable horror. Bruno Fischer (1908–92) was among the top tier of original mystery and crime novelists who rose to prominence during the first success of the paperback boom. His earlier titles, tinged with horror, include* So Much Blood *(aka* Stairway to Death, *1939),* Quoth the Raven *(1944), and* The Spider Lily *(1946), plus series featuring private eyes Rick Train (*The Hornet's Nest, *1944) and Ben Helm (*The Dead Men Grin, *1945). However, he really hit his stride with a string of 1950s hits, including* The Lady Kills *(1951),* The Fast Buck *(1952),* So Wicked, My Love *(1953),* Knee-Deep in Death *(1956),* Murder in the Raw *(1957), and* Second-Hand Nude *(1959). As "Russell Gray" he wrote* The Lustful Ape *(1950). In 1960 Fischer returned to his first profession, editing, in*

New York City. His final book was The Evil Days *(1974), after which blindness forced him to retire fully from writing.*

Of all the images spawned by horror literature in the twentieth century, only one set has actually not only been unaffected by a natural twenty-first century, postmodern numbness but also can also still arouse outrage.

These are the covers of the "shudder" or "weird menace" pulps of the American 1930s. *Horror Tales. Terror Tales. Dime Mystery.* Gorgeous half-clad women being tortured by hunchbacks and dwarves and men in hoods was the usual vivid, primary, four-color fare for the artists. These paintings sear, amuse, and disturb still. Copies of the magazines in good shape fetch astronomical prices on eBay. Mutant cousins to the giant of pulp horror, *Weird Tales,* the "shudder pulps" had stories that stuck to one successful formula: their melodramatic tales had all the elements of the most outrageous supernatural entities; however, by the end, the author had to tie things up to show that no physical laws were actually broken. In other words, like William Hope Hodgson's "Carnacki" stories, the ghosts and goblins and vampires, in the light of day, are from natural origins.

I adore the "shudder" pulps. Their stories own a strange putrefaction. They smell of dusty, forgotten, unredeemable pulpwood. Like good hunks of stinky French or German washed-rind cheese, they just get better with age.

In the mid-1930s, the editor of a socialist magazine, Bruno Fischer, was complaining of his poor salary to a publishing friend. Fischer was told of the roaring Depression success of the garish pulp magazines. He read a pile and felt an inclination toward the "shudder" titles. Fischer immediately began selling stories with titles like "Satan Calls His Slaves" and "Monsters of the Pit," and became prolific enough to need to use the pseudonyms "Russell Gray" and "Adam Train."

By the 1940s, with the horror pulps selling from behind newsstand counters, stalwarts of morality like Mayor Fiorello LaGuardia of New York City outlawed them. Fischer went on to easily adapt to writing for the multitude of pulp mystery and detective magazines, and began selling hardcover mystery novels as well.

In 1949 Fawcett Publications was running out of options for reprints and decided to enter pulp territory and publish original material. Under the Gold Medal imprint they joined the booming market for paperback books. One of the first titles was Bruno Fischer's *House of Flesh*.

Without the constraints of hardcover expectations of mystery and crime novels, Fischer was able to fashion a creepy and queasily odd tale—a horror novel, like one of his old shudder pulp tales. It uses the elements of the supernatural literary tradition to inform the naturalistic *noir* sensibilities of John Hersey and James M. Cain and create a book whose power perhaps grows in retrospect.

A lover of pulp fiction since a kid, I stumbled across the *noir* paperbacks of the 1950s a few years ago. Largely collected because of their fabulous covers, these books still stand up as entertaining reading. Because there seems to have been a paradigm shift in style in popular fiction between the 1930s and early '50s, paperback *noir* is more readable now than its pulp forebears.

What strikes me, particularly in *Manhunt* magazine—a kind of 1950s *noir* digest—was how these stories opened up a horrific view of modern male psychology. You get the feeling that "the greatest generation" that fathered the baby boomers had married in haste and was repenting in resentful, violent leisure.

Fischer wrote for *Manhunt* magazine. After *House of Flesh*, I don't think he ever used the "shudder" pulps formula again. Maybe once was enough.

House of Flesh tells the story of a Manhattan pro basketball player seeking rest and sanctuary from a divorce in a sleepy rural town in upstate New York. There he encounters dark secrets, a sinister vet, and an odd but intensely compelling femme fatale. The effective back cover declares: "In the forbidding old house, guarded by vicious dogs, lived exotic, mysterious Lela. Murder was done there, it was said, and other deeds, wanton and eerie."

Like the "shudder" pulp stories, *House of Flesh* is pervaded by the existential dread of the "skull beneath the skin." While there's no actual mention of the supernatural, the sweaty summer here is drenched with its feel. Fischer's implication seems to be that the wholesome façade of Americana forces the natural to become the supernatural. The results of this repression are horrific. In fact, the title *House of Flesh* is derived from an A. E. Houseman verse cited at the beginning of the book:

> If the heats of hate and lust
> in the house of flesh are strong
> Let me mind the house of dust
> Where my sojourn will be long.

It's a Gothic novel for males—who then read fiction more than nowadays—addressing modern man's self-hatred, his obsession-yet-repulsion with sex and emotional slavery. Beneath the smooth, sleek lines of modernity lurks chaotic horror. Tightly cohered by vivid prose and sex scenes oddly steamier than those in postmodern prose, like classic ironic French and Russian stories, this novel entertains wildly but leaves behind a gloomy and haunting resonance.

While out of print now, in its day *House of Flesh* sold two million copies in North America alone. Other writers of crime fiction, such as Jim Thompson, Charles Williford, Robert Bloch, and Cornell Woolrich, doubtless took note of its success.

Mystery has always been one step away from horror. *The Hound of the Baskervilles* (a prototype shudder pulp story) is a perfect example. However, horror is generally not thought of as a progenitor of kitchen-sink naturalistic *noir* crime stories.

It should be.

Other powerful original paperbacks with psych-horror elements include Charles Williams' *The Hot Spot*; Bloch's *Psycho*; and another, even more lurid male Gothic, Gil Brewer's *13 French Street*, which I strongly suspect is a direct editorial result of *House of Flesh*'s success.

However, because I love shudder pulp horror stories, *House of Flesh* remains my favorite.

DAVID BISCHOFF (b. 1951) was born in Washington, D.C., and now resides in Eugene, Oregon. He graduated from the University of Maryland with a Bachelor of Arts degree in television, radio, and film, and worked for NBC-TV for five years before becoming a prolific fiction writer. Working in various genres, including science fiction, fantasy, horror, and mysteries, his numerous novels include a young adult version of *Phantom of the Opera, Nightworld, Vampires of Nightworld,* the trilogy *Day of the Dragonstar, Night of the Dragonstar,* and *Dragonstar Destiny* (all with Thomas F. Monteleone), *Bill the Galactic Hero #3* and *#5, Philip K. Dick High, J. R. R. Tolkien University, The H. P. Lovecraft Institute,* and *The Tawdry Yellow Brick Road.* Bischoff also is the author of a number of film, television and gaming novelizations, such as *WarGames, The Manhattan Project, The Blob, Gremlins II: The New Batch, Star Trek: The Next Generation: Grounded, Aliens: Genocide, Aliens vs. Predators: Hunters' World, SeaQuest: The Ancient, Space Precinct: The Deity Father, Space Precinct: Demon Wing* and *Space Precinct: Alien Island, The Crow: Quoth the Crow* and *FarScape: Ship of Ghosts.* As "Brad Quenton" he has written six books in *The Real Adventures of Jonny Quest* series, aimed at younger readers. The author of more than seventy short stories in magazines such as *Omni, The Magazine of Fantasy & Science Fiction, Amazing, Analog, Fantastic,* and *Pulphouse,* his collection *Tripping the Dark Fantastic* appeared in 2002. Bischoff's television credits include scripts for *Star Trek: The Next Generation* ("Tin Man" and "First Contact") and episodes of the animated shows *Centurions, Dinosaucers,* and Disney's *Darkwing Duck.* He also has worked in comics, computer games, and magazine publishing.

32 [1951]

ANNE BILLSON on

Fancies and Goodnights
by JOHN COLLIER

London-born John Collier (1901–80) was a successful Hollywood screenwriter whose credits include Sylvia Scarlett *(1935),* I Am a Camera *(1955),* The War Lord *(1965), and an unproduced adaptation of* Paradise Lost *(circa 1968). He also wrote for television, adapting his own stories for* Alfred Hitchcock Presents *(1955) and* Tales of the Unexpected *(1979), and produced a collection of poetry and several novels, of which the best known are* His Monkey Wife *(1931) and* Defy the Foul Fiend *(1934).* Fancies and Goodnights *(1951) collects fifty short stories written between 1931 and 1951. Some were originally published in the* New Yorker, *the* Atlantic Monthly, Harper's Bazaar, Harper's Magazine, *and* Esquire; *twenty-four had previously been collected in* Presenting Moonshine *(1941). Among Collier's best-known short stories are "Green Thoughts," "Evening Primrose," "Thus I Refute Beelzy," "Bird of Prey," and "The Lady on the Grey," all included here. In 2003,* Fancies and Goodnights *was reissued by the New York Review of Books with a new introduction by Ray Bradbury. Many of the stories have been adapted: "Evening Primrose" became a Broadway mini-musical by Stephen Sondheim, which was produced for television in 1966 with Anthony Perkins; "Green Thoughts" is the unacknowledged source of Roger Corman's film (and the later Broadway musical)* The Little Shop of Horrors *(1960); and "Sleeping Beauty" was filmed by James B. Harris as* Some Call It Loving *(1973), with Zalman King and Tisa Farrow. The stories from this collection have frequently been used on anthology TV shows: "De Mortuis" on* Suspense *(1951); "The Chaser" on* The Twilight Zone; *"De Mortuis," "Back for Christmas,"* and "Wet Saturday" on Alfred Hitchcock Presents; "Special Delivery" (as "Eve") on Journey into the Unknown; and "Back for Christmas," "Youth from Vienna," "De Mortuis" (as "Never Speak Ill of the Dead"), "Wet Saturday," "Bird of Prey," and "In the Cards" all on Tales of the Unexpected. *In 1958 Orson Welles adapted "Youth from Vienna" as a pilot for an anthology series,* The Fountain of Youth.

"IT WAS ON the second-floor landing that they found the shoe, with the man's foot still in it, like that morsel of a mouse which sometimes falls unnoticed from the side of the jaws of the cat." John Collier has a knack for rounding off a short story with the sort of deliciously understated unpleasantness that immediately makes you want to jump back to the beginning of the tale and read it all over again, just to verify that it really was as nasty as you suspected.

I first stumbled across his work in the anthologies of ghost and horror stories that were the staple reading matter of my adolescence. His name didn't register in my brain back then, but his stories most certainly did, the payoffs lodged like glittering splinters in my memory: "At that moment a log rolled on the hearth, and a little flame flickered up, and he saw his long and hairy fore-legs, and he knew." Twenty years later (by which time I had managed to attach an author's name to those glittering splinters) the highlight of a productive rummage through a secondhand bookstore in West Los Angeles was a battered but still readable copy of *Fancies and Goodnights.*

Each of the fifty short stories in this collection is a little miracle of elegant and sardonic writing, capped not so much by a narrative twist as a vicious little kick that makes it the literary equivalent of a dry martini that some malicious prankster has garnished with a coiled worm instead of an olive. There's whimsy aplenty, but of the dark, unsettling kind that teeters on the edge of nightmare and sometimes falls right in. Collier is the missing link between Saki and Roald Dahl, and beneath the polished veneer of his exquisite and often very funny prose seethes a maelstrom of perverted passion and murderous greed.

His protagonists are adulterous spouses and serial philanderers, concupiscent demons and lovelorn fleas, jealous pigs or performing mice whose misplaced trust in humans proves their undoing, statisticians driven to murder by badly mixed cocktails, or ghosts who drift through their old routines, unaware that they've died. Though Collier's tone is classically English in its ironic detachment, he travels easily between Old Europe and the New World, as much at home in Malibu or Chicago as he is in Piccadilly Circus, the south of France, or indeed hell itself, parts of which, in "The Devil, George and Rosie," "proved to have an aspect not unlike that of the Great West Road, where it approaches London. On every hand, rows of cells were being run up. To add to the total refinement of misery, they were designed exactly like houses in a modern building project."

Collier's sense of dialogue is keen, and he doesn't waste words. In "Collaboration," a wife's infidelity is exposed (to the alert reader, if not her blinkered husband) through nothing more than the speech patterns of her offspring. There's a peppering of movie in-jokes: in "Pictures in the Fire," a screenwriter wriggles out of a deal with the Devil thanks to his familiarity with the intricacies of Hollywood contracts, while "Over Insurance" begins, "Alice and Irwin were as simple and as happy as any young couple in a family-style motion picture. In fact, they were even happier, for people were not looking at them all the time and their joys were not restricted by the censorship code." Since this is Collier, though, you know that such happiness is fated to end in tears.

For every protagonist prepared to go to baroque lengths in pursuit of romantic or erotic satisfaction—the narrator of "Squirrels Have Bright Eyes" pretends to be a stuffed hunting trophy in order to infiltrate his loved one's penthouse, while in "Season of Mists" a man who has posed as his own identical twin to facilitate a bigamous marriage ends up cuckolding himself twice over—there is another whose marriage has turned sour, like the husband in "Three Bears Cottage" whose attempt to kill his wife with a poisonous mushroom goes awry when he eats it himself and is duly subjected to "giddiness, nausea, spots before the eyes, palpitations, convulsions, flatulence, and other symptoms too hideous to mention."

The pursuit of romantic happiness and its unhappy sequel finally dovetail in "The Chaser," the last story in the collection, in which an old man sells a cheap love potion to an eager young romantic, secure in the knowledge that he will one day be back in search of the more expensive antidote—a tasteless, colorless liquid "quite imperceptible to any known method of autopsy." Delicious, understated, unpleasant: it's Collier in a nutshell.

> **ANNE BILLSON** (b. 1954) was born in Southport, England, and currently lives in Paris. Growing up in Exeter and the South London suburb of Croydon, she took a foundation course in art and design at Wolverhampton Polytechnic (1971–72) and a degree course in graphic design at London's Central School of Art and Design (1972–76). She worked as a bookshop assistant, signwriter, window dresser, secretary, cookbook illustrator, unqualified English teacher, lyric-writer for Japanese pop singers, movie cashier, and once appeared as a Dutch girl in a Japanese television commercial. As a stills photographer her pictures have been published in *Time Out, Event, Illustrated London News, Mode et Mode, Fashion News, Men Only, Tatler, Options, Elle, Vogue, Daily Express, Soho Weekly News,* and other periodicals, and she has had exhibitions of her work in Tokyo and London. Her articles have appeared in the *Sunday Telegraph, Monthly Film Bulletin, The Erotic Review, GQ, Time Out, Event, City Limits,* the *Times, Vogue, Elle, Harpers & Queen, Esquire, Just Seventeen, Cosmopolitan,* the *Guardian,* the *Independent,* the *Observer,* the *Sunday Times,* and *Playbirds,* and she was the regular film critic for *Today* (1986), *The Sunday Correspondent* (1989-90), *Tatler* (1989-90), *New Statesman & Society* (1991–92) and the *Sunday Telegraph* (1992–2001). Her 1989 novelization

of *Dream Demon* was deemed to be too good to tie in with the film, and she followed it with the revisionist vampire novel *Suckers* (which earned its author a place on *Granta*'s "Best Young British Novelists" list) and the darkly comic ghost story *Stiff Lips*. Billson's non-fiction books include *Screen Lovers*, *My Name is Michael Caine*, and a study of John Carpernter's *The Thing* for the *BFI Film Classics* series.

33

[1952]

NANCY A. COLLINS on

The Killer Inside Me
by JIM THOMPSON

The prolific Jim Thompson (1906–76) might have felt he enjoyed little luck in his lifetime, but his posthumous reputation has mushroomed thanks to respectful reprints of novels issued originally as paperback ephemera, high-profile film adaptations like Stephen Frears's The Grifters *(1990) and a definitive biography (Robert Polito's* Savage Art, *1995).* The Killer Inside Me *was Thompson's fourth novel and began a productive three-year streak in which he turned out eleven tough, strange, brief, innovative thrillers. Thompson wrote books that sold to Hollywood (*The Getaway, *1959) and worked on early Stanley Kubrick films (*The Killing, *1956;* Paths of Glory, *1957), but alcoholism, political troubles (as a sometime Communist, he was often blacklisted), and seismic shifts in the paperback market made for a bibliography* studded with work-for-hire gigs like novelizations of the television pilot Ironside *(1967)* and the Western film The Undefeated *(1969)*. He has one lone credit as an actor, as the aged tycoon married to a slut murderess in Farewell My Lovely *(1975)*. Killer *is one of two Thompson novels narrated by a corrupt small-town cop (the other is* Pop. 1280, 1964*);* Killer *was turned into a much-underrated 1976 film by director Burt Kennedy, with an outstanding Stacy Keach in the lead (few other actors could manage Deputy Lou Ford's sham folksy imbecile with murderous intellect glittering through the eyes) and one of those supporting casts that make B-movie buffs' eyes water: Susan Tyrrell, Tisha Sterling, Keenan Wynn, John Dehner, Royal Dano, Julie Adams, Don Stroud, and (in one of his best 1970s cameos) John Carradine.*

Although widely acknowledged as one of the defining works of American "crime *noir*", Jim Thompson's *The Killer Inside Me* is also important in the context of the sub-genre known as "psychological horror."

It could be argued that Thompson's "protagonist," Deputy Lou Ford, is the literary precursor to such American psychos as Norman Bates and Hannibal Lecter. Like his better-known fictional kin, Lou Ford isn't the giggling, ax-wielding lunatic of Gothic literature or the twitchy, hand-washing sadist of the Grand Guignol. The human monster on display in Thompson's novel is far more disturbing because of his unnerving ability to pass for "normal" among his friends, loved ones, and coworkers.

Thompson's years of working as a stringer for *True Detective* had given him unique insight into the workings of the sociopathic mind. Although the sex scenes are exceptionally tame by today's standards, the story retains the ability to shock the reader, even more than fifty years after its initial publication. The way the first-person narration recounts a secret life filled with sexual sadism, child molestation, rape, murder, and acts of cruelty as if they were all as natural as the sun rising is far more unnerving than any gruesome description of mayhem ever could be.

A particularly inspired bit of character development by Thompson comes from Ford's deliberately playing himself for a fool, so those who think they know him underestimate him as a likable oaf. Or, as the narrator explains it, "Striking at people that way is almost as good as the other, the real way."

Imagine, if you can, Sheriff Andy Taylor of the good town of Mayberry beating naked women with a belt until the blood comes and putting out cigars in the palms of homeless panhandlers in between dishing out cornball homilies and you will understand the disconcertment *The Killer Inside Me* can trigger within a reader.

As a writer I stand in awe of how Thompson refuses to succumb to the temptation of allowing his viewpoint character to soften or become a "nice guy," even though it's clear by the end of the novel that many of the citizens of Central City, Texas, are as corrupt and evil as Ford, in their own way.

Every time you start to feel something like empathy for the character, or think there might be the faintest glimmer of hope for his redemption, you hit a passage like this one, where he's discussing the woman he admits to loving all his life: "I knew I had to kill Amy; I could put the reason into words. But every time I thought about it, I had to stop and think why again. I'd be doing something, reading a book or something, or maybe I'd be with her. And all of a sudden it would come over me that I was going to kill her, and the idea seemed so crazy that I'd almost laugh out loud. Then I'd start thinking and I'd see it, see that it had to be done, and . . ."

In the decades since the publication of *The Killer Inside Me,* the real-life equivalents of Lou Ford have become far more plentiful. Strange that a novel published during an era we now choose to remember as far more bucolic and "simpler" than the one today should presage the likes of Scott Peterson, BTK, Ted Bundy, Herb Baumeister, John Wayne Gacy, and other such ogres who hide in plain sight in modern society, masquerading as "perfectly average" family men until that fatal moment when all masks are dropped and the fiend within is revealed in all its horrid glory.

The Killer Inside Me is a reminder that the knowledge a novel is "ahead of its time" isn't always a source of comfort for its author.

NANCY A. (AVERILL) COLLINS (b. 1959) was born and raised in Arkansas and currently makes her home in Atlanta, with her dog, Scrapple. She is the author of several novels and numerous short stories, served a two-year stint as the writer of DC Comics' *Swamp Thing*, and created *Dhampire: Stillborn* for DC/Vertigo. She has received the Horror Writers Association's Bram Stoker Award, the British Fantasy Society's Icarus Award, and the Deathrealm Award, and was nominated for the Eisner, International Horror Guild, and World Fantasy Awards. Her books include her 1989 debut *Sunglasses After Dark* (which introduced undead-vampire-hunter Sonja Blue), *In the Blood, Paint It Black, Darkest Heart, A Dozen Black Roses, Tempter, Walking Wolf, Angels on Fire,* and *Lynch: A Gothik Western*. Her short fiction has appeared in numerous anthologies and magazines and has been collected in *Nameless Sins, Dead Roses for a Blue Lady: The Sonja Blue Short Fiction Collection, Dead Man's Hand: Five Tales of the Weird West, Knuckles and Tales: Southern Neo-Gothic* (illustrated by Steve Bissette), and *Avenue X and Other Dark Streets*. As an editor Collins has co-compiled the erotic horror anthologies *Dark Love* (with Edward E. Kramer and Martin H. Greenberg) and *Forbidden Acts* (again with Kramer), while *Gahan Wilson's The Ultimate Haunted House* features stories loosely based on the artist's work.

34

[1955]

LAURENCE STAIG on

The Third Ghost Book
Edited by LADY CYNTHIA ASQUITH

Lady Cynthia Asquith (Mary Evelyn Charteris, 1887–1960) was private secretary to J. M. Barrie, creator of Peter Pan, *from 1918 until the author's death in 1937. To earn extra money she wrote biographies, children's books, and an occasional ghost story. Calling upon her large circle of literary friends and acquaintances, she edited a number of superior horror anthologies, including* The Ghost Book *(1927),* The Black Cap *(1928),* Shudders *(1929),* When Churchyards Yawn *(1931), and* My Grimmest Nightmare *(1935). She finally compiled* The Second Ghost Book *in 1952, and followed it with a third volume four years later.* The Third Ghost Book *was originally published by James Barrie Publishers and contained twenty-seven original stories by Elizabeth Bowen, Lord Dunsany, L. P. Hartley, Robert Aickman, Rosemary Timperley, Nancy Spain, Angus Wilson, and others, including the editor's own tale "Who is Sylvia?" When it was reprinted by Pan Books in 1957, the cover of the paperback depicted a man surprised in bed by a spectral pirate. The cover Laurence Staig recalls was on a 1960s reissue. After Cynthia Asquith's death, the series was revived in 1965 and continued by James Turner, Rosemary Timperley, and Aidan Chambers.*

I'VE NEVER BEEN in any doubt about my love of "the dark side." Growing up in numerous fairgrounds and the circus (my father was a showman), I remember all too well the attractions of my bizarre surroundings. I especially liked the ghost trains with graphic flashes showing yawning graveyards and dancing figures in shrouds.

But my first "literary" introduction to the macabre (when I was just ten years old) was ghost stories, with M. R. James's *Ghost Stories of an Antiquary*—the Penguin edition. James's stories were bliss: nasty creatures from dark, damp tombs were definitely my kind of thing. However, at about the same time, I discovered another collection, which I have only recently realized has played just as significant a part in my own writing, and love of the genre.

I still remember the day I found the book. I had been playing with school friends at "the flats," a huge tower block estate of council flats in Brixton, South London. It was a Saturday lunchtime, getting late, and I had to return home. Stopping by a newsstand, I was intrigued by a circular (and rickety) metal paperback display. I gave it a twirl, and there it was. A Pan paperback sat in a wire pocket, a bit dog-eared, but it had an interesting cover showing an arched black cat, standing on a coffin and staring at an assembly of spectral graveyard figures. The tagline read: "Stories that will take you in a cold embrace—twenty-seven startling tales of the tormented and the damned." It was a week and a half's pocket money, but I had enough—two shillings and sixpence—and I had to have it: *The Third Ghost Book,* edited by Lady Cynthia Asquith.

I seldom read anthologies from start to finish. I treat collections like a box of chocolates. Not unsurprisingly at that time, I had never heard of any of the authors, so I started with titles I was drawn to. Although described as *The Third Ghost Book,* the introduction (an excellent essay on the genre) by L. P. Hartley referred to this as being Cynthia Asquith's seventh collection. The book is dedicated to Walter De La Mare and includes stories by such literary luminaries as Elizabeth Bowen, Angus Wilson, Ronald Blythe, and Robert Aickman. It is a very English collection, and the general tone is specific: dry and sometimes understated. At other times it is simply quite shocking.

Although described as a "ghost book," many of the stories do not feature ghosts, although they most definitely lean toward the macabre and the horrific. The settings include hotels, country houses, and East Anglian coastal resorts with a mixture of mannered characters among "the lost." It is also an eclectic mix stylistically, with Ronald Blythe's humorous take on Suffolk country life in "Take Your Partners"; Lord Dunsany's "The Ghost of the Valley," which shimmers with its sensitive poetic references to the passing of time and sense of place; and then there is Ursula Codrington's "Shades of Sleepe," which similarly evokes the transition and synergy of place. I have never forgotten these stories, but a particular few significantly affected me when I first read them. I believe these represent some of the finest and genuinely most disturbing ghost stories ever written.

For me, the best story in the collection is "The Tower," written by Marghanita Laski. This tells the story of a lone lady tourist who in the early evening chooses to take in one final attraction—a climb to the top of a medieval Florentine Tower via 470 stone steps. The creeping sense of menace that Laski creates is truly horrifying, and you begin to care desperately about the unfortunate and vulnerable woman in the story. When I reached the end with its terrible twist, it frightened the life out of me.

There is a postscript. In the 1980s I did a stint on the Arts Council's Literature Panel, which was chaired at the time by . . . Marghanita Laski. Upon hearing how much I liked the story, Marghanita revealed that it was the only ghost story she had ever written. After passing a biscuit she then asked me, "Do you think I should have written more?"

This collection also includes what must be one of Robert Aickman's best stories, "Ringing the Changes." This was my first introduction to Aickman, and this story hooked me to his work for life. Much has been written on the psychological interpretation of his fiction and, as with the best literary horror stories, this works on many levels. It is the honeymoon from hell: A newly married couple arrive at Holihaven, a desolate East Anglian coastal town. He is twenty-four years her senior. They arrive to a pealing of bells throughout the town. The townspeople are ringing to wake the dead, and at the moment at which the bells suddenly stop you may well catch your breath and you truly realize they have been with you throughout the story. What happens next is a fantastic depiction of a horrifying descent into loss of innocence. "Ringing the Changes" is about as disturbing a piece of fiction as you will find.

Finally, I mention a story I have often revisited, partly because to this day I have never been entirely certain what happens in it. L. P. Hartley's "Someone in the Lift" was a devastating read for me as a child. Hartley perfectly adopts the young Peter Maldon's point of view as an observer of a possibly imagined occupant of an elevator. Elevators were never the same for me after reading this and I easily identified with Peter, as I had a similar fascination with elevators and elevator shafts. They terrified and attracted me, and if we sometimes stayed in hotels I was always wary of them. Reading this, you will see why it chilled me and brought back memories. It is a grim story of childhood fascination with insubstantial shadows and premonition—the stuff that scares most children. The ending is quite a shock.

Cynthia Asquith wrote a little under a dozen or so ghost stories herself, but it is as an important early anthologist that she will be best remembered. Her other collections are equally as rich and memorable as this one. But this was my first encounter with an anthology to which I not only related, but that also unconsciously had a part to play in my own involvement in supernatural and horror fiction. My thanks, Lady Cynthia, for a very important collection.

LAURENCE STAIG (b. 1950) was born in Bristol and educated at Manchester and London universities. He grew up among fairground and circus folk, and having a magician uncle (the illusionist Robert Harbin) and a sideshow showman father, he was easily attracted to the macabre. After a short teaching career in the 1970s and a stint working for the Arts Council of England, he became an author in 1986. His horror and dark fantasy novels for young adults include *The Network, The Glimpses, Digital Vampires, Shapeshifter, Fear of the Dark* (as "Christopher Carr"), *Carnival of the Dead,* and *The Bestiary. The Invasion of the Wire Ones, Nightwing Towers, The Haunting of Aisle Number Nine, The Tick-Tock Man,* and *The Polkadot Wash-*

ing Machine are aimed at younger readers, while his short stories are collected in *Dark Toys and Consumer Goods* and *Technofear*. Staig writes obituaries for the *Independent* newspaper and teaches film and media studies part-time at a college in Cambridge, England. He has never won the Booker Prize or received an Arts Council grant.

35

[1955]

ANDY DUNCAN on

The Body Snatchers
by JACK FINNEY

Jack Finney (1911–95) was a proud member of that forgotten literary tradition, the slick (as opposed to pulp) writer. First published as a serial in Collier's *magazine in 1954,* The Body Snatchers *recounts the takeover of a small California town by doppelgängers who—it turns out—sprout from alien seed pods that have drifted to Earth. The film rights were immediately purchased by producer Walter Wanger—on the advice of genre expert William K. Everson—and the project assigned to director Don Siegel. The 1956 film was titled* Invasion of the Body Snatchers, *to prevent confusion with the film of Robert Louis Stevenson's* The Body Snatcher *(1945). Despite a studio-mandated frame story that suggests that the invasion* might *be defeated, the film is a rare case of Hollywood changing the happy ending of a novel (in which the aliens are defeated) in favor of a terrifyingly downbeat finale (in which the invasion spreads and the hero's warnings are ignored). There have been two official remakes, and a string of imitations in film (*The Day Mars

Invaded Earth, *1963) and television (*The Invaders, *1967–68). Part of Finney's appeal was that, like John Wyndham in England, he wrote science fiction or fantasy but with a more direct, mainstream appeal than the material coming out of the genre magazines. He is among the most imitated of writers—Rod Serling, Richard Matheson, and Stephen King have all "remade" Finney stories (Serling repeatedly and without according credit), and the George Clayton Johnson-scripted movie Ocean's Eleven (1960) owes a debt to Finney's first novel,* Five against the House *(1954). Finney's other novels (almost all filmed) include the comic fantasy* Marion's Wall *(1973), the heist thriller* Assault on a Queen *(1960), the marital comedy* Good Neighbor Sam *(1963), and the linked time-travel stories* Time and Again *(1980) and* From Time to Time *(1995). His outstanding short stories are collected in* The Third Level *(1957) and* I Love Galesburg in the Springtime *(1963).*

M EDICINE HAS A name for it: Capgras's syndrome, the insistence that a spouse, parent, or child has been replaced by an impostor. Some believe the disorder is caused by a short circuit in the brain's ability to recognize faces. The sufferer gets enough input to recognize, say, her husband, but not enough input to feel the appropriate emotional connection.

Much scarier is the explanation so memorably offered in Jack Finney's novel *The Body Snatchers:* Madam, your spouse really *has* become someone else, from someplace not of this Earth.

This theme was not new when Finney's novel first was serialized in *Collier's* in 1954, the year of *Brown v. Board of Education,* the Army-McCarthy hearings, Ike's acknowledgment of the H-bomb tests, and Dr. Wertham's anticomics hysteria. Aliens-among-us paranoia was commonplace. Finney's immediate predecessors include Robert A. Heinlein's 1951 novel *The Puppet Masters* and two 1953 movies, *Invaders from Mars* and *It Came from Outer Space.*

But *The Body Snatchers* became the definitive novel on the theme. Its just-the-facts-ma'am approach is as insidiously effective as Finney's alien spores. It has been repeatedly filmed (by Don Siegel in 1956, by Philip Kaufman in 1978, and by Abel Ferrara in 1993) and endlessly imitated because it works on many levels, beginning with the literary allusion in its title. Robert Louis Stevenson's famous 1884 story "The Body Snatcher" is about grave robbers, but Finney's snatchers needn't wait until we are dead and buried to trundle us away. The novel also evokes ancient folk beliefs of doppelgängers, evil doubles that herald our doom; and of fairies that abduct human children and leave changelings in their place. The novel's emphasis on the dreadful consequences of sleep makes no sense as alien biology but is a powerful echo of the midnight fancies of childhood, when fighting sleep can seem a matter of life and death. And what childhood fear is greater than the fear that one's parents might one day, without warning, become someone else?

The Body Snatchers is also a political novel—though the opening paragraph tells us to expect an ambiguous one:

> I warn you that what you're starting to read is full of loose ends and unanswered questions. It will not be neatly tied up at the end, everything resolved and satisfactorily explained. Not by me it won't, anyway. Because I can't say I really know exactly what happened, or why, or just how it began, how it ended, or if it has ended; and I've been right in the thick of it. Now if you don't like that kind of story, I'm sorry, and you'd better not read it. All I can do is tell what I know.

At the time of publication, *The Body Snatchers* was seen both as anti-Communist and anti-McCarthyist, depending on the reader's point of view, and half a century later the novel retains its ability to unnerve everyone equally. After all, what an outsider sees as mindless robot conformity always looks to the conformist like the way things ought to be, or even like the one true path to salvation.

I first read *The Body Snatchers* when I was fifteen and enjoyed it as a straightforward bogeyman tale. At the time I attended one of the all-white private academies erected across the American South in the 1960s and '70s in a wave of protest and panic by white parents fleeing the desegregation of public schools. In hindsight I marvel that

I wasn't made more uneasy by Finney's description of one's humanity being leached away unnoticed, "absorbed like static electricity," leaving only "a pile of gray fluff. It can happen, does happen, and you know that it *has* happened; and yet you will not accept it." I was too conformist at fifteen to accept it myself.

The passing decades have added resonance to Finney's setting, Mill Valley in Marin County. What seemed in 1954 a generic middle-American county has become famous since for hot tubs, New Age beliefs, and the Skywalker Ranch. Aliens among us, indeed!

At novel's end, Mill Valley seems to be returning to normal, but the reader gets little reassurance from the closing paragraph:

> But . . . showers of small frogs, tiny fish, and mysterious rains of pebbles sometimes fall out of the skies. Here and there, with no possible explanation, men are burned to death inside their clothes. And once in a while, the orderly, immutable sequences of time itself are inexplicably shifted and altered. You read these occasional queer little stories, humorously written, tongue-in-cheek, most of the time; or you have vague distorted rumors of them. And this much I know. Some of them—*some* of them—are true.

Finney's other famous novel is *Time and Again* (1970), a time-slip fantasy in which a disenchanted New Yorker wills himself back to 1882, to a Manhattan he finds more to his liking. *Time and Again* implies that the entirety of the modern world is a sort of mass hallucination from which a strong individual can fight free. Those of us who don't make that effort, Finney ultimately seems to be saying, are no better off than the Pod People. Is anyone feeling sleepy?

ANDY DUNCAN (b. 1964) was born in Columbia, South Carolina, and currently lives in Northport, Alabama. After graduating from the University of South Carolina with a B.A. in journalism, he worked as a writer and editor for the Greensboro *News & Record* for seven years. He first attended the Clarion West writers' workshop in 1994, and returned a decade later to teach. A winner of the Theodore Sturgeon Memorial Award and the World Fantasy Award for his short fiction, his stories of southern fantasy and regional Gothic have appeared in such magazines and anthologies as *Asimov's, Realms of Fantasy, SciFiction, Weird Tales, Mojo: Conjure Stories, New Magics, Polyphony 1, Starlight 1* and *3, The Year's Best Science Fiction, The Year's Best Fantasy and Horror, The Mammoth Book of Best New Horror, Year's Best Fantasy,* and *The Mammoth Book of Best New Erotica*. His World Fantasy Award-winning collection *Beluthahatchie and Other Stories* was published by Golden Gryphon in 2000, he co-edited the anthology *Crossroads: Tales of the Southern Literary Fantastic* with F. Brett Cox, and he wrote the non-fiction study *Alabama Curiosities*.

36 [1955]

JOHN GORDON on

The Talented Mr. Ripley
by PATRICIA HIGHSMITH

Patricia Highsmith (1921–95) introduced her psychopathic antihero Tom Ripley, an American whose stamping ground is Europe and area of interest is art collection, in her third novel, The Talented Mr. Ripley *(1955). She returned and found him older, more assured, and just as dangerous in* Ripley under Ground *(1970),* Ripley's Game *(1974),* The Boy Who Followed Ripley *(1980), and* Ripley under Water *(1991).* The Talented Mr.

Ripley *has been filmed twice, by René Clement as* Plein Soleil *(*Purple Noon, *1960), with Alain Delon as Ripley and Maurice Ronet as the gilded youth he replaces; and by Anthony Minghella in 1999 (onscreen title:* The Mysterious Yearning Secretive Sad Lonely Troubled Confused Loving Musical Gifted Intelligent Beautiful Tender Sensitive Haunted Passionate Talented Mr. Ripley*), with Matt Damon and Jude Law. However, the first adaptation was a live television drama done on* Studio One *in 1956, with Keefe Brasselle and William Redfield. Minghella's well-known film simplifies Ripley, depicting him as a tormented gay man. Though all the novels feature odd relationships between Ripley and other men, Highsmith's character (who has a strangely normal marriage) is far more complicated. Other screen Ripleys have included Dennis Hopper in Wim Wenders'* The American Friend *(1977, from Ripley's Game), John Malkovich in Liliana Cavani's* Ripley's Game *(2002), and Barry Pepper in Roger Spottiswoode's* Ripley Under Ground *(2005).*

IT WOULD BE a pleasure to meet Mr. Ripley. He is polite, even diffident, can be very considerate, talks amusingly and has a really great talent for mimicry. Yet, if he saw profit in it, he would kill you. *The Talented Mr. Ripley* is one of the most chilling books I have read. When we first meet Tom Ripley he is in a bar on Fifth Avenue where he has been followed by a stranger. Tom is nervous, and has reason to be. Although outwardly harmless and holding down a reasonable job, he has been working a postal scam. The stranger could be a policeman.

So we know Ripley is a small-time crook, but otherwise he seems sensible and decent. It is a great relief when the man trailing him turns out not to be a policeman but the father of one of Tom's friends. He is seeking help in a project that is perfectly legal and at the same time very profitable for Tom.

It's hard not to be on Tom Ripley's side. He loves pictures, architecture, and travel, and the new project offers them all, with enough money for clothes and good hotels. Patricia Highsmith has encouraged us into a dream with just the hint of guilt that often comes with dreams. Things are turning out well for Tom, but we do not quite forget that he is, or has been, a petty crook.

At some time in the past, Tom Ripley had met a young man of his own age, a rich young man, Dickie Greenleaf, and it is Greenleaf Sr. who has, in effect, hired Tom to encourage Dickie to give up his ambition to be a painter and come home to the family business. Dickie is living abroad on his own money.

Within a week Tom is in Italy with an allowance generous enough to make him feel at home among wealthy expatriates, and before long he is living in Dickie's house.

It is then that a subtle shift in the narrative begins to have its full effect. We know that Tom Ripley is capable of theft and is very afraid of being caught, that he almost panics at the thought of punishment, but what has not been so clear is that he is incapable of feeling guilt. Eyes devoid of feeling look out from his friendly face. Patricia Highsmith has lured the reader into the skin of a cold-blooded, self-seeking psychopath and in the process has transferred the guilt Tom Ripley does not feel onto the reader.

But Tom is enjoying himself. He is accepted by Dickie Greenleaf, who is leading exactly the type of life Tom covets. The two even have a physical resemblance, and Tom is one day discovered trying on clothes from Dickie's wardrobe, to the great disgust of Dickie's girlfriend Marge. She believes Tom Ripley is homosexual, and there is a hint of it in the way he behaves, but he is as near asexual as makes no difference. His great happiness is to be alone among his possessions—or the possessions of others.

Frictions develop and gradually the dream darkens. Tom Ripley may have become an alien character, but his grip on the reader tightens. Patricia Highsmith never allows the talented Mr. Ripley to do the impossible. He is a good liar and so inventive that whenever he seems at the point of being unmasked as an unscrupulous villain, he can turn the moment to his own advantage. But he is not universally liked. Marge, in particular, begins to see through him. And Tom begins to sense that the wealthy Dickie Greenleaf is shoving him out into the cold.

Then comes "a crazy emotion of hate, of affection, of impatience and frustration" ... and Tom Ripley knows that he himself can become

Dickie Greenleaf. They are the same height and build, he can do everything that Greenleaf does, and Tom is a brilliant mimic. Only one person stands in his way.

The two young men are in a small boat, just far enough from land for no one to see what is happening, when "Tom lifted the oar and came down with it on the top of Dickie's head."

The body, stripped of its valuables, carefully weighted, goes over the side, and Tom Ripley steps ashore as Dickie Greenleaf. Tom can never hope to be safe masquerading as his victim, but he is totally unscrupulous. More, almost casual, murder follows, but the talented Mr. Ripley is hardly aware of the nightmare he is living. It is the reader who feels the relentless buildup of the horror.

> **JOHN GORDON** (b. 1925) was born in Jarrow-on-Tyne and now lives in Norwich with his wife, Sylvia. As a child he moved with his family to Wisbech in the Fens of Cambridgeshire, where he went to school. After serving in the Royal Navy on minesweepers and destroyers during World War II, he became a journalist on various local newspapers. His first book for young adults, *The Giant Under the Snow*, was published by Hutchinson in 1968 and garnered praise from Alan Garner, among others. Since then Gordon has published a number of fantasy and horror novels, including *The House on the Brink*, *The Ghost on the Hill*, *The Quelling Eye*, *The Grasshopper*, *Ride the Wind*, *Secret Corridor*, *Blood Brothers*, *Gilray's Ghost*, *The Flesh Eater*, *The Midwinter Watch*, *Skinners*, and *The Ghost of Blacklode*. Gordon's short stories are collected in *The Spitfire Grave and Other Stories*, *Catch Your Death and Other Stories*, and *The Burning Baby and Other Stories*. He was one of five authors who contributed to the Oxrun Station "mosaic novel" *Horror at Halloween*, edited by Jo Fletcher, and his autobiography *Ordinary Seaman* appeared from Walker Books in 1992.

37 [1957]

NORMAN PARTRIDGE on

The Hunger and Other Stories
by CHARLES BEAUMONT

Charles Leroy Nutt (1929–67) understandably adopted the pseudonym "Charles Beaumont" and then legally took it as his name. A busy professional who turned his hand to the slicks, radio, television (notably episodes of The Twilight Zone, One Step Beyond, Thriller, *and* Alfred Hitchcock Presents*) and the movies (*Queen of Outer Space, Mister Moses*), Beaumont is best remembered for his short fiction.* The Hunger and Other Stories *was issued in hardcover by Putnam in 1957 in the United States, and reprinted in abridged form as* Shadow Play *by Panther in the United Kingdom in 1964 (although it doesn't include a source story for Beaumont's* Twilight Zone *episode of that name).* The Magic Man, *published by Fawcett in 1965 (topped and tailed by comments from Ray Bradbury and Richard Matheson), and* The Edge, *from Panther in 1966, have overlapping contents with* The Hunger, *as do* Best of Beaumont *(1982), edited by his son Christopher, and* Charles Beaumont: Selected Stories *(1988), edited by Roger Anker (reissued in 1992 as* The Howling Man*). Beaumont's screenplays include adaptations of other significant genre writers: Edgar Allan Poe's tales (*The Premature Burial, The Masque of the Red Death*), H. P. Lovecraft's "The Case of Charles Dexter Ward" (*The Haunted Palace*), Fritz Leiber's* Conjure, Wife *(*Night of the Eagle/Burn, Witch, Burn*), and Charles G. Finney's* The Circus of Dr Lao *(*The 7 Faces of Dr. Lao*).* The Intruder *(1959), Beaumont's only solo novel, became a strong 1962 film from his own script, directed by Roger Corman and starring William Shatner, with Beaumont in his only acting role as* *a liberal Southerner opposed by a mob that includes fellow* Twilight Zone *writers William F. Nolan and George Clayton Johnson. Though he died of premature-onset Alzheimer's disease in 1967, his script* Paranoia—*written for Corman in the early 1960s—was finally made by director Adam Simon in 1990 as* Brain Dead. *"Miss Gentibelle" became an unsettling 1961 short film,* Ursula. The Hunger *is, of course, not to be confused with Whitley Strieber's 1981 novel, the 1983 Tony Scott film adaptation, or the 1997–2000 anthology TV show.*

R OD SERLING INTRODUCED me to a couple of damn fine writers.

Not personally, of course. I hadn't yet seen my second birthday when *The Twilight Zone* debuted in 1959, and I was still in high school when its creator died. But I was just the right age to grow up watching Serling's signature anthology television series, which was a re-run staple on American television.

So you might say that I first encountered Charles Beaumont and Richard Matheson in *The Twilight Zone*. After Serling, those writers were the two most frequent contributors to the show. As a teenager armed with a library card, I set about tracking down short story collections by both men. Finding Matheson's work was easy; his career was still going strong in the mid-1970s. Finding Beaumont's books was harder—he'd died in 1967 at age thirty-eight, a victim of Alzheimer's disease.

But I was persistent in my quest. Eventually I found a beat-up Bantam paperback of Beaumont's *The Hunger and Other Stories* in a used bookstore. In it, I found the kind of tales I'd admired on *The Twilight Zone*, but I also discovered that Beaumont on the page was different from Beaumont on the screen. Freed from the restraints imposed by television, his dark work was darker, while his comedy was definitely more sardonic.

This was Beaumont *unfiltered*. It was also very good stuff.

Rereading that old paperback copy of *The Hunger* now, I'd have to conclude that in one sense Beaumont was very much a writer of his times. His stories appeared in the best markets of the day—*Playboy*,

Esquire, the *Saturday Evening Post, Collier's*—and for the most part his subject matter fit solidly within the template of the 1950s and the "what kind of man reads *Playboy*?" generation. Jazz musicians, disaffected businessmen, bohemian hipsters, and juvenile delinquents populate the stories in *The Hunger,* while Beaumont's themes included racism, alienation, and sexual repression. He often worked with genre conventions mined by other writers of his day, and this, too, is evidenced in the collection—there's a tale about an escaped asylum patient on the prowl, a few black comedies featuring murders gone wrong, and even one story featuring the familiar setup of a fortyish spinster encountering a satyr in the woods.

In the hands of a less-talented writer, this material might have become pedestrian. The difference with Beaumont was that he wrote beyond the idea. Unlike the typical genre writer who focused almost exclusively on plot, Beaumont used plot as a point of departure. The gimmick was not his primary concern. His stories contained a different level of characterization (and emotion) than you'd find in the average genre tale. Beaumont wrote about people. That was his great secret . . . and his great strength.

It's also why Beaumont's best work has stood the test of time. Though the *Playboy* aesthetic is long gone, and the concerns of the 1950s may seem simple exercises in nostalgia, Beaumont's characters retain a pulsebeat on the page. You still feel that pulse when you read stories like "The Vanishing American" and "A Point of Honor." I don't know if Beaumont understood that, or if thoughts of fictive longevity ever crossed his mind. I do know that while the world has changed in the past fifty years, the dynamics of the human heart remain the same. I also know that Beaumont understood the human heart, and that his understanding formed the core of his fiction. That's why his work endures.

Beaumont's people stick with you. They're loners, or underdogs, or outsiders. Many are haunted in a not quite expected sense of the word. They aren't easily forgotten. The trapped boy in "Miss Gentibelle," the lonely woman in "Fair Lady," the busted flush of a writer in "Open House," the boy intent on becoming a man in "Tears of the Madonna"... they'll leave you with an ache you'll feel long after closing the covers of *The Hunger*.

Apart from his skill with characterization, Beaumont had a way of catching the reader stylistically, too. One example is "Free Dirt," a story about a miserly suburbanite who landscapes his yard with soil taken from a cemetery. Beaumont's tale opens with a straight comic tone that's reminiscent of Robert Bloch's work, but then the story becomes progressively darker, stranger, and extremely unsettling. There's nothing at all overt about the ending; still, it disturbs in a way few stories can.

There are a lot of great endings in *The Hunger*. Beaumont was a master of closing with a single line that was both a summation and a coup de grâce. You'll find that most often in quieter stories like "The Dark Music" and "Last Night the Rain." It's a difficult technique to describe—on the one hand packed with emotion, on the other hard and cold and final. Searching for an analogy, I can only think of a door slamming in a very quiet house. The door itself isn't capable of emotion, but the person who slammed it . . . well, that's another story.

Perhaps Beaumont's finest work climaxes the collection. "Black Country" is the tale of a terminally ill musician and his young protégé. Again, it's a story very much of its time; the narrator tells the tale in the vernacular of 1950s jazz. You'd think the technique would date "Black Country," but Beaumont never crosses the line into parody, and the story still works marvelously today.

The ending of "Black Country" is a flat-out *tour de force,* and maybe the best thing Beaumont ever got down on paper. Many writers have tried to capture music through words. Few have succeeded. Beaumont does the job and then some. For a few pages, his typewriter truly becomes a jazzman's battered trumpet.

And, man, does Beaumont play that thing. His phrasing is impeccable, his rhythm driving and perfect, his music by turns dark and bright. There's a paragraph near the end of the tale describing a solo gone wild and "the heart of jazz." I'll resist the temptation to quote it here. But experiencing it as both a climax to "Black Country" and

The Hunger itself, I found myself thinking of that block of black type as the best music a writer could possibly conjure. It's an enduring testament not only to Beaumont's own talent, but also to the people and stories he left behind on the page.

NORMAN PARTRIDGE (b. 1958) was born in Vallejo, California, and lives in the San Francisco Bay Area with his wife, Canadian writer Tia V. Travis. Patridge grew up listening to his father tell ghost stories in the backyard on summer nights—tales of haunted houses, bloody footprints, and Pennsylvania's own private haunt, the "Green Man." The first book he remembers buying on his own was a copy of Peter Haining's *The Ghouls*. A two-time Bram Stoker Award winner for Best Collection, for *Mr. Fox and Other Feral Tales* (1993), and *The Man With the Barbed-Wire Fists* (2002), he also won the International Horror Critics Guild Award for his 1995 short story "The Bars on Satan's Jailhouse." Partridge is a frequent contributor to anthologies and magazines. His novels range from horror to *noir* to suspense, including *Slippin' into Darkness, Saguaro Riptide, The Ten-Ounce Siesta, Wildest Dreams,* and *To Hell and Gone,* the latter set in the universe of Joe R. Lansdale's "God of the Razor" character. *Bad Intentions* is another collection, and he also edited *It Came from the Drive-In* (with Martin H. Greenberg), an anthology of short stories that might have been drive-in movies. He contributes a popular column of the same name, featuring movie reviews and commentary, to *Horror Garage* magazine. An expanded edition of *Mr. Fox and Other Feral Tales* was published in 2005 and featured early tales and extensive commentary, plus advice for young writers looking to break into the horror market. A movie adaptation of his original novel, *The Crow: Wicked Prayer,* stars Edward Furlong, David Boreanaz, Tara Reid, and Dennis Hopper.

38

[1957]

ROBERT IRWIN on

The Blind Owl
by SADEGH HEDAYAT

Sadegh Hedayat (1903–51) originally published this short novel in Persian as Buf-i Kur *(1937)*; the English translation, by D. P. Costello, appeared in 1957 as The Blind Owl. The unnamed narrator scrapes a living working in a suburb of Teheran as a painter of pen boxes. As he reaches for a jug of wine, he glimpses through a hole in the wall a beautiful woman robed in black, who leans toward a sinister old man robed like an Indian fakir and offers him flowers. The old man's laughter is chilling. The painter becomes obsessed with this vision or hallucination. Weeks later the woman enters the painter's hovel, lies down on his bed, and dies. He paints a portrait of the corpse's face before cutting up the body to squeeze the pieces into a suitcase that he takes to a graveyard. In digging her grave, he finds an ancient vase bearing an identical portrait of the woman. In the second part of the story, a man, apparently the same narrator but now married and sickly, is frantically jealous of his young wife (whom he thinks of as the "harlot"). He suspects her of having an affair with that same sinister old man, whom, in his earlier identity, he had glimpsed laughing at the woman in black. The narrator makes love to his wife and in a frenzy of passion kills her. He then looks into the mirror and sees that he has the face of the old man. Although The Blind Owl is a very short novel, its hallucinatory plot defies sensible summary.

"THERE ARE SORES which slowly erode the mind in solitude like a kind of canker." This is the opening to what is almost certainly the greatest Iranian novel of the twentieth century. The Blind Owl faithfully reflects its author's fastidious, melancholy, and even suicidal temperament. Sadegh Hedayat was born in Teheran. Though he belonged to an aristocratic landowning family, he was without social or political ambition. Early in life he went to Europe and studied dentistry in Belgium. Fortunately for the history of the novel, orthodontics swiftly lost its appeal. Thereafter, though he occupied various low-level civil service posts in Iran, he spent much of his life traveling and writing. Since he was intensely proud of his country's past, by that very token he was bitterly disappointed with the tyranny, corruption, and poverty of the age he lived in. He produced novels, short stories, plays, and satires. He also translated Kafka's writings into Persian, though he only became aware of Kafka after completing *The Blind Owl*. That story's blasphemy and eroticism meant that it was impossible to publish it at first in Shah Reza's Iran. It first appeared in India in mimeographed samizdat form, before being serialized in an Iranian newspaper in 1941. In Paris in 1951, Hedayat gassed himself and was at last successful in exiting from the world he despised.

The Blind Owl's painter of lacquer pen boxes paints those boxes for the same reason that he takes opium and drinks alcohol. He is a man in hiding from life and people and, as the claustrophobic atmosphere of his story intensifies, his room will come to resemble his tomb. Though he had hoped to stupefy his senses, visions still come to him—most specifically, the vision of the woman in black and her eyes: "frightening, magic eyes, those eyes which seemed to express a bitter reproach to mankind, with their look of anxiety and wonder, menace and promise—and the current of my existence was drawn to those shining eyes charged with manifold significance and sank into their depths. That magnetic mirror drew my entire being towards it with inconceivable force." The story coils and turns in upon itself like smoke from an opium pipe. Is the woman in black with the brilliant eyes the same as the bitch-wife in the second part of the story? How many stories are being told? The pen-box painter both is and is not the same as the husband of the bitch-wife. There is little logic to the narrative, which works with echoes, ambiguities, and sinister metamorphoses. There is a Dostoyevskian intensity to the description of the burial of the suitcase and its maggoty, bloody aftermath. The reader is drawn into the squalor and dread of the narrator's world. The reading experience is that of being horribly drunk—too drunk to find a door out.

Toward the end, the narrator comes to consider everyone—the odds-and-ends man, the butcher, the uncle, the nanny, the bitch-wife, and the sinister old man—as shadows of himself, "shadows in the midst of which I was imprisoned. I had become like a screech-owl, but my cries caught in my throat and I spat them out in the form of clots of blood. Perhaps screech-owls are subject to a disease which makes them think as I think. My shadow on the wall had become exactly like an owl, and, leaning forward, read intently every word I wrote." As a youth, Hedayat tried to drown himself. His masterpiece is a novel to drown in. But note that drowning is rarely pleasant.

ROBERT IRWIN (b. 1946) studied modern history at Oxford and taught medieval history at the University of St. Andrews before resigning in 1977 to become a house-husband and write books. Since then he has published six novels: *The Arabian Nightmare* (chosen by Brian Stableford for his essay in *Horror: 100 Best Books*), *The Limits of Vision, The Mysteries of Algiers, Exquisite Corpse, Prayer Cushions of the Flesh,* and *Satan Wants Me.* He has also published a few short stories. He is a director of a publishing company and a commissioning editor at the *Times Literary Supplement.* He has also pursued an intermittent career as a freelance scholar and has published *The Middle East in the Middle Ages: The Early Mamluk Sultanate 1250–1382, The Arabian Nights: A Companion, Islamic Art, Night and Horses and the Desert: An Anthology of Classical Arabic Literature,* and *The Alhambra.* Irwin is a fellow of the Royal Society of Literature, a fellow of the Society of Antiquaries, a fellow of the Royal Asiatic Society and a fellow of the London Institute of Pataphysics.

39 [1957]

MARK MORRIS on
The Midwich Cuckoos
by JOHN WYNDHAM

After The Day of the Triffids *(1951),* The Midwich Cuckoos *is the best-known novel of the English author John Wyndham Parkes Lucas Beynon Harris (1903–69), who usually signed himself with his first two names but occasionally used "John Beynon" or "Johnson Harris" and once (*The Outward Urge, *1959) claimed to be collaborating with himself as "John Wyndham and Lucas Parkes." It is one of a run of very different Wyndham stories dealing with the effects of alien species on mankind and the Earth, physically and socially: the human-born but alien-souled cuckoos follow the genetically engineered killer plants of* Day of the Triffids *and the Jovian invaders who take up residence in the sea's deeps in* The Kraken Wakes *(1953), while prefiguring the ambiguous mental contact made by an alien with a human child in* Chocky *(1968). Along with Penguin's H. G. Wells reprints, the novels of Wyndham-influenced disastermongers like John Christopher and John Blackburn (even the early J. G. Ballard), and television like the* Quatermass *serials,* Doctor Who, *and* The Avengers, *Wyndham's books maintained a tweedy, down-to-earth, post-war British style of science fiction/horror as an alternative to pulpier American forms. The novel was filmed as* Village of the Damned *by Wolf Rilla in 1960, with George Sanders and Barbara Shelley as the "parents" of well-spoken Midwich kid Martin Stephens; oddly, the script was by an American (Stirling Silliphant), and the film lets stand some of his mistakes (the movie Midwich has a "general store" instead of a "village shop"). It was successful enough to inspire a thematic sequel,* Children of the Damned *(1963). An unsatisfying John Carpenter remake (1995) stars*

Christopher Reeve and Kirstie Alley; it relocates Midwich in modern California but weirdly keeps the children not only in 1960 British school uniforms but also makes them gray to match the black-and-white of the earlier film. Thanks to the persistent fame of the first Village of the Damned, *Wyndham's novel received an ultimate accolade when its creepy kid characters were caricatured in the distinctive Matt Groening style as the cast of* The Bloodening, *an imaginary film which features in "Wild Barts Can't Be Broken," a 1999 episode of* The Simpsons.

REMEMBER THE MOVIES? Remember the spooky blond-haired kids who could control people with their minds? In the 1960 version—and, by the way, the movie adaptations of Wyndham's book were renamed *Village of the Damned*, thus consolidating the cinematic supposition that these were the devil's children, evil to the core—the kids' eyes even glowed with an eerie light when they made people do bad things.

It's a cracking little film, but thematically it is so radically different from Wyndham's thoughtful, talky, ideologically complex novel that seeing it should not discourage potential readers from tracking back to the source material. For what makes Wyndham's book so frightening is not the spooky children themselves, but the fact that their presence serves to strip away, layer by layer, the political, religious, and moral foundations of our so-called civilized society. The children are a rogue element, a fly in the ointment, a cuckoo (as the title suggests) in the nest, and as such are used by the author to raise fundamental questions about the way we structure our society and run our lives.

But let's backtrack. Let's talk about the plot. *The Midwich Cuckoos* is a relatively simple story, which takes place almost exclusively in a sleepy little village in the heart of England, "a place where things did not happen." The story, related by Richard Gayford, who quickly adopts a largely passive role of observer and reporter, begins when he and his wife, Janet, try to return to their Midwich home one September morning, only to discover that the village has been enclosed in a (for want of a better term) "sleep barrier." For twenty-four hours any living thing who enters the village limits falls instantly and profoundly asleep. Afterward it is discovered that every childbearing woman in the village is pregnant. When the sixty-one children are born they appear to be normal, except for an odd golden hue to their eyes. Soon, though, it becomes apparent that the children are anything but normal—physically identical, they appear to share a group mind (albeit delineated by gender), and most terrifying of all, have the ability to mentally influence and control whomever they wish.

As far as the plot goes, that's about it. The final third of the book, by which time the children are nine years old but are as physically developed as children almost twice that age, chronicles a series of escalating encounters between themselves and the increasingly hostile villagers, which inevitably leads to a—literally—shattering climax.

Even here, however, the "action" mostly takes the form of a series of theoretical discussions in various country pubs and genteel English drawing rooms—though this is not to suggest that the book is dry or dull. The issues raised by the children's presence and actions are fascinating and thought-provoking. The mouthpiece for most of these ideas is tutor, philosopher, and grandfatherly academic Gordon Zellaby, a friend of Gayford's who brings to mind a retired version of Nigel Kneale's Professor Quatermass (and it is feasible that Wyndham had Quatermass in mind when he wrote the book; the initial BBC production of *The Quatermass Experiment* preceded publication of *The Midwich Cuckoos* by some four years). It is Zellaby who first propounds the theory that the children are "intruders, changelings: they are cuckoo-children." Evidence—in particular the discovery that other groups of children have been simultaneously born in other small communities throughout the world—suggests that the children may be the first stage of an "interplanetary invasion". However, if so, theirs is a low-key, parochial, insidious invasion. It is also nonaggressive. When they attack, they do so with devastating force, but their actions are always reactive rather than proactive. Their motive, Zellaby states, is simply to survive: "They have an instinct for survival, an instinct characterized by utter ruthlessness."

That human beings and the "cuckoos" will ultimately not be able to survive in tandem is made abundantly clear. When a villager clips a cuckoo child with his car and injures him, the others react spontaneously, forcing the villager to commit suicide by driving his car at speed into a wall. Later the brother of the dead villager, seeking revenge, shoots and wounds one of the children and is then forced to turn his gun on himself. These two incidents illustrate that the children are unpunishable, which in turn brings to light the frailty of our universal system of law and order, coupled with our ideas of what constitutes "justice." Zellaby states, "What these incidents really make clear . . . is that the laws evolved by one particular species, for the convenience of that species, are, by their nature, concerned only with the capacities of that species—against a species with different capacities they simply become inapplicable."

This is only one of many fascinating and disturbing dilemmas raised in the book. At its heart, though, lies the most tragic dilemma of all. Both sides *know* that only one species can survive, yet even while being aware that ultimately there can be no mutually satisfactory solution, both can discuss the situation with the other calmly, intelligently, and without rancor. "What are you going to do to liquidate us?" one of the boys bluntly asks Bernard Westcott, who represents the interests of the military. When Westcott asks why the subject can't be approached in a civilized manner, he is told, "This is not a civilized matter . . . it is a very primitive matter. If we exist, we shall dominate you—that is . . . inevitable. Will you agree to be superseded, and start on the way to extinction without a struggle? Can *any* state, however tolerant, afford to harbor an increasingly powerful minority which it has no power to control? Obviously the answer is . . . no."

There are many more issues raised by this timeless novel than I can possibly discuss here. My advice is to watch the movie for its spooky kids and read the book for its terrifying ideas. That way you won't be disappointed by either.

MARK MORRIS (b. 1963) was born in the mining town of Bolsover and spent his childhood in the English towns of Tewkesbury, Newark, and Huddersfield, as well as

Hong Kong. He became a full-time writer in 1988 on the Enterprise Allowance Scheme, and a year later saw the publication of his first novel, *Toady* (aka *The Horror Club*). Since then he has had eight further novels published: *Stitch, The Immaculate, The Secret of Anatomy, Mr. Bad Face, Longbarrow, Genesis, Fiddleback* (as "J. M. Morris") and *Nowhere Near an Angel*, along with the *Doctor Who* novelizations *The Bodysnatchers* and *Deep Blue*. His short fiction has appeared in such magazines and anthologies as *Fear, Skeleton Crew, Peeping Tom, The Third Alternative, Interzone, Cemetery Dance, Subterranean, Final Shadows, Dark Voices 3, Darklands, Darklands 2, Blue Motel, Dark Terrors, The Mammoth Book of Werewolves, Taps and Sighs, Best New Horror, Fourbodings,* and *Night Visions 12*, and has been collected in *Close to the Bone*. He is the editor of *Cinema Macabre*, a multi-authored collection of essays on horror films avowedly modeled on *Horror: 100 Best Books*.

40 [1958]

HOWARD WALDROP on

A Scent of New-Mown Hay
by JOHN BLACKBURN

In the proud tradition of gruesome stories about mushroom plagues, A Scent of New-Mown Hay *is worthy of comparison with William Hope Hodgson's story "The Voice in the Night" (1907), inspiration for*

Ishiro Honda's underrated film Matango *(aka* Attack of the Mushroom People, *1963), and* The Fungus *(1985) by Harry Adam Knight (John Brosnan and Leroy Kettle). John Blackburn (1923–93), who wrote about* The Tragedy of Macbeth *by William Shakespeare in* Horror: 100 Best Books, *continued to alternate science fiction-themed horrors with the supernatural in novels like* A Ring of Roses *(1965),* Children of the Night *(1966),* Nothing but the Night *(1968, filmed 1972),* For Fear of Little Men *(1972), and* Our Lady of Pain *(1974). A 1968 New English Library paperback reprint of* A Scent of New-Mown Hay *uses the cover line "Now an outstanding BBC serial"—referring to a four-part radio adaptation.*

I AM GOING TO tell you about the power of books.
When I first read this, at age twelve, when it came out, it scared the crap out of me.

I remember the opening chapter: men lost in a cold fog on the Russian Arctic coast; villages deserted or burning, *something* coming across the tundra after the lost men in the night.

I carried the memory of that chapter around with me for forty-seven years; whenever I needed a little frisson, I'd conjure it up.

So when I just reread it, you could have knocked me over with a feather: the opening chapter takes place on a rare, sunny bright July day at the Foreign Office in London.

The chapter I mostly remembered is chapter three: there *is* fog, but it's still July. It's mostly daytime when the shipwrecked British sailors find the deserted village (the burning village is in another chapter, told from the point of view of a Russian officer). Something *does* come across the tundra for the men.

What makes the chapter so chilling and effective is that until the survivors of a rammed British cargo vessel land in the lifeboats and find the deserted huts, it has been a straightforward, realistic report on abandoning a sinking ship, of navigating the lifeboats, and a description of how *not* to get lost in the fog, walking on marshy ground, roped together, with the lifeboat sirens going off every thirty seconds so you can echolocate yourself back to the boats. The three men find the huts, which had been abandoned in a hurry. Then, going back toward the boats, they realize that something large is following them. We leave them waiting, and we know that those three, and everyone in the lifeboats, are going to die without seeing any of it happen. (*They* see something; we don't.)

This, Blackburn's first novel, is subtitled *A Novel of Action, Horror, and Emotion*, which pretty much sums it up. What it reminds me of (forty-seven years on) was *Quatermass II* as imagined by a cross between John Le Carré and C. P. Snow—a horror novel involving various British bureaucracies and departmental denizens. It is, even for 1958, a solidly old-fashioned novel, with all the strengths and weaknesses the term implies. It is almost as full of coincidence as a novel by Dickens or Wilkie Collins, but the coincidences in service of the plot come out of the characters' very human emotions and motivations.

The plot: (stick with me) General Kirk, a gentleman missing all but two fingers on one hand (never specified), is head of Foreign Service Intelligence. He gets a report that the Russians are evacuating a huge area of their Arctic coast. There's lots of speculative palaver—perhaps they need it for a new atomic missile they're testing?

Then we follow Marcia and Tony Heath (a name, appropriately enough, right out of Defoe's *A Journal of the Plague Year*). She's the wife (but not a cipher); he's a teacher of biology at a small university, but was formerly the brightest guy at Farhill, a high-powered research institute. Then we get the *swell* chapter with the crew of the *Gadshill* (Dickens's last house) forced to leave with only two-thirds of a load of timber from a Russian port by the evacuation order; hit by what seems to be a Russian aircraft carrier and sinking; the lifeboat journey to land and the unshown deaths of the crew. Then we see Russian officers burning other villages: there's a United Nations meeting at which the current decent-bureaucrat ambassador is replaced at the last minute by the last of the hard-line Stalinist (author's description) leftovers (who breaks down and cries and asks the British and Americans for help).

It devolves that there's some kind of fungoid human-based horror loose in Russia. (You imagine they look like the Heap in the old *Air-*

boy Comics of the 1940s and '50s), which goes back to a sociopathic genius orphan German girl named Rosa Steinberg, who was the brains behind SS experimental Camp Ruhleben during the war—much is made of the fact that Himmler was afraid to use her plans earlier—and only authorized it in late 1944.

One of the coincidences: Ruhleben was liberated by a unit headed by Professor Roberts, who also teaches at the same university as Tony Heath and who tried to warn the British War Office in 1945 that something very dangerous and nasty had been going on there. (The Nazis destroyed most of the equipment before the Allies arrived.) Rosa Steinberg escaped.

Tony is called back by his former boss at Farhill for a conference at the Foreign Office after the Russians ask for help. There is—as in the *Quatermass* movies, wherein in all three—we get glimpses of mystifying things as shown in films or other media—a first glimpse of the mutated fungus creatures—still not really described—in a foggy, badly lit bouncy, handheld film as the Russian cameraman runs. There's a scene in Germany—on the Reeperbahn, where the Quarrymen would be playing in a few years—an agent starts out on the very cold trail of Rosa Steinberg. The British scientists think they have at least four days before the wind changes to the east, bringing the spores to the rest of Europe. Then we follow a lady shoplifter from a small English peninsular village who has developed what seems to be a toothache.

Then the book kicks into high gear.

Needless to say, everyone ends up at the same place at the same time with (like in a 1940s movie serial) one of the fungus things coming to get them all.

Earlier there's even a (mild) sex scene (between married people).

Once things start to move in the book, they *really* move. But it's not the plot you come to this book for.

No one has ever written a horror novel like this—a novel told mostly from within the operations of big science and big government.

The narrative POV jumps around to tell you what you need to know without spilling all the beans.

All this is in the context of the just-austerity-ended Britain. (Cozy was gone; despair and nicotine poisoning had not yet set in.) The book has a charm it didn't have when it was published; you can see the changes nearly fifty years have brought to the sceptered isle—they *still* did things the old ways then, even, as Dylan Thomas said, "In this Hydrogenous Age."

Something ugly is loose in the world, and they try to stop it. If you're twelve, it's a scary book. Forty-seven years later, it's still scary, but you can admire how Blackburn scares you, and the architectonics of the narrative engine.

And there's still that third chapter, which is as frightening as anything you've ever read.

HOWARD WALDROP (b. 1946) was born in Houston, Mississipi, and has lived in Texas since he was four years old. His stories are filled with images from contemporary American culture—rock 'n' roll music, bad science fiction movies, cartoons, comic books, and real-life characters have all found their way into his uniquely comic/tragic fiction. A winner of the World Fantasy and Nebula Awards, his novels include *Texas-Israeli War: 1999* (with Jake Saunders), *Them Bones, A Dozen Tough Jobs,* and *You Could Go Home Again.* Waldrop's highly distinctive short fiction is collected in *Going Home Again, Howard, Who?: Twelve Outstanding Stories of Speculative Fiction, All About Strange Monsters of the Recent Past, Strange Things in Close-up: The Nearly Complete Howard Waldrop, Night of the Cooters: More Neat Stories, Dream Factories and Radio Pictures, Custer's Last Jump and Other Collaborations* (with A. A. Jackson, Leigh Kennedy, George R. R. Martin, Joseph F. Pumilia, Buddy Sanders, Bruce Sterling, and Steven Utley), and *Heart of Whitenesse.* His novella *The Search for Tom Purdue* was recently published by Subterranean Press, while Old Earth Books is issuing two chapbooks with covers by Carol Emshwiller.

41 [1958]

ED GORMAN on
A Stir of Echoes
by RICHARD MATHESON

"Out of the nightmare mists of darkness, the pale silent woman came in a macabre dream of terror." In the 1950s, before there was a marketable publishing category of "horror" fiction, Richard Matheson (b. 1926) tended to write science fiction or crime novels that sidled up to the genre: I Am Legend *(1954)* and The Shrinking Man *(1956)* in science fiction and Someone is Bleeding *(1953)* and Ride the Nightmare *(1959)* in crime. A Stir of Echoes *flirts with the parapsychology that comes to the fore in* Hell House *(1971) and finds a murder mystery at the heart of its haunting, but it is the first Matheson novel to deal with the supernatural. Its plot pattern, as a haunted protagonist is nagged by a ghost to solve a murder, may be influenced by Dorothy McCardle's* The Uninvited *(1942) but is presented in a more grounded, credible setting.* Stir of Echoes *(1999), a film adaption scripted and directed by David Koepp, updates the story from the 1950s but is remarkably faithful, with an especially strong central performance from Kevin Bacon as a typically paranoid Matheson protagonist. It was eclipsed by the box-office success of* The Sixth Sense *that summer, but its reputation is slowly building.*

IN THE LATE 1950s, aircraft plant worker Tom Wallace goes to a party with his pregnant wife, Anne, and his brother-in-law Phil, a psych major at Berkeley.

Phil, who is not adverse to showing off a bit, puts on a demonstration of hypnotism with Tom as the subject. While the guests are amused, Tom finds himself oddly troubled by the experience. In nights to follow, unable to sleep, he begins to hear voices, among them, ultimately, the voice of the ghost who shows herself to him, demanding that he solve her murder. Equally as troubling, he begins to hear the most intimate thoughts of those around him, voices that in the end help him find the killer of the ghost-girl who appeared to him.

The conventional wisdom is that Richard Matheson created a new kind of horror—kitchen-table everyday kind of horror—almost as soon as he appeared on the scene.

True enough, but I think that the novel that best proves this theory is not one of his two widely acknowledged early masterpieces, *I Am Legend* or *The Incredible Shrinking Man*. While the latter certainly turns the hero's home into a house of horrors for the ever-diminished protagonist, the central dilemma is so powerful that the everyday moments of the story begin to fade quickly.

A Stir of Echoes takes as its milieu the working class of 1950s Southern California. Pregnancy, the price of groceries, labor conditions, the upkeep of the era's automobiles, evening meals, in-laws, backyard barbecues, neighborhood relationships, *Ozzie and Harriet,* crew-cut time—the book is packed with cultural references that ground it in the hopes and fears of the Cold War era in America.

Because he places his novel in a realistically depicted historical moment, and because the *I* narrator presenting this story is believable in every respect, the reader accepts without question the only unrealistic elements of the book—the paranormal scenes. It is the quiet, informal tone of the novel that gives the fantastic aspects their reality.

The real theme of the book is in harmony with all Matheson's great work (and I can't think of another author who has so many novels and short stories that live up to that adjective)—a man in isolation not only from his loved ones, from his society and also from himself. The last is especially important. No fearless pulp hero is to be found in Matheson. He is as fearful, neurotic, and existential as his time.

As in *I Am Legend, The Incredible Shrinking Man, The Beardless Warriors, The Night Stalker, The Journal of the Gun Years,* and *What Dreams May Come,* this novel is about working alone in search of a particular truth. Sometimes the truth is about himself (*Gun Years*) and sometimes the truth is much greater (*Dreams May Come*). But there is always that question, whether internal, external, or both—Matheson's unlikely (even unwilling) protagonists always need a truth that will redeem them. The last page of *Shrinking Man* speaks to this theme brilliantly.

For all that *A Stir of Echoes* relies on its historical period to create its reality, the book is as vital and fresh as it was when it first appeared nearly half a century ago. This is likely because of the shifting relationship between Tom and Anne—at times she is afraid for him; other times she is afraid of him. Given her pregnancy, and the added concern for the child she's carrying, Anne's moods are as much a part of the drama as the ghostly visitor, and give the reader one more compelling reason to keep flipping those pages so quickly. The marriage dynamic is as current as tonight's news.

While *A Stir of Echoes* isn't as high concept as *I Am Legend* or *The Incredible Shrinking Man* (or even another Matheson masterpiece, *Hell House*), my feeling is that in every other way it's just as strong, just as cohesive, and just as unforgettable.

> **ED GORMAN** (b. 1941) was born in Minneapolis and currently lives in Iowa with his wife, Carol, who is also a writer. He spent twenty years in communications, working at various times as a political speechwriter, a writer-director of television commercials, a copywriter for several advertising agencies, and owner of his own small agency. Gorman has been a full-time fiction writer for almost a quarter century, working in suspense (his favorite genre) and Westerns, with a handful of horror short stories and novels. His fiction reflects his primary influences—Richard Matheson, Robert Bloch, and Cornell Woolrich—and among his best-known books are *The Autumn Dead* (mystery), *Cage of Night* (horror), and *Wolf Moon* (Western). He recently collaborated with Dean Koontz on *City of Night*, the second novel in Koontz's modern *Frankenstein* series.

Though Gorman's writing output has slowed in recent years, his work has still managed to win the International Horror Guild Award, the Anthony, the Shamus, and the Spur. He has also published six collections of his short fiction, and has contributed to a wide variety of publications, including the *New York Times, Redbook, Penthouse, Ellery Queen, The Magazine of Fantasy & Science Fiction, Poetry Today,* and *Interzone*. With Martin H. Greenberg he has edited more than twenty anthologies. Gorman is the father of two sons and grandfather of five grandchildren, each of whom take turns showing him how to use his DVD player.

42 [1960]

MURIEL GRAY on

The Weirdstone of Brinsingamen
by ALAN GARNER

Alan Garner (b. 1934) set his first novel in Alderley Edge, Cheshire, where he attended primary school. Collins published the book in 1960 as The Weirdstone of Brinsingamen: A Tale of Alderley, *while the 1961 American edition, from Watts, was retitled* The Weirdstone. *In 1962 the author adapted the book for BBC Radio. For its paperback appearance from Penguin's famous Puffin children's imprint in 1963, Garner slightly revised the text. The* Moon of Gomrath *(1963) is a direct sequel, but his later novels—*Elidor *(1965),* The Owl Service *(1967), and* Red Shift *(1973)—take darker, more personal courses and seem less and less like "children's books."*

GARNER : 43

For lovers of horror who occasionally turn to the fantasy novel in search of alternative explorations of the supernatural, there remains the obstacle of searching for such among reams of derivative pish that make any sensible reader wish to ram an elf up some wise old wizard's backside by page thirty.

The disquieting elements of evil that fascinate discerning horror fans—that it is never tidy, predictable, containable, or conclusive—are generally neutered in the poor fantasy novel by rigid and formulaic lines drawn between good and bad. Brave and honorable protagonists encounter good creatures with pretty names like Gelflindlings or Brindlelashes, who battle bad opponents with names consisting of phlegm-creating consonants, and nothing much more complex or unsettling gets in between.

Given the subject matter of Alan Garner's 1960 children's novel *The Weirdstone of Brinsingamen*—an Arthurian tale in which two children find themselves unwitting guardians of medieval warriors, slumbering deep in a mountain in enchanted reverie until an England in peril deems their awakening necessary, (which, if true, the poor bastards would have been woken up every five minutes by *Daily Mail* editors)—one might imagine that the book must therefore be dismissed into this clichéd category and passed up by serious horror buffs.

This would be very wrong.

As a young person's introduction to horror, *The Weirdstone of Brinsingamen* resides with the classics. The reason it transcends its enjoyable wizard and troll romp is that Garner quickly establishes an evil that is not confined to remote magic kingdoms. By bringing the canker of moral corruption into the modern human community—in the form of witches and warlocks who have been dwelling covertly right under the noses of the solid and decent if emotionally retarded Yorkshire men and women who never suspected their neighbors—Garner's tale begins to toy with sophisticated ideas of paranoia and corruption that are more usually found in works of superior horror than in elves-in-tights books.

The children first enter an Alderly Edge straight out of Enid Blyton, played host to by Gowther and Bess Mossock, who stop short at offering lashings of ginger beer but nevertheless represent normal, clean-living country wisdom, getting on with nothing more demanding than the arduous task of bastardizing the English language as only a Yorkshire person can. Susan comments that the Edge is creepy (that's the location, and not U2's balding guitarist), to which Gowther replies, "Ay, theer's some as reckons it is, but yon munner always listen to what folks say." Er, quite so.

So against the backdrop of this English rural solidity, when the children encounter a local witch, the Morrigan (whose human form is the terrifying Selina Place, the posh lady from the big house), the human landscape alters. Selina Place, on recognizing the stone that Susan wears around her wrist as the missing key to the warriors' dorm, tries to force them into her car with hissing, demonic, Latin incantations, succeeding only until a dog barking breaks the spell.

From this moment on we are out of that safe childhood division between the real world and the fantastic, more in Stephen King territory, where the shifting sands of a normal society are gradually blown from the surface to reveal nasty things beneath.

What follows includes the truly gripping entrapment of the children in the Morrigan's house, there to retrieve the stone, but in the process witnessing from their hiding place the summoning of supernatural forces. These are described by Garner in true M. R. James understatement when he tells us that the column of smoke created by the witch contained strange shapes whose "forms were indistinct, but the children could see enough to wish themselves elsewhere." When their sanctuary is sniffed out by a supernatural hound with a head, ears, snout, but no eyes, the reader is deliciously chilled to the marrow.

Of course, the romp in the enchanted underworld that ensues is familiar, although beautifully crafted and with darker and nastier shadow-dwelling creatures than most rival works. But the climax of the book, back in the real world where innocent ramblers in anoraks cannot be trusted and even Gowther and Bess are forced to stop torturing vowels and defend their home and lives against these terrifying human as well as supernatural foes, is a horror rather than fantasy *tour de force*.

It's Garner's breathtaking ability not just to make profound ideas accessible to children and adults alike but also to merge two genres and create something unique and terrifying that keep *The Weirdstone of Brisingamen* rightly in a position of literary importance. As Gowther Mossock says, "I've seen nowt like it: it's enough fer t'send you mazed." I'm sure he's right. Whatever the hell he means.

MURIEL GRAY (b. 1958) was born in Glasgow, Scotland. Educated at the Glasgow School of Art, she went on to become assistant head of design in the National Museum of Antiquities in Edinburgh. At the same time she followed a parallel career as a member of the rock group the Von Trapp Family. With her trademark bleached hair and sharp wit, during the 1980s Gray became familiar as the post-punk presenter of a range of British television programs, including Channel 4's late-night cult music show *The Tube* (1982) and *The Media Show* (1987–89). She started her own TV production company, Gallus Besom, in 1989 and was responsible for such shows as *Art is Dead, Long Live TV* (1991), and *The Munro Show* (1991). Her company Ideal World is now the biggest television production company in Scotland. In the mid-1990s Gray reinvented herself as a mother and successful horror novelist whose books include *The Trickster, Furnace,* and *The Ancient,* while *The First Fifty* is a non-fiction work from Mainstream Publishing. Known for her outspoken views, she writes regularly for various newspapers and became the first female rector of the University of Edinburgh (1988–91).

43 [1961]

TERRY DOWLING on

Tales of Terror
Edited by CHARLES HIGHAM

Tales of Terror, *the first of six paperback anthologies from Australian imprint Horwitz Publications (better known for crime thrillers and naval adventures), was edited by the British-born Charles Higham (b. 1931). Produced not long after wartime paper restrictions in Australia were lifted in 1958, the books were distinguished by pulpy cover art and predominantly Victorian selections.* Tales of Terror *was quickly followed by* Weird Stories *(1961),* Tales of Horror *(1962),* The Curse of Dracula *(1962),* Spine-Tingling Tales *(1962, reprinted 1965) and* Nightmare Stories *(1962). All are rare and highly collectible today. As an editor, Higham mined a vein that would later be tapped by Robert Aickman, Mary Danby, R. Chetwynd-Hayes, and others in the British* Great Ghost Stories *and* Great Horror Stories *series from Fontana Books. Eleven of the forty tales in his collections were drawn from Montague Summers'* The Supernatural Omnibus *(1931). He also reprinted classic stories by Frederick Marryat, Guy de Maupassant, Wilkie Collins, J. Sheridan le Fanu, Erckmann-Chatrian, Ambrose Bierce, Théophile Gautier, E. Nesbit, Honoré de Balzac, Sir Walter Scott, Amelia B. Edwards, and others. Just once, Higham published an original—"The Mummy's Curse" by Horwitz house writer John Workman (aka "James Dark"), which appeared in* Nightmare Stories. *Higham left Australia in 1970 for America, where he became known as a Hollywood biographer; among his subjects are Cary Grant, Louis B. Mayer, and Howard Hughes. With Joel Greenberg, Higham wrote* Hollywood in the Forties *(1968), an important and influential critical work with a rare appreciation for the fantastic in genre cinema.*

It's so often about context, isn't it, how and when we come to something?

For me it was at age fifteen in 1962. Somewhere in between discovering Fritz Leiber's "A Bit of the Dark World" in the June issue of *Fantastic* magazine that year and Jack Vance's "The Dragon Masters" in the August issue of *Galaxy*, I chanced upon *Tales of Terror*, compiled by Charles Higham. It was a compilation of ten horror reprints published by Horwitz Publications (the "Australian Pocket Book," the back cover said), and though London was included with Melbourne and Sydney at the foot of the title page, the book probably never made it far beyond the antipodes.

The stories were mainly late nineteenth-century pieces, though I never knew that then. They had a mannered, antiquarian caste certainly, a syntactical quaintness, but somehow that seemed right, too, making for a curious refrain of people telling stories in front of warming fires while the wind howled outside and rain lashed the windows. You'll find something of that antique "fireside" quality in my own work—"The Daemon Street Ghost-Trap" comes to mind—just as Charles Dickens's "The Signalman" gets a nod in my story "Scaring the Train." You pay your dues where you can.

Maybe it was the running order that did it. Higham opened his anthology with two tales from the same author, F. Marion Crawford, a curious enough practice in any day but, then as now, an excellent way to set the mood.

The opening piece, "The Screaming Skull," was too good a title and too striking an image for the book's uncredited cover artist to resist. There it sits, midshriek, in the top left of a deep green nightscape, ably illustrating this tale of a retired sea captain holding forth in true old salt fashion and inadvertently providing a husband with the perfect means for murdering his wife. Here the MO was drugging the victim and pouring molten lead in her ear through a tiny funnel. (The *Grand Guignol* has a definite appeal when you're fifteen.)

Later the husband is found with his throat torn out, and our sea captain comes into possession of a skull that can only be that of the murdered wife. It screams, it bites, and, yes, there's a little piece of lead rolling around inside. Horrific premise. Simple story. Just add wind, a rainy night, and presto! I read "The Screaming Skull" on a sunny late autumn afternoon and considered myself lucky to have escaped so lightly.

"The Upper Berth," Crawford's haunted-stateroom story, made an ideal second offering—all very safe and quaint until that locked porthole began unscrewing and the bed was no longer empty. Crawford—and Higham—had done it again.

"The Body Snatcher" was the third in a run of unforgettable titles and themes, and author Robert Louis Stevenson taught me the Writing 101 essential of always trying for a strong ending, a surprise if you can manage it, though an uncanny flourish will certainly do. It also gave the artist a second powerful image for the cover. The screaming skull keeps watch over two body snatchers carrying a shrouded yet distinctly—alarmingly then!—feminine shape away from an opened grave.

W. W. Jacobs's "The Monkey's Paw" at fourth place was all the more powerful for its economy, delivering the sort of sudden nugget of horrific understanding later to be found in much of Ray Bradbury's earlier work. Just that one swift reading in 1962 and I learned how understatement, implication, and imagination can work better than mere words ever can—a precious lesson to have at any age. By this stage *Tales of Terror* had well and truly earned its keep.

A. M. Pushkin's "The Ace of Spades" came next (Alexander S. Pushkin misnamed and robbed, too, of his preferred title "The Queen of Spades"), a slight, elegant *conte cruel* that worked mostly by contrast. This respite was followed by Wilkie Collins's "The Dead Hand," more potent in its chilling central premise—the narrator passing the night with a corpse in the next bed—than in its rather forgettable conclusion. Like having a skull screaming, it again showed the power of a good title and a solid narrative hook.

Charles Dickens's "The Signalman," then as now, was eerie, full of portent and dread, while Edgar Allan Poe's "The Tell-Tale Heart" provided not only a first taste of that seminal author's work, but also threw together the sort of uncanny and disturbing notions you could never have quite imagined without one or two such examples to set you on your way. Shining the light of a lantern on a sleeping man's "dead" eye was one such.

Just as Higham opened his compilation with two works from a single writer, he closed it the same way: with two from Bram Stoker. "Dracula's Guest," a chapter omitted from his famous 1897 novel, was smooth and atmospheric, but safe fare for someone already conditioned by horror movies. It was the final tale, "The Squaw," that shocked and delighted me with its unforgettable iron maiden finale.

It would be overly sentimental and wrong to say that *Tales of Terror* was *the* single contributing factor in my own fascination with the darker side of storytelling. There were soon many other roads to the same destination: *Told in the Dark,* edited by Herbert van Thal, *Creeps by Night* from Dashiell Hammett, *Perturbed Spirits* from R. C. Bull, the work of Lovecraft, Bradbury, and Robert Bloch, and other Higham compilations.

But for form, feel, and sheer cumulative effect, *Tales of Terror* sits as the work that first helped me distill a sense of what good horror is and what it should always try to do. More importantly, since for many of us it is always about context and paying dues, there's something right in Charles Higham editing his book then and me thanking him for it now. All of us take our turn and try to pass it on.

TERRY DOWLING (b. 1947) was born in Sydney and is one of Australia's most awarded and internationally acclaimed writers of science fiction, fantasy, and horror. He has been called "Australia's finest writer of horror" (*Locus* magazine) and "Australia's premier writer of dark fantasy" (*All Hallows*). A communications instructor, musician, and songwriter, he has reviewed genre books for *The Weekend Australian* for the past sixteen years. His novels and collections include the "Tom Rynosseros" saga, comprising *Rynosseros, Blue Tyson,* and *Twilight Beach, Wormwood, The Man Who Lost Red, An Intimate*

Knowledge of the Night, Antique Futures: The Best of Terry Dowling, and *Blackwater Days.* Dowling is also the author of the best-selling computer adventures *Schizm: Mysterious Journey, Schizm II: Chameleon,* and *Sentinel: Descendants in Time.* His short stories have appeared in numerous anthologies, including *The Year's Best Science Fiction, The Year's Best SF, The Year's Best Fantasy, Best New Horror,* and *The Year's Best Fantasy and Horror,* as well as *Dreaming Down Under, Centaurus, Gathering the Bones,* and *The Dark.* He is also co-editor of *Mortal Fire: Best Australian SF* and *The Essential Ellison,* while a collection of his best horror stories recently appeared from Cemetery Dance Publications.

44 [1961]

PETER ATKINS on

Some of Your Blood
by THEODORE STURGEON

This novel by Theodore Sturgeon (1918–85) is brief enough to be included whole in anthologies: Robert Arthur, who actually edited the books credited to Alfred Hitchcock, selected it for Stories My Mother Never Told Me *(1963). In telling its story through interview transcripts and medical memorandums, the novel updates the collage of diaries and news cuttings Bram Stoker used in* Dracula *(1897), pioneering a format that became familiar in thrillers like Lawrence Sanders's* The Anderson Tapes *(1969).* Some of Your Blood *concerns a medical inquiry into* the mental health of an American serviceman of Eastern European origin who is called "George" throughout the file, though a single slip gives away his significant real name ("Bela"). Actor-writer-director Ken Campbell, of The Science Fiction Theatre of Liverpool, adapted the novel as a play, Psychosis: Unclassified *(1977).*

THE WRITER WHO died as Theodore Sturgeon in 1985 had been born as Edward Waldo in 1918. The "Sturgeon" came from his stepfather, the "Theodore" was (I'm guessing) reverse-engineered from the diminutive it has in common with his real first name. He wrote prolifically from the late 1930s to the early 1960s and sporadically thereafter. The life is over now, but the work survives. And the work is wonderful.

Sturgeon was of that generation of fantasists whose fiction was routinely classified always as science fiction, whatever its actual nature. Certainly Sturgeon wrote science fiction (and the best of it was genre-expanding, influential, and quite marvelous stuff), but he also wrote Westerns, mysteries, and fantasies—some whimsical, some not so much, and some downright horrifying.

The science fiction field is keeping Sturgeon's memory alive and his fiction in print, for which we should all be grateful—but it means that some of his work, marginal to science fiction proper, is in danger of not being remembered or celebrated. Case in point: *Some of Your Blood,* an almost unacknowledged masterpiece of unflinchingly dark vision and, at least for the popular fiction of its day, innovative execution.

This refreshingly short 1961 novel begins with medical and military curiosity regarding a minor piece of violence in the army, moves to a long story of a particularly deprived childhood in rural Kentucky, and ends as a reminder of how and where, and perhaps why, there are monsters among us.

Readers unfamiliar with the book who don't want part of its pleasures compromised should perhaps stop here and read it, because there's kind of a punch line to the novel—not quite an O. Henry or Fredric Brown all-in-the-last-line zinger, more a series of cumulative revelations in the last thirty pages—which I will have to reveal at this point.

Though the nature of what's going on in *Some of Your Blood* is unveiled slowly, it eventually becomes clear that it is in fact a vampire novel, albeit one blessedly free of the ossifying and irritating conventions of the genre. It overtly stacks the deck against there being any supernatural cause for its psychotic protagonist's condition, though his parents "come from the old country" and his father's phonetically rendered accent is a contextually disguised joke—"Poy, dat schmells goot!" is the kind of line, we realize in retrospect, that could have come from the mouth of another, more well-known, bloodsucking émigré had the latter not been of a more aristocratic lineage.

Another nod to *Dracula* is that *Some of Your Blood* is, like its predecessor, an epistolary novel (or, more precisely, that particular riff on the form that includes various found documents, not all strictly letters) that allows the story to reveal its secrets obliquely, in patchwork glimpses of alternating analysis and revelation.

Some of the voices in the surrounding documents—the vernacular of middle-class military men of their time—may strike the modern reader as a little dated, but the central voice of the book, a beautifully observed prose that never steps outside the halting and uneducated voice of its "writer" but nevertheless achieves a poignant folk-art poetry, is not only assured and masterful but also is a sustained demonstration of the bravura hide-in-plain-sight technique by which Sturgeon conceals the truth about his protagonist. Sentences that make perfect (if disturbing) contextual sense in what we believe to be the novel's reality take on deeper significance upon a second reading.

There are moments in the book that, nearly fifty years later, retain a stunning power. The protagonist's innocent readings of the Rorschach tests given to him by a well-intentioned psychiatrist, for example, are both revelatory and deeply disturbing, exposing the utterly alien drives within a character for whom we have previously felt at least pity and perhaps sympathy and affection.

Though *Some of Your Blood* is also, in its own bizarre way, a love story, it is by no means a "vampire romance" and it's sobering and sad to compare this neglected gem to today's best-selling bodice-rippers-with-blood, those fantasies (in the least generous sense of the word) in which the legions of Anne Rice imitators trot out their wearying tales.

Richard Matheson's *I Am Legend* and Stephen King's *'Salem's Lot* both receive deserved praise as novels that revivify vampire mythology by marrying it to well-observed contemporary (or, in Matheson's case, near-future) settings. It's easy to forget, of course, that that was also true of Stoker's *Dracula* upon its first appearance. Sturgeon's novel more than deserves a place in that particular pantheon. It recasts an ancient bogeyman as a terrifyingly and truthfully rendered contemporary monster. Over and above its real-world milieu, it possesses an emotional and behavioral truth that renders it a timeless classic of dark fantasy.

PETER ATKINS (b. 1955) was born in Liverpool and now lives in Los Angeles, with his wife, Dana. A childhood friend of Clive Barker's, in 1974 he joined Barker's experimental theater company, which also included Doug Bradley (future horror icon Pinhead). He worked with them for the next six years and was flayed alive in Barker's short film, *The Forbidden.* Atkins trod the boards for another half decade as composer, musician, and singer before establishing himself as a novelist and screenwriter. He has published the novels *Morningstar* (1992) and *Big Thunder* (1997), and the collection *Wishmaster and Other Stories* (1999). His short fiction has appeared in the anthologies *Best New Horror, Don't Turn Out the Light, 365 Scary Stories,* and *The Museum of Horrors,* and he has been a contributor to *Fear, Demons and Deviants, Skull: The Magazine of Dark Fiction, Weird Tales,* and *The Magazine of Fantasy & Science Fiction* as well as the non-fiction anthologies *The Hellraiser Chronicles, Clive Barker's Shadows in Eden, Cut! Horror Writers on Horror Film, Pandemonium, The Tiger Garden, Dancing With* the Dark, and *My Favorite Horror Story.* He has twice been nominated for the British Fantasy Award and has served as a judge for the World Fantasy Awards. Atkins is perhaps best known for his work in the movies, where he has authored the screenplays for *Hellbound: Hellraiser II, Hellraiser III: Hell on Earth, Hellraiser: Bloodline, Fist of the North Star,* and *Wishmaster.* He has also written for television, comic books, and the stage.

45

[1962]

JACK WOMACK on

We Have Always Lived in the Castle
by SHIRLEY JACKSON

Shirley Jackson (1916–65) remains a frequently invoked name in the horror genre for her story "The Lottery" (1948) and novel The Haunting of Hill House *(1959), but her works stretch to a mainstream novel about multiple personalities,* The Bird's Nest *(1954), memoirs of her life as a parent,* Raising Demons *(1957), and the children's history* The Witchcraft of Salem Village *(1956).* We Have Always Lived in the Castle, *her second best-known novel, takes place in an America that is at once horribly credible and strange enough to seem fable-like. Lisa Tittle wrote about* The Haunting of Hill House *in* Horror: 100 Best Books.

FEW WRITERS WERE as adept as Shirley Jackson at the art of never wasting words. *We Have Always Lived in the Castle* opens as sparely, and perfectly, as any novel can:

> My name is Mary Katherine Blackwood. I am eighteen years old and I live with my sister Constance. I have often thought that with any luck at all I could have been born a werewolf, because the two middle fingers on both my hands are the same length, but I have had to be content with what I had. I dislike washing myself, and dogs, and noise. I like my sister Constance, and Richard Plantagenet, and *Amanita phalloides,* the death-cup mushroom. Everyone else in my family is dead.

Mary Katherine—Merricat, to those who know her—is one of literature's most unreliable narrators: hungry for revenge, perversely imaginative, suspicious of all around her, as patient and cunning as her beloved cat Jonas, possessed of a heart like one of Jupiter's moons—forever frozen yet magma-hot within. She lingers on the cusp of adulthood, staring cold-eyed into the abyss beyond, opting to go no farther. Her story seems at first half-remembered: fragments of a child's dream, scattered verses of a murder ballad, a New England fairy tale bereft of moral, yet rich in poetry.

> Merricat, said Connie, would you like a cup of tea?
> Oh no, said Merricat, you'll poison me.
> Merricat, said Connie, would you like to go to sleep?
> Down in the boneyard ten feet deep!

Every day for nearly six years she has walked to the village for groceries and library books, hearing the villagers—young and old alike—chanting this rhyme (if often hearing it only in echoes, bouncing off the walls of her skull). Constance, a decade older, never leaves the house, but serves tea to neighborhood ladies who ask boldfaced what drove her to poison her parents and younger brother with arsenic in the sugar bowl (their uncle Julian survived, though wheelchair-bound and a bit addled, and still lives with them). They wonder, too, what led her to spare Merricat.

As Jackson's masterpiece unfolds, and Merricat alludes to her true feelings for the villagers and the world in general, the mood darkens, yet becomes ever more entrancing. However mad the reader's head perceives Merricat to be, the more the reader's heart embraces her. As she wanders in the woods, burying coins and nailing books to trees, casting spells meant to protect the family against the villagers, you hope her magic will work. When it fails and their cousin Charles slips through, all smiles and lies and greed, it's impossible not to take her side as he openly plots to drag Constance (and the family's money) back into the world while sending Merricat away, where she'll be a bother to no one but herself.

As is always the case in Shirley Jackson's work, the greatest horrors in her books are those people who are most keen to inflict pain upon others (and often themselves). In most of her work, there is no escape—think of Mrs. Hutchinson screaming as the stones begin to hit her, and of Eleanor, held tight in the grip of Hill House. So after Charles's pipe has set the house on fire; after the villagers, having extinguished the flames, begin to hurl rocks through the house's few unbroken windows; after they smash and steal the Blackwoods' possessions; after they seem moments away from lynching Merricat and Constance; after they slink off into the night, leaving behind the women, the ruins, and their uncle lying dead in the grass—afterward the reader can only breathe a sigh of relief when Constance decides to remain with her sister thereafter in the ruin, staring up beyond where the roof had once been at the moon, where Merricat has always wished they could live, far away from the terrible world down below.

They have always seemed two sides of the same woman; and now, for all intents and purposes, they *are* the same woman. And they are as happy in their castle as they will ever be.

Remarkably, a stage play was somehow adapted from the book soon after its publication—it ran on Broadway for three days. I am genuinely horrified to hear that a movie is in the works—had Val Lewton lived into the 1960s he might have pulled it off, but I doubt anyone can these days.

Ultimately this novel, like Merricat, like Shirley Jackson herself, remains sui generis.

JACK WOMACK (b. 1956) was born in Lexington, Kentucky, and moved to New York City in 1977, where he has since resided with his wife and works as publicity manager for all the science fiction and fantasy titles at HarperCollins Publishers. He is the author of the novels *Ambient* (1987), *Terraplane, Heathern,* the Philip K. Dick Award-winning *Elvissey, Random Acts of Senseless Violence,* and *Going, Going, Gone.* Set mostly in two alternate New Yorks—one that never was, but could have been; the other might never be, but then again might—these six books make up a single interrelated narrative called by some the "Dryco," or "Ambient" cycle, although the author always called it "WomackWorld." *Let's Put the Future Behind Us* is a contemporary novel set in Moscow in about 1994, and he is currently working on a new book, *Lying to Children.* Womack's infrequent short stories have appeared in such anthologies as *Walls of Fear, A Whisper of Blood, The Year's Best Science Fiction and Fantasy,* and *Little Deaths,* and he has contributed non-fiction to *Spin,* the *Washington Post Book World, Science Fiction Eye, The Magazine of Fantasy & Science Fiction,* and the *New York Review of Science Fiction.* He has both written short pieces for and appeared on BBC-TV and the BBC World Service, as well as Radio Bavaria. His novels have been translated into German, French, Spanish, Italian, Hebrew, Japanese, Czech, Polish, Greek, and Norwegian, but he has no idea how any of them read in these languages.

46 [1962]

DARRELL SCHWEITZER on

The Case Against Satan
by RAY RUSSELL

Ray Russell (1924–99) was the anonymous editor of The Playboy Book of Horror and the Supernatural *(1967), which Ellen Datlow writes about elsewhere in this volume. His novella-length horror fiction inclines to the Gothic, most memorably the much-anthologized conte cruel "Sardonicus," but his comparatively few horror novels have contemporary American settings and tend to be well ahead of breaking waves in the genre.* Incubus *(1976) is an early entry in the small-town-infiltrated-by-a-supernatural-murderer cycle, while* The Case Against Satan *is a template for the wave of Satanic terrors that followed* Rosemary's Baby *(1967) and reads like the seed of William Peter Blatty's franchise blockbuster* The Exorcist *(1971). A sharp, polished, to-the-point piece free from bloated best-seller mannerisms,* The Case Against Satan—*originally subtitled* A Melodramatic Novel—*was published by Oblensky in the United States and Souvenir in the United Kingdom at a time when very few modern-set American supernatural novels were being written.*

THIS TAUTLY WRITTEN psychological thriller, by far a better book than William Peter Blatty's later, more sensational reworking of the same material in *The Exorcist*, is a *Turn of the Screw* for modern Catholics. The scenario is familiar: a priest with something of an alcohol problem transfers into a new parish where he must cope with not merely the usual nosy parishioners, hints of prior scandal, and the disapproval of his bishop, but also what seems to be a genuine case of demonic possession in a teenage girl.

Yet the "supernatural" manifestations are equivocal, even when the girl is burned by the touch of a crucifix. Could her sudden lapses into extreme licentiousness and profanity be some form of schizophrenia? The modern, liberal priest-hero, Father Sargent, is all too inclined to such explanations. Is this just one more of the Devil's wiles to prevent us from believing in him? When the Father of Lies, within the girl, is forced to speak (after a vomiting scene and bedroom acrobatics like those in *The Exorcist*), he explains his purpose as an attempt to drive the girl to suicide. But is it really a more elaborate plot to undermine Father Sargent's faith and possibly that of his bishop? The delicate balances among paranoia, narcissism, and superstition are enough to drive anyone over the edge. Is one young girl actually worth the Devil's time? Is Father Sargent?

Like the governess in *The Turn of the Screw*, Father Sargent has to make tough choices. He is ultimately assisted by the bishop, even as parishioners, the girl's father, and the police oppose him. (What *about* those female screams coming from the rectory at all hours? Exorcism in the modern world takes some explaining.)

The real strength of *The Case Against Satan*, other than the compulsive readability of its prose, is how every detail sets a further trap for Father Sargent in a manner—if one will pardon the expression—truly diabolical. When it is revealed that the girl may have suffered sexual assault, and that the criminal will be the next person to knock on the rectory door, and a knocking is heard, Sargent, still tottering between belief and non-belief, can only pray that it isn't his predecessor, Father Halloran (whom we know is on his way to the rectory just then). The dilemma is neatly summed up by a quote from H. C. Goddard, which Russell puts at the front of the book:

> Whether the insane man creates his hallucinations or whether insanity is precisely the power to perceive objective existences of another order, whether higher or lower, than humanity, no open-minded person can possibly pretend to say.

Father Sargent is open-minded if he is anything, but is he thus falling prey to yet another Satanic snare? What Russell has focussed on is both a serious theological question—can even someone who believes in God truly believe in an active, personal devil?—and the core issue of all supernatural fiction. What is truly supernatural, and what is merely produced by abnormal psychological states? If all data come from the senses, how do we know that we are not deceived? Ultimately characters like James's governess or Russell's priest have to go with gut instincts. The priest is victorious. He knows that his own faith is on a more solid foundation when he is able to casually describe the girl's fate to his brother-in-law over the phone: "She was possessed by the Devil. They cast him out. She's fine now."

The Case Against Satan may be one of the very few supernatural horror novels ever published in a special edition for the Catholic Book Club, but it is much more than a philosophical conundrum and is anything but a religious tract. There are more moments of genuine fear evoked by this fifty-thousand-word short novel than in most bloated bestsellers. That a subtle, thoughtful book can also be paced like a series of hammer blows makes it all the more remarkable.

This was Russell's first novel, written shortly after he resigned as fiction editor of *Playboy*. He is better known for the novella *Sardonicus*, written at about the same time, but is generally, despite a World Fantasy Award for Lifetime Achievement in 1991, a neglected writer. *The Case Against Satan* is a model of what a good horror novel should be. It is a lost gem that cries out to be reprinted.

> **DARRELL SCHWEITZER** (b. 1952) has lived all his life in the Philadelphia area, though he is widely traveled. He has been publishing fantastic fiction and critical commentary since the early 1970s. His work has appeared in *Twilight Zone Magazine, Realms of Fantasy, Interzone, Whispers, Amazing Stories, Fantasy Tales*, and elsewhere. His three published novels are *The White Isle, The Shattered Goddess*, and *The Mask of the Sorcerer*. His short story and poetry collections include *Tom O'Bedlam's Night Out, Transients, Refugees from an Imaginary Country, Nightscapes: Tales*

of the Ominous and Magical, Necromancies and Netherworlds: Uncanny Stories* (with Jason van Hollander), *The Great World and the Small: More Tales of the Ominous and Magical, Sekenre: The Book of the Sorcerer,* and *Groping Toward the Light: Poems for Midnight and After.* His nonfiction books include a collection of essays, *Windows of the Imagination,* book-length studies of Lord Dunsany and H.P. Lovecraft, and numerous critical symposia such as *The Thomas Ligotti Reader, Discovering Modern Horror Fiction I* and *II, Discovering Classic Horror Fiction,* and *Speaking of Horror: Interviews With Writers of the Supernatural.* He is a regular contributor to the *New York Review of Science Fiction* and has been co-editor of the revived *Weird Tales* since 1987, for which he won the World Fantasy Award in 1992 with George H. Scithers.

47 [1963]

PETER CROWTHER on

Something Wicked This Way Comes
by RAY BRADBURY

Ray Bradbury (b. 1920) sketched the tale that would become Something Wicked This Way Comes *in the story "The Black Ferris" (*Weird Tales, *May 1948)—perhaps in homage to Charles G. Finney's* The Circus of Dr. Lao *(1935), though weird doings in carnivals and amusement parks are also central to the Lon Chaney-Tod Browning films Bradbury watched as a child. That the theme was especially personal to the* author can be gauged from the title of his first collection from Arkham House, Dark Carnival *(1947)*. According to Bradbury, the title "was supposed to be a long story about an evil carnival which arrived in a small town late one October night. I never finished the story, at that time, so the book came out minus its title story!" Impressed—unlike 98 percent of other viewers—by Gene Kelly's "art movie" Invitation to the Dance *(1956)*, Bradbury reworked Dark Carnival *as an original screenplay for Kelly to direct. When Kelly could not raise the budget, Bradbury converted his script into the novel* Something Wicked This Way Comes. *Bradbury, at various times, approached David Lean and Steven Spielberg with the project, and Sam Peckinpah worked on an abandoned adaptation. In 1983 Jack Clayton finally directed a film from Bradbury's script, with Jonathan Pryce as the sinister Mr. Dark and Pam Grier interestingly cast as "the most beautiful woman in the world." After studio interference, which included removing scenes and replacing a Georges Delerue score with one from James Horner, Clayton and Bradbury distanced themselves from the film—though it has some good things in it.*

"First of all, it was October, a rare month for boys."

While that oh-so-familiar first line in Ray Bradbury's most complete and damn near perfect novel *seems* to say it all—October, wood smoke, Halloween, dark nights, boys, adventure, et al.—it actually tells only half of the story. For, though it's a wholly appropriate opener (and, make no mistake, this *is*—at least on the surface—a boys' book), the eternal October in which Bradbury dwells, and with which he has filled his voluminous output, is simply a metaphor for that almost-end section of life, the winding-down time wherein we can see the first faint glimmer of light reflecting from the Grim Reaper's scythe as it waits for us all at the allegorical year's end: the swan song of the party that is life. And, of course, that holds true even if you're a girl.

But in addition to gender-spanning, *Something Wicked This Way Comes* also builds a bridge across that other great divide in our culture, age, reuniting traditionally opposite if not necessarily opposing sides against the common enemy of death. The two sides in question are not male and female but rather young and old—or, more specifically, children and adults—and this is where Bradbury's novel, like so many of his short stories, scores most highly, in that it speaks so eloquently of the yawning gulf of time between those age streams. Sneakers versus slippers, if you will.

For anyone who doesn't know the story, here it is in a nutshell: Will Halloway and Jim Nightshade, two thirteen-going-on-fourteen-year-old boys, encounter "Cooger & Dark's Pandemonium Shadow Show," a traveling troupe of ageless soul-stealers, masters of the arcane arts, and altogether general ne'er-do-wells. Masquerading as carnival sideshow-and-ride hosts, they come to visit their mayhem on the sleepy midwestern community of Green Town, Illinois, and go off replenished with a few souls for their efforts. Mister Dark, the carnival's cadaverous proprietor, gets wind of the fact that the boys are onto him and of their intention to foil him. So he sets out to steal them away . . . particularly the fatherless Jim Nightshade, in whom Dark senses a young ward's great potential. Quickly recognizing that they are completely outclassed when pitted against the preternatural strength and powers of the Pandemonium Shadow Show players, Will and Jim decide to enlist an ally—Will's father, the town librarian.

It's in this very special relationship—a melding far beyond anything that could reasonably be normally expected between parent and progeny—that we're able to dissect life's greatest fear, its end, and through that, the prospect of loss, of bereavement, and of loneliness. This, surely, is the essence of all horror—it's not the lycanthrope or the shambling zombie; nor is it the patchwork man made up of dead parts, or the multi-limbed "Old Ones" set to retrieve dominance through ancient volumes of arcane law; it's not even slavering aliens or malevolent ghosts—it's what these things can *do* to us that scares us. In short, it's not the weapon nor its wielder—it's the act, and the act's consequences: the fact that they can kill us. That's what scares us: the end of all things. It's what all of us wake up thinking about from time to time, wondering how and where and when and why everything will stop. And that is what Bradbury achieves in this ostensibly gentle and optimistic work: he reminds us of our own frailty.

What will it be like when it comes, that ending... that gentle taking of a last cherished breath, the dawning realization that we're slipping away from everything we have ever known, a darkness creeping up across the edges of our vision and our very being, as the final glimpse of a loved one dims and a once-cherished and familiar voice grows faint? What will it be like, that final breath, that oh-so-slender cusp of existence and nothingness? Will it *hurt*?

As the story comes close to its finale, we're treated to the inevitable confrontation between the middle-aged Halloway—carrying on his weary shoulders the memories of a life of missed opportunities and gentle regrets—and the carnival's proprietor, confident, calm and polite, self-assured and thorough, uncaring and unafraid. It is here that the librarian faces a Sophie's Choice of sorts: hand over the two boys and, Dark promises, he will receive a reduction of years—perhaps as many as thirty—to live again, and to experience *life* again, to revisit questionable decisions and play them again. It's a tempter, but Halloway stands firm. Unperturbed, Dark turns away, but not without exacting a grim punishment:

> "Stay there," he directed. "Listen to your heart. I'll send someone to fix it. But, first, the boys."

Something Wicked This Way Comes is that rare find, a work of literary genius that bears repeated readings, each time revealing more of itself while, paradoxically, each time turning slightly darker at its core. Cunningly disguised as a gentle tale of strength against adversity and redemption despite almost impossible odds, it's a tale filled with all manner of 3:00 A.M. lingerings... when, perhaps the only one awake in your house, you'll cast a thought to the manner of your own passing and wonder what it will be like.

PETER CROWTHER (b. 1949) was born in Leeds and now lives in the northeast of England, close to the sea, with his wife, Nicky. While employed by one of the biggest financial institutions in the United Kingdom, he also worked as a freelance music and arts journalist. He has since become a full-time author, editor, critic/essayist, poet, and, most recently—with the multiple award-winning PS imprint—publisher. Crowther is the editor of more than twenty anthologies, including such titles as *Narrow Houses, Touch Wood, Blue Motel, Taps and Sighs, Fourbodings, Destination: Unknown, Tales in Time, Tales in Space,* and *Tombs* and *Dante's Disciples* (both with Edward E. Kramer). His 1996 Bradburyesque novel *Escardy Gap* was written in collaboration with James Lovegrove, and some of Crowther's more than one hundred short stories and novellas have been collected in *The Longest Single Note,* the British Fantasy Award-winning *Lonesome Roads, Cold Comforts, Songs of Leaving,* and *Dark Times.*

48 [1963]

IAN MacLEOD on

The Collector
by JOHN FOWLES

John Fowles (b. 1926) made a best-selling debut with The Collector—*a canny mix of literary fiction, suspense thriller, and perversity—and delivered two more of the signature novels of the 1960s, both inflected with fantasy,* The Magus *(1966) and* The French Lieutenant's Woman *(1969). All three have been filmed, though the depths of the novels have proven difficult for the movies. William Wyler directed* The Collector *in 1965, with Terence Stamp in a bad haircut as the butterfly-collecting Clegg and Samantha Eggar tied to the bathroom pipes as art student Miranda. Far less well known is Mike DeLeon's Tagalog-language remake,* Bilanggo sa dilim *(Prisoner of the Dark, 1986), from the Philippines. An entire sub-genre of "imprisonment" Grand Guignol springs from this source: Stephen King willingly acknowledges the debt in* Misery *(1987), but other examples include the Hammer film* Fanatic *(aka* Die! Die! My Darling, *1965) and the Korean movie* Oldboy *(2004).*

IF THERE WAS ever a book that expressed the banality of evil, *The Collector* is it. The tone and structure couldn't be blanker, simpler, or more horrifying. In the long canon of works about obsession, few get closer to what lies beneath, or find so terrifyingly little there.

I'd read almost everything Fowles had written by my early twenties, and reached *The Collector* after I'd already enjoyed most of his later work. I remember that for all I'd grown to expect twists and surprises, it came as something of a shock. At the time he wrote *The Collector*, Fowles was unpublished as a novelist, although he'd already produced most of what later came out as *The Magus*. He felt, probably rightly, that he was unlikely to get very far with such big, complex works. *The Collector*, which is as blunt as *The Magus* is elusive, was the result.

Clegg, a youngish man of no particular accomplishments, becomes obsessed with Miranda, a pretty young art student whom he lacks the courage ever to approach. Instead he follows her, dwells upon the fragments of her life. When he gets the windfall of a pools win, he quits his dowdy job, buys a house in the country, kidnaps her, and keeps her in the cellar.

Nothing so very new there, at least now, when bookshops echo to the helpless cries of imprisoned females. Indeed, with the success of *The Collector*, Fowles as much as anyone could be blamed for starting this misogynistic trend. But his concerns, his approach, are very different. The book is written exclusively—indeed, claustrophobically—in diary form by the two main characters. Not only that, but Fowles's focus is unwavering; there's none of the switching back and forth between narrators that you might expect. What we get is almost Clegg's entire story in the first half, then Miranda's in the second. That, apart from a few final entries by Clegg, is it.

Clegg's tone, in particular, rings out. Fowles, once a teacher, had plainly had long and bitter exposure to the flat tones of underachieving middle England. There's no brightness, no verve, no passion. We don't doubt that Clegg, in his own bland, introverted way, loves Miranda—but it's a love that, on the page just as when he's in her presence, he's quite incapable of expressing. By the time we do get to hear from Miranda, for all Clegg's obsessive detailing, we still know very little about her. Partly—after all, she's an *art student*—we're hoping for brightness and relief from her: indeed, escape. But we already know, from what Clegg has set down about their deteriorating relationship and her rapidly weakening health, that it's too late. I can't think of another book where the unrelentingly thinning number of pages waiting to be read is more ominous.

Miranda, as it turns out, is nothing more nor less than what she appears: a pretty, moderately intelligent art student from a wealthy if not especially privileged background. If anything, we come to find her surprising initial optimism about the situation she finds herself in—and then her willingness to treat Clegg like a normal human being—irritating. She's not really passionate or resourceful enough to find a realistic way of escape, or of bringing the situation to a head. Instead she details her metropolitan life, and in particular a relationship with an older painter whose main interest, although she seems incapable of realizing it, is getting into her knickers. As she natters on about style and taste and art and a mother who drinks too much and a father who's a little cold, she reveals herself to be shallow and snobbish. Only when she starts to become delirious toward the end of her section does her writing ever take flight.

The Collector isn't a book about sex; sex, in its passion, is something neither of the two narrators can understand. It touches, a couple of times, lightly, and in passing, on the Nazi Holocaust, and I think that that points us closer to the truth. Evil isn't about monstrous people doing monstrous things; it's about gray lives dragged through day by day in vague incomprehension and dull resentment. It's about problems at work and people looking down on each other and thinking they know better, or not caring if they don't. It's about hope turned sour. The true place of horror, Fowles is telling us, isn't a railroad junction in Poland or a damp cellar in the country. It's inside all of our heads.

> **IAN MacLEOD** (b. 1956) currently resides in Bewdley, Worcestershire, where he divides his time between teaching English and writing. After an early diet of *Doctor Who*, he fell in love with ghost stories in his early teens, and then "scary" science fiction novels such as *The Day of the Triffids*. For MacLeod, unease has always been a key part of what's important in storytelling. As a writer—and, indeed, a reader—he is particularly interested in the boundaries of the real and the unreal, and what makes or unmakes genre and mainstream fiction. His books include the Arkham House collection *Voyages by Starlight*, *Breathmoss and Other Exhalations*, *Past Magic* and the novels *The Great Wheel*, *The Light Ages*, *The House of Storms*, and *The Summer Isles*. The latter two titles are both set in a historically twisted version of England, where the industrial revolution took place with the aid of magic. He is currently working on an eschatological novel of the very near future about God, death, and a technological afterlife. MacLeod's "The Summer Isles" won the 1999 World Fantasy Award and the Sidewise Award for Best Alternate Fiction Novella, while his story "The Chop Girl" received both the Asimov's Readers' Award and the World Fantasy Award in 2000. He has also been nominated for the BSFA, James Tiptree, Arthur C. Clarke, Nebula, and Hugo Awards.

49

[1963]

GLEN HIRSHBERG on

Who Fears the Devil?
by MANLY WADE WELLMAN

Taking its title from a game song once popular with Southern children, Who Fears the Devil? *was first published by Arkham House in an edition of 2,058 copies with a jacket illustration by the regional artist Lee Brown Coye. The eleven stories about John, a wandering balladeer with a silver-stringed guitar, and his supernatural encounters among the people of the Appalachian hill country, originally appeared in the* Magazine of Fantasy and Science Fiction *between 1951 and 1962. August Derleth convinced Manly Wade Wellman (1903–86) to revise the stories for the collection and give them a thread of continuity with brief, atmospheric, linking vignettes (four origin to the book). Wellman returned to the character of John in five novels,* The Old Gods Waken *(1979),* After Dark *(1980),* The Lost and the Lurking *(1981),* The Hanging Stones *(1982) and* The Voice of the Mountain *(1984).* John the Balladeer *(1988), edited by Karl Edward Wagner, collects all the stories from* Who Fears the Devil? *in their original form, along with six further tales about the character that appeared between 1979 and 1987. Hedge Capers starred as John in John Newland's low-budget 1972 film of* Who Fears the Devil? *(aka* The Legend of Hillbilly John*), which adapted Wellman's stories "O Ugly Bird!" and "The Desrick on Yandro" while adding an original story and an original voodoo tale.*

WHEN HE WAS growing up young and poorish in Ohio, my father spent his Saturdays pretending he was the Lone Ranger, Captain Marvel, Elvis, and Cleveland Symphony Orchestra conductor George

Szell. In my own suburban Detroit neighborhood, we had kids who played at being G.I. Joe, Luke Skywalker, Ted Nugent (I have no idea what happened to that kid, so don't ask me), and even Malcolm X. I didn't know anyone who actually wanted to be Frank or Joe Hardy, but there were guys around who'd read about them, and a few who traded Robert Arthur's quirkier, friendlier Three Investigators novels. My friends were the kids who aspired to be "stocky" (as in *fat*), brilliant, defiantly independent Jupiter Jones. But I wanted to be Silver John.

It's not an experience typically associated with our genre. To walk (with whatever else walks) the wood and stone of Hill House, sure. To sit in on one of Straub's Chowder Society storytelling sessions, sight the ghost-pirates from the deck of Hodgson's "Morzestus," hear—just once—the bells ringing the changes in Aickman's Holihaven, you bet. But few horror books worthy of the designation create life maps, or inspire that specifically personal kind of daydreaming that drives children (and not only children) to remake themselves. This one does, or at least it did for me.

It also gave me nightmares. For all its tree-dappled mountain sunlight and wisps of folk music ("Fare thee well, my charming girl/Fare thee well, I'm gone") and colloquial speech, *Who Fears the Devil?* is full of monsters. One of the little vignettes scattered through the book, "Find the Place Yourself," delivers some of the most memorable haunted-house imagery I have ever encountered: "In the trees over you will be wings flapping, but not bird wings. Roundabout you will sound voices, so soft and faint they're like voices you recollect from some long-ago time, saying things you wish you could leave forgotten . . . look back, and you'll see the path wiggle behind you like a snake after a lizard." There are giant blackbirds in these valleys, and behinders, and a train whose cars are coffins.

But the people are worse. Characters use every power they possess or inherit or steal from the landscape to terrorize their neighbors, settle ancient scores, horde treasure, lure one another's wives and daughters. Even the gentler stories have barbs buried in them, as in "Dumb Supper," in which a lonely—and, it turns out, dead—woman performs an ancient ritual to call her living lover home. Though Wellman dedicates the book to the backcountry people from whom he collected the inspiration for these stories, calling them "High on top of the mountain/Away from the sins of the world," the culture he portrays is every bit as sin-soaked and hunger-driven and unforgiving as the one in the teeming American cities below.

And yet, through it all strides Silver John, comfortably solitary but capable of love, using music like campfire light to chase back loneliness. I love his sense of justice, which is site-specific, derived partially from Native American traditions and partially from Judeo-Christian theology but mostly from intuition. Told that witches can't prevail against a pure heart, John says, "I can't claim that," and he can't. But he listens, and he learns, and he sorts for himself, and his judgments aren't global, and his fights are his own even when they benefit others.

All of this might make me admire the character. But it's Silver John's wanderlust that binds me to him and that keeps this collection tucked forever on my bedside night table. At the opening of *The London Adventure*, a book primarily about getting lost, Arthur Machen mentions "a certain tavern in the north-western parts of London which is so remote from the tracks of men and so securely hidden that few people have ever suspected its existence." The allure of such hidden people and places, for Machen—and for Silver John, and, I hope, for me—isn't the promise of joining some private club, or gaining privileged knowledge to keep for oneself. It is, instead, the promise of discovery, the opportunity to be let in on a secret to share, the confirmation that even the dreariest days are *lived* days, which automatically makes them magical. In "Nine Yards of Other Cloth," when John finally finds a woman he would stop wandering for, she tells him, "'You have what you need. There's music on the way you walk, John. I want to hear the music. I want to help the song.'" Then she comes wandering, too.

Corny, that. A drifter's pipe dream. But if there's a bittersweet quality to most great horror writing—and I believe there is—it derives from conceits like Silver John's commitment to musicmaking as a method of making peace with (as opposed to making sense of) the way people treat each other, to dreaming by day at least as much as by night. More, it comes from his conviction that if he can just make it over that next hilltop, to the porch of that house in the woods no one visits anymore, up that last, dark hollow, he'll catch a glimpse of a bird he can't name, a well he can't sound, a home he forgot he knew, the edge of the world, another story worth telling.

GLEN HIRSHBERG (b. 1966) grew up in Detroit and in San Diego, and currently lives in the Los Angeles area with his wife and children. A very early discovery of Ramsey Campbell's stories and the series of RKO Radio films produced by Val Lewton in the 1940s led to a lifelong love of the eerily alluring aesthetics and quietly crushing impact of much good horror fiction. Hirshberg has written film and music and literary criticism for alternative newspapers such as *Seattle Weekly* and *L.A. Weekly*, where he was a regular contributor for a number of years, in addition to his fiction, which blurs genre boundaries but draws heavily from the ghostly. He is the author of the serial-killer novel *The Snowman's Children* and the supernatural collection *The Two Sams*, both published by Carroll & Graf in the United States. His work has also appeared in various anthologies, including *The Mammoth Book of Best New Horror*, *The Year's Best Fantasy and Horror*, *The Mammoth Book of New Terror*, *Acquainted With the Night*, *Shadows and Silence*, *Dark Terrors 6*, *Trampoline: An Anthology*, and *The Dark: New Ghost Stories*. In 2004, both his story "Dancing Men" and *The Two Sams* garnered him International Horror Guild Awards. The collection was also selected by *Publishers Weekly* as one of the Best Books of 2003. Hirshberg's latest novel is a ghost/love/lighthouse story called *Sisters of Baikal*.

50 [1965]

SIMON CLARK on

A Wrinkle in the Skin
by JOHN CHRISTOPHER

A series of earthquakes and volcanic eruptions in the southern hemisphere prompt the press to call it a "Quaking Spring." On Guernsey, an affluent island that is a microcosm of all that is cozily English, an earthquake reduces everything to rubble, killing almost everyone. Tomato grower Matthew Cotter wanders through the desolation, eventually setting out for the mainland in search of his daughter. However, he finds that the harmony of post-war New Elizabethan England has yielded to the dissonance of barbarism. John Christopher (b. 1922) authored many disaster novels for adults and children. His 1956 novel The Death of Grass *was filmed by Cornel Wilde as* No Blade of Grass *(1970). The author's most famous work,* The Tripods *trilogy, with its* Catcher in the Rye *aesthetic of liminal angst, became an engaging family serial from BBC-TV in 1984–85. Christopher's work may well have flavored Terry Nation's compelling BBC drama series* Survivors *(1975–77) as well as influenced a tranche of contemporary apocalyptic tales such as* The Day After Tomorrow *(2004).*

JOHN CHRISTOPHER'S NOVELS are the news stories of today. *The Death of Grass* is pure eco-horror; grass and cereal crops die. The world starves. *The World in Winter* expounds on a new ice age. The Thames River freezes solid; civilization collapses. Even in his children's novels such as *Empty World,* its young hero is confronted with a corpse-strewn England after a plague.

As a John Wyndham fan, I'd heard that Christopher wrote disaster yarns in the same vein. Many critics, however, were dismissive of the author, suggesting he merely recycled Wyndham for the not very discerning reader. Though I resisted for a while, naïvely believing that to read Christopher would be disloyal to Wyndham, my eye was snagged by the dramatic covers of Christopher's Sphere paperbacks. One showed the Houses of Parliament surrounded by glaciers. Then I found *A Wrinkle in the Skin*. Here, New York is being torn by seismic convulsions, the sky's on fire, cars are hurled into the air. In a rush of blood I bought the book and hurried home to enjoy my guilty pleasure. I soon learned that Christopher isn't derivative of Wyndham, despite scenarios of global destruction. Wyndham, dubbed the master of the "cozy catastrophe," depicts his heroes bearing up in the face of rampaging Triffids and GM kids. Stiff upper lips never become flaccid. That's no criticism of Wyndham's work. I love it. I really do. It was a product of its age. Christopher, however, is the tightrope between the tightly laced fiction of the 1950s and the raunchy storytelling of the '60s, when you read your gaudy paperback as the Who hollered teenage rebellion from the radio.

Christopher can be summed up in one word: subtraction. His characters arrive on page one as successful, contented men with breeding and education. In fact, very much your typical Wyndham hero. However, when disaster strikes, Christopher's men lose everything—home, money, possessions, wives, and even their home turf. Invariably the hero is forced to undergo a journey. And you've seen nothing yet. This is a real Nekyia—a Jungian night-sea journey of both body and soul. The process of subtraction is remorseless. Material possessions are only the start. The hero loses pride, his peace of mind, his self-image. Nothing is sacred. Ultimately they're robbed of what the imperial Englishmen treasured most; the thing they believed they'd never abandon. They lose that stiff upper lip. This was real horror for the 1950s reader, the moment when the gallant hero breaks down and weeps, because everything they value has gone and they are helpless as a baby.

A Wrinkle in the Skin is still my favorite Christopher novel. Here his iron rule of subtraction is absolute. It begins with Mathew Cotter losing his home when a ferocious earthquake strikes Guernsey. Soon he discovers that every building on the island is shattered, with its population lying dead in the ruins. The birds have vanished. He has no shelter, no human company. Subtraction, subtraction. He reaches the coast and looks out across the beach: "It was like a glimpse of another planet, a strange and savage barren world . . . the blue sweep of wave was gone." Subtraction! Even the sea has vanished.

Eventually Cotter joins fellow survivors. They trek across the ocean floor that has been raised by the quake. It's become a land of evil enchantment, a desert-like place littered with ships and ancient wrecks shrouded in weeds. In dwindling pools, whales, porpoises, and fish wallow. Once the survivors reach the mainland, they encounter bands of Englishmen reduced to savagery. Civilization is subtracted from the world. It's kill or be killed. Yet Cotter still treasures hope that he will somehow find his grown-up daughter on the mainland. With everything else of value gone from his life, he desperately hangs on to the illusion that he'll be reunited with her despite the fact that England's cities are dust.

What proves to me that Christopher is no rehasher of Wyndham is when Cotter thinks he's saved a group of women from being raped. This is one of the real shock scenes in the book. Just as Cotter is being almost smug about his chivalrous intervention, one of the group tells him that she was raped along with the others. My blood ran cold as I read this chapter, especially when she reveals it's happened several times before. For women in that shattered world, rape is a regular occurrence. They accept that that's the way it's going to be. It's impossible not to be deeply affected by their fatalism.

Cotter's ego is gone. He sheds his illusion that he can find his daughter alive. Subtraction, subtraction. Other than the loss of Cotter's life, there's nothing left to subtract. And only now, when he hits rock bottom, can he begin to rebuild one Matthew Cotter.

SIMON CLARK (b. 1958) was born in Wakefield, England, and currently lives in Doncaster with his wife and children. He attended Whitwood Technical College, where he learned what he considers one of his most useful skills, touch typing. He began writing for small-press magazines before his first novel, *Nailed by the Heart,* made it through the slush pile in 1994. With the advance safely banked, he became a full-time writer. His subsequent novels include *Blood Crazy, Darker, King Blood, Vampyrrhic, The Fall, Judas Tree, Stranger, Vampyrrhic Rites, Darkness Demands, In This Skin,* and *The Night of the Triffids,* which continues the story of John Wyndham's classic dystopian novel *The Day of the Triffids.* His revival of the ambulatory Triffid plants won the British Fantasy Society's August Derleth Award for Best Novel in 2002. His short stories have been collected in *Blood and Grit* and *Salt Snake,* and since making his first professional sale to local radio, Clark has also created and co-presented the series *Winter Chills* for BBC regional television. His latest book is another short-story collection, *Hotel Midnight.*

51 [1967]

NANCY HOLDER on

Rosemary's Baby
by IRA LEVIN

One of the first horror novels to climb the best-seller lists, Rosemary's Baby *confirmed the status of Ira Levin (b. 1929) as a major popular author; he virtually reprised the novel's structure in* The Stepford Wives *(1972), in which another wife learns that paranoid fantasies about her husband's involvement in a conspiracy against her are well founded, and delivered a tardy, disappointing sequel in* Son of Rosemary *(1997). The book was filmed in 1968 by writer-director Roman Polanski, with Mia Farrow as Rosemary Woodhouse; John Cassavetes as her husband, Guy; and an Oscar-winning Ruth Gordon as the witch next door. Among many films to lift outright Levin's premise are* The Omen *(1976) and* Blessed *(2004). Sam O'Steen, Polanski's editor, directed a television movie sequel,* Look What's Happened to Rosemary's Baby *(1976), with Patty Duke Astin as Rosemary, George Maharis as Guy, Stephen McHattie as teenage Antichrist Adrian, and Gordon reprising her role. Ray Bradbury's essay/story "A New Ending to Rosemary's Baby," written in response to the film, somewhat presumptuously suggests an alternative outcome to Levin's story.*

IN HIS INTRODUCTION to the twenty-fifth-anniversary edition of *Rosemary's Baby* (published in 1990 by the Armchair Detective Library), Ira Levin says:

> It's one thing to refer to the book in my bio as being generally credited or blamed for having sparked the current revival of occultism, and another to recognize, as I have in the past few years, that the blame may be real and weighty. It was *Rosemary's Baby*—both the novel and Roman Polanski's faithful film of it—that led us to exorcists, omens, and all manner of supernatural nonsense, which in turn led us to a time when people, presumably schooled, detect backward demonic messages in rock music, and Satan's symbol on bars of soap.

Why was *Rosemary's Baby* so influential?

Certainly a lot of the book's commercial success was the result of timing. Levin was already on the literary radar after his first novel, *A Kiss Before Dying*. And in the above-mentioned introduction, Levin reminds us that his editor was fond of saying that *Rosemary's Baby* wasn't about witchcraft, it was about motherhood. The novel originally came out in 1967, during the hippie era. Middle-class parents were terrified by the behavior of their children, who were seemingly possessed: running away and joining communes, taking drugs, and sleeping with each other. Then the nightmare came true: some of them joined a murderous cult led by Charles Manson, butchering, among others, a nine-months-pregnant actress named Sharon Tate. She was the wife of director-actor Roman Polanski.

In 1968, one year after publication (and one year before the murder of his wife), Roman Polanski directed the film version of *Rosemary's Baby*. The hit film continued the momentum of the novel's success. After all, Stephen King wrote *Carrie* in 1974; the film version came out in 1976, and King's career was launched. A similar thing happened to Peter Straub. His first "Gothic" novel, *Julia* (filmed as *Full Circle*, aka *The Haunting of Julia* with Mia Farrow, who starred in *Rosemary's Baby*), paved the way for *Ghost Story* and his stellar literary carrier.

But *Rosemary's Baby* was there before King and Straub. Or Anne Rice, for that matter. It is the foundation stone for the horror boom that was to follow.

Again: why?

A story, about an American teenager (that would be me) who had just moved to Germany to become a ballet dancer. Ironically (in the context of this essay), Polanski's *Dance of the Vampires/The Fearless Vampire Killers* (*Tanz der Vampire*) was in the German movie theaters, and I was so shy and inarticulate that it took me two days to purchase a ticket and go inside.

The film started; it was in German with no subtitles, and although it was very broad and slapstick and I could follow the action, I was only watching it. I wasn't "in" the movie because I couldn't suspend my disbelief. Because it wasn't "speaking my language," it seemed too alien to me to really get into it.

Then at one point in the film, the professor character whispered in the dark to his assistant (Polanski): "Wo . . . wo bist du?" ("Where are you?"). And Polanski whispered back, "H-hier."

These were the first two lines of the movie that I actually understood. I burst out laughing so hard that everyone started staring at me. It was not a particularly funny moment in the film. I was reacting purely out of a shock of recognition.

I think tremendous numbers of readers and moviegoers connected with *Rosemary's Baby* in a similar way. Yes, because of the timing, and the *Weltgeist*, and because Levin's details—a concurrent papal visit to New York, a newspaper strike—lent such an air of verisimilitude that, it's been claimed, Polanski called him up during filming and asked him which issue of the *New Yorker* Rosemary's husband, Guy, is reading in a particular scene.

There's also Levin's writing itself. His straightforward narrative style—like that of King and, to a lesser degree, Straub, who is more elegant—provided readers a shock of recognition, a sense of being truly present. As echoed by Rosemary in the dream sequence when Satan impregnates her: "This is no dream! This is really happening!"

Ironically, I first read *Rosemary's Baby* after *Carrie* had come out, because I wanted to see what all the fuss had been, now that I was hooked on this horror stuff.

I read it in German. And it really creeped me out.

NANCY HOLDER (b. 1953) was born in Palo Alto, California, and has lived in Japan, Germany, South Carolina, Hawaii, and back to California. She studied ballet for many years, but her career was cut short by a number of injuries and the realization that the best she could hope for was a position in innumerable productions of *Swan Lake* as the 1,217th swan on the left. Holder was encouraged at a young age to become a writer, and in 1981 she sold her first novel, a young adult romance retitled (to her chagrin) *Teach Me to Love*. She sold five more romance novels before Charles L. Grant bought her first horror short story, "Blood Gothic," for *Shadows 8*. Since then she has sold more than two hundred short stories and essays and approximately sixty-five more novels. The latter include *Dead in the Water, Making Love* and *Witch-Light* (both with Melanie Tem), *Pretty Little Devils, Cannibal Dwight's Special Purpose, Spirited,* and *The Wicked Saga* (*Witch, Curse, Legacy,* and *Spellbound*). She has written various novelizations for *Sabrina the Teenage Witch*, *Highlander*, *Smallville*, *Angel*, and more novels, novellas, short stories, essays, and show guides about *Buffy the Vampire Slayer* than any other writer in the galaxy. She also recently co-edited the anthology *Outsiders: Stories on the Edge of the Fantastical* with Nancy Kilpatrick. Holder has received four Bram Stoker Awards from the Horror Writers Association, and her work has appeared on recommended lists from the American Library Association, the American Reading Association, and the New York Public Library. She teaches writing at the University of California at San Diego through their Extension Department, and also at the Maui Writers Retreat.

52 [1967]

ELLEN DATLOW on

The Playboy Book of Horror and the Supernatural
Edited by THE EDITORS OF PLAYBOY

Though the introduction is vaguely signed by "the editors of Playboy," *who also get listed on the title page, this was in fact put together by novelist and screenwriter Ray Russell (1924–99), who held various positions on Hugh Hefner's magazine from 1954 and deserves credit for ensuring that the magazine genuinely was bought for the quality of its writing as well as the attractions of its centerfold "Playmates." Russell's (contractually enforced?) modesty did not keep him from including two of his own (excellent) stories, "Sardonicus" (filmed by William Castle* as Mr. Sardonicus *in 1961) and "Comet Wine" (which concludes the book). Several other selections have been dramatized—David Ely's "The Academy" on* Night Gallery *(1971), Richard Matheson's "No Such Thing as a Vampire" on the BBC's* Late Night Horror *(1968) and in the made-for-television movie* Dead of Night *(1977). Taking stories not from traditional genre markets but the trend-setting (and high-paying) men's magazine, Russell showcased mostly American authors who began their careers in pulps but moved up in the 1950s and '60s to the "slicks." These "gray flannel suit" horror writers remain anthology mainstays, and are as liable to be adapted for TV or film as they were in the days of* Alfred Hitchcock Presents, The Twilight Zone, *and* Thriller. *Among authors represented are Charles Willeford, John Collier, Charles Beaumont, Henry Slesar, Robert Bloch, William F. Nolan, Mack Reynolds, John Christopher, John Tomerlin, Jack Finney, Ken W. Purdy, Charles Schafhauser, John Reese, Hugh G. Foster, Calvin Tomkins, and Ray Bradbury.* Playboy's *most famous horror story—George Langelaan's "The Fly" (1957)—was left out because Russell had just used it in* The Playboy Book of Science Fiction and Fantasy *(1966). The series also included* The Playboy Book of Crime and Suspense *(1966) and* Playboy's Stories of the Sinister & Strange *(1969).*

*P*LAYBOY WAS LAUNCHED by Hugh Hefner in December 1953, and from the very beginning it showcased great genre writing. The Playboy *Book of Horror and the Supernatural,* reprinting stories from the first four years of the magazine's existence, was published as a hardcover by Playboy Press in 1967 and then reprinted the following year as a mass-market paperback.

That paperback, dog-eared and moldy, is still a cherished possession. I first read it when I was about eighteen. I was already a voracious reader throughout my childhood and as a teenager—consuming historical novels, mysteries, science fiction, fantasy, and horror. And short stories. I read *Bulfinch's Mythology,* the brothers Grimm, Hans Christian Andersen, Oscar Wilde, and the Andrew Lang colored fairy books; stories by Guy de Maupassant, O. Henry, Edgar Allan Poe, Nathaniel Hawthorne, and collections and anthologies by Harlan

Ellison and Ray Bradbury. Nothing could intrude—except my mother yelling for me to come and eat, dinner was getting cold.

Although university put a crimp in my reading schedule, I made up for it during semester breaks and summer holidays. It was during this period that *The* Playboy *Book of Horror and the Supernatural* introduced me to wonderfully disturbing stories by writers whose names I was already somewhat familiar with: Ray Bradbury for his luminous descriptions of a Mars and his often bittersweet, sometimes dark tales of small-town U.S.A. Gahan Wilson for his ghoulish, hilarious cartoons. Fredric Brown for his science fiction short shorts. I was also reading Richard Matheson's collections *Shock!*, *Shock II*, and *ShockWaves*. And although I didn't know it at the time, I was watching Matheson's and Charles Beaumont's work regularly on *The Twilight Zone*.

Perusing the table of contents of *The Playboy Book of Horror and the Supernatual* recently—more than thirty years after I first devoured it—I still recalled some of the odder titles: "Burnt Toast," "Heavy Set," "Nasty," "Sardonicus," "Weird Show," "Black Country," and "The Sea Was Wet as Wet Can Be." Did I remember the actual stories at first glance? Not really, but as soon as I started rereading them it was like encountering old friends. I realized that these literate, well-told terror tales embedded themselves into my conscious, my subconscious, and even my temperament. This is one of the books that created a horror editor.

As I re-read the book, I discovered that the stories I remembered best were those with titles that were familiar to me. They were still deliciously creepy and unsettling, and retained their bite. But *all* the stories are good, and overall the book provides a glimpse at the sheer variety of what encompasses what we call "horror fiction." The psychological horror story about insanity, the terror tale, the *conte cruel*, the monster story, deal with the Devil—these stories represent some of the best of their type and, after all the vitriol spewed over the past twenty years about "quiet horror vs. splatter horror," this book clearly focuses on what the horror field *should* be concerned with: the *story*.

The individual stories capture snapshots of specific places and times—New York City, Hollywood, Paris, small-town America in the 1950s. The characters are con men, innocents, schlubs, femmes fatales, musicians, dreamers, the guilt-ridden, and the selfish.

"Heavy Set," a story about a strange young man and his mother, represents Ray Bradbury at his sinister, subtle best, reminding contemporary readers that throughout his long career the author has maintained a chilling, cutting edge to his fiction.

A bit of harmless Americana—the "weird" or spook show, during which children and teenagers watched grade-B horror movies while being pelted by "worms" (macaroni) or terrorized by a man in a gorilla costume—is used in "Weird Show," Herbert Gold's only horror story of the thirty-six he wrote for *Playboy*.

"Black Country" by Charles Beaumont is one of the most amazing stories about playing great jazz music ever written. I wasn't a jazz aficionado at eighteen, so although I enjoyed the story when I first read it, I appreciate it more today when I can "hear" the music played in the story.

"The Sea Was Wet as Wet Can Be" by Gahan Wilson has always been one of my favorites because it transforms Lewis Carroll's "The Walrus and the Carpenter" into as macabre a story as I've ever read.

The above stories are only a hint of the treasures in *The Playboy Book of Horror and the Supernatural.* For me, one of the most interesting things about the anthology (aside from the sheer overall quality) is that all these stories were originally published in a slick, high-paying, *non*-horror or non-science fiction magazine. Many of the writers in the anthology also wrote for genre titles: the *Magazine of Fantasy and Science Fiction, If, Orbit, Imagination, Ed McBain's Mystery Magazine,* etc. But it seems that the boundaries between genre and nongenre were as fluid then as they sometimes are today.

Now, *that* is an important tradition we should all continue to embrace and nurture.

ELLEN DATLOW (b. 1949) was born and lives in New York City. She earned a B.A. in English literature before traveling around Europe for a year. Having spent the latter half of the 1970s attempting to work in the book publishing industry, she was eventually hired as associate fiction editor at *Omni* magazine in 1980. When Robert Sheckley left as fiction editor, Datlow was promoted to his job. After editing twelve *Omni* anthologies for various publishers, in 1989 she became the editor of a string of acclaimed horror and science fiction anthologies, including *Blood is Not Enough, Alien Sex, A Whisper of Blood, Little Deaths, Off Limits: Tales of Alien Sex, Twists of the Tale: Stories of Cat Horror, Lethal Kisses: Revenge and Vengeance, Vanishing Acts,* and *The Dark: New Ghost Stories.* With Terri Windling she has co-edited the successful series of fairy-tale anthologies *Snow White Blood Red, Black Thorn White Rose, Ruby Slippers Golden Tears, Black Swan White Raven, Sirens and Other Daemon Lovers, Silver Birch Blood Moon, Black Heart Ivory Bones, A Wolf at the Door and Other Retold Fairy Tales, The Green Man: Tales from the Mythic Forest, Swan Sister: Fairy Tales Retold, The Faery Reel,* and *The Coyote Road: Trickster Tales.* For sixteen years, since 1988, Datlow and Windling co-edited the multiple award-winning *The Year's Best Fantasy and Horror* series from St. Martin's Press, with Datlow handling the "horror" material. From the seventeenth volume onward, Windling's role has been taken by Kelly Link and Gavin Grant. A winner of seven World Fantasy Awards, the Bram Stoker Award, the International Horror Guild Award, and the 2002 Hugo Award, Datlow is currently editor of *Sci Fiction,* the fiction area of SciFi.Com, the SciFi Channel's Web site, and a consulting editor at Tor Books.

53 [1968]

TERRY LAMSLEY on

Pages from Cold Point
by PAUL BOWLES

Though most of the nine stories in this collection were written in the 1950s and published in America at that time, the title story and "The Delicate Prey," perhaps due to the subject matter, did not become available in the United Kingdom until 1968, when the book was published by Peter Owen. After World War II, author and composer Bowles (1910–99) moved to North Africa, where many of his stories are set, remaining a voluntary exile there until the end of his life. Sometimes associated with the "beat" writers with whom he shared friendship and a keen interest in literature and smoking kif, his writing is nothing like theirs, being detached, elegant, lucid, and deeply pessimistic. The term "African Gothic" has been applied. Bowles said that his mother read Edgar Allan Poe to him when he was seven or eight—an experience that gave him many sleepless nights and, he was sure, influenced his own fiction thirty years later. Other writers he read in his early years were Arthur Machen, M. P. Shiel, Lautreamont, Conrad, and Kafka; it is possible to detect echoes of the last two in his mature work. Bowles claimed that his grandmother told him that his father, jealous of the attention the baby Paul was getting from his mother, had tried to kill him by leaving him naked in a basket by an open window in the depth of winter. With such a start in life, it is no wonder Bowles became the creator of a dark, cruel, and godless world. Bowles's best-known fiction is his first novel, The Sheltering Sky *(1949)*; he appears enigmatically as himself in the 1990 film. Among other manifestations in popular culture, he inspired the character played by Ian Holm in David Cronenberg's film of William Burroughs' Naked

Lunch *(1991) and lent his surname to Christopher Isherwood for the character of "Sally Bowles," heroine of his Berlin stories (and later the musical* Cabaret*).*

The story that starts this collection, "Pages from Cold Point," caused some controversy when it first appeared, and may seem even more disturbing to the politically correct nowadays, as it describes the seduction of a father by his young son. Even the supposedly unshockable Tennessee Williams took exception to it, and other writers advised Bowles to put it to one side for fear that people would think he was a monster. Norman Mailer, however, described it as "one of the best stories ever written by anyone." Sure enough, it's a nasty little tale, written in the author's most detached and amoral style, and its ending somehow leaves one amused and shuddering at the same time.

Next comes "The Time of Friendship," an account of the grotesque relationship between an elderly female Christian teacher and a young Muslim boy she decides to befriend, that explores the huge and, for her, agonizing gaps between her beliefs and his. Very relevant today, this is one of Bowles's gentler efforts, though it is full of pain and closes on a note of despair. "The Hyena" is a savage and elliptical little fable that reads like a folk tale but is almost certainly the author's invention. Then comes "He of the Assembly" in which a man named Ben Tajah sees "a letter lying on the pavement. He picked it up and found that his name was written on the envelope." When he opens it he finds "a paper which reads: The sky trembles and the earth is afraid, and the two eyes are not brothers." This discovery leads him to believe "that Satan was nearby." Later he fails to find the letter in his pocket and wonders if he ever really found it. Then meets He of the Assembly, a very stoned boy who seems to know something about the letter. What follows is a nightmare of superstitious dread and *kif*-induced disorientation that convincingly creates a mood of entrapment and paranoia that will be uneasily familiar to anyone who has ever done much too much dope.

"The Garden" is a tight little jewel of a story of jealousy, poison, and the fear and destruction of innocence. Next comes "The Story of Lahcen and Idir," a tale of two aimless and predatory young men, one addicted to brandy, the other to *kif,* who spend their days pursuing and abusing women. At one point, as Idir sits smoking in his room, he notices a tiny bird walking slowly along the floor next to him. He captures it and slips a ring Lahcen has given him around its neck. Then, when he tries to take the ring off, he finds he can't pull it back over the bird's head. The bird struggles and escapes. When Lahcen returns drunk and is told about the incident he says angrily, "So he stole my ring"—an example of the sublime unreasonableness of many of Bowles's characters that creates a particular kind of tension and often leads to cold, absurd violence.

The following story, "The Delicate Prey," my main reason for choosing to recommend this particular collection, is Bowles at his gruesome and relentless best. The events, which I see no point in describing, are related as if from a very great distance, but with absolute clarity, and the reader is led into somewhere dreadful and left there. The conclusion of the story, a paragraph of three short sentences, still sends my head spinning. Two stories, "A Friend of the World" and "The Wind at Beni Midar," which both deal with false magic and spiteful acts of revenge and casual cruelty, bring the collection to a bleak, downbeat end.

I hope the above book will lead the reader into a wider consideration of Bowles's four novels and many short stories collected in *Call at Corazon, A Thousand Days for Mokhtar,* and *Midnight Mass.* He never wrote specifically for the horror genre, but many of his tales are much more strange and disturbing than those by some writers who do. One such, "Kitty," about a girl who wants to turn into a cat, was written for a children's book and rejected by the publisher as being far too gruesome. I have never come across any of his stories in a horror anthology.

By all accounts a fastidious, totally unpretentious, polite, and compassionate man, Bowles was nevertheless essentially solitary and chose to live in somewhat sordid and uncomfortable circumstances. Reluctant to discuss his own or anyone else's sexual activities and private life, his autobiography, *Without Stopping*, reads like an exercise in devious self-concealment. He tells us where he went, but not much of interest about what he did when he got there. William Burroughs suggested it should have been called *Without Telling.*

I'll finish with a few enigmatic words from Bowles himself, taken from a 1988 film called *Paul Bowles: The Complete Outsider*. When asked, "What is your idea of a good time?" his reply was, "Forgetting myself, laughing. It requires the presence of other people to forget oneself. Man is gregarious. I don't want to be gregarious. I don't even want to be human. But what can I do? I'm in the land of the living!"

TERRY LAMSLEY (b. 1941) was born in the south of England, but lived in the north for most of his life. He eventually moved a few years ago to Amsterdam. His first collection of supernatural stories, *Under the Crust*, was published in a small paperback edition in 1993. Originally intended to appeal only to the tourist market in Lamsley's hometown of Buxton in Derbyshire (the volume's six tales are all set in or around the area), its reputation quickly grew, helped when stories from the book were included in two of the annual "Year's Best" horror anthologies. The book was subsequently nominated for three World Fantasy Awards, eventually winning for Best Novella. Ramsey Campbell accepted it on the author's behalf, and Lamsley's reputation as a writer of supernatural fiction began to grow. In 1997 Canada's Ash-Tree Press reprinted *Under the Crust* as a handsome hardcover, limited to just five hundred copies and now as sought after as the long-out-of-print first edition. A year earlier, Ash-Tree had issued a second, equally remarkable collection of Lamsley's short stories, *Conference With the Dead: Tales of Supernatural Terror,* which has recently been reissued by Night Shade Books, and it was followed in 2000 by a third collection, *Dark Matters.* The author's short stories have been published in a wide variety of magazines and anthologies, including *Cemetery Dance, Dark Terrors, Lethal Kisses, The Mammoth Book of Dracula, Midnight Never Comes, Subterranean Gallery, White of the Moon: New Tales of Madness and Dread, Taps and Sighs, Meddling With Ghosts: Stories in the Tradition of M. R. James, By Moonlight Only, The Mammoth Book of New Terror, Taverns of the Dead,* and *Fourbodings.*

54 [1968]

JOHN FARRIS on

Outer Dark
by CORMAC McCARTHY

Though born in Rhode Island, Cormac McCarthy (b. 1933) was brought up in Knoxville, Tennessee, and writes literary fiction rooted in the American West—which takes on an infernal, horrific feel in his Blood Meridian, or the Evening Redness in the West *(1985).* Outer Dark, *his second novel, is set in Appalachia, perhaps around 1900, and opens with the birth of a baby born of an incestuous union between brother and sister. The father (Holme) abandons the child and tells the mother (Culla) it has died, whereupon she sets out in search of the lost infant, and both siblings undergo dangerous, Gothic-inflected journeys in a degraded landscape, encountering grotesque characters and appalling situations. Among McCarthy's other novels are* Child of God *(1973), a study of an alienated necrophiliac, and the slightly mellower Tex-Mex Western* All the Pretty Horses *(1992).*

Most of Cormac McCarthy's literary life has been spent as an isolato: for the most part he appears not to like talking about himself or his work. In the one photo of McCarthy I recall seeing, reprinted in my Vintage edition of *Outer Dark,* he looks annoyed, in that bred-in-the-bone black Irish manner, that anyone should be trying to steal his soul with an Instamatic. His arms are folded in an attitude of stern passivity. Could he have been having a clairvoyant moment, "seeing" across decades to his inclusion in a compendium that offers up what I consider to be his greatest work as a "horror novel"?

Sorry, Cormac. Labels are onerous, but "horror novel" in no way compromises your achievement. I first read *Outer Dark* almost forty years ago and recently reread it to see what I'd forgotten, but I had forgotten very little: the book has been burning in my creative unconscious for quite a long time.

The title itself nails the stark, strange, apocalyptic landscape in which the novel exists, as well as its cast of wandering souls: the abandoned, the despised, the hopeless, and the damned—"from nowheres," McCarthy writes, "to nowhere bound." Symbolized in the birth of a child conceived by siblings, on the dark side of Eden, left to die in a wood by Culla Holme, the father, taken up by a tinker, and eventually destroyed, in the novel's biblically searing denouement, its throat cut and the frail body burned so that only "a little calcimined rib cage" remains when its mother stumbles into that charnel, burned-out place, in which, "half-wild and haggard," she falls asleep, her circular fate concluded.

McCarthy's formidable talent has been celebrated elsewhere, abundantly. I might add that what elevates talent to brilliance or perhaps genius in the creation of fiction is (and here I'd like to borrow an observation of Raymond Chandler's) "a perfection of control over the movement of a story similar to the control a great pitcher has over the ball."

From the opening paragraph of *Outer Dark* in which Culla Holme awakens from a dream that is nothing short of an apocalypse of the soul to Culla's metaphoric encounter with the mendicant blind man and, finally, his arrival at "a spectral waste ... A faintly smoking garden of the dead that tended away to the Earth's curve," McCarthy is in command of his story. On the road that leads to wasteland Culla has a sole moment of introspection, a vague apprehension of the evils his corruption of virginal innocence has wrought: "Someone should tell a blind man before setting him out that way."

What frightens in *Outer Dark*—slowly, offhandedly at times, but inexorably—is McCarthy's tight control; for all of his gifts, seldom needing to go to his fastball. Once we are acquainted with the phantasmal, murderous trip crossing and recrossing the landscape, all McCarthy need write of them is, "The men when they came might have risen from the ground. The tinker could not account for them. They gathered about the fire and looked down at him. One had a rifle and was smiling" to evoke the desired reaction: creeping fear.

Sorry again, Cormac. You did your work well.

You wrote a hell of a horror story.

JOHN FARRIS (b. 1936) was born in Jefferson City, Missouri. He began writing at age fifteen and has persevered through his adult years, which have, inevitably, become numerous. He began his writing career in the late 1950s with a series of young adult books published under the pseudonym "Steve Brackeen." Described by Stephen King as "America's premier novelist of terror," Farris is best known as the author of the 1976 novel *The Fury* (filmed by Brian De Palma in 1978, starring Kirk Douglas and Amy Irving). He followed it with the belated sequels *The Fury and the Terror, The Fury and the Power,* and *Avenging Fury.* His more than thirty books also include *When Michael Calls* (filmed as a television movie in 1971), *All Heads Turn When the Hunt Goes By* (which David J. Schow wrote on in *Horror: 100 Best Books*), *Catacombs, Son of the Endless Night, Wildwood, Nightfall, Fiends, Soon She Will Be Gone,* and *Phantom Nights.* The author of twenty screenplays (including *Dear, Dead Delilah,* 1972, which he also directed), poetry, and a book-length collection of aphorisms, his horror short stories have been collected in *Scare Tactics* and *Elvisland.* A recipient of the Horror Writers Association Grand Master Award, he never plots anything in advance—because if he isn't interested in finding out what happens next, nobody else will care either.

55 [1971]

STEPHEN BAXTER on

The Book of Skulls
by ROBERT SILVERBERG

Four American college boys seek out a secretive desert sect with an extraordinary promise—immortality, but for only two of them: "Eternal life... An existential gamble. Two to live forever, two to die." The pressure of this dreadful bargain tears the boys apart. Robert Silverberg (b. 1935), who kicks off this present volume with his essay on The Revenger's Tragedy, *is among the most prolific writers of his generation;* The Book of Skulls *is one of* twelve *books that appeared under his byline in 1971. In addition to the novels* The World Inside, A Time of Changes, *and* Son of Man *and the non-fiction* Before the Sphinx, Clocks for the Ages: How Scientists Date the Past, To the Western Shore: Growth of the United States 1776–1853, *and (with Arthur C. Clarke)* Into Space, *Silverberg edited the anthologies* Four Futures, The Science Fiction Bestiary, To the Stars, *and* New Dimensions *that year. Published in 1971 by Scribner in the United States and in 1978 by Gollancz in the United Kingdom,* The Book of Skulls *has tended to be packaged in science fiction lists, stressing the author's science fiction credentials, but the apt strapline of the 1981 Coronet paperback is "a thriller fantasy."*

THE BOOK OF SKULLS was first published in 1971. Robert Silverberg was thirty-six. Having established himself as a master of genre science fiction—his first science fiction novel was published in 1955—he was in the middle of a remarkable eight-year period of creative experimentation.

The material, the idea, and the artistry were the drivers, not genre forms. Silverberg told me of *Skulls*, "I never consciously thought of the book as being a horror novel, or SF, or fantasy. I had a story to tell, inspired by a reproduction I saw of a medieval manuscript page bearing a row of skulls (it was used on the U.S. hardcover edition), and the category it might fall into was not anything I spent time considering. . . . I also had set a technical challenge for myself—to tell the story through four different first-person narrators."

Those narrators are carefully constructed. All American, all aged roughly twenty, the four boys are polarized types ethnically, sexually, intellectually. But Silverberg is seeking a more enduring fable. A hint of his design, perhaps, is contained in a reference to "an ethnographical film about some African bushmen out hunting a giraffe [, which] drew a structural metaphor of society." Similarly, here is a metaphor of American society in four college kids out pursuing a dream (or a nightmare). So you have a shaman in Eli the bookish New York Jew, a headman in Timothy the spoiled preppy rich kid from Chicago, a clown in Ned the overtly homosexual Boston Irish Catholic, and a beautiful one in Oliver the repressed Kansas farm boy.

To approach their goal, the boys must first endure a long drive into the heart of a desert that seems alien to them all. The strangeness of their quest is contrasted with the mundane surfaces of their lives: it's all a game—but what if it isn't? And the stress has been mounting since even before they left Manhattan.

When they do find their monastery, populated by ageless, leathery-skinned "fraters," Silverberg makes the immortality project utterly convincing. Science fiction writers are practiced in making the impossible seem plausible, so there are references to the familiar, allusions, compelling details, and irresistible hints of roots going back all the way to the Ice Age: "You have come to us out of Altamira, out of Lascaux, out of doomed Atlantis itself." It's all smoke and mirrors, of course; you don't really see anything, but you're left feeling that you do.

But all the while the approaching crux of the boys' quest ratchets up the psychological pressure: "This frightens me. I'm likely to find out something about myself I don't want to know." The trick of four first-person narrators works beautifully. The characters' outer layers and inner levels are built up in intense detail; on one level this is a parable of how little we know each other, how alone we humans are. And through long, fluent, first-person passages you are locked firmly into the heads of the four narrators and drawn into their conflicts inner and outer, until the final disintegration overwhelms.

On still another level the book captures its moment in time. The late 1960s was an age of intense psychological (some of it drug-fueled) experimentation, of self-awareness, of a restless search for something new and spiritual. Perhaps Silverberg can be criticized that his four twenty-year-olds are a little too knowing, of themselves and their position in time; and perhaps in some ways the book has dated. Nevertheless, Silverberg's characters are archetypes of an age that survives in the imagination, so enduring has 1960s culture proven to be, demonized or eulogized in turn.

When I first read this book a few years ago I was deeply impressed with its technical quality, but it was the sheer intensity of the prose that really hooked me. I read it in a sitting, and it reads as though it were written that way. Silverberg himself may not have defined this as a horror novel, but at its deepest core the book is an extended meditation on the ultimate horror, the inevitability of personal death in an immense and ancient universe. And it is a story of personal disintegration brought about purely through psychological pressure, with nary a special effect in sight, it foreshadows *The Blair Witch Project*, perhaps.

The Book of Skulls is a technical *tour de force*, deeply unsettling, astounding. Read it in a sitting, as I did; you'll remember it for a lifetime.

STEPHEN BAXTER (b. 1957) was born in Liverpool. He has degrees in mathematics, from Cambridge University; in engineering, from Southampton University; and in business administration, from Henley Management College. He worked as a teacher of math and physics, and for several years in information technology. He is also a chartered engineer and fellow of the British Interplanetary Society. Baxter applied to become a cosmonaut in 1991—aiming for the guest slot on *Mir* eventually taken by Helen Sharman—but fell at an early hurdle. Best known primarily as a "hard" science fiction author, like Robert Silverberg he has been known to dabble in horror from time to time. His first professionally published short story appeared in 1987, and he has been a full-time writer since 1995. His acclaimed SF novels include *Anti-Ice, The Time Ships, Evolution,* and the "Destiny's Children," "Manifold," "Mammoth," "NASA," "Xeetee," and "The Web" series. He has collaborated with Sir Arthur C. Clarke on *The Light of Other Days, Time's Eye,* and *Sunstorm,* while his short fiction has been collected in *Traces* and *The Hunters of Pangaea.* Baxter's books have won the Philip K. Dick Award, the John W. Campbell Memorial Award, the British Science Fiction Association Award, the Kurd Lasswitz Award (Germany), and the Seiun Award (Japan). He helped develop the BBC television series *Invasion: Earth* (1998) and scripted an episode of the Sky One series *Space Island One* (1998), while his novel *Voyage* was dramatized for BBC Radio and broadcast in six weekly parts in 1999.

56

[1973]

ELIZABETH MASSIE on

Harvest Home
by THOMAS TRYON

Under the name "Tom Tryon," the future novelist (1926–91) had a midrange acting career that spanned lead roles in I Married a Monster from Outer Space *(1958) and Otto Preminger's* The Cardinal *(1963). The story goes that Tryon was so bullied by Preminger, whom he worked for also on* In Harm's Way *(1965), that he resolved to quit acting and find something else to do. Impressed by the book, film, and success of Ira Levin's* Rosemary's Baby *(1967), Tryon wrote the ghost-themed* The Other *(1971)—which he then scripted for Richard Mulligan's 1972 film.* Harvest Home, *Tryon's second horror novel, stands in the 1970s run of strangers-in-a-strange-small-town novels, including Stephen King's* 'Salem's Lot *(1975) and Peter Straub's* Ghost Story *(1979), but it also has some echoes of the pagan, ritual, sacrificial concerns of the film* The Wicker Man *(1973). It was adapted into a two-part television miniseries,* The Dark Secret of Harvest Home *(1978), with Bette Davis top-billed as the sinister Widow Fortune, David Ackroyd as the threatened incomer, Joanna Miles as his wife, Rosanna Arquette memorably sexy as the teenage daughter, and narration from Donald Pleasence (video releases are of an unsatisfactory feature-length cut-down that ruins director Leo Penn's slow, unsettling buildup). Though Tryon never excluded the macabre, horrific, and magical from his fiction, his subsequent novels and collections tend to be less squarely in the genre; his most personal writing might be the four linked Hollywood-themed novellas in* Crowned Heads *(1976).*

By sheer virtue of being cast in our own bodies at birth, we are destined to lives of isolation and alienation. With few exceptions, we spend our remaining years in an attempt to leap or crawl from ourselves into some collective better, emotionally and physically. There is a hard-wired need in most people to seek out and to belong to a communal whole. Not necessarily a need to go as far back as the bicameral mind, but an urge to find a group with whom we have things in common, with whom we feel most often comfortable, a group that accepts us for the unique oddities we are.

Often coupled with the desire to belong comes the desire for a life free of the shoulder-crushing minutiae of modern life, the mindless tedium that clogs our brains like sticky cobwebs, the blaring white noise that makes us think we have, or even drives us to, adult ADD.

I understand both these needs. Born and raised in a small town and presently living in rural Virginia, I remain aware of my separateness. I have family and friends who love me and whom I love, yet there are times when I am acutely conscious of how different I am from them, them from me, and even more so from the world at large. And I get on edge when the kid in the car behind me has his stereo system so loud that it drives its enormous fists into the side of my own vehicle or when I go into a "superstore" and am accosted by countless ads and displays that scream "buy me!" at every turn.

Thomas Tryon's *Harvest Home* gets right to the heart of these very real, very human matters. He understands that the greatest horrors in life might not be that is outside us but that which is within. He knows that to be human is to try to make life better for ourselves and for those we love, but such an attempt is never as simple as it should be. We carry our baggage, our dark secrets, with us into our supposed paradises. And we encounter the dark secrets of others of the collective.

Tryon's main characters, the Constantines, seek an escape from the crime, noise, filth, and clutter of life in New York City. They discover Cornwall Coombe, a New England town that seems frozen in a time long past. As the family drives into the town, Ned, the first-person narrator, witnesses farmers planting corn on a hillside and is moved:

> I could not then—nor can I now—describe, a vague stirring inside me, some fugitive longing, a desire to stop the car, get out and feel my feet upon that earth, to be among those farm people planting seeds that would grow.

Ned, his wife, Beth, and daughter Kate decide this humble place will be their salvation.

But it can never be as simple as that, can it? The dark secrets come out to play, and play with a vengeance.

Tryon weaves a beautiful, touching, claustrophobic, and horrifying story of a family in need of peace, and a community in need of, well, something else altogether. From the outset the reader senses something isn't quite right with the folks of Cornwall Coombe—the wise and outspoken Widow Fortune, the overly chatty peddler Jack Stump, the women's sewing circle with their "ways" that carefully follow and mimic the cycles of nature, the blind neighbor to whom the Invisible Voice reads classics the whole day long, the odd child Missy and the respect given her by the villagers. The communal whole with which the Constantines have surrounded themselves and that have accepted them tightens its cold, purposeful grip. Two will mold themselves happily to the pressure, to become one with the village. The third will resist and be crushed in the vise.

There is nothing supernatural in *Harvest Home* save the villagers' beliefs in oracles and the power of magic. Thus, for me, it is all the more frightening. I read the novel soon after it was published, and at the tender age of twenty was shaken. I do not doubt its enormous impact on my decision to write on the darker side of fiction. Tryon's book is a brilliant blend of the graphic and the downplayed, the violent and the idyllic. It is a story with characters so genuine—so likable or pitiable or callous—that one can easily find himself or herself there in Cornwall Coombe as the suffocating, caring circle closes in.

ELIZABETH MASSIE (b. 1953) grew up in the Shenandoah Valley of Virginia and has lived her life there. Her first published short story, "Whittler," appeared in David B. Silva's magazine the *Horror Show* in 1984. She became a full-time writer in 1994, and continues to create novels, short stories, poetry, and non-fiction works. Her books include the Bram Stoker Award-winning *Sineater, Dark Shadows: Dreams of the Dark* (with Stephen Mark Rainey), *Welcome Back to the Night, Wire Mesh Mothers, Shadow Dreams, The Fear Report, 1863: A House Divided, 1776: Son of Liberty, 1609: Winter of the Dead, 1870: Not With Our Blood, The Great Chicago Fire: 1871, Buffy the Vampire Slayer: Power of Persuasion, Maryland: Ghost Harbor, The Little Magenta Book of Mean Stories,* and *Abaddon Inn: Twisted Branch.* She is the author of about eighty short stories and novellas (including the Bram Stoker Award-winning "Stephen"), which have appeared in various magazines and anthologies, and her story "Lock Her Room" was developed into a short film that premiered on the Showtime Network in 2003. Her teleplay for the PBS special *Rhymes and Reasons* was the recipient of a 1990 Parents' Choice Award. A World Fantasy Award finalist, Massie acknowledges that living in the rural southern United States has certainly influenced her fiction, creating works that some have classified as "Southern Gothic."

57 [1973]

P. N. ELROD on

The Night Stalker
by JEFF RICE

In January 1972 ABC-TV aired The Night Stalker, *a made-for-television movie about a vampire in Las Vegas, produced by Dan Curtis, directed by John Llewellyn Moxey, and scripted by Richard Matheson. It scored a record-setting 75 million viewers and was followed by a sequel,* The Night Strangler *(1974), also starring Darren McGavin as crusading newspaperman Carl Kolchak.* Kolchak: The Night Stalker, *a short-lived TV series with McGavin, followed in 1974–75. The original TV film was based on an as-yet unpublished novel by journalist Jeff(rey) Grant) Rice (b. 1944), originally titled* The Kolchak Papers. *It belatedly appeared in December 1973 under the title* The Night Stalker *as a Pocket Books paperback original, and has been reissued as* The Kolchak Papers #1: The Night Stalker. *Rice's novelization of Matheson's* The Night Strangler *script was issued by Pocket Books in January 1974. In 2003 Gauntlet Press published Richard Matheson's Kolchak scripts, which also includes an unproduced third teleplay (co-written with William F. Nolan),* The Night Killers. *Mark Dawidziak's* Night Stalking: A 20th Anniversary Companion *(1991), a guide to Kolchak's career, was revised as* The Night Stalker Companion: A 25th Anniversary Tribute *(1997).*

THE KOLCHAK PAPERS began as a yet-to-be published novel adapted by Richard Matheson into a screenplay with the catchy title *The Night Stalker.*

It was January 1972, and I was a nut for vampires, having seen every film, read every book (at least twice), and was a loyal disciple of my much-loved *Dark Shadows*. A serious scholar of the critters, I'd even waded through Montague Summers' hefty tomes on the topic. There are vampires everywhere now, but not then. They were thin on the ground, and the formula established by Bram Stoker of evil-vampire-comes-to-town-sucks-necks-gets-staked-by-good-guys had been done to undeath. I was young and cynically certain there would never be anything new on the theme.

But . . . the all-too-fleeting previews of *this* version of the myth promised something different and dynamic, and—oh, gosh!—against all odds, it *delivered*. The television movie exceeded my expectations, and I love it to this day, but the *book* that followed was something truly special.

I first glimpsed its gaudy cover on the revolving wire rack at the elderly grocery store up the street from my house, seized the book with a squeal, and blew half my allowance then and there. I knew it would be worth the extravagance if it bore even a cousinly resemblance to the completely cool movie I'd watched the previous year.

At that time I was vaguely familiar with such early attempts at media tie-in books. The genre had yet to achieve the bookstore staple status of this era. Then as now, many adaptations were more often than not hack work written for the money, particularly in cases where the writer had never seen the show.

But in December 1973 my find was an out-of-the-blue treat, and I gave it the respect it deserved. I whisked away Jeff Rice's book and read it in one sitting.

It wasn't what I'd expected.

Yes, it was like the movie, only a whole lot more so. In a good way. From the eye-opening autopsy to the gruesome and graphic climax I could *not* put it down. As soon as I finished I read it all over again, caught my breath, then began a third reading. I was in gleeful shock; I was in love with Carl Kolchak, and Jeff Rice was my new god.

I'd never met any other literary character quite like Rice's Kolchak. He was overweight, drank, was wholly unglamorous, and suffered a number of personality problems that never made it to the screenplay, and still I *loved* him. For all those faults, he burned to bring the truth to the people, and his ongoing frustration when thwarted hit a deep chord in my own developing personality. He was not a crazed knight tilting at windmills, but going after *real* giants, and craziness be damned. He *knew* he was right; the world was flat after all.

That book was also ahead of its time.

It chronicled brutal slayings and profiled the background of a serial killer when the term had yet to be coined by Robert K. Ressler, who had joined the FBI's budding Behavioral Science Unit only the year before.

It delved into the dark and nasty world of political coverups, which didn't become popular grist for the news mills until Alfred E. Lewis reported a break-in at the Watergate Hotel in June 1972. Colleagues Woodward, Bernstein, and others would keep things stirred up, but chronologically, the then-unpublished *Kolchak Papers* predated them.

It had a detailed description of an autopsy and the use of forensics to help track and identify the killer, anticipating this century's abundance of crime scene investigation shows by more than three decades.

It used date, time, location, and a straightforward, no-frills reporting style, giving the narrative a documentary feel. So convincing was this that I biked down to the university library to spin through microfiche files in search of the reality behind the fiction, and by default learned how to research the books I would someday come to write.

Its setting was not a creepy castle or an isolated old house, nor was it peopled with stock heroes tracking a stock villain to a morally satisfying demise. This vampire moved and killed freely in the most frivolous and garish of modern American cities. His predatory prowlings were glossed over and to some extent aided by the powers that be, anticipating one of the plot drivers for Peter Benchley's *Jaws* in 1974.

All those factors and more made for a very scary and thrilling read, and they still work for me.

It is no accident that the vampire hero in my first series of novels started out being a reporter. Jack Fleming was no Carl Kolchak, but they might have understood one another—providing Kolchak wasn't about to stake my guy in the heart for his drinking habits.

Carl, I still love you; I always will.

Jeff Rice, I revere you for firing my young imagination and helping me to begin to learn my craft.

Thank you and thank you again; I would love to buy you both a beer.

See you in Vegas?

P. (PATRICIA) N. ELROD (b. 1954) was born and lives in Texas. She is the author of more than twenty novels since 1990, most notably the best-selling *The Vampire Files* series featuring Jack Fleming and comprising *Bloodlist, Lifeblood, Bloodcircle, Art in the Blood, Fire in the Blood, Blood on the Water, A Chill in the Blood* (winner of the 1998 Lord Ruthven Award for Best Vampire Novel), *The Dark Sleep, Lady Crymsyn, Cold Streets, Song in the Dark,* and *Dark Road Rising.* Her other books include *I, Strahd: The Memoirs of a Vampire* and *I, Strahd: The War Against Azalin* for Wizards of the Coast, three collaborations with actor Nigel Bennett (*Keeper of the King, His Father's Son,* and *Siege Perilous*), *Quincey Morris Vampire,* and *The Adventures of Myhr,* while her four books about Jonathan Barrett, Gentleman Vampire (*Red Death, Death and the Maiden, Death Masque,* and *Dance of Death*) were collected into an omnibus edition by the Science Fiction Book Club. She has edited the anthologies *Time of the Vampires* and *Dracula's London* (both with Martin H. Greenberg), *Stepping Through the Stargate,* and *My Big Fat Supernatural Wedding,* while her short fiction has been published in *Dracula Prince of Darkness, Vampire Detectives, Tales of Ravenloft, Celebrity Vampires, Murder Most Romantic, Assassin Fantastic, Death by Horoscope, Presidential Pet Detectives, Familiars Fantastic, Vengeance Fantastic, Death by Dickens,* and *Rotten Relations,* among other titles.

58 [1974]

MICHAEL SWANWICK on
Blood Sport
by ROBERT F. JONES

Robert F. Jones (1934–2002) was a journalist who specialized in outdoor subjects, from manly sports to combat; allegedly he was the writer who popularized the term "hippie." Besides Blood Sport, *a fantastical yarn of father-son bonding and conflict set along a bizarre river, Jones was the author of several other novels about field sports:* The Diamond Bogo: An African Idyll *(1977),* Slade's Glacier *(1982), and* The Run to Gitche Gumee *(2001). His Westerns include* Tie My Bones to Her Back *(1996),* Deadville *(1998), and* The Buffalo Runners *(1998). Slightly more inclined to be classed as non-fiction, though equally concerned with shooting and hooking things, are* Upland Passage: A Field Dog's Education *(1992),* Dancers in the Sunset Sky: The Musings of a Bird Hunter *(1996), and* Hunter in My Heart: The Sportsman's Salmagundi *(2002).*

It BEGINS WITH one hell of a narrative hook: "The Hassayampa River, a burly stream with its share of trout, rises in northern China, meanders through an Indian reservation in central Wisconsin, and empties finally into Croton Lake not a mile from where I live in southern New York State."

After swallowing that, the reader is committed to believing anything—and the author takes full advantage of it, populating the wilderness around the Hassayampa with buffalo and mastodon, elk and aurochs, manticores and mandiggers, even a Sad Sack of a unicorn. Jones plays the reader like a trout.

Blood Sport can best be understood as North American magic realism. A man and a boy travel up the mythic river of self-discovery. They have no names, though they will earn them later. The father wants to toughen up his son. The son wants his freedom. They are heading for their separate confrontations with the outlaw Ratnose—ugly, one-eyed, cunning, murderous, and possibly unkillable.

But it's also an early work of postmodernism. Drinking the water of the Hassayampa, we are told, turns men into liars. Important parts of the plot happen offstage and are learned of from men who may well be lying. Much of what we see is literally unbelievable. At the beginning of the novel, the man knows of Ratnose only by things he seems to recall hearing. By the time they meet, they have a long and bitter history. The text casts constant doubt on its own reliability. I don't think that the title's initials are coincidental.

The action plays out in the uneasy borderland between nightmare and tall tale. Father and son are on internal voyages back to the Stone Age, where each will get in touch with his inner savage. Their stories overflow with testosterone. Not just the swagger and crudeness of being male, but the easy violence born of boredom and the casual brutalization of women as well. (*Blood Sport* has a cult following, but I doubt that many of its admirers are female.) The pleasures the son experiences as an outlaw include massive drug use and frequent public sex. Both are presented in a down-and-dirty fashion sure to offend the moralists, and they are not portrayed with disapproval.

Indeed, one of the chief virtues of *Blood Sport* is how bracingly free it is of moral judgment. Nobody blames the son for running away, or the father for his numerous acts of murder and even torture. For all his treachery and guile, Ratnose in person is as charming as the Devil on a bright blue day. And it is only when madness and suffering have transformed the father into someone as cruel and remorseless as Ratnose himself that he can finally face off against the outlaw in a climactic duel to the death at the source of the Hassayampa, using fly rods with poisoned flies.

All of this could easily devolve into whimsy and self-indulgence were it not for the delicate precision and iron control of the writing.

The passages dealing with hunting and fishing, which Jones covered for twenty-four years as a writer for *Sports Illustrated*, are particularly fine, but the prose burns with a lean and holy elegance throughout. Much in this book that a reader might otherwise find repugnant is redeemed by the beauty with which it is told.

Ultimately, Robert F. Jones has created a myth of manhood, and like all myths it resists being reduced to a single reading. Consider it instead a map of the far reaches of the male psyche, the primitive lands upriver where monsters lurk and only the strong and tough and violent can survive. Up there lie the anarchic territories of the spirit where mothers and wives are conveniently absent and women are little more than opportunities for men to display sexual prowess. The proving grounds are deep in the subconscious where we go to experience things that cannot be allowed in the real world, and thus become, briefly, heroes and gods.

Blood Sport presents an unflattering portrait of the male gender, warts and all, with no apologies whatsoever. You may not agree with it, but its power is undeniable. We are men, Jones says. These are our fantasies. This is the way we are.

MICHAEL SWANWICK (b. 1950) was born in Schenectady, New York. Committed to being a writer at age seventeen, he attended the College of William and Mary in Virginia but graduated with no marketable skills. Settling in Philadelphia, he finished his first story when he was twenty-nine. It didn't sell, but every story he has written since has. His first two published stories were both Nebula Award finalists. He has since been honored with five Hugo Awards and the Nebula, Theodore Sturgeon, and World Fantasy Awards, as well as receiving nominations for the British Science Fiction Award and the Arthur C. Clarke Award. Swanwick is one of the most acclaimed science fiction and fantasy writers of his generation. His novels include *In the Drift, Vacuum Flowers, Griffin's Egg, Stations of the Tide, The Iron Dragon's Daughter, Jack Faust,* and *Bones of the Earth*. His stories have appeared in *Omni, Penthouse, Amazing, Asimov's Science Fiction, High Times, New Dimensions, Starlight, Universe, Full Spectrum, Triquarterly,* and elsewhere. Many have been reprinted in "Best of the Year" anthologies, and his short fiction has been collected in *Gravity's Angels, A Geography of Imaginary Lands, Moon Dogs,* and *Tales of Old Earth.*

59 [1975]

NICHOLAS ROYLE on

Nightshade
by DEREK MARLOWE

An English couple, Edward and Amy Lytton, are on vacation in the Caribbean. At the port of Revenants, a light aircraft has crashed into the side of a volcano, killing the plane's two occupants. Edward, unsettled in the tropics, encounters a mysterious stranger, Daniel Azevedo, who appears out of nowhere and vanishes as suddenly. Ambiguous signs lead Edward to cultivate a vague suspicion that Amy is enjoying the company of another man. Moving on to Haiti, the Lyttons meet a voodoo priest who tells them that if someone dies in an accident they are likely to reappear as a restless soul in search of company for their return to the grave. Spooked, Edward is surprised to find himself attracted to an Englishwoman staying in the same hotel and feels equally drawn to the charismatic Azevedo, while Amy's behavior becomes increasingly unpredictable. England seems impossibly distant. Finding success with his first novel, A Dandy in

Aspic *(1966)*, Derek Marlowe *(1938–96) wrote five more, among them* Echoes of Celandine *(1970, filmed and reissued as* The Disappearance*) before publishing* Nightshade. *Associational with horror is* A Single Summer With L. B. *(1969), about the Byron-Shelley ménage of 1816 that produced* Frankenstein. *Marlowe also wrote for the* Adventures of Sherlock Holmes *television series and co-scripted the 1988 two-part TV drama* Jack the Ripper.

THROUGHOUT HIS CAREER, Derek Marlowe flirted with genre. And not just one. *A Dandy in Aspic* was a spy novel. *Echoes of Celandine,* about a professional assassin, would be shelved with crime—if it were in print today—alongside his detective novel *Somebody's Sister* (1974), assuming that was available, too.

Let me save you some time. *Nothing* Marlowe wrote is in print, including his wonderfully creepy ghost story/horror novel *Nightshade* (at the time of writing, abebooks.com lists sixty-eight second-hand copies from $1.00 to $85.00).

For a voodoo tale, it's remarkably restrained, far more suggestive than explicit. Instead of rotting corpses in ragged shrouds dragging themselves from their graves (and I enjoy reruns of *Zombie Flesh Eaters* and *The Living Dead at the Manchester Morgue* as much as the next gore-hound), Marlowe gives us silk shirts, straw hats, blue blazers, panatelas, backgammon, and cocktail lounges.

Edward and Amy have not come away without baggage. Dark hints are dropped about a terrible event involving Amy's late sister Blanche: "what had happened in Tewkesbury need never happen again." If the vacation is an opportunity to heal the wounds of the past, however, it is soon lost. Edward picks up signs (damp patches on the beach chair next to Amy's, the smell of cigarette smoke in their room), and in the tropical heat suspicion is quickly cooked up into paranoia. Untrustworthy faces pop up: Lapotre, the cane-wielding hotelier who ambushes the couple at the airport and persuades them to switch accommodations; Jean-Dantor, the voodoo priest or *houngan*, polite but persistent and perceived by Edward as leading Amy astray; Daniel Azevedo, the cultured and charismatic stranger who appears and disappears at will, seemingly the guardian of any secrets of the island to which the *houngan* is not privy.

Edward tries to convince himself that his suspicions are unnatural and unwarranted. He remembers reading that it's the light and the fact of being on an island. "Commonplace behaviour suddenly appeared sinister." It's that, but it's more than that. Emotionally repressed, Edward can barely bring himself to touch his wife. They sleep apart and have yet to consummate their marriage. Witnessing a couple fornicating in a cornfield severely discomfits him. Returning from Mass, he thinks he spots a figure on their balcony but can't be certain it's theirs. Noises are heard coming from the room upstairs, which is unoccupied. But on investigation, a blue dress and shoes are discovered, just like Blanche's. The urbane, personable Azevedo is a light in the gathering darkness to which both Edward and Amy, in their different ways, are attracted like moths.

In the *Times*, Amy reads that the woman on the plane that crashed at Revenants was English, though the man was not. When Amy wears too much makeup for a proposed evening that the two of them will spend with Azevedo, Edward objects. Is it Amy's being attracted to Azevedo that upsets him, or Azevedo's suspected attraction to Amy? Their marriage is approaching total breakdown. "If only, she wished, he would hit her. Just once. She deserved that at least. To feel his hand on her body, no matter what the intention." But Edward is burdened with his own secret: he is attracted to Alice, a woman he has seen and spoken to around the hotel.

"An eel, as you know, has a fondness for human flesh. It enters a drowned body through the eyes," the *houngan* tells Edward. It's a powerful image and a telling one. With his aversion to touch, Edward relies on the evidence of his eyes. An observer, he takes everything in.

Marlowe's style—his rich, lyrical prose with its love of detail and parentheses—is intimate. He apostrophizes the reader, drawing us in: "Let me just place you discreetly outside her half-open shutters in such a way that you may peer into the room." The relationship he sets up between the narrator and the story—"It is a clumsy image, to be sure, but it is Edward's and so one is stuck with it"—encourages trust and acceptance. It falters once, when Edward feels so detached he imagines he's no more than a character in a book, but this self-conscious blip merely demonstrates that Marlowe was, in fact, only human.

Appropriately, he contrives, elegantly and cleverly, to work in a reference to Matthew Gregory Lewis ("The driver of the white Packard had said he owned a plantation that used to belong many years ago to Monk Lewis. The writer of ghosts.") and even allows a surprising eruption of Lovecraftian horror: "He had thought he had seen things moving inside . . . semi-human creatures huddled one within the other . . . he heard the scuffling again, and above it a kind of indefinable sliding, scraping, as if something living was dragging itself with great difficulty over damp earth."

Sly, bewitching, and devilishly paranoid, *Nightshade* is a masterpiece of dark fiction.

NICHOLAS ROYLE (b. 1963) was born in Manchester, England, and recently returned to that city with his wife and two children after years of living in London. He is the author of five literary and disturbing novels—*Counterparts, Saxophone Dreams, The Matter of the Heart, The Director's Cut,* and *Antwerp*—in addition to more than a hundred short stories, which have appeared in a wide variety of anthologies and magazines. He has edited twelve anthologies: *Darklands*; *Darklands 2*; *A Book of Two Halves*; *The Tiger Garden: A Book of Writers' Dreams*; *The Time Out Book of New York Short Stories*; *The Agony and the Ecstasy: New Writing for the World Cup*; *The Ex Files: New Stories About Old Flames*; *Neonlit: Time Out Book of New Writing*; *The Time Out Book of Paris Short Stories*; *Neonlit: Time Out Book of New Writing, Volume 2*; *The Time Out Book of London Short Stories, Volume 2*; and *Dreams Never End.* He has written about books, film, art, and music for a wide range of publications and is a regular contributor to *Time Out,* the *Independent,* the *Guardian,* and the *Independent on Sunday.* Royle has won the British Fantasy Award three times and the Bad Sex Prize once. In case anyone doesn't know, the latter is also a literary prize.

60

[1975]

ROZ KAVENEY on

Peace
by GENE WOLFE

Gene Wolfe (b. 1931), who wrote on H. G. Wells's The Island of Dr. Moreau *in* Horror: 100 Best Books, *is among the most important contemporary fantasy authors, though none of his works can easily be slotted into genre brackets.* Peace *is a small-town portrait, narrated by a man who might be a ghost, full of truncated stories about the inhabitants of a midwestern town that has a certain kinship with such archetypal locales as Thornton Wilder's* Our Town, *Henry Bellamann's* King's Row, *and the Bedford Falls of* It's a Wonderful Life—*all of which nurture deep darknesses behind the folksy façades and picket fences. Perhaps best known for the far future cycle* The Book of the New Sun *(1980–83), Wolfe has written other novels of the fantastic and sinister, including* There Are Doors *(1988) and* Castleview *(1990).*

THE TITLE IS one of the most disturbing things about this subtle book; throughout its length, people sleep or die, but peace is the last thing they find in their dreams and the stories told there. It is one of the earliest of Gene Wolfe's novels and still one of his best; it demonstrates that it is possible to evoke a truly disturbing unease while using almost none of the standard material of the horror novel.

Peace is a novel in which it is almost impossible to be sure of anything, but some things appear most of the time to be the case. Alden Weer is an old man, wandering the empty rooms of his large house. Some of the time he is a young man taking medical advice for his old age, and a child doing the same and telling that doctor of the imminent death of the doctor's son Bobby, whom Alden, almost certainly, killed. At other times he is old and brooding and uncertain whether he has had a stroke, and whether he can get up to walk around some more; the fire at which he is sitting is no more than smoldering and he himself may only be the ashes of the dead.

At one level this is a novel of deep nostalgia in which Alden mourns a long-ago small-town America in which he was briefly innocent; at another, it is a reminder that lost paradises were never quite what they seemed. Heartbreak and cruelty are part of the human condition; his past is too full for comfort of maiden aunts who aged into eccentricity, and solitary bachelors for whom a collection of curios has become a substitute for life. The people Alden knew have far too much in common with the hungry ghosts about whom they tell stories. Alden Weer speaks for us as well as to us, and he is an uncomfortable spokesman in his vague malice and hints of worse.

We know that people in Alden Weer's life have met with misfortune, and it is never entirely clear to us how much he had to do with any of it. His habit of avoiding telling us things and of telling us only parts of stories comes to seem like an evasion. Some of his stories are open to far more terrible interpretations than the one we assume at first hearing; the world Alden inhabits is one in which the nightmarish is always available. If this is the case about the little lives whose memories drift around Alden, how much more so the godless but haunted universe of his tales in which genies and ghouls and banshees lurk, and even Christian saints can only offer release from pain into death?

Wherever Alden is, people tell him stories, most of which never end; those that do end, end badly in heartbreak and unfulfilled promises. Stories are interrupted by other stories, or set aside so Alden can discuss his future health with the people of his past; this is a book about frustration that delivers its fair share of frustration as it goes. Wolfe is writing about the limits of narrative and the capacity possessed by the act of refusing a sense of an ending; he gives us instead the evocation of a complex mood. Everyone Alden has known or loved is dead, and the promise of their futures comes to nothing but his ramshackle memories. This is perhaps the most horrid thing of all.

Because this is, after all, a Gene Wolfe novel, it includes a number of deeply precious literary jokes. One of the more obvious is the unnamed—or rather nameless—presence in it of a copy of the *Necronomicon* as well as of other books from the H. P. Lovecraft mythos; the copy is a forgery of an imaginary book, and yet that, in a sense, makes it a real one. Certainly Alden seems as bound by other characters' endless repetition of his name as other spirits are by the book's rituals. The allusion to Alden's stone pillow is perhaps a reference to the unwritten tale with that title which was to be the culmination of Robert A. Heinlein's unfinished "Future History."

Above all, Alden's tale, which loops back and forth through his life without resolution and without any clear sense of who ultimately he is and what he has done, is an allusion to another book about memory. *Peace* ends as Proust's *Remembrance of Things Past* begins, with a fractious child trying to sleep. Time cannot be regained, Wolfe seems to be saying, and what is lost is gone—including the soul of the damned Alden Weer.

ROZ KAVENEY (b. 1949) was born in London. She studied English at Oxford and did research on William Morris there. After brief periods in the civil service, teaching, and television, she started working as a reviewer and publisher's reader, intermittently involving herself in civil liberties and anti-censorship work as well as queer and trans politics. She is best known in the science fiction and fantasy fields as an anthologist, editing the two *Tales from the Forbidden Planet* volumes as well as co-editing *Villains!* and both volumes of *The Weerde* with Mary Gentle. She is also the author/editor of *Reading the Vampire Slayer* and author of

From Alien to the Matrix: Reading Science Fiction Film, as well as a variety of short stories. As a reviewer, she covers everything from science fiction to thrillers, classical music to literary biographies.

61

[1976]

DAVID DRAKE on

The Year of the Sex Olympics: Three TV Plays
by NIGEL KNEALE

With apologies to Rod Serling, Brian Clemens, Gene Roddenberry and Joss Whedon, the Manxman, Thomas Nigel Kneale (b. 1922), is probably the most important horror/SF writer to work primarily in television. Though he published an early collection of short stories (Tomato Cain, *1949*) and was perhaps the last major writer launched by Strand Magazine, *his sole novel—developed in parallel with a serial script—is* Quatermass *(1979). Otherwise he has written exclusively for the small and large screens, often adapting other authors in and out of the genre, like George Orwell (the TV version of* Nineteen Eighty-Four, *1954),* John Osbourne (the films of Look Back in Anger, *1958, and* The Entertainer, *1960),* H. G. Wells (the film First Men in the Moon, *1964),* Susan Hill (the TV film of The Woman in Black, *1989), and Kingsley Amis (the TV serial* Stanley and the Women, *1991). The scripts of his first three* Quatermass *serials were published in paperback by Penguin (Stephen Laws wrote about* Quatermass and the Pit *in* Horror: 100 Best Books*) and reissued by Arrow in 1979.* The Year of the Sex Olympics *collects three of Kneale's original genre teleplays, all writ-*

[253]

ten and produced for the BBC. *The broadcast of* The Road *no longer exists (criminally, much 1960s British television was not preserved), but* The Year of the Sex Olympics *(sadly in black-and-white rather than the garish color it was designed for) and* The Stone Tape *have been issued on DVD in the United Kingdom. The book, published by George Locke's Ferret Fantasy imprint, is hard to find, but all three scripts are included on the DVDs.*

IN THE 1950S Nigel Kneale wrote three television serials for BBC in which Professor Bernard Quatermass saved the world from invading monsters. Because he focused on human beings and human reactions rather than on the monster, they are some of the best and most effective of the SF horror films of the period.

When Kneale returned to SF/horror teleplays with *The Road* (1963), *The Stone Tape* (1972), and *The Year of the Sex Olympics* (1969), he dispensed with the monster altogether. The horror is implied by the actions of the human characters rather than stemming from the phenomena they're investigating.

The scripts were collected by a London bookseller in 1976. I discovered them the next year and reread them not only for pleasure—though always with pleasure—but also to hone my craft as a writer.

That they remain teleplays instead of being novelized doesn't detract from their effectiveness. Kneale was an award-winning short-story writer before he turned to screen writing. His settings and stage directions are crisp, clear, and sufficient for a full understanding of the action.

The Road is set in 1770. A country squire, an amateur of natural philosophy, is investigating sounds heard annually in a stretch of woods. His young, bored, very resentful wife has invited a rationalist to watch—and to mock—her husband's endeavors. Both the proto-scientist and the rationalist are men of their own time; and they, as well as the supporting cast, are rounded, believable human beings.

The rationalist knows the truth by deduction: the power of the mind will perfect mankind by eliminating both labor and superstition. The proto-scientist has no certainties beyond the need to devote himself to an empirical search for truth. His humility and determination make him far more attractive than his sneering, arrogant, and close-minded, rationalist rival.

But it's the rationalist who understands the true horror of the terrifying climax and who understands also that it's men like the quietly decent proto-scientist who will create that horror in a single-minded pursuit of truth. The interplay of characters in 1770 is a paradigm of the horror to come.

The Stone Tape has a contemporary setting: the research division of an electronics firm moves into a haunted house and begins investigating the phenomena with an eye toward making a breakthrough in recording technology. The scientists don't have as much time as they think, however, and corporate infighting forces the division's ruthless, charismatic head to cut scientific corners as he has in his professional and personal life.

This time he can't bull through with drive and arrogance. The tragedy that follows is complete, crushing—and forever.

The final play, *The Year of the Sex Olympics*, is set a generation or two in the future. Government exists to eliminate "tension"—emotional spikes of all descriptions. The population is divided at age nine into "high-drives" who maintain society, and "low-drives"—by far the majority—who are fed, housed, and entertained by television. TV programming is didactic, convincing the low-drives that food is disgusting and sex is a spectator sport only, thus conserving resources that wouldn't stretch if they bred to capacity.

A pair of high-drives, more bored than repelled by their society, go to an island to be filmed as entertainment while living a "natural" life with their daughter. The inevitable tragedy—they're completely out of their depth—is accelerated when their former television colleagues add sparkle by placing a murderous sociopath on the island with them.

Unlike the faceless rulers of *1984*, the TV executives of *Year* aren't after power or privilege; they're working hard and responsibly to keep society together, preventing war and mass starvation. They'll do *anything* to achieve those results even if it means arranging to film the deaths of women and children.

Kneale in recent interviews plays down the importance of the "prophecy" of reality television in *Year*. That's simply a tool the executives use, the way the gentleman amateur in 1770 uses an electroscope or present-day researchers use a thermograph. They're pragmatists: they'll use any available tool to achieve their immediate goals; and they all ignore the question of where those goals—laudable in themselves—will lead in the longer term.

The gentleman amateur of 1770 has no intention of creating a nuclear holocaust. He wouldn't halt his search for truth if he did know, however; and neither did his twentieth-century successors.

The dangers here aren't monsters or evil men; they're innate in mankind itself. Kneale shows horrors that no human can escape.

DAVID DRAKE (b. 1945) was born in Dubuque, Iowa. He graduated from the University of Iowa with a B.A. in history and Latin in 1967. While an undergraduate, he sold his first story, "Denkirch," to August Derleth's Arkham House anthology *Travellers by Night* (1967). Derleth bought three more stories from the young author, mailing the check for the last on July 3, 1971; Derleth died the following morning. Drake entered Duke Law School in 1967, was drafted in 1969, and spent two years in the army, with service in Vietnam and Cambodia. He returned to finish law school in 1972, and practiced law as assistant town attorney for Chapel Hill, North Carolina, for eight years. After driving a city bus for a year, he became a full-time freelance writer in 1981. With Karl Edward Wagner and Jim Groce he was one of the three partners in Carcosa, the World Fantasy Award-winning small-press publishing house, and was assistant editor of Stuart David Schiff's *Whispers* magazine from the second issue onward. Drake has sold more than a hundred short stories and has written, co-written, or edited about 150 books, including *Killer* (with Karl Edward Wagner), *Old Nathan, The Sea Hag,* and the popular *Hammer's Slammers* and *The Crisis of Empire* military SF series. He bought *The Year of the Sex Olympics* in 1977, during his first visit to London, and has treasured and often reread it since.

62

[1977]

MARC LAIDLAW on

Our Lady of Darkness
by FRITZ LEIBER

Fritz Leiber Jr. (1932–92), the son of a familiar character actor, appeared in a few tiny movie bits (e.g., James Whale's The Great Garrick, *1937, and Mark McGee's* Equinox, *1969), and was a significant force in at least three popular literary genres. He brought the ghost story to modern America (cf. the 1947 collection* Night's Black Agents*) and arguably did more than anyone else to make horror a contemporary genre. Furthermore, he added wit and humor to sword and sorcery in his "Fafhrd and Grey Mouser" stories and published much outstanding science fiction. Gerald W. Page wrote about Leiber's* Conjure Wife *(1943) in* Horror: 100 Best Books, *and* Our Lady of Darkness—*following Shirley Jackson's* The Haunting *the last time around—won an unofficial poll as most requested title from this crop of contributors. We assigned the book to Marc Laidlaw, against stiff competition, because we felt it needed to be covered by another San Francisco writer. Leiber sketched out the story in the novella* The Pale Brown Thing, *written in 1974–75, which he swiftly expanded into the World Fantasy Award-winning novel.*

IN 1976, JUST shy of my sixteenth birthday, I drove four hundred miles to meet Fritz Leiber, the culmination of several months of correspondence. I had pictured him living in luxury befitting his status as one of science fiction's grand masters. Instead, I was shocked to find him occupying one small room of a seedy San Francisco residence hotel, its squalor relieved mainly by walls of books. Far from the professional office I had imagined, he perched on the edge of his unmade bed to type on a cluttered coffee table. Yet Fritz made me feel at home. He signed my books in purple ink; he showed me his annotated copy of Lovecraft's *The Outsider;* and from the window of his room, he pointed out the Twin Peaks TV tower and the pale brown shape of Corona Heights above the cityscape. I left with a deepened respect for Fritz, and a sense of sadness because of his circumstances.

When, shortly thereafter, *The Pale Brown Thing* appeared in *The Magazine of Fantasy & Science Fiction*, I experienced first a shock of recognition and then the slow magic of artistic transformation. The story of Franz Westen, a writer struggling with grief and alcoholism after the death of his wife, was mixed up not only with my visit but also with photocopied letters Leiber sent to his correspondents in this period. In his letters, Fritz detailed the vagaries of his career, his adventures in the city, and even his "self-experiments" with alcohol. There was little separation between the tone and content of these letters and the circumstances of *The Pale Brown Thing*. Westen's apartment was Fritz's own. Westen's deceased wife, "Daisy," was Leiber's own "Jonquil." The low bed covered with books and magazines, which Westen called his "Scholar's Mistress," was the same low bed where Leiber composed his book. When Leiber described the supernatural impinging on this instantly recognizable world, it created in me a kind of thrill I had never felt before—supernatural novel as confessional, eerie love song to a fog-swept city with which I was falling in love myself.

Our Lady of Darkness (its eventual title) is the quintessential San Francisco horror novel. It borrows techniques from M. R. James and H. P. Lovecraft, and uses them to visit nightmares on the Bay Area's literary dreamers: Jack London, George Sterling, Dashiell Hammett, and Clark Ashton Smith. Yet rather than populate the customary scenic attractions of Golden Gate Bridge or Coit Tower with Barbary Coast ghosts, Leiber grimly obsesses on the city's depressing financial district skyline with its focal Transamerica Pyramid, and develops a modern metropolitan mythology that is completely unique.

This is not a book for tourists. It is a piercing look at the heart of a city so full of lonely individuals that they have achieved critical mass. The soul of the city itself is racked with terror and despair, albeit shot through with glimmers of hope. No other horror novel so well evokes the feeling of huddling with friends on a windswept sidewalk, telling stories that both deepen and push back the surrounding dark. Amid the crush of steel and cement towers, Leiber poignantly summons the spirit of friendship and demonstrates the cost of its absence. For in their desperate loneliness, Westen and his troubled peers grant inanimate objects the kind of significance intended for human companions. Corona Heights, observed through binoculars, stirs and wakes, as if grateful for Westen's inspection. His research disturbs the long-forgotten specter of a man who might be either an occult visionary or a fraud fantastically twisted by his lies. Scattered through the book is a breadcrumb trail of speculation about the line between sanity and madness, truth and art. Leiber leaves plenty of hints to suggest that his real concern is the manner in which frustrated creativity turns inward upon itself, transforming dreamers into addicts, deviants, madmen, or (more rarely) artists. Westen continually grapples with the question: Which am I?

Yet a hallmark of the book is its continual optimism. Westen is a white-knuckled drunk, holding so tightly to sobriety and sanity that his hands cannot stop trembling. Terrified of losing his grip and slipping into the abyss beneath existence, Westen resolutely refuses to look down. He fixes his gaze on hilltops, TV towers, stars. He pushes aside all thoughts of his dead wife; he refuses offered drinks and avoids backsliding into unconsciousness or oblivion; he resists all the obvious temptations but overlooks his most telling vulnerability. For Westen finds his false solace in a form of escapism well known to Leiber's audience. He buries himself in books, in words, in cold print. He lies down with his Scholar's Mistress and comes very close to never rising again. From this bloodless partner, this paperwork simulacrum, only his links of friendship, fragilely forged through the rest of the book, save Franz Westen in the end by binding him to life. And Leiber's spirit of friendship, which I recognize in this supernatural journal, still means exactly this to me. The dark mirror he raised up to the cold city still shows the warm imprint of Fritz's foggy breath. It reminds us that we are more than merely readers.

MARC LAIDLAW (b. 1960) was born in Los Angeles and lived in San Francisco for fifteen years, before moving to Washington State to learn how to write and design video games. He is the author of numerous short stories, and his novels include *Dad's Nuke, Neon Lotus, Kalifornia, The Orchid Eater, The Third Force,* and the International Horror Guild Award-winning *The 37th Mandala* (1996). In 1997 Laidlaw joined Valve Software to write and design computer games, beginning with the successful *Half-Life*, which was noted for its innovative storytelling technique and has sold about 3.5 million copies to date.

63

[1978]

PAUL McAULEY on

The Cement Garden
by **IAN McEWAN**

Of his early, creepy work, Ian McEwan (b. 1948) has said, "I always used to deny this, but I guess what I'm really saying is that I was *writing to shock. . . . And I dug deep and dredged up all kinds of vile things which fascinated me at the time."* McEwan's second published book, following the short-story collection First Love, Last Rites *(1975),* The Cement Garden *came to the attention of genre fans when Stephen King and Douglas E. Winter listed it in the "further reading" sections of their important studies* Danse Macabre *(1981) and* Faces of Fear *(1985); Winter even spelled McEwan's name correctly. With a premise that distantly echoes Julian Gloag's 1963 novel* Our Mother's House *(filmed in 1967 by Jack Clayton) and even the incest gothics of V. C. Andrews,* The Cement Garden *fits into a tiny sub-genre of children-left-to-their-own-devices stories that descend from* The Lord of the Flies *(1954). Though McEwan has worked as a screenwriter (*The Ploughman's Lunch, *1983),* The Cement Garden *was filmed by writer-director Andrew Birkin (scriptwriter of* The Final Conflict*) in 1993, with his niece Charlotte Gainsbourg and future Titus Groan Andrew Robertson in the lead roles of Julie and Jack.*

A<small>LTHOUGH IAN MCEWAN'S</small> place at the top table of the British literary establishment is firmly established, several of his novels have flirted with the borderlands of genre. *The Comfort of Strangers* is a psychological thriller; *The Child in Time* a near-future dystopia; *The Innocent* is a Cold War spy story. And *The Cement Garden* not only displays his consummate skill in dissecting pathological extremes of human behavior and evoking macabre menaces from ordinary events, but also is a cunning variation on that good old horror staple of an odd family with dark secrets and something nasty lurking in the basement.

In McEwan's accomplished first novel, a family of four children, living in an isolated house in a down-at-the-heels urban area that's slowly being demolished, have grown used to taking care of themselves during their mother's long illness (their father suffered a fatal heart attack while laying the first batch of the cement with which he planned to cover his garden). When they're orphaned by their mother's death on the last day of the summer term, they're afraid that they will be put into care and split up, and hide her body inside a trunk in the basement of their house and bury it under cement. The children have already reimagined their lives through dreams, masturbatory fantasies, pulp science fiction, and games of dressing up as doctors and nurses. Concealing their mother's death enables them to reinvent their lives for real, to create new rules and an alternate morality, and assume the power of the grown-ups who have previously governed every aspect of their lives. But without the yardstick of adult authority they are unable to express their grief properly, and their collective guilt divides rather than binds them.

McEwan atomizes the slow decay of the children's fantasy world with stripped-down, high-precision prose (at about fifty thousand words, the novel is a perfectly structured marvel of compression), and fastidious psychological acuity. The narrator, fifteen-year-old Jack, becomes obsessed with the various secretions of his body and possessed by a pathological torpor; his introverted younger sister, Sue, retreats into her bedroom and books; his young brother, Tom, regresses toward babyhood. Only Julie, Jack's older sister, makes a serious attempt to keep the family together as, during a gruelingly hot summer (the novel was written during the fag end of Britain's long, hot summer of 1976), food rots in the kitchen and their mother's body bursts its cement casing.

The claustrophobic heat invokes a postapocalypse landscape similar to those of J. G. Ballard, a strange new world in which the rules of ordinary civilization have melted away, while the children's isolation and skewed notions of self-sufficiency recall William Golding's subversion of desert-island fictions in *The Lord of the Flies.* But while the absence of adults allowed the schoolboys in Golding's novel to revert to violent, primitive savagery, what's released or unrepressed in *The Cement Garden* is sexuality. Although Julie does her best to assume the role of her dead mother, she also brings into the house the agent of her family's destruction in the form of her boyfriend Derek. Just twenty-three, an only child with an overprotective mother, Derek, as Julie tells Jack, "wants to be one of the family, you know, big smart daddy." But when Derek surprises Julie and Jack in bed together, his jealous rage drives him to smash open the family's secret.

The best horror novels are solidly rooted in fastidiously detailed evocations of ordinary, everyday life; we're only willing to be seduced into believing in monsters and supernatural events after we've been convinced that the fictional worlds into which they erupt are precisely congruent with our own. Like the best horror novels, *The Cement Garden* evokes an utterly convincing and recognizable world that gradually mutates into a weird fantasy, and while the monsters remain inside the heads of the protagonists, they are as disturbing as any vampire or werewolf.

McEwan has earned an undeserved reputation as a connoisseur of the sordid and perverted outer edges of human behavior, yet his work carries a powerful imaginative charge precisely because it acknowledges and anatomizes what lies beneath the thin skin of civilization and civilized behavior—what, despite our most fervent denials, lies as unrealized potentials inside all of us. That's the true wellspring of horror, and *The Cement Garden*'s pellucid nightmare, which ends with a wakening and an ironic and rhetorical question ("There," she said, "wasn't that a lovely sleep."), is a pure and bracing draft drawn deep from the depths.

PAUL McAULEY (b. 1955) was born in Stroud, Gloucestershire. He received a B.Sc. in botany and zoology from Bristol University in 1976, and went on to get a Ph.D. in botany in 1980. A former research scientist at Oxford University and UCLA and a former lecturer at St. Andrew's University, he became a full-time writer in 1996. He sold a story to *If* when he was just nineteen, but the magazine folded before it could appear, and his first published short story, "Wagon, Passing," appeared in *Asimov's* in 1984. With his debut novel, *Four Hundred Billion Stars,* he became the first British writer to win the prestigious Philip K. Dick Memorial Award, and he established his reputation as one of the best young science fiction writers in the field by winning the John W. Campbell Memorial Award in 1995. His other novels include *Secret Harmonies* (aka *Of the*

Fall), *Eternal Light*, *Red Dust*, *Pasquale's Angel* (winner of the Sidewise Award for Best Long Form Alternate History fiction), the Arthur C. Clarke Award-winning *Fairyland*, *Child of the River*, *Ancients of Days*, *Shrine of Stars*, *Ship of Fools*, *The Secret of Life*, *Whole Wide World*, *Doctor Who: Eye of the Tyger*, *White Devils*, and *Mind's Eye*. McAuley's short fiction is collected in *The King of the Hill and Other Stories*, *The Invisible Country*, and *Little Machines*, while his story "The Temptation of Dr. Stein" was awarded the 1995 British Fantasy Award. *Making History* was a novella from PS Publishing, and he co-edited the 1986 anthology *In Dreams* with Kim Newman.

64

[1978]

JO FLETCHER on

Darkness Weaves with Many Shades
by KARL EDWARD WAGNER

Karl Edward Wagner (1945–94) is remembered at the insightful editor of fifteen volumes of The Year's Best Horror Stories series (DAW Books, 1980–94) and an author of superior horror fiction. While attending medical school, inspired by the sword and sorcery heroes of Fritz Leiber and Robert E. Howard, Wagner set about creating his own fantasy character, the immortal, red-haired, dark-hearted Kane. Darkness Weaves With Many Shades *(1970; revised 1978) was a paperback original from West Coast porn imprint Powell Publications, which introduced numerous changes and typographical errors rooted out in later editions.* Darkness Weaves *set the tone for the series as Kane, the Mystic Swordsman, finds himself involved in the political machinations of a hideous ruler and opponents both human and supernatural. Wagner relinquished his chance to become a doctor and turned to writing full-time.* Death Angel's Shadow *(1973), a collection of three original Kane novellas, was followed by the novels* Bloodstone *(1975) and* Dark Crusade *(1976).* Night Winds *(1978) collects six previously published Kane tales, including the British Fantasy Award-winning "Two Suns Setting." Silver Eel Press published nine Kane verses in* Songs of the Damned *(1981), a thin chapbook limited to three hundred copies; a revised and expanded version was published by the Sidecar Preservation Society as* Red Harvest *(2002). The* Book of Kane *(1985) contains five reprint stories,* Gods in Darkness *(2002) is an omnibus of the three Kane novels, and* Midnight Sun *(2003) collects all the Kane short stories and poetry in one volume. Roger Zelazny narrated two audio volumes of Kane stories in 1993.* In the Wake of the Night, *a proposed fourth Kane novel, was much discussed but never actually written. Karl Edward Wagner wrote on E. H. Visiak's* Medusa *(1929) in* Horror: 100 Best Books, *while Ramsey Campbell contributed an essay on Wagner's collection* In a Lonely Place *(1983) to the same volume.*

> Two centuries: they are as nothing to Kane. Years are only flickering moments to a man who has seen ages roll past him, empires rise and crumble, mankind emerge from infancy, and the elder races crumble into darkness. . . . He is not, as you had supposed, a mere pirate lord who has been kept living past his time by a freak of fate. No, Efrel! Pirate, thief, beggar, king, sorcerer, warrior, scholar, general, poet, assassin—his roles have been myriad. This man who measures centuries like years has been many things in his endless wandering. Kane was one of the first true men.
>
> —from *Darkness Weaves With Many Shades*

In the late 1970s I met Kane, and my life, like the countless numbers who had already encountered this pirate, thief, beggar, king, sorcerer, warrior, scholar, general, poet, assassin, changed. Kane, an assumer of myriad roles, was at that time wandering the Earth in his endless quest for who-knew-what in the guise of Karl Edward Wagner, a giant of a man with flaming Viking-red hair and beard, ice-blue eyes (the "Mark of Kane," I later discovered, although with added twinkle), a fierce intelligence, and a ready wit.

I should perhaps add that at this point I didn't recognize him as Kane: I wasn't, as many of my friends were, a child of the pulps; I had grown up veering wildly between the hard science fiction of Philip K. Dick, Isaac Asimov, and Eric Frank Russell and the high fantasy of Lord Dunsany, George MacDonald, and James Branch Cabell, and the horror I knew was from the hands of Kipling and Poe, Hawthorne and Haggard, all those grimy volumes squirreled away from Girl Guide rummage sales and the dusty junk shops that pervaded my seaside town home.

But I fell in with Wagner, who introduced me to Manly Wade Wellman, and Frances Garfield, and E. Hoffman Price, and Hugh B. Cave, and many others, and the stories told by these vibrant, articulate older people reliving their glory days as pulp writers at a cent a word opened my eyes to a treasure trove awaiting my plundering. That was the first of the ways Kane changed my life: he opened the gates to the wonderful world of pulp fiction, for he was a knowledgeable and avid collector and reader himself.

So my days were filled with stories of musclebound barbarian heroes and beautiful snake sorceresses with hearts harder than the jade that echoed the color of their eyes, and my nights with nightmares of tentacled horrors suppurating in uncharted deeps and unwary neophytes chanting tortured syllables to waken ravenous elder gods . . . and then I moved on to Wagner himself, and read, in quick succession, *Bloodstone*, and *Dark Crusade*, and *Darkness Weaves With Many Shades*.

This was the second way Kane changed my life: now my much-loved and very dear friend, and genial host of so many Chapel Hill and Tennessee and "Dead Dog" gatherings, including my surprise twenty-first-birthday party, was a sorcerer indeed.

At the end of the 1970s there were no shortage of Conan reprints, revisions, and rip-offs, and much as I loved Wagner, I wasn't expecting much more than a better-than-averagely written Conan pastiche. His Bran Mak Morn book *Legion from the Shadows* was fast and furious and terrific fun, and his Conan novel *The Road of Kings* darker and more intense than its predecessors, but he was working with someone else's characters. With Kane, Wagner found his own voice and, en route, not only revitalized the moribund genre of sword and sorcery, but also at the same time started his own journey into horror with characters like Efrel, the once-beautiful sorceress twisted and flayed into an unrecognizable obscenity after being tied to a maddened bull and dragged through the city—her punishment for betraying her emperor husband with his own brother and trying to steal his empire. But Wagner was never content with linear characters or plots: in *Darkness Weaves* Efrel, herself a rare monstrosity and without doubt providing quite enough evil in one story for most writers, calls up even more unpleasant supernatural help in the guise of the Scylredi, an ancient and unspeakably noisome race armed with alien technologies, and the Oraycha, deep-ocean-dwelling monsters that owe a passing wave to H. P. Lovecraft's own Cthulhu Mythos. Kane is hired to lead Efrel's rebellion against her erstwhile husband, Netisten Maril, king of Thovnos, to repay him for ruining her body and her life, but she has plans for Kane, too, once he has handed over to her Maril's empire, his beauteous daughter M'Cori, and Maril himself. Efrel's vengeance has been long in the planning, and it is going to be neither quick nor easy. Kane himself has his own plans for all of the above . . . but this is a Wagner story, and that means nothing is ever going to be quite as simple as it might appear at the beginning.

Though Wagner may have been playing with by now familiar tropes, both in heroic fantasy and Gothic fantasy archetypes, his intelligence, introspection and dark humor make him stand out from his contemporaries, not least thanks to the many intriguing secondary characters, such as the assassin Arbas in *Darkness Weaves*, with whom he peoples his tales. And that was the third way Kane changed my life: *Darkness Weaves* was the start of my own journey into modern horror.

There is a fourth way, too: Wagner was not just an extraordinary writer in his own right, but also was a seeker and nurturer of talent, the likes of whom are too seldom seen. Many of today's big names got a helping hand, a first start, or a leg up thanks to the selfless efforts of Karl Edward Wagner, who would search out the cheapest and smallest mimeographed fanzines searching for contributions to his *Year's Best Horror Stories* series, which he edited for DAW Books. It redefined the horror genre and showed readers that great horror writing could be found in the most unlikely places.

Karl Edward Wagner was a prolific novelist in the first years after he gave up his psychiatric training to be a full-time writer, but illness and depression took their toll too soon and we have been robbed of the many extraordinary tales that were waiting to be set free from his always fertile mind. I at least was one of the few who have the memories of many late-night sessions passing the jack and listening to Wagner revealing more about his previous lives as a pirate, thief, beggar, king, sorcerer, warrior, scholar, general, poet, assassin. And wherever he is now, you can be sure he's raising hell and living the legend to the full.

> **JO FLETCHER** (b. 1958) is a poet, writer, critic, journalist, and publisher. She won the International Society of Poets' Editors' Choice Award in 1996, the British Fantasy Society's Karl Edward Wagner Award in 1997, and the World Fantasy Award in 2002. She has been published widely, and her work has appeared in, among other titles, *The Mammoth Book of Werewolves, The Mammoth Book of Frankenstein, The Mammoth Book of Dracula, Now We Are Sick, The Tiger Garden: A Book of Writers' Dreams, Dark of the Night, White of the Moon, Freaks Geeks and Sideshow Floozies, Cthulhu and the CoEds, Short Trips: A Christmas Treasury* and *Daughter of Dangerous Dames*. As "featured poet" she

contributed a zodiac cycle to the *Urbanite* magazine. She has edited a number of anthologies, including *Gaslight & Ghosts* and *Secret City: Strange Tales of London* (both with Stephen Jones), and the mosaic children's novel *Horror at Halloween*. Her first poetry collection, *Shadows of Light and Dark*, was short-listed for the British Fantasy Award. Non-fiction has included *The World's Greatest Mysteries* and a number of military and historical works. In 1985 she joined the fledgling independent publishing company Headline and masterminded the launch of Headline's fantasy, SF, and horror list, introducing award-winning writers like Dan Simmons, Michael Bishop, and Charles L. Grant's acclaimed horror anthology series *Shadows* to the United Kingdom. She left Headline in 1988 and worked for Mandarin (1988–90), then moved to Pan to run the newly revitalized genre list. She is currently editorial director of Gollancz, which she took over in 1994.

65

[1979]

SIR CHRISTOPHER FRAYLING on

The Bloody Chamber and Other Stories
by ANGELA CARTER

The Bloody Chamber and Other Stories *is a collection of Gothic short stories, reworkings of traditional fairy tales for modern readers—from "Beauty and the Beast," "Little Red Riding Hood," and "Puss in Boots" to legends of the vampire and the werewolf. In each story the traditional* "moral" is challenged—as is the tyranny of good taste—and the lion learns to lie down with the lamb (or, sometimes, vice versa). Angela Carter (1940–92) deliberately sets out to subvert the homogenized, Disneyfied, consolatory version of fairy tales that dominate the market today and to bring some of the nastiness back. Earlier drafts of some of the stories appeared in Vogue, Bananas, the Iowa Reader, South West Arts Review, *and Emma Tennant's anthology* The Straw and the Gold *(1979). With writer-director Neil Jordan, Carter elaborated two of the stories, "The Werewolf" and "The Company of Wolves," into the script for the film* The Company of Wolves (1984).

IN THE EARLY summer of 1976—which happened to be the five-hundredth anniversary of the death of Vlad the Impaler—I visited the Carpathian Mountains in Romania, with notebook and camera on the backseat of a Dacia 13, known to the rest of the world as a Renault 12, to unearth some visual and historical material on vampires for a study I was preparing on "the vampyre" in literature.

At the same time, my good friend the novelist Angela Carter was beginning to prepare her BBC radio play *Vampirella*, which subsequently became the magical short story "The Lady of the House of Love" in her collection of reworked fairy tales *The Bloody Chamber*. Angela's story was very loosely based on my escapade, and it grew out of the many midnight conversations we had at that time about the tainted bloodline of the literary Count Dracula; also about Sawney Beane the Midlothian cannibal and amateur anarchist, a particularly choice specimen whose favorite meal was roast leg of justice of the peace, which (we fantasized) was consumed to the sound of bagpipes in a cave near Edinburgh.

In both play and story, the central character is a dashing young *Boys Own* paper chap called Hero, who decides to go on a tour of the land beyond the forest on his bicycle. Hero is rather naïve and overly enthusiastic (thanks, Angie), has studied the good old English tradition of literature at university, looks as though he has "the head of a lion," and believes that words are facts—always a mistake in Angela

Carter's world. Indeed, when confronted with the delectable vampire countess in her dark glasses—and in her glittering castle, school of Cocteau's *La Belle et la Bête*—the strapping Hero tries to reassure himself by clinging onto the world of facts:

> Soon it will be morning; the crowing of the mundane cock and the first light will dissolve this gothic dream with the solvent of the natural. Yes, perhaps I shall take her to Vienna; and we shall chip off her fingernails and take her to a good dentist, to deal with her fangs. Perhaps, perhaps . . . one day, when she is cured . . . mother, I want you to meet . . . There are some things that, even if they are true, we must not believe them.

In the end, what protects Hero from the vampire countess are not the traditional weapons of religion—holy water and the crucifix—or even of folklore and the old religion—garlic and a wooden stake—but the fact that he has been brought up to repress his imagination, and he simply doesn't recognize a bloodsucker when she is standing right in front of him. Desire is best coped with by "blessing the cold showers of my celibacy." He hopes to cure her by the innocence of his kiss, like in *Sleeping Beauty*. This lack of a Gothic imagination gives heroism to the hero (thanks again, Angie!). Then off he goes to die—this being 1914—in a war that turned out to be more ghastly by far than any superstitious imaginings. "Next day," as the story version briskly concludes, "his regiment embarked for France."

I can still remember talking to Angela about the effects of World War I on the borders of the land of Nosferatu, and about *haematodipsomania*—my word for the pathological thirst for blood; like alcoholism only much, much worse. And, more generally, about whether human relationships must always be about asset-stripping.

The Bloody Chamber and Other Stories is Angela Carter's cabinet of fairy tales, or folktales, reinterpreted with sympathy, wonder, and excess as well as with cynicism for a late-twentieth-century audience. These short stories are about lions and lambs, carnivores and herbivores, desire and anxiety, romance and bawdy humor—and they are variations on the theme of the lion and the lamb reaching some kind of mutual understanding rather than the one always tearing the other to pieces. On the whole, the lamb is expected to join the lion's side. They are also a challenge to traditional myths about the role of women—and what used in those days to be called "the battle of the sexes."

So in "The Tiger's Bride," one of the stories, the virginal heroine discovers that she, too, is an animal and all the better for that. In the three wolf stories—"The Werewolf," "The Company of Wolves," and "Wolf-Alice"—the little girl discovers, in different ways, that she is "meat for no one," she takes control by refusing to be frightened, and she learns that there is much more to life than "eat or be eaten"; also, that being a victim is not much fun. She comes in the process to a particularly useful realization: that some wolves are hairy on the inside.

In the title story, Bluebeard meets his match in the form of the heroine's formidable mother, who has spent time shooting man-eating tigers in Indochina. And in "The Courtship of Mr. Lyon," the beast is transformed into a herbivorous human being by the power of mutual love, which conquers stereotyping and aggression.

As Margaret Atwood has wittily noted, these stories are organized by categories of meat-eater—from cats ("sleepily cruel by nature") via woodland spirits and vampires to wolves ("fearful of gift rather than plunder"). Nosferatu meets *La Belle et la Bête* in finely worked prose that combines extravagant, sometimes nasty fantasies, seductive forests, gorgeous images, Gothic tracery, and carnival jokes.

In *The Bloody Chamber*, Angela Carter is reacting against what she called "the tyranny of good taste," and against the modern tendency to treat fairy tales as nothing more than "consolatory nonsense." For her, these tales carry important truths about everyday life. They are also, she later wrote, "the most vital connection we have with the imagination of ordinary men and women whose labour created our world." *The Bloody Chamber and Other Stories* renews an age-old tradition and is now recognized—as it should have been since the late 1970s—as a contemporary classic of horror fiction.

SIR CHRISTOPHER FRAYLING (b. 1946) was born on Christmas Day, which lore at least as ancient as Hammer's *The Curse of the Werewolf* (1961) suggests leads to lycanthropy. Author, broadcaster, academic, and arts administrator, he has written sixteen books, among them *Vampyres: Lord Byron to Count Dracula*, *The Face of Tutankhamun*, and *Strange Landscape and Nightmare: The Birth of Horror* (all three made into BBC television series), *Spaghetti Westerns, Clint Eastwood and Sergio Leone: Something to Do With Death*, *Ken Adam: The Art of Production Design*, and *Mad, Bad, and Dangerous?: Images of the Scientist in the Movies*. His broadcast credits include the Channel 4 television series *The Art of Persuasion* (winner of the Gold Medal at the New York Film and TV Festival) and *Busting the Block*, plus the BBC Radio series *America: The Movie, Britannia: The Film, Print the Legend, How the West Was Shot*, and *Cinema Cities*. Frayling is rector of London's Royal College of Art and professor of cultural history there, as well as being chairman of Arts Council England and the longest-serving trustee of the Victoria and Albert Museum. He has several honorary doctorates and fellowships, and lists his recreation in *Who's Who* as "finding time."

66 [1979]

THOMAS LIGOTTI on

Sweeney Todd
by STEPHEN SONDHEIM and HUGH WHEELER

Whether a barber named Sweeney Todd ever kept shop on London's Fleet Street, murdering customers for money and turning corpses over to the widow next door as material for her pie shop, is impossible at this date to discern. It seems likely that the tales scramble stories of the Scots cannibal Sawney Beane. Todd became famous in the nineteenth century thanks to George Dibdin Pitt's play The String of Pearls; or the Fiend of Fleet Street *(1847) and a penny dreadful probably written by Thomas Pecket Prest,* The String of Pearls; or the Sailor's Gift *(1846–47). The barber didn't become the title character until 1862, when Frederick Hazleton wrote (then novelized) a play,* Sweeney Todd, the Barber of Fleet Street; or the String of Pearls. *The story was a warhorse of repertory theater for a hundred years, and the most notable stage Sweeney was Tod Slaughter, who also "polished them off" in a 1936 film. The musical, with music and lyrics by Stephen Sondheim and book by Hugh Wheeler (who also adapted Shirley Jackson's* We Have Always Lived in the Castle *as a play), is based closely on a 1974 play by Christopher Bond that reimagines the story, adding revenge and social injustice themes from Tourneur's* The Revenger's Tragedy *and Dumas'* The Count of Monte Cristo. *The Broadway and London productions were led by Len Cariou and Angela Lansbury (who are on the original cast album) and Denis Quilley and Sheila Hancock; George Hearn, Cariou's replacement, partners Lansbury in a 1984 TV record of the show issued on DVD and also takes the lead in a recent* Sweeney Todd *in concert performance, also available on disc. The musical is often revived—very successfully in London at Sadler's*

Wells in 2003. *The script was published in 1991 by Nick Hern Books, with useful introductory material by Craig Zadan, Robert Kimball, and Christopher Bond.*

> Every normal man must be tempted at times to spit upon his hands, hoist the black flag, and begin slitting throats.
> —H. L. Mencken

PEOPLE, FOR LACK of a better term, see things in different ways. If this were not so, we would all be living in harmony with one another, which never has been and never will be the case. Actually, universal harmony, which is a mere metaphor, would not eliminate differences, which can mean anything from a good-natured divergence of opinion to dreams of genocide. To put things truly right, to make a world truly just, assonance itself would need to dissolve into a single pitch sung by a multitude of voices—an impossible unison outside of heaven or a fairy tale. So we fall back into harmony, because without harmony, there can be no music, no singing, no anything. Harmony is difference. At its extreme, it is dissonance. Our common crime on this earth is that we prefer difference to unity, dissonance to monotony. ("For what's the sound of the world out there? . . . It's man devouring man, my dear.") To claim otherwise is a lie and a sham. We do not love oneness and cannot abide sameness, let alone endure the ultimate redemption of eternal silence. What we want—the sound of what we embrace—is the screech that cuts the air and signals the opening to Stephen Sondheim (b. 1930) and Hugh Wheeler's (1912–87) melotragic telling of the Demon Barber of Fleet Street.

If it were not for tragedy, the human race would have become bored into extinction long ago. No one knows this better than the entertainers among us, who could not sell a book or a song or a seat in a theater without drawing upon the screams and tears arising out of that primal pit of twisting shadows from which every life emerges and to which every life returns. Thus each action and consequence in Sondheim and Wheeler's *Sweeney Todd* flows out of, and feeds into, the tragic. It is the groaning pedal tone over which everything else—for instance, beauty and love—serves as fleeting grace notes that only *seem* to suggest the existence of something other than the tragic, yet are actually part of the piece as much as the grossest monstrosity that stalks the stage. And tragedy *(Oedipus, Hamlet, Long Day's Journey into Night)* begins at home.

"There was a barber and his wife." Like every horror that has wormed its way from the muck of the organic, *Sweeney Todd* begins with a desired union that spreads its seed by the blood of progeny ("Wake up, Johanna, it's another bright red day"). This reproduction, however, only promises to perpetuate the pain when one offspring meets another. "I feel you, Johanna," sings Anthony to his beloved, who together compose another innocent and inane couple whose purpose is to provide a ray of "hope" into the mayhem of the drama. However, to anyone who has been paying attention, this new Adam and Eve are only being readied for the meat grinder of their future life, just as were a barber named Benjamin Barker and his wife, Lucy. It is only when Benjamin and Lucy have been dragged through the inferno of their lives that they are fit to sate our hunger for tragedy. They are positioned within the innermost circle of hell, while Mrs. Lovett, Judge Turpin, Toby, and others radiate concentrically about them with their own fateful cravings (for beauty and love, of course), pushing them closer to the barber's blade and the fire-belching oven.

Ultimately all of us end up as filling for one of Mrs. Lovett's meat pies. In the purported last words of Thomas Lovell Beddoes, the poet and physician called himself "food for what I am good for—worms." While worms do not get to feast on many of us in modernized nations, the point of our essential ignobility still resonates. That anyone cares about nobility or dignity or any of those other traps we set for ourselves is part of the whole sloppy mess of our lives. This is where tragedy performs a crucial function for us by providing us with grandeur and style, qualities of the theatrical world and not the everyday one. This is why we are thrilled with the horror of Sweeney Todd and envy, if only as gawking spectators, the qualities he possesses and we lack. He is as illuminated as any sage when he declares that we all deserve to die, given the fact that none of us can unmake the tragedy of our birth. He has a sense of purpose that few who are made of flesh and blood rather than of music and poetry will ever know ("But the work waits/I'm alive at last/And I'm full of joy"). Most of all, he has the courage and bravado to do what he knows needs to be done. "To seek revenge may lead to hell," he says, to which Mrs. Lovett answers, "But everyone does it and seldom as well . . . as Sweee-ney." Since harmony and unity are beyond our talents, we might as well admit universal villainy as the lot of our species and get to work. Alas, hardly any of us has the gifts required for this duty. And those among us who are so gifted are precisely the ones, in my opinion, who would be most justly seated in the barber's chair. Ah, how the mind dreams of those righteous throats.

Reading these words, some might suspect that their writer is leaning toward derangement himself. To that charge I cannot honestly give an answer. Nevertheless—you, sir, how about a shave?

THOMAS [ROBERT] LIGOTTI (b. 1953) was born in Detroit and currently lives in Florida. After training as a teaching assistant, he took a series of editorial jobs at Gale Research Company before going freelance. Ligotti's horror fiction has been critically praised for its richly evocative prose style and its ability to suggest the nightmarish essence of existence itself, and his first collection of short stories, *Songs of a Dead Dreamer,* was published in 1986 with an introduction by Ramsey Campbell. He followed it with the World Fantasy Award-nominated *Grimscribe: His Lives and Works, Noctuary, The Agonizing Resurrection of Victor Frankenstein and Other Gothic Tales, In a Foreign Land in a Foreign Town, I Have a Special Plan for This World, This Degenerate Little Town,* the International Horror Guild and Bram Stoker Award-winning *My Work is Not Yet Done, Sideshow and Other Stories,* and *Death Poems.* His 1996 retrospective collection *The Nightmare Factory* featured an introduction by Poppy Z. Brite and won the Bram Stoker Award and the British Fantasy Award, as well as being a World Fantasy Award finalist. *Crampton: A Screenplay* was co-written with Brandon Trenz, while *The Unholy City* included a CD featuring voice and music by the author. *The Thomas Ligotti Reader*, edited by Darrell Schweitzer, was published by Wildside Press in 2003. Ligotti has also won the Bram Stoker Award for superior achievement in novella, and the Small Press Writers and Artists Organization (SPWAO) Award for best author of horror/weird fiction.

67 [1980]

D. F. LEWIS on

The Collected Stories of Elizabeth Bowen
by ELIZABETH BOWEN

The Irish authoress Elizabeth Bowen (1899–1973) turned out a great many eerie or ghostly tales between mainstream novels of haut bourgeois *middle age, like* The Last September *(1929),* The House in Paris *(1939), and* The Heat of the Day *(1949).* Collected Stories, *first published in the United Kingdom by Jonathan Cape in 1980, assembles stories written between 1923 and 1956 and draws on several earlier collections, notably* The Cat Jumps and Other Stories *(1934) and* The Demon Lover and Other Stories *(1945, aka* Ivy Gripped the Steps and Other Stories*). (She is not to be confused with Marjorie Bowen, whose* The Last Bouquet *(1932) was the subject of an essay by Jessica Amanda Salmonson in* Horror: 100 Best Books.*) Elizabeth Bowen wrote a handful of stories that remain staples of ghost anthologies. Although*

67 : BOWEN

her mainstream novels have occasionally been adapted as classy vehicles for the likes of Patricia Hodge, Maggie Smith, and Michael Gambon, her ghostlier works have been overlooked by television and the movies, though Peter Hammond directed an hour-long version of "The Demon Lover" retitled The Dream Lover *(1986) with Adrienne Corri, Hugh Grant, Robert Hardy, and Miranda Richardson.*

> Ivy gripped and sucked at the flight of steps, down which with such a deceptive wildness it seemed to be flowing.
> —from "Ivy Gripped the Steps"

Her stories and novels are all that one needs; because knowing about Elizabeth Bowen as a person may well undermine what they give you. However, to satisfy the curious, she was born in Dublin, traveled a lot, and lived at various times in Ireland and England (particularly London). She wrote fiction about her sort of higher social class people and the contemporary historical events that surrounded them.

Let's get to the point. Elizabeth Bowen is my favorite writer of all time. Many have been surprised at this, when I have enunciated the fact in many places over the years. A lot of well-read people have never heard of her; she is usually ignored by those in the world of English literature, where she often finds her place. I claim that her work more naturally resides in the horror genre of fiction and that her huge volume of *Collected Stories*—containing seventy-nine stories published in various separate collections from the 1920s to the '50s—is a seminal work of this genre.

Each story needs special care and attention to wring out the horror and, once wrung out, lodges in the mind and haunts you most effectively—not always wrung-out horror, but often delightfully in your face. The language itself sets traps and surprises you with unexpected turnings of structure and meaning, giving a ivy-like grip upon the reading mind, insinuating within you and fortifying the concentration required to open the prose's dark charms. The stories consistently have this special tentacular power in style and subject matter, teetering on the edge of a subtly surreal and/or fragmented world, a world that is contrastively generated by her high social (and sometimes more mundane) world of events—comprising, typically, tales of childhood and evocative depictions of the London Blitz era.

One has to *infer* ghosts; otherwise many of the stories' plots wouldn't make sense. Some have real ghosts without the need for inference, as in "The Demon Lover." There is also a visionary strength similar to Arthur Machen, as in "Mysterious Kôr." The one titled "Love" has the puckish absurdism but enduring nightmarishness of Robert Aickman. "The Cat Jumps" horrifies me beyond words. "The Apple Tree" applies falling apples—*thump thump* . . . equally horrifying.

The streets of lonely seaside towns. The opening of a silver cigarette case, the match flaring. The characters with inexplicable (or gratuitous) motives: for instance, climbing into a stranger's car, or spurning the one they love as bombs rain down like spilled hot jam. London's World War II is made to appear paradoxically more real by giving it an unreal veneer—as if that sort of history (one only witnessed in monochrome newsreels) is simply waiting to be brought back to life with some instinctive flourish of the fictional art. And fiction, at its best, disfigures as well as reflects. We are ever in a nightmare of angst. Life without disfigurement would lack humor as well as credibility; it can only be brought truly to life with ominous imagination.

Elizabeth Bowen's imagination is ominous, leaning out to grab you back before even *you* know that you are about to fall down the flight of ivied steps she has just created. But will she lean far enough? Elizabeth Bowen (as I infer) didn't understand her own powers; she is a conduit for a creative force that yearns to bring to life the figments and fragments of our recent history with the added ingredient of alternately subtle and blatant elements of supernature. Her many fine novels often demonstrate these features, too.

In the end, one has to return to the language, the incredibly rich texture of the prose, the syntactic/semantic traps—because these elements, above all, are where the previously mentioned "conduit" resides. One cannot do justice to all these stories, written along different threads of subject matter and in different strengths of horror as they are. They do contain, in varying degrees, the fissured soul of someone who was Elizabeth Bowen or, equally, someone who was not Elizabeth Bowen. The stories do carry her label, however. I return to her work at all times. Peter Ackroyd compares her to a hybrid of Saki and Edgar Allan Poe. I compare her to Charles Dickens, Marcel Proust, Ivy Compton-Burnett, Walter De La Mare. She is, in fact, a major figure in the universal reservoir of creative fiction that underpins and is underpinned by our beloved horror fiction, a genre that rightly comprises all manner of styles and methods to create that horror.

D. (DES) F. LEWIS (b. 1948) was born in 1948 in Essex, England. He qualified for a B.A. degree from Lancaster University in 1969, and worked for an insurance company from 1970 to 1992 while living in Croydon, Surrey. He has now returned to live by the North Sea coast near Walton-on-Naze with his wife of thirty-five years. Creatively influenced by a nontechnical enjoyment of classical music, Lewis had approximately fifteen hundred surreal and idiosyncratic stories published from 1986 to 2000, many of which appeared in hard-to-find small press outlets, plus literary journals and professional book anthologies. The latter includes three volumes of the *Best New Horror* series edited by Stephen Jones and five volumes of the *Year's Best Horror Stories* edited by Karl Edward Wagner. Other anthologies Lewis has contributed to include *Shadows Over Innsmouth, Horror of the Next Millennium, Signals, Cthulhu's Heirs, Touch Wood,* and *The Ultimate Zombie.* Sixty-seven of his stories were recently collected in *Weirdmonger* from Prime Books, and he is currently the editor/publisher of the acclaimed series of *Nemonymous* anthologies. He received the British Fantasy Society's special Karl Edward Wagner Award in 1998.

68 [1980]

CHRISTOPHER GOLDEN on

Dark Forces:
New Stories of Suspense and Supernatural Horror
Edited by KIRBY McCAULEY

Kirby McCauley (b. 1941) made an underappreciated but significant contribution to horror as a New York literary agent, representing Stephen King and Peter Straub early in their careers and also less best-selling but equally major writers like Ramsey Campbell, Dennis Etchison, and Karl Edward Wagner. A devotee of horror from his early teens and an avowed disciple of August Derleth, McCauley edited the original anthologies Night Chills *(1975),* Beyond Midnight *(1976), and the World Fantasy Award-winning* Frights: New Stories of Suspense and Supernatural Terror *(1977). These were well received enough to convince Anthony Cheetham, then an editor at Futura in the United Kingdom, that McCauley was the man to put together something more ambitious; vowing to do for the horror field that was undergoing a metastasis in the late 1970s what Harlan Ellison's* Dangerous Visions *(1967) had done for science fiction—namely, get new stories from established greats that showed they were still abreast of current developments in the field, showcase the works of names that were only just becoming major presences on the weird shelf, and introduce newcomers who would proceed to amass considerable bodies of work. Containing twenty-three original stories by authors on McCauley's client list,* Dark Forces: New Stories of Suspense and Supernatural Horror *won a World Fantasy Award, a Balrog Award, and was voted thirteenth best anthology of all time in a 1999* Locus *magazine poll.*

I was thirteen years old when editor Kirby McCauley presented the world with the gift of *Dark Forces*, widely regarded as the most influential horror anthology of its era, and doubtless among the most important such collections of all time. Words like "quintessential" and "seminal" are bandied about until they lose their power. *Dark Forces*, and the stories inside, have never suffered the same fate.

Thirteen—the perfect age, I think, for discovery. By that time I had read most of Stephen King's early works, but that was the sum of my knowledge of "modern" horror fiction. Soon enough I would discover a vast array of books and authors I still recall today, some of whose stories are capable of making me uneasy even as mere memories. I would devour those writers. On the beach during misspent summers and during recess at my Catholic school, I would devour all I could find of what the early 1980s had to offer. I was fortunate to come of age during what I still believe to be the most creatively fertile time in the genre's history.

My first exposure to many of the authors who would make such an impression on me came courtesy of Charles L. Grant, editor of numerous anthologies, most notably the long-lived *Shadows* series. It may seem oddly tangential to discuss *Dark Forces* by talking about Charlie Grant, but you can't really separate the two. Though McCauley and Grant were working on volumes of horror fiction simultaneously, Grant would go on to become the seeming patriarch of a generation of horror writers due to his reputation as a cultivator of talent and his mission to bring fresh, intelligent modern horror stories to the reading public.

But if Charles L. Grant was on a mission, Kirby McCauley's *Dark Forces* is the mission statement.

Prior to 1980, horror fiction had been gathering steam, garnering more and more attention. Stephen King and Peter Straub had already published massively influential novels, emerging as the Young Turks in a genre dominated by writers such as Richard Matheson, Ray Bradbury, and Charles Beaumont, whose specialty was not simply horror, but stories of the fantastic that defied the boundaries publishers would later place on genre fiction.

Dark Forces represented a bridge of sorts from one generation to the next, and the beginning of an era where the idea of being a "horror writer" was brand new. The anthology approached horror as literature with a sturdy defiance, McCauley recruiting Isaac Bashevis Singer and Joyce Carol Oates, among others, to contribute unsettling tales. Within those pages I discovered Bradbury and Matheson, Robert Bloch and Theodore Sturgeon, Davis Grubb and Manly Wade Wellman, masters of the form who had been writing since before I was born, in some cases, long before. Yet also within those pages were tales by the "new wave" of writers of the fantastic, including Stephen King, Ramsey Campbell, Dennis Etchison, Lisa Tuttle, Edward Bryant, T. E. D. Klein, and Charles L. Grant.

Dark Forces was a bridge, and perhaps there is no better example than "Where There's a Will," a gut punch of a story about unwelcome resurrection by Richard Matheson and his son, Richard Christian Matheson.

The anthology is perhaps best remembered by most readers as the book in which King's story "The Mist" first appeared, and if that had been where the book ended, it would already have been a landmark. "The Mist" took up 130 pages of *Dark Forces,* and it is prime Stephen King, an absolutely essential read, and still one of my favorites. The story of a government facility whose experiments tear a hole into another reality, unleashing an unearthly mist and all manner of monstrosities, has been on director Frank Darabont's wish list to translate to celluloid since long before he found success in Hollywood. The ugly microcosm of humanity that finds temporary sanctuary in a local supermarket provides the intimacy and character work that had already become King's hallmark and that other writers have been attempting to replicate for a quarter century.

Yet "The Mist" is, as noted, only the beginning of *Dark Forces.* Each story is a gem, from Etchison's cheap zombie labor in "The Late Shift" to Gene Wolfe's fascinating "The Detective of Dreams."

But I find that the ones that really got under my skin then, that filled my head with images and ideas I simply couldn't shake, are the same ones remaining with me today. A quarter century has passed, and so many of the stories in *Dark Forces* are fresh in my mind even now. It is rare to find a single story with such resonance, but a book full of them?

Edward Bryant's "Dark Angel" is brutal and shocking, laying bare human fragility in one of the finest, most affecting tales of vengeance I have ever read. Joyce Carol Oates's "The Bingo Master" is a story of loneliness worthy of Shirley Jackson. Gahan Wilson's insidiously absurd short short "Traps" was my first exposure to an absolute master, known to so many only from his extraordinary career as a cartoonist but equally talented in prose. Charles L. Grant's "A Garden of Blackred Roses" remains with me to this day, particularly its final image, and the atmosphere of utter damnation in every line.

Most of all, however, the images from T. E. D. Klein's "Children of the Kingdom" linger. Klein, legendary editor of *Twilight Zone* magazine, is rarely heard from today, but he was on a roll during the early 1980s. This was one of a handful of remarkable stories he produced in that period, and its sense of hidden history, the quiet menace of every scene, and the vividness of the elderly characters, make it unforgettable.

A bridge, a mission statement, the quintessential collection of horror stories from the 1980s, *Dark Forces* is one of horror's finest moments, a landmark that seems even more remarkable today than it did twenty-five years ago.

CHRISTOPHER GOLDEN (b. 1967) was born and raised in Massachusetts, where he still lives with his wife and three children. After twelve years in Catholic school, he attended Tufts University, graduating with honors. His first book was as editor of the non-fiction study *Cut! Horror Writers on Horror Film* (1992), which won the Bram Stoker Award. Golden is the author of such novels as *Of Saints and Shadows, Strangewood, The Ferryman, Straight on 'Til Morning, The Boys Are Back in Town, Wildwood Road*, the *Prowlers* series, *The Veil* trilogy, and the *Body of Evidence* series of teen thrillers (several co-written with Rick Hautala). Working with actress/writer/director Amber Benson, he co-created and co-wrote *Ghosts of Albion*, an animated supernatural drama for BBC Online that is now a book series from Del Rey. With Thomas E. Sniegoski he is the co-author of the dark fantasy series *The Menagerie* as well as the young-adult fantasy series *OutCast*. Golden and Sniegoski also wrote the graphic novel *BPRD: Hollow Earth*, a spin-off from the fan favorite comic book series *Hellboy*. Golden has authored the original *Hellboy* novels, *The Lost Army* and *The Bones of Giants*, and edited two *Hellboy* anthologies. He has also written or co-written (many with Nancy Holder) numerous novels, non-fiction guides, video games, and comic books set in the world of *Buffy the Vampire Slayer*. His other media tie-ins include *X-Men*, *Daredevil*, and *Justice League*, along with the novelization of *King Kong* (2005). There are more than eight million copies of his books in print.

69

[1981]

JOHN BURKE on

Tales from the Nightside
by CHARLES L. GRANT

Published by Arkham House with a dust-jacket painting by Michael Whelan, Tales from the Nightside *collects fifteen stories by Charles L. Grant (b. 1942), who, at that time, was emerging as the leading proponent for "quiet horror." With a foreword by Stephen King and interior illustrations by Andrew Smith, several stories in the book were originally published in* The Magazine of Fantasy & Science Fiction, Midnight Sun, *and the* Year's Best Horror Stories. *Charles L. Grant wrote on Bernard Taylor's* Sweetheart, Sweetheart *in* Horror: 100 Best Books, *while Guy N. Smith covered Grant's novel* The Pet *in the same volume.*

IN HIS FOREWORD to this collection of short stories, Stephen King rightly emphasizes that "None of them takes place on distant planets, none of them takes place in any environment more exotic than suburban England. Most of them could have happened two streets over and one block down from where you yourself live."

To me this is a more effective way of writing really macabre tales than by piling on the gore and sadistic torture. The author himself speaks of "those shadows over in the corner that do not quite resolve themselves into objects familiar."

With evocative illustrations by Andrew Smith, this volume contains some of the finest examples of what I like to call "Tales of Unease" rather than blatant horror stories. They are full of sinister whispers rather than repetitive screams. Even coming to them for the third or fourth time over several years, I still get the frisson provoked by subtle, disturbing suggestiveness that leaves an uneasy bewilderment at the end but that can unexpectedly erupt into stark terror.

The book is divided into three sections. "Tales from Oxrun Station" encompasses five stories set in a small New England township bedeviled by strange forces that rarely show their shapes or purposes but that are all the more disquieting for that. In "Coin of the Realm," a man in a routine job, collecting money at a highway toll office, begins to find that strange coins are showing up in his takings. Previous employees have walked off the job or simply disappeared without explanation. It all seems so drab and ordinary, a boring way of earning a living in a place hardly worth living in, until he, too, decides to get out, and drives off along the highway, only to find himself saddled with one of those coins with a strange, symbolic head on it. The last two lines of dialogue in the story deliver a ghastly blow for which nothing in the earlier development has prepared the reader.

The other four stories in this section take us through the revenge of a boy whose supposed fear of darkness turns into an unexpected strength; the puzzling sight of an eccentric old man who sets up garden swings for children who are not there; a domestic clash between parents and child that might seem like a contemporary TV situation drama but that leads us in a darker direction; and what, yet again, might seem a predictable situation, this time a séance about which we are as skeptical as the journalist sent to report on it . . . until the time comes to leave.

Always with Grant there is a distortion of things familiar, as if, walking along your own street toward your own cozy home, you are tripped by a loose paving stone and thrown sideways into another dimension; or disorientated by a swirling fog. Grant is much preoccupied by fog, shadows, and dreams.

By the end of these experiences you can feel sure of only one thing: you're lucky not to be living in Oxrun Station.

Yet are the "Tales from Hawthorne Street" going to be any more comforting?

In fact, we are still in a world where everyday situations are gradually contaminated by a sly menace that has been lying in wait all along, biding its time. We are told that on Hawthorne Street "all families were neighbors and all children friends," but then it emerges that just one house has a reputation for being "unlucky." We soon realize that it's the neighbors who are unlucky.

In "Something There Is," a tired schoolmaster longs for a dream to start so that it he can find in it the Muse who has so far eluded him. I once wrote a story in which a dream beckoned more alluringly than everyday routine, and I'm wondering whether it was provoked by some half-forgotten experience of a kind that this author, too, might have gone through. There are places I still visit in dreams that bear only a fleeting resemblance to anywhere in the real world. But what is *real*? Sometimes when I wake I'm not sure I'm really awake, and have to make a great effort to avoid being dragged back into those unidentifiable places. Charles Grant is skilled at nudging you just over the edge in either direction.

The final section of the book, called "Tales from the Nightside," contains a miscellany of six unrelated stories, of which the most horrific is set in England, with an ending that needs to be brooded over . . . if you are really hungry for a foul, lasting nightmare.

So many scenes in this book are so eerily close to my own experiences that I find it hard to believe that other readers will not feel the same kinship, the same fear of normality becoming not so much abnormal as a different, more perverse normality.

All right, Mr. Grant, in every story you have been way ahead of me. But I don't want to look over my shoulder to glimpse what the hell is behind me.

The last, innocent-sounding line in the whole book is "'Daddy's home,' the boy whispered. 'You said you wanted to meet him.'"

Frightening or not frightening? That depends on how intently you have been following the preceding narrative.

JOHN BURKE (b. 1922) was born in Rye, Sussex, and now lives with his wife in Kirkcudbright, Scotland. Brought up in Liverpool, where his father was a chief inspector of police, he became an early member of the Liverpool branch of the Science Fiction Association and founded an early fanzine, the *Satellite*, which for a brief period became the official journal of the SFA. Following World War II he worked in publishing as production manager for Museum Press and editorial manager of Paul Hamlyn Books for Pleasure Group, while in the 1960s he was European story editor for Twentieth Century Fox Productions. Burke's first novel, *Swift Summer* (1949), won an Atlantic Award in Literature from the Rockefeller Foundation. He has since published numerous books in all genres under a bewildering array of pseudonyms. He edited three volumes of *Tales of Unease* for Pan paperbacks and was story editor on the television series of that name and on *The Frighteners*. Author of the "Dr. Caspian" trilogy and "The Laird and the Law" series, his numerous film and TV novelizations include such titles as *Dr. Terror's House of Horrors, The Hammer Horror Omnibus, The Second Hammer Horror Omnibus, Moon Zero Two,* and the Beatles tie-in *A Hard Day's Night*. A chapter on his original screenplay for the Michael Reeves film *The Sorcerers* appears in Benjamin Halligan's study of the British filmmaker, published by Manchester University Press in 2003.

70 [1981]

YVONNE NAVARRO on

They Thirst
by ROBERT R. McCAMMON

Acclaimed as the "War and Peace *of vampire novels,*" They Thirst *was the fourth novel—and first epic—from Robert R. McCammon (b. 1952). In* Horror: 100 Best Books, *McCammon wrote about Walter van Tilburg Clark's* Track of the Cat *(1949), while his apocalyptic novel* Swan Song *(1987) was selected by Eddy C. Bertin. Among many, many presences in* They Thirst *is Karloff-Lugosi-Chaney-style classic horror star "Orlon Kronsteen," whose make-up kit also figures in the story "Make-up," adapted with Billy Crystal for the* Darkroom *anthology television show in 1981. McCammon returned to the theme of a vampire-dominated world by editing the Horror Writers of America anthology* Under the Fang *(1991), to which he contributed the story "The Miracle Mile." In an essay on* They Thirst, *which he began as a Chicago-set vampire street-gang novel that would have been called* The Hungry, *McCammon notes, "I think a Vampire King would find Los Angeles a wonderland. He would know that such a beautiful beast has a huge dark belly. And in that darkness, surrounded by pallid forms who fall at his feet in worship, even a Vampire King might become a star."*

People have been saying for years that vampire stories are all the same, little more than old clichés and legends retold so often that no one wants to hear them anymore. What a shame that the folks who insist this is true can't see beyond their own time frame—as long as there are children learning to read, there will eventually be readers who have never read those "old clichés and legends," who will pick up Bram Stoker's *Dracula* or Anne Rice's *Interview With the Vampire* or Stephen King's *'Salem's Lot* and come away craving more.

I hope these readers will be lucky enough to find and read Robert R. McCammon's *They Thirst*.

Anxiety, energy, excitement, and terror—ask anyone to name the components of a great horror story and he or she will come up with a hundred different descriptions, but they always come down to these four things. Thanks to too many relocations, my copy of this wonderful book has been in storage for the better part of seven years, and I probably haven't read it cover-to-cover in close to fifteen. My memory is average at best, and yet after a decade and a half, I can still recite the opening and closing sentences of *They Thirst*. In an exceptional story, anxiety can be called a synonym for anticipation, and McCammon goes straight for the heart with his classic first line: "Tonight there were demons in the hearth."

A book deserves to be called the best when you can't forget the characters, when its opening line still brings a dark, pleasurable smile to your face nearly a quarter of a century (yes, I am that old) after you first read it. Beginning to end, the scenes in this wonderful novel stay with you, and while I won't divulge it here, I also can still recall the last, two-word sentence, that simple line that wraps it all up. With a master's touch, Rick McCammon took a theme that even in the 1980s was wrongly labeled passé and showed horror fans how much depth, life, and *death* were still to be discovered within the forever intertwined concepts of vampires and the end of the world.

To make it better, he spread that idea over one of the most vibrant cities in the world: Los Angeles. While this unforgettable adventure starts in a humble Hungarian village, it quickly catapults forward to the City of Angels. There, in the City of Dreams, is Hollywood, movies, gangs, riches beyond imagination, and for so many, the heart of the search for youth and fame and all things fabulous. That search, as McCammon shows, can take you to Heaven . . . or Hell.

Evil feeds on evil, multiplying to the nth power. So far, so typical. But it isn't just vampires who show their dark truths here. McCammon portrays with chilling accuracy the evil that hides in humanity and how quickly some would join it, revel in it, and help it to procreate. Los Angeles is a world unto itself, and McCammon misses none of it. We don't just read about the gangbanger's pregnant girlfriend, the haunted police detective, the ever-curious reporter, and the Hollywood star made successful by a mystical woman he wins in a poker game. Instead we go with them on their journeys. We live and die, *endure,* as they do, being caught between the holy and the unholy in a terrifying and unexpected apocalypse. With others, such as the serial killer, the biker who exists only to serve his dark master and spread death, and the relentlessly hungry being who sees the city as the stepping-stone to a world aching to be destroyed, we cringe as we're pulled along on their dark and irresistible ride. Mesmerized, we shudder as via one devastating move after another, the great City of Angels folds in on itself and crumbles.

For me this wasn't just a great book. It wasn't even a best book.

It was, in complete honesty, a life-*changing* book. This novel, a first-printing paperback I bought off a drugstore rack in 1981 despite (or maybe because of) its hideous, toothy-mouth-dripping-blood cover, worked magic for me. The prose was so smooth and compelling, so *immersing*, that it sparked something inside my mind and my heart, inside *me*. A seed, an idea, a *dream* that worked on me month after month and year after year. *They Thirst*, and Robert McCammon, made me want to be what I am today . . .

A writer.

YVONNE NAVARRO (b. 1957) grew up and lived mostly in Chicago until 2002, when she finally realized her nearly two-decade-old dream of moving out of that frigid climate to Arizona, where she now lives with her husband, author Weston Ochse, and two Great Danes, Lily and The Gobin. Her writing career has included original novels and media tie-in projects (both original and adaptations), including *AfterAge* (1993), *Deadrush, Final Impact, Red Shadows, That's Not My Name, DeadTimes, Mirror Me, Species, Species II, Aliens: Music of the Spears* (based on the graphic novel by Chet Williamson), *Buffy the Vampire Slayer: The Willow Files* (two volumes), *Buffy the Vampire Slayer: Paleo, Buffy the Vampire Slayer: Tempted Champions, Wicked Willow Books 1–3, Hellboy, Elektra,* and *Ultraviolet*. Also the author of about a hundred short stories and one reference book, Navarro has won the Bram Stoker Award, the CWIP Award for Excellence in Adult Fiction, and the IWPA's Mate E. Palmer Communications Contest for adult novel, first and second place young-adult novel, and the short-story category (where she swept first, second, and the third places). She has also won the NFPW Communications Contest, and the *Rocky Mountain News* "Unreal Worlds" Award for Best Horror Paperback.

71 [1983]

POPPY Z. BRITE on

The Face That Must Die
by RAMSEY CAMPBELL

Ramsey Campbell's second novel under his own name, The Face That Must Die, *was originally published as a paperback original in the United Kingdom (Star Books/W. H. Allen, 1979), with the text pruned against the author's wishes. A break with the supernaturally based horror of* The Doll Who Ate His Mother *and most of Campbell's earlier short fiction, it is an intensely interior account of psychosis, establishing a thread of personality-based horror that has often resurfaced in his work, notably the later novel* The Count of Eleven. *Reputedly "too strong" for the New York publishing establishment,* The Face That Must Die *appeared in America in 1983 from Jeff Conner's California small press imprint Scream/Press in a trade hardcover edition and a one-hundred-copy numbered boxed edition, signed by the author and artist J. K. Potter. This was the first edition of the author's preferred text and includes an additional short story, "I Am It and It Is I," plus a new foreword by Robert Bloch and Campbell's frank, revealing autobiographical essay (later adapted by Bill Wray as a comic strip, "At the Back of My Mind," for* Saturday Mourning Fly in My Eye *and reprinted as "Near Madness" in* Ramsey Campbell, Probably, *2002). This edition (minus Bloch's piece) has subsequently been reprinted with a 1989 afterword by Campbell that serves as an addendum to his very personal introduction. Jack Sullivan wrote about Campbell's collection* Dark Feasts *(1987) in* Horror: 100 Best Books.

THE FACE THAT MUST DIE is probably the best slasher novel ever written. It's more than that, too, but we are concerned with horror superlatives here, so that will be its present distinction. Many are gorier, many are flashier, but *The Face That Must Die* stars John Horridge, and John Horridge is the only fictitious serial murderer who has ever wholly convinced me. (I enjoy Hannibal Lecter, but I don't believe in him, if you see what I mean.)

Horridge is no cliché, no product of a colorfully abusive home, no clothespins on his privates or Grandma's false teeth compelling him to kill. His father beat him once for masturbating and urged him to "be a man" during painful visits to the dentist—a far cry from the lurid tortures found in most such characters' childhoods. Nor (refreshingly, given his virulent homophobia) was he molested by a man or an older boy; he has only a memory (or at least a dream) of being trapped among some garbage cans by girls who ordered him to "make it stand up," then called him a queer when he couldn't. These events suggest a bleak childhood but not a freakish one. Like most of his real-life counterparts, Horridge is simply an ineffectual creep, his disposition toward mental illness stirred by a nasty experience or two, who eventually wills himself into being dangerous; he's never explained or excused.

Yet he is handled with humor and even, I daresay, a macabre affection. His restless but not especially keen mind occupies itself by making endless paranoid puns and associations: a poor-visibility weather forecast on the radio becomes "poor disability" to mock his limp; the Social Security—police—need only jackboots to live up to their initials; masturbation for him is like "pumping away as though to make a reluctant toilet work." He has a naïveté that's almost touching at times: passing an army barracks, he thinks, "At least there couldn't be any homosexuals in there: soldiers were men." He has a voracious sweet tooth, even forgetting his boiled dessert while savaging a victim with his straight razor, then rediscovering the dessert rattling against his teeth afterward.

The perfect foils to this muttering creation are the young couple Cathy and Peter, she painfully earnest and exasperatingly patient, he self-indulgent and self-loathing in about equal parts. She saves money, hoping to buy a house; he spends it on grass, acid, and comics. The other residents of their apartment building are picked off by Horridge, and eventually they must tangle with him, which they do with a welcome lack of the resourcefulness, heroics, or sudden attacks of wit common to the protagonists of so many slasher novels.

My copy of *The Face That Must Die* is the 1983 Scream/Press hardcover edition that includes J. K. Potter's disturbing illustrations, Robert Bloch's laudatory foreword, and Campbell's own remarkably candid autobiographical essay, "At the Back of My Mind: A Guided Tour." During a recent visit to Liverpool I had the good fortune to visit, in the author's company, both John Horridge's joyless concrete home Cantril Farm and the house where Campbell lived for twenty years with his increasingly unstable mother. I found Cantril Farm far less unsettling than I'd expected it to be, and the former Campbell home far more so. I'm not sure what this demonstrates: his ability to transform a rather innocuous housing estate into a fictional landscape of sunless dread? His power to make us see the demons of the mind in an ordinary house where no splashy disasters occurred, just a real woman going quietly, wrenchingly insane and doing her best to take her only child with her? Or both?

In his foreword, Robert Bloch compares *The Face That Must Die* to the early Graham Greene novel *Brighton Rock*. Both are wonderful books; both feature a riveting antihero and an unparalleled sense of place. I think perhaps Campbell's novel is a little better. *Brighton Rock*'s Pinkie is a type; he's flawlessly drawn, but we have seen him elsewhere and will see him again, a young man hardened by his own ignorance and self-pity. John Horridge, by contrast, is a complete original; I can't think of another character like him anywhere in fiction. This seems to me one of the finest things an author can achieve—a character who is wholly his own and utterly memorable.

POPPY Z. BRITE (b. 1967) was born in New Orleans, where she still lives in the French Quarter with her husband, Christopher, a chef. After briefly attending the University of North Carolina at Chapel Hill, she dropped out to write her first novel. *Lost Souls*, a punk Gothic vampire fable that introduced a number of recurring characters and themes in her fiction, was published to instant acclaim in 1992, and became a Book-of-the-Month Club alternate selection (Brian Hodge writes about it in this volume). Winner of the British Fantasy Society's Best Newcomer Award in 1994, she followed her debut with the novels *Drawing Blood, Exquisite Corpse*, and *The Lazarus Heart*. Her short fiction has been published in the collections *Wormwood* (aka *Swamp Foetus*), *Are You Loathsome Tonight?* (aka *Self-Made Man*), *The Devil You Know, Wrong Things* (with Caitlín R. Kiernan), and *Triads* (with Christa Faust), while *His Mouth Will Taste of Wormwood and Other Stories* was a compilation of four stories published as part of the "Penguin 60s" series to celebrate the influential imprint's sixtieth anniversary. *Guilty But Insane* is a collection of non-fiction, and she also edited two volumes of the erotic vampire anthology *Love in Vein*. She appeared in the erotic art film *John Five*, directed by Jim Herbert (the video director for the band REM, not the horror writer), and also has written a bestselling biography of rock personality Courtney Love. In recent years Brite has moved away from horror, drawing on her extensive knowledge of the New Orleans restaurant scene for a series of novels and short stories about Rickey and G-man, two young New Orleans cooks who make a name for themselves by opening a restaurant whose menu is based entirely on liquor. Brite's restaurant tales include the novels *Liquor, Prime*, and *The Value of X*, and she is currently working on another book in the series.

72 [1983]

DAVID STUART DAVIES on

The Woman in Black
by SUSAN HILL

*This slim novel by Susan Hill (b. 1942) is at once a playful pastiche, stitching together references to Victorian ghost and mystery tales, and a genuinely terrifying horror tale, returning nastily to Henry James's "turn of the screw" in its imperiling of children. Hill, a prolific writer, has dipped again into ghostliness (*The Mist in the Mirror*, 1992), edited anthologies of the supernatural (*Ghost Stories*, 1983), and produced the authorized sequel to Daphne du Maurier's* Rebecca *(*Mrs. de Winter*, 1993).* The Woman in Black *was adapted by actor Stephen Mallatratt into a two-handed stage play, which has been running in London's West End since 1987 and been produced widely around the world. In 1989 Nigel Kneale scripted a made-for-TV movie adaptation for Christmas broadcast; Kneale eliminated an H. G. Wells reference by renaming protagonist Arthur Kipps "Arthur Kidd."*

I DON'T KNOW WHAT it is about the human psyche that enjoys being scared witless. Isn't it strange to actively seek to frighten yourself by picking up a horror novel or ghost story? Maybe, but there is a perverse and satisfying pleasure in being frightened by literature. It happened a lot to me when I was a child.

The school library was a wonderful receptacle of spooky stuff. I remember quivering to *A Christmas Carol,* particularly when the ghost of Christmas Present reveals the two shivering children Want and Ignorance beneath his dark, voluminous robe; being chilled by the stories of Algernon Blackwood, especially a tale in which a child's doll comes to life and begins walking in a strange, stiff, mechanical way up the bedspread toward its victim; and shuddering to the gloriously frightening *Hound of the Baskervilles*, which disappointed me in the end when it turned out to be a real dog.

In adulthood I have rarely been as frightened by a story as I was in my salad days, except by *The Woman in Black*. I remember first reading it one wet and rainy evening in November in the mid-1980s. I was alone in the house as the wind shook the windows, howling like a banshee outside—or was it the Woman in Black trying to gain entrance? No longer was I an impressionable kid, but nevertheless I was genuinely frightened. And yet I couldn't put the book down.

Of course, *The Woman in Black* is a pastiche. Susan Hill has gathered a whole raft of clichés from the genre, including isolated houses, strange noises in the night, unexplained happenings and portends of death, and woven them so cleverly into the fabric of her story that she has come up with something fresh and genuinely chilling. Throughout the novel there are nods to her literary predecessors. The title itself is a play on Wilkie Collins's *The Woman in White*, and one of the chapters is called "Whistle and I'll Come," which is a touch of the cap to one of M. R. James's most frightening tales, "Oh Whistle and I'll Come to You, My Lad." In fact, the influence of James, his ability to build up the suspense infinitesimally slowly and make the ordinary seem odd, is felt throughout the book. And we get some Dickensiana, too, for good measure. Hill's wonderful description of the fog in the early chapter, "A London Particular," is not only rich in detail but also echoes the opening scene in *A Christmas Carol*. Arthur Kipps, the central character, also refers to Eel Marsh House as being like "the house of poor Miss Havisham." This is a deliberate ploy. Hill is giving us a dark wink to show us that she knows where she's coming from. These are witty little jokes along the way, as when Kipps, learning about his trip to Eel Marsh House, confesses to the reader, "The business was beginning to sound like something out of a Victorian novel."

Indeed, although the period of the tale is the early part of the twentieth century, the trappings of the Victorian age are felt within the story, not least in the leisurely and circumspect tone and language

Hill employs to create her chills. It is not for her the urgent, graphic prose of a Stephen King or a Dean Koontz. Hill plays gently with the reader's imagination by suggestion and implication—for the most part, that is, so when she does shock, it is unexpected and therefore more brutal.

By having the story told in the first person, Hill allows the reader to follow the same road as Arthur Kipps, a levelheaded fellow who states on arriving at Eel Marsh House that he does not believe in ghosts. The unsettling and frightening experiences he endures force him to change his mind and, caught up in the story, we, too, share his fears. For example, the scene where Arthur hears the sound of rocking emanating from the darkened nursery undermines our rationality. He recognizes the sound from his own childhood, "from a time before I could clearly remember anything else." It was comforting then, associated as it was with his nurse sitting by his bed in a rocking chair. This warm memory gives him courage to enter the haunted nursery.

The book begins with a ghost story-telling session; but Arthur, whose story is real, cannot bear to tell it. Thank goodness Susan Hill does tell it, and in doing so she creates one of the greatest chillers of all time.

DAVID STUART DAVIES (b. 1946) was a teacher of English for twenty years before becoming a full-time writer. His work is heavily influenced by the Sherlock Holmes stories of Sir Arthur Conan Doyle, and he is the author of five Holmes novels: *Sherlock Holmes & the Hentzau Affair*, *The Tangled Skein*, *The Scroll of the Dead*, *Shadow of the Rat*, and *The Veiled Detective*. The editor of various anthologies, including *Return from the Dead* and *Tales of Unease*, his non-fiction work includes *Holmes of the Movies* and *Starring Sherlock Holmes*. Davies has provided authoritative commentaries to the DVD releases of the remastered Basil Rathbone Sherlock Holmes films, and also has worked on DVDs of the Jeremy Brett Holmes series and with David Jason on the *Frost* releases. Davies' award-winning one-man play *Sherlock Holmes: The Last Act,* has been touring with the actor Roger Llewellyn since it premiered at Salisbury Playhouse in 1999. Llewellyn has performed the play all over the United Kingdom, as well as in Hong Kong, Malta, France, Canada, and the United States. Davies has edited the crime fiction magazine *Sherlock,* and *Red Herrings,* the monthly publication for members of the Crime Writers Association. His latest novel, *Forests of the Night,* features his own detective, Johnny One Eye, a private investigator operating in London during World War II. A second adventure about the character is in the pipeline, along with a collection of vintage detective and mystery stories titled *Baffled.*

73 [1983]

MICHAEL MARSHALL SMITH on

Pet Sematary
by STEPHEN KING

Taglined (on the U.K. edition at least) as "the ultimate horror novel," Pet Sematary *was reputedly written by Stephen King (b. 1947) and then bottom-drawered as liable to be too upsetting even for his regular audience. If* The Shining *(1977) is a book by a father who wonders what he might do to his family, this is a book by a father who wonders* what he might not do for them. It's a sustained riff on W. W. Jacobs's classic short story (and play) "The Monkey's Paw" (from The Lady on the Barge, 1902), which several contributors to this volume offered to write about even though it's not an actual book, about the dangers of wishing for the dead to return. In light of the fact that Michael Marshall Smith has never actually finished reading Pet Sematary, he might be interested to learn that Ramsey Campbell has argued that the zombie-stalked last chapters aren't horrific enough. King scripted Mary Louise Lambert's slightly too-on-the-nose 1989 film, starring Dale Midkiff, Fred Gwynne, and Denise Crosby (who features in a memorable, subtly gruesome last shot), but had no involvement in Lambert's Pet Sematary II (1992), featuring Edward Furlong, Clancy Brown, and Anthony Edwards. A 1997 BBC Radio serial written by Gregory Evans stars John Sharian (best known for his sinister role in the film The Machinist) and has been released on CD and audio cassette. Perhaps the best media adaptation of the novel is the Ramones' film theme song, "I Don't Wanna Be Buried in (Pet Sematary)." Al Sarrantonio wrote about Stephen King's 'Salem's Lot (1975) in Horror: 100 Best Books, and Peter Straub covered The Shining (1977), while King himself contributed a piece on Robert Marasco's Burnt Offerings (1973).

WHY PET SEMATARY?
Because it changed my life.

I'm sure there are many, many people currently plying the word juggler's trade who know that without Stephen King they'd be doing something else. In pure cause-and-effect terms, it was *The Talisman* that did it for me. That was the book a friend recommended while I was on a long theater tour, the summer after I finished university.

I spent the following three months hunting down every King book in the land (and as *The Bachman Books* had just come out, there were plenty to get my teeth into): reading them during rehearsal breaks, or perched on windowsills in stuffy bed-and-breakfasts, or while killing afternoons around a series of theater-equipped towns. Until then I assumed I'd join the family business and become an academic. In fact, partly through spending too much time writing comedy shows and being a third-rate performer, I'd wound up with a degree good enough to win a doctorate place but not good enough to secure a grant. By the end of the summer this didn't matter so much to me: I'd decided I wanted to be a horror writer instead. *The Talisman* was the book that flicked the switch. But *Pet Sematary* was the one that glued it permanently in the "On" position.

And the weird thing is, I didn't even finish it.

The book's plot is simple, as the best ones usually are. Dr. Louis Creed relocates his family from urban Chicago to meadowed Maine. They move into a rambling old house and all is well until one night when the wife and kids are away and their much-loved cat gets killed by one of the big trucks that thunder along the highway outside. Luckily, the old guy who lives across the way has a solution. Unluckily . . . well, it just doesn't work too well. But when the same kind of accident befalls the Creeds' baby son, a grief-stricken father thinks he knows what he must do.

And bam—that was me *out of there.*

I put the book down and went for a walk. I bought another King book the next day—something gentle and soothing, like *The Shining*—and started reading that instead. I have still never gotten to the end of *Pet Sematary,* and I've tried twice since. The reaction was the same each time, and occurred at the exact same point: great, thanks very much, Mr. King, really enjoyed it so far, but no fucking *way* am I following you down that road.

I was twenty-one that first time, and the reaction was out of all proportion. I didn't have a wife or children or a job. I hadn't lost anyone whose absence turned the world sour and bleak and flat. *Pet Sematary* abruptly hurled me forward twenty years, showing me things I'd suspected but not yet learned. Among its other qualities the novel is a heartrending reimagining of the old tale of the Monkey's Paw, with its terrible, melancholy lesson of how death is not only immutable, but also so life-structuring that you'll stop wishing it wasn't so. As Creed's neighbor Jud Crandall says at one stage, "Sometimes dead is better."

Sometimes in life you've just got to let it go.

In general, I'm not a wuss. I have never stopped watching a horror movie, nor shirked the husbandly duty of going downstairs to check what's making that weird noise. *Pet Sematary*'s just different. It's too real, too mythically sharp. It doesn't achieve this through gore or Gothic, but by conjuring a covetable everyday life and introducing a waking nightmare, the kind that can enter the lives of someone like you or me: by presenting the reader with a scenario where you agree the character has no credible option but to walk a dark and terrible path.

Where you know you'd do the same.

Pet Sematary represents the quintessential Stephen King and contains some of his very best prose. The writing is focused, intent, austere, a distilled master class in how King managed to reinvent horror and bring it to people who "don't normally read that kind of thing": by proving the genre works best when the emotional core drives the story. This is King in no mood to kid around, either: he's out to cause damage, and he's coming in low and fast. It's like Annie Wilkes suddenly dropping the folksy stuff and swinging the ax out from behind her back: you dismally realize you've been suckered in, tied to the bed by King's storytelling genius, and all you can do is watch the hammer coming down.

We all know how our life stories are going to end. But that doesn't mean you actually want to, like, *know*.

This afternoon, nearly twenty years after first picking up *Pet Sematary*, I have another copy in front of me. It's a new edition, without my decades-old reading creases, which stop at a certain point. Many things have changed for me during that time. I am married. I have lost people dear to me. My experience bag is fuller now.

Also, I have a baby son.

Can I read this book now? Do I really want to go there—and this time for real? Do I want to walk into those woods and follow that path to the end? Three times I have woken from this nightmare just in time. Can I do the same again?

Neither I, nor the boy I was, are sure.

MICHAEL MARSHALL SMITH (b. 1965) was born in Knutsford, Cheshire, and grew up in the United States, South Africa, and Australia before moving to North London, where he lives with his herbalist wife, Paula, his son, and two cats. After earning a degree in philosophy from Cambridge University, he spent some time as a comedy writer and performer for BBC Radio. In 1991 he won British Fantasy Awards for Best Newcomer and for his debut story, "The Man Who Drew Cats," and he followed those with two more for his short fiction, some of which is collected in *What You Make It* and the International Horror Guild Award-winning *More Tomorrow & Other Stories* (discussed in this present volume by Tim Lebbon). The author of three science fiction novels, *Only Forward* won the August Derleth and Philip K. Dick Awards, *Spares* was optioned by Steven Spielberg's DreamWorks SKG and translated into seventeen languages, and *One of Us* was optioned by Warner Brothers. Seven of Smith's short stories are also under option. Writing as "Michael Marshall" he has recently completed a series of three thriller novels—*The Straw Men*, *The Lonely Dead* (aka *The Upright Man*), and *Blood of Angels*—which have been *Sunday Times* and international bestsellers. He has also written a number of film and television scripts for companies in Hollywood and London.

74 [1984]

ANTHONY TIMPONE on

Clive Barker's Books of Blood Volumes One, Two, and Three
by **CLIVE BARKER**

Clive Barker's Books of Blood Volumes One, Two, and Three *were first published in the United Kingdom by Sphere Books as paperback originals. Though it was conceived as one gargantuan six-hundred-page collection called* The Book of Blood, *Clive Barker (b. 1952) was convinced to split the stories into three simultaneously published volumes. Volume One contains Ramsey Campbell's introduction and the stories "The Book of Blood," "The Midnight Meat Train," "The Yattering and Jack," "Pig Blood Blues," "Sex, Death, and Starshine," and "In the Hills, the Cities." Volume Two presents "Dread," "Hell's Event," "Jacqueline Ess: Her Will and Testament," "The Skins of the Fathers," and "New Murders in the Rue Morgue." Volume Three offers "Son of Celluloid," "Rawhead Rex," "Confessions of a (Pornographer's) Shroud," "Scapegoats," and "Human Remains." The Liverpool-born writer's first published efforts, the* Books of Blood *were an instant critical and eventually financial success. Barker delivered three additional* Books of Blood *a year later. The books' complex printing history is lampooned in Kim Newman's short story "The Man Who Collected Barker," which hasn't stopped variant editions from appearing to the present day. The first two volumes became a Sphere book club omnibus hardcover in 1984, and California's Scream/Press issued all three volumes in a single hardcover the following year, with illustrations by J. K. Potter and Harry O. Morris. Numerous variations and permutations include a run of prestige format comics adaptations,* Tapping the Vein. *In 1986, "The Yattering and Jack" became an episode of the* Tales from the Darkside *television series and "Rawhead Rex" a low-*

budget feature film; both were scripted by Barker but failed to serve his work well. Clive Barker wrote about The Tragical History of Doctor Faustus *(c. 1592) by Christopher Marlowe in* Horror: 100 Best Books, *while Adrian Cole contributed an essay on Barker's debut novel,* The Damnation Game *(1985).*

On both personal and professional levels, I first discovered Clive Barker in the summer 1985 when, prophetically, I had just begun work as a lowly editorial assistant at the New York-based *Fangoria* magazine. The first issue I contributed to, no. 48 (September), included a rave review of the Sphere edition of *Clive Barker's Books of Blood.* A few weeks later, out of the blue, a polite Englishman called the office.

"Hi, this is Clive Barker," he said. "I would like to thank *Fangoria* for the kind review of my book." "Whoa," I thought, "if all horror people were this cool, who cares if I have to type up all those free subscribers ads?"

In the months before I started, word of Barker's horror wake-up call had filtered to *Fangoria* via transatlantic phone calls from newly minted British correspondent Philip Nutman. It would be two years before most Americans would discover these dark delicacies for themselves, courtesy of paperback editions published by Berkley Books in two-month intervals, beginning in June 1986 (with images of cheesy rubber monster masks leaping off the covers). By this time I had been groomed to take over the editorship of *Fangoria,* and Barker himself had visited us "in the flesh" to personally show his gratitude for all the glowing press.

Before Barker's *Books of Blood* came along, short horror fiction was in a sorry state. The stories I read came from dated Scholastic Books collections and Alfred Hitchcock and Rod Serling anthologies—tales that struggled to come up with O. Henry-style or *Twilight Zone* twists. Stephen King's 1979 *Night Shift* collection had several winners (the wryly clever "Quitters, Inc." and the achingly personal "The Woman in the Room"), but a few clinkers, too (silly B-movie-inspired yarns such as "Trucks" and "The Mangler," which themselves inspired dopey

B-movies of their own). Overall, *Night Shift* could not compete with the mastery of King's long-form novels of that period (*Carrie*, *'Salem's Lot*, and *The Shining*).

Once I began devouring the *Books of Blood*, however, I realized from the get-go that *every* story was a winner. Each was unique in its outrageousness, refreshing inventiveness, and chilling gruesomeness. Volume One's introductory "The Book of Blood" worked just fine as a stand-alone, but how could I not be hooked by the grisly charnel house express ride called "The Midnight Meat Train"? I *rode* that line that Barker described so well, a subway rich in doom and gloom in a pre-Giuliani New York; and I read "The Midnight Meat Train" and each subsequent story as I traveled those city rails to my job at *Fangoria*. What could be more appropriate?

Though almost whimsical on the surface, "The Yattering and Jack" had a subversive naughtiness, while "Pig Blood Blues" came close to turning me into a vegetarian. With the sublime ghost story "Sex, Death, and Starshine," Barker first fused horror with the erotic. I think that many readers, myself included, never realized they could get sexually aroused while reading a horror story until they found Barker's prose. Volume One closes with one of Barker's greatest stories ever, the breathtakingly original "In the Hills, the Cities," about the citizens of warring towns who tie themselves together to tussle as towering giants.

Volume Two opens with the nasty ditty "Dread," which, like many of the stories in these books, would make a doozy of a motion picture. Not some big-budget fx fest, but an intimate, skin-crawling psychological thriller on the order of *Saw*. Barker's writing throughout the *Books of Blood* shows an affinity for outré cinema, from the body horror of David Cronenberg to the flesh-eating zombie flicks of Lucio Fulci. The ultimate expression of female empowerment, "Jacqueline Ess: Her Will and Testament" plays out like Brian De Palma's *Carrie* and *The Fury* times ten, while "The Skins of the Fathers" serves as the perfect precursor to Barker's own movie *Nightbreed* (based on his novella *Cabal*). Barker even pays homage to Edgar Allan Poe and Roger Corman with "New Murders in the Rue Morgue," which also asks us to love our monsters, particularly the ones that shave.

Speaking of movies, imagine what a David (*Eraserhead*) Lynch could do with Volume Three's "Son of Celluloid," about a cancer imitating dead movie stars in a fleatrap grindhouse. "Rawhead Rex" would have made the ultimate monster movie if Tobe Hooper or Eli Roth had directed it, and not some guy named George Pavlou, who screwed up the 1986 film version. The powerful, full-throttle "Rawhead Rex" rates as one of the best monster stories of all time. The vicious gangland vendetta antics and subsequent spectral revenge in "Confessions of a (Pornographer's) Shroud" would make Martin Scorsese blanch, while the water-logged ghouls of "Scape-goats" manage to echo both the grossness of Fulci and poetry of Val Lewton. With the golem tale "Human Remains," Barker once again finds compassion for his "monsters," as both ancient sculpted doppelgänger and the reader himself shed tears at a moving graveside conclusion.

Clive Barker's Books of Blood announced a literary force to be reckoned with, but within a few years, Barker abandoned the short form. He soon graduated to ambitious, large-scale epics of dark fantasy, such as *The Great and Secret Show, Everville, Imagica,* and the *Abarat* series. More than twenty years after the publication of his *Books of Blood,* Barker's imagination continues to show no limits.

ANTHONY TIMPONE (b. 1963) is the long-time editor of both *Fangoria* magazine and its sister Web site (fangoria.com). He is the author of *Men, Makeup, and Monsters,* which the New York Public Library named one of the "Best for the Teenage 1997." He also edited *Fangoria Vampires, Fangoria Masters of the Dark: Stephen King and Clive Barker, Fangoria's 100 Best Horror Films You've Never Seen,* and *Fangoria's Best Horror Films.* During the early 1990s he helped guide the first three Fango movies for Columbia/TriStar Home Video: *Mindwarp, Children of the Night,* and *Severed Ties,* and in 2004 he served as a producer on the five-hour documentary series *The 100 Scariest Movie Moments.* He currently serves as a producer at Fangoria TV and as an acquisitions chief for *Fangoria*'s three video/DVD labels: Fangoria Presents GoreZone, Fangoria International, and Fangoria's Midnight Classics. For Koch Vision he co-created and co-produced *Fangoria Blood Drive*, a short film search and magazine-format DVD hosted by Rob Zombie. For television he was a consulting producer for the *Horror Hall of Fame* special and served on the award show's Board of Directors. Timpone has been a frequent media spokesman for the horror industry, appearing on MTV, *Nightline, Geraldo, Entertainment Tonight, Showbiz Today, CBS Evening News*, and many more, as well as numerous documentaries such as *Horror Business, The Many Lives of Jason Voorhees, Halloween: A Cut Above the Rest, Haunters, Full Tilt Boogie*, and *Hollywood's Creepiest Creatures*.

75

[1986]

NANCY KILPATRICK on

Perfume: The Story of a Murderer
by PATRICK SÜSKIND

The German author and playwright Patrick Süskind (b. 1949) ventured very successfully into the grotesque with Perfume, *which appeared in German in 1985 as* Das Parfum: Die Geschichte eines Mörders *and was translated into English (by John E. Woods) a year later. An international bestseller, the book has been in development as a film for nearly twenty years, though a version directed by Tom Tykwer (of* Run, Lola Run *fame) seems likely to appear in 2006 with Ben Whishaw as the odious but not odiferous* Grenouille *(French, of course, for "frog") and support from Dustin Hoffman and Alan Rickman. Among the novel's fans was the late rock star Kurt Cobain, whose song "Scentless Apprentice" is allegedly inspired by the book. Süskind has not been prolific, but delivered a modern-day tale of the obsessive and macabre in* The Pigeon *(1988). In partnership with director Helmut Dietl, Süskind has scripted several major projects in a black comic vein for German televison and film:* Monaco Franze: Der Ewige Stenze *(1983),* Kir Royale *(1986),* Rossini *(1997), and* Vom Suchen und Finden de Liebe *(2005).*

I SAT ON THE crowded Air Canada plane, flight number 928, aisle seat 22B, directly in front of seat 23B, where my then-husband, Mike, sat. We were headed to Puerto Vallarta, Mexico, on our first vacation together. It was 1989. Clean aircraft, friendly crew, smooth ride, polite passengers.... All was right in my little world, specifically and generally. I felt good.

I cracked open the paperback I'd bought a few days before, knowing nothing about it or the author other than the descriptive subtitle on the cover: "The story of a murderer."

Instantly I was transported to another time and place. France. July 17, 1738. A child is birthed beneath a market stall onto the filthy street by a woman who dropped four others over the years on the same spot, all stillborn or half stillborn. This time, despite what the mother intended, the baby survives. Found on one of the hottest days of the year beneath a "swarm of flies, and amid the offal and fish heads" is a sociopath who will come to be named Jean-Baptiste Grenouille, and live his life as a serial killer like no other.

Before I had read more than the first two pages I was astonished, charmed, captivated, and revolted by the exquisite prose of this translated-from-the-German novel by Patrick Süskind. I remember leaping out of my seat several times and exclaiming to my husband, "This book is extraordinary!"

What Süskind does in the novel *Perfume* is describe events largely by how they smell. There may have been other novels written prior to this in which scent is used as the major descriptive element, but

I hadn't read them. Most authors rely on the visual. Sometimes the audile. Less often the tactile. Even more rarely, the sense of taste is employed. Smell is used in fiction so infrequently that to encounter it in a major way opens up a new, fresh world or, in the case of *Perfume,* a rank world.

Perfume is a dark journey through the life of this born-bad mass murderer Grenouille, which means "frog" and which describes his hideous appearance. His voyage of evil is portrayed mostly by scent because of Grenouille's unique gift. His body does not emit any odor, yet something comes from him that, throughout his life, repels others. Meanwhile, his own sense of smell is so acute that he can detect the precise elements that composed any scent his olfactory nerves focus on.

But despite the novel's title, the smells are not pretty, and that is part of what makes this such a deliciously insidious read. Right from the get-go Paris is presented as a revolting cacophony of odors, all the more offensive because they compose a breeding ground for harmful bacteria that, in reality, would not be addressed by the world until closer to the end of the eighteenth century. Süskind writes that the streets stank of "manure, the courtyards of urine, the stairwells stank of moldering wood and rat droppings, the kitchens of spoiled cabbage and mutton fat." Individuals were worse, reeking of more than the sweat and filthy clothing we would expect from the era. The author continues, "from their mouths came the stench of rotting teeth, from their bellies that of onions, and from their bodies, if they were no longer very young, came the stench of rancid cheese and sour milk and tumorous disease."

Having been all my life a fan of eighteenth- and nineteenth-century literature, I love the imitative style of this work. The writing is complex, dark, and moody. It also does what fiction of the past did so well—encourages the reader to feel both sympathy and revulsion toward a character. Grenouille is a murderer, thoroughly insane, and yet his life is agonizingly hard from birth onward; I feel sorry for him even as I am repelled by his hideous violence. Grenouille does not possess the brilliant personality of a Hannibal Lecter, nor is he crisp and corporate like many modern serial killers. In fact, Grenouille seems to have little personality at all; the story takes place more *around* him than *through* him. What makes it work is his unique obsession, which is both fascinating and thoroughly absorbing.

Perfume is a twisted tale that reveals the grim underbelly of society; it horrifies to the core. Only a wordsmith and a historian such as Süskind could weave such a cleverly brutal *tour de force*. I still marvel at and treasure every page of this magnificent novel.

NANCY KILPATRICK (b. 1946) was born in Philadelphia and currently resides in Montréal, Québec, where she lives with her black cat Bella and travels the world in search of cemeteries, ossuaries, mummies, and *danse macabre* artwork. Her generational "Power of the Blood" vampire series comprises *Near Death, Child of the Night, Reborn, Bloodlover,* and *Transformation,* while her other novels include *As One Dead, Dracul, Eternal City* (with Michael Kilpatrick), *Mercedez: Day of the Dead, Jason X: Planet of the Beast,* and *Jason X: To the Third Power.* She is a winner of Canada's Arthur Ellis Award for her story "Mantrap," and her short fiction has been collected in *Sex and the Single Vampire, Endorphins, The Vampire Stories of Nancy Kilpatrick,* and *Cold Comfort.* As an editor, she has a number of anthologies to her credit, including *Outsiders: Stories on the Edge of the Fantastical* (with Nancy Holder) and *Graven Images* and *In the Shadow of the Gargoyle* (both with Thomas Roche). She is the author of the non-fiction book *The Goth Bible: A Compendium for the Darkly Inclined* and has scripted various issues of the Brainstorm Comics series *VampErotica.* Her play *Ghost Rails/Les Fantômes Déraillent,* written with Benoit Bisson, was staged at the Fringe Festival, Toronto, in 1996. Under the pseudonym "Amarantha Knight" she has written a number of explicit novels in *The Darker Passions* erotic series, including *Dracula, Dr. Jekyll and Mr. Hyde,*

Frankenstein, The Fall of the House of Usher, The Portrait of Dorian Gray, Carmilla, The Pit and the Pendulum, and *Curse of the Mummy,* as well as editing the anthologies *Love Bites, Flesh Fantastic, Sex Macabre, Seductive Spectres,* and *Demon Sex.*

76

[1986]

BILL SHEEHAN on

Finishing Touches
by THOMAS TESSIER

Thomas Tessier (b. 1947), who contributed an essay on Jeremias Gotthelf's The Black Spider *(1842) to* Horror: 100 Best Books, *is an American writer who spent much of the 1970s in London. Like* The Nightwalker *(1979), his effective and unusual werewolf novel,* Finishing Touches *brings an informed outsider's eye to the British cityscape, digging deep to find particularly appalling horrors. Among the mysteries confronted uncomfortably in the book is the disappearance of the murder suspect Lord Lucan, who is here brought to some kind of terrible justice. Though Tessier often deals with the unconventionally supernatural, as in* The Fates *(1978),* Phantom *(1982), and* Fog Heart *(1997),* Finishing Touches *was the first of a run of non-supernatural mystery and suspense novels that continued with* Rapture *(1987) and* Secret Strangers *(1990).*

HORROR FICTION, BY definition, invites us to contemplate extreme situations and equally extreme states of mind. At its best, this sort of fiction can be disquieting, exhilarating, and revelatory all at once. Few modern horror novels succeed on all these levels as thoroughly—and frighteningly—as Thomas Tessier's *Finishing Touches*. An unsparing meditation on the human capacity for cruelty and corruption, *Finishing Touches* is Tessier's masterpiece and is one of the dark landmarks of late twentieth-century fiction.

In its early stages, the narrative bears a resemblance to John Fowles's *The Magus*. In Fowles's novel, a callow young Englishman named Nicholas Urfe travels to the Greek islands in search of "a new mystery," encounters Maurice Conchis (the "Magus" of the title), and finds himself enmeshed in a labyrinthine psychological experiment known as "The Godgame." In Tessier's novel, Tom Sutherland, a young American doctor, travels to England for an extended final fling before settling into his chosen career. Over drinks in a hotel bar, Tom encounters a Magus-like figure of his own: Dr. Roger Nordhagen, a successful cosmetic surgeon and advanced alcoholic whose bland exterior conceals an unspeakable secret life.

Nordhagen is the master and creator of a grotesque variation of the Godgame that takes place in a high-tech dungeon beneath his lavish Mayfair home. (I won't reveal the precise nature of Nordhagen's "game," since readers should be free to discover it for themselves. Suffice it to say that it is a breathtaking exercise in what Tessier calls "the politics of cruelty.") When Tom first meets Nordhagen, Tom sees only a harmless, somewhat inebriated old man. But Nordhagen sees something different—something special—in Tom. Quoting Pascal, he tells Tom, "'If I had not known you, I would not have found you,'" a remark that implies a profound, if unspecified, affinity and sets the stage for the multifaceted seduction to come.

What follows is, in fact, a seduction—or a series of seductions—that lead Tom (a pliable, unfinished young man about to undergo some very special finishing touches) from his initial aimless state to a condition of pure, transcendent evil. The seduction takes place in stages, and Tessier describes those stages with quiet, systematic brilliance. It begins with Tom's first brief glimpses of a "private London"—a world of power, privilege, and erotic possibility—and reaches a new level when Tom meets Lena Ravichol, Nordhagen's ravishing personal assistant. Blinded by his feelings for Lena, Tom quickly realizes that he will do anything—literally anything—to win and keep her love. This deeply sexual Faustian bargain propels Tom out of his old life and into an unexplored universe where everything is permitted.

Finishing Touches is a profound—and profoundly moral—examination of the lengths a man will go in pursuit of his deepest, most secret desires. Through a series of increasingly disturbing episodes, the novel circles and recircles a single fundamental question: are there any limits to human behavior? The answer, as Tessier sees it, is no. The interconnected stories of Tom, Lena, and Nordhagen reflect a world balanced precariously over a moral abyss, a world where every act of cruelty and degradation leads downward to newer, darker possibilities. At every step of his descent—which encompasses erotic obsession, sexual violence, and murder—Tom learns to accommodate himself to his own capacity for evil. He may, on occasion, be deeply shocked by the things he sees and does, but the shock, no matter how profound, eventually subsides. (Tom's discovery of Nordhagen's underground kingdom precipitates the novel's sharpest moral crisis. But that, too, passes, leaving Tom to resume his pursuit of a life unhindered by moral reservations.)

At bottom, *Finishing Touches* concerns the power of fantasies to shape our lives for better or, in Tom's case, for worse. The novel is filled with "scenarios of enactment" that, once realized, make the next fantasy, the next scenario, both possible and inevitable. By the novel's end, Tom and Lena have created a mutual, self-contained fantasy world that keeps the "real" world increasingly at bay. At first their shared fantasies are invariably sexual. (Eros is a powerful element of this novel, as it is in so much of Tessier's work.) But sex, as Lena tells Tom early on, is only the "first wave. Beyond that, are the *real* fantasies." As those "real fantasies" become more extravagant and destructive, *Finishing Touches* attains the level of an authentic, fully realized nightmare.

This isn't by any means a comfortable novel. (What real horror novel ever is?) But it is, I believe, a memorable and important one, the rare sort of book that invades your consciousness and takes up residence forever. Very few novels—very few works of art of any kind—can do this. If you've read *Finishing Touches*, you'll know exactly what I mean. If you haven't, then a memorable, unsettling experience awaits you. I envy you the encounter.

BILL SHEEHAN (b. 1950) lives outside of Philadelphia with his wife and two daughters. His insightful and perceptive essays, articles, interviews, and reviews have appeared in *The Washington Post Book World*, *The Magazine of Fantasy & Science Fiction*, *Locus*, the *New York Review of Science Fiction*, and numerous other publications. Sheehan's book-length critical study of Peter Straub, *At the Foot of the Story Tree*, won the World Fantasy Award, the International Horror Guild Award, and was a finalist for the Horror Writers Association's Bram Stoker Award. He edited the original anthology *Night Visions 11* (containing original stories by Kim Newman, Lucius Shepard, and Tim Lebbon) and, with William K. Schafer, co-edited the anthologies *Embrace the Mutation* and *Lords of the Razor*.

77 [1987]

KELLY LINK on

Strange Toys
by PATRICIA GEARY

Patricia Geary (b. 1951) made a splash with her debut novel, Living in Ether *(1982), which mixes psychic phenomena; lightly satirized Californian New Ageness; and an intensely odd set of family relationships, especially between siblings.* Strange Toys *shifts the locale to New Orleans, stirring in a little voodoo, and explores three stages in the life of Pet, which is wound-up with that of her sister Deane. The book apparently suffered from a bizarre piece of publishing office politics, wherein a senior figure at Bantam Books was locked briefly in a closet and opted to blame Geary's editor. The decision to release the book as a genre paperback, without the benefit of a hardcover edition, paid off in that* Strange Toys *won the Philip K. Dick Award for best genre paperback original, but Geary took an enforced break from publishing for fifteen years before returning with* The Other Canyon *(2002) and* Guru Cigarettes *(2005).*

> We are magicians! Our heads are ravens, our wings are purple, studded with nails. When we fly overhead, sleeping women feel the breath of frost on their cheeks. Children dream of the seven tongues of fire. We fear only the Master Wizard. Now he is on us. His arms are giant radishes with revolving razor blades. Each blade can cut a piece of paper into two thinner pieces of paper. We feel the heat on our cheeks. Without the magic formula, we will be torn to ribbons!

THIS QUOTE COMES from a game that Pet, the narrator of *Strange Toys*, plays with her sisters June and Deane. Maybe you once played games like this, too. I did. Riding tricycles in a loop down their driveway, they take turns describing what they see. Pet is fond of fairy tales; bossy, greedy June invents a suburban Candyland where swimming pools brim with M&M's. Deane, beloved and feared by her younger sisters, describes nightmarish landscapes from which only she can save them.

The novel itself has the feel of a childhood game or a fairy tale: prickly; loopily endearing and private; dangerous when one doesn't know the rules; and described with the inventive, hallucinatory textures of the best and most convincing nightmares. What I felt reading Geary was: childhood is like this. Magic is like this, and families are like this.

Family vacations are boring and enchanted, exactly like this. Tourist attractions are gates into other worlds. Malevolent supernatural forces are focused on the ones you love, and only certain rituals or tokens can protect them, if only you could figure out which rituals, what tokens.

I love the first section of this book best: it's the most enchanted, the spookiest, and the most gonzo. It begins with the mysterious disappearance of the oldest sister (Deane manages to disappear in the second part as well, and again in the third) and ends with the failure of Pet's magical efforts to protect her family from her sister Deane with souvenir necklaces.

Pet is nine, and Geary gets childhood and magic perfectly. Every time I read it, I'm convinced that if magic worked, it would work exactly as Geary says. There are bizarre and unmagical ceremonies, as when Pet and June painstakingly build an elaborate village of vacation tepees for their plush-toy stuffed poodles. There are rituals of protection and rituals to accumulate power: when Deane disappears for the first time, she leaves behind Marmalade—Pet's missing kitten—whom she's killed and amateurishly stuffed, and even worse, her diary/*grimoire*.

Despite the three-page warning—DANGER! TURN THE PAGE AT YOUR OWN RISK! / FINAL WARNING: A CURSE ON THE PERSON WHO STEALS THIS BOOK, OR READS IT UNLAWFULLY / ANCIENT MAGICS AND SECRETS, THE UNKNOWN—Pet reads her sister's diary. Of course she does! Wouldn't you?

Disaster falls on her immediately; further disaster follows, and her family leaves their home in a kind of involuntary, perpetual vacation: part *On the Road*, part on the lam. (Pet's mantra, repeated throughout the book, is "Don't farewell. Fare forward." Not the best mantra for a writer, but it works for a reader of this book.)

Later, Pet will transform herself into a kind of tourist attraction, a monument to her own wrecked childhood. Rituals of childhood become rituals of self-empowerment and Pet becomes the splendid destination she never found in her journeys: large enough to contain both the ordinary and the supernatural world, strong enough to pick up herself and keep moving forward. Sex becomes a doorway into mystic realms, and so do shopping malls and upscale restaurants.

Here's one of the things I love about Patricia Geary's book: every place that looks like a destination turns out to contain an even stranger journey. Pet, abandoned as a child in Disneyland, discovers that her favorite ride is closed and instead boards a boat on the mysterious Sammy's Snowland attraction. She ends up sailing, in isolated, ghostly silence, through a cheerfully supernatural beta-version of It's a Small World and then is carried away even farther, into service tunnels leading straight into the underworld. Perhaps you've been on this ride. Or perhaps you'd know better.

Geary turns the dingiest of tourist attractions—Madame Miraculo's Crazy House, the Snake-a-Torium, Ripley's Believe It or Not Museum—into something more: dangerous, alluring, and almost affordable. The supernatural world is always pressing against the seams of the real world, and sometimes the seams give and the supernatural world seeps right through. Every purchase or ticket is imbued with magical possibility, just like the advertisements promise.

KELLY LINK (b. 1969) lives in Northampton, Massachusetts. She grew up reading Helen Hoke's alliterative anthologies of uncanny tales, and graduated to the short stories of Joan Aiken, John Collier, E. F. Benson, M. R. James, H. P. Lovecraft, Shirley Jackson, Angela Carter, Fritz Leiber, Robert Westall, and Robert Aickman. Link is the author of two acclaimed collections, *Stranger Things Happen* and *Magic for Beginners*. With her partner Gavin J. Grant she runs Small Beer Press and edits the fiction magazine *Lady Churchill's Rosebud Wristlet*. Together they also edit the fantasy half of *The Year's Best Fantasy and Horror* anthology series, with Ellen Datlow handling the horror. Over the past few years Link has been writing mostly ghost and horror stories, especially those featuring zombies, and these will be appearing in such anthologies as *Undead, Firebirds Rising, Coyote Road,* and a *McSweeney's* young adult benefit volume with a ridiculously long title. Her surreal and literary short fiction has won the Nebula, World Fantasy, and Tiptree Awards.

78

[1987]

ALLEN KOSZOWSKI on

The Dark Descent
Edited by **DAVID G. HARTWELL**

Initially published by Tor Books at the height of the 1980s horror boom as a single, thousand-plus-page hardcover, The Dark Descent *was an attempt by editor David G. (Geddes) Hartwell (b. 1941) to chart the entire spectrum of horror fiction up to that time, as well as to make a case for considering horror as central to contemporary literature. Hartwell's experience as editor in chief of Berkley Science Fiction, director of science fiction for Timescape/Pocket Books, and a consulting editor at Tor allowed him to assemble some of the biggest names in the genre, from Ray Bradbury, Richard Matheson, H. P. Lovecraft, and Theodore Sturgeon to Robert Aickman, Ramsey Campbell, Harlan Ellison, and Stephen King (three contributions). The fifty-six stories are broken down into three sections: "The Color of Evil," "The Medusa in the Shield," and "A Fabulous Formless Darkness." In paperback the book has been split into three volumes:* The Dark Descent: The Color of Evil, The Dark Descent: The Medusa in the Shield, *and* The Dark Descent: A Fabulous Formless Darkness. *Hartwell followed* The Dark Descent *with another* magnum opus *horror anthology,* Foundations of Fear *(1992).*

In the first edition of what we can now safely call at least a two-volume series, David Hartwell chose Boris Karloff's 1946 anthology *And the Darkness Falls* as one of the picks for *Horror: 100 Best Books,* and an excellent choice it is. Naturally, modesty would have prohibited him from choosing his own landmark anthology *The Dark Descent,* published the previous year. I have no such constraints, so I will go on record as saying I feel this blockbuster anthology to be the Mount Everest of horror anthologies, to which all other serious editors must aspire.

According to editor Hartwell, the seed of this collection sprouted during a panel discussion at a dark fantasy convention, one of the many panels that fill most of the conventions to which enthusiasts from all over the world flock every year. This panel concerned literary influences, and it occurred to David Hartwell that with the exception of Stephen King, all the authors mentioned were primarily known as short-story writers. Further thoughts on this observation, and talks with such novelists as Peter Straub, led Mr. Hartwell to the tentative conclusion, or theory, that since the late 1960s and early '70s the field had been moving from primarily a short story to a novel genre. Mr. Hartwell's ruminations went much deeper than this, of course, and I don't have enough space here to expand on them. It would be much better for you to purchase the collection and read his wonderful, thoughtful introduction.

Anyone who has more than a passing interest in the field must own a copy of this book for his or her permanent library.

And what about the stories? You will not find a better assemblage of horror stories from the 1700s until the present (in the case of this book, 1987) anywhere. There are a whopping fifty-six stories included in the collection, and there is not a weak tale among them. Longtime readers will have read many before, but never enshrined as they are here, or put into the critical context in which Mr. Hartwell wraps them. It was wonderful to be prodded into reading these classics again, to remind me why I fell in love with the genre to begin with, to show me, as if I needed showing, to what literary heights horror fiction can climb.

There will always be those who will carp, "Why not that Lovecraft story over this one?" or "This Ellison over that one?" That is a waste of time. Editor Hartwell obviously could not include every classic. The superb roster of stories he has amassed here speaks for itself and illustrates the thoughts expressed in his introduction well. He has even managed to use a small gem of a story I was not familiar with: Lucy Clifford's "The New Mother" (1882). I was also pleased to see that he did not neglect a favorite sub-genre of mine, the science fiction-horror story. Michael Shea's "The Autopsy" is an excellent inclusion.

Obviously I can't name every writer and story included, but I will say that editor Hartwell has managed to collect an impressive number of my favorites: Ramsey Campbell's shivery "Mackintosh Willy," Ray Bradbury's paranoid "The Crowd," Fritz Leiber's groundbreaking "Smoke Ghost" (which I once read to my English class in high school), M. R. James's frightening "The Ash Tree," Theodore Sturgeon's gruesome "Bright Segment," Poe's "The Fall of the House of Usher"—I could go on and on. Each story is a classic. I loved rereading them. Each story shines, and in the company of all the rest it is a bright firmament indeed.

I have been reading horror fiction for many years, and I have a collection of books and magazines that number in the many thousands. Among those are the volumes that contain the original appearance of many of these stories, but that did not stop me from purchasing this collection. I now have these tales enshrined in a more permanent form than those crumbling old magazines. This anthology now holds a treasured place in my collection and is among the best anthologies in the field.

If you ever want to hook friends on horror fiction, to show them how classy, how thoughtful, how atmospheric, how *scary* the field can be, I urge you to steer them to this anthology. I cannot recommend this book highly enough. It truly is a classic collection.

ALLEN KOSZOWSKI (b. 1949) was born in Upper Darby, Pennsylvania, and has lived there all his life, except for a stint of about ten years on the mean streets of southwestern Philadelphia. He spent four years in the U.S. Marines, with thirteen months of that time in Vietnam. He has had an interest in science fiction and horror ever since he saw the original *Godzilla* in 1956 at a local movie theater, and his collection of horror, SF and fantasy books, comics, and magazines numbers in the tens of thousands. His distinctive and highly detailed stipple artwork has appeared in such publications as *Fantasy Tales, Whispers, Weirdbook, Asimov's Science Fiction, The Magazine of Fantasy & Science Fiction, Analog, Weird Tales, Cemetery Dance, The Horror Show,* and many others. He has also contributed art to such publishers as Subterranean Press, Midnight House, and Midnight Marquee Press, to name only a few imprints. Koszowski has won the L. Ron Hubbard Illustrator of the Year Award, the World Fantasy Award for Best Artist, and the Small Press Writers and Artists Award a number of times. Despite mostly working in black-and-white illustration, he has been the artist guest of honor at the World Fantasy Convention, The World Horror Convention, Albacon, Necronomicon, and Eeriecon. In 2003 Koszowski launched his own fiction title, *Allen K's Inhuman Magazine.*

79

[1987]

GRAHAM JOYCE on

Misery
by STEPHEN KING

Stephen King (b. 1947) has described Misery *(which was originally going to be published under the author's "Richard Bachman" alias) as illustrating "the powerful hold fiction can achieve over the reader." Although the story has echoes of John Fowles's 1963 novel* The Collector, *King's book was inspired by a meeting the author had with an intense autograph-seeker who asked to have his photograph taken with King and described himself as the writer's "number one fan." The admirer allegedly turned out to be Mark Chapman, who subsequently shot John Lennon to death in New York City on December 8, 1980. Director Rob Reiner and screenwriter William Goldman adapted the novel into a 1990 film starring James Caan as novelist Paul Sheldon, while Kathy Bates won a Best Actress Oscar for her performance as the demented Annie Wilkes. Less well known is a 1992 stage play by Simon Moore, which opened in London with Bill Paterson and Sharon Gless. In 2004, Moore's play became a radio drama with Nicholas Farrel and Miriam Margoyles. Other stage Annies include Sara Morsey, Carolmarie Stock, Merry Evans, Cathy O'Brien, Barbara Chisholm, Hazel Maycock, Lisa Marie Daugherty, Sheila Sheffield, Catherine LeClair, Kristina Baker, and Deborah Lobban.*

EXEMPLARY HORROR, EXEMPLARY writing. Once, when I was lost in what I was doing as a writer, I went back to this book and examined its structure. I made notes about how the story worked, how the cogs turned, how the characters held each other in orbit. It was like discovering laws of physics, but applied to writing. After I'd ended my note-making and closed the book, what I was trying to write at the time all started to make sense again. If I get lost again, I'll go back to *Misery*.

Quite recently Stephen King was honored with the National Book Foundation Medal for Distinguished Contribution to American Letters. It aroused a bit of controversy, but not from anyone who matters. One egregious sack of gas huffed and puffed and pronounced Stephen King not literary enough to merit the award. Shameful, and yet wonderfully ironic when you think that *Misery*, in addition to being a flight of brilliantly executed horror, was at the same time a discourse on literary writing values.

In fact it's the double intention at large in this novel that makes it so spectacular. The narrative grabs you like an eagle's claw, while the multiple layering is what carries you into the air. On one plane, in a clever inversion of Scheherazade, it is about a male storyteller kept prisoner by a monster of a woman; on another, it is an exploration of the alarming nature of the writer's muse. The novel is often described as being about obsessive fans, and maybe that's another level. But then again, the fan and the muse ultimately melt down to the same thing.

The rich layering in *Misery* cannot have been rationally apprehended at the time Stephen King wrote it. These things tend to happen much deeper in the psyche, and it is the gift of the true literary author to have the mental capacity to hold two possibly contradictory ideas at the same time and run them in parallel. Overly rational apprehension would compromise either the narrative or the poetic message of this book. This is why some critics don't get Stephen King. They operate on inferior lines: more intellectual but less humane; more academic but without compassionate insight. This is why we need artists more than we need critics, and Stephen King is an artist.

The trouble is that people say "literary" when they mean "about language." Many so-called literary authors merely paddle about in language, employing a kind of exhibitionist verbosity, sometimes hysterical, sometimes lyrical, sometimes bloody boring. Stephen

King, like many popular authors, deliberately erases style. It's a literary form that might be called "non-style." It avoids self-conscious playfulness with language. But that's *not* the same thing as not being literary. The craft of narrative is a much higher literary quality than any amount of lyrical word-slinging. Character play is far more subtle and elusive an art than genteel finessing of a sentence. And Stephen King shows in *Misery* that he is a grand master of these and many other eminently literary qualities.

When recommending *Misery* I don't know whether to talk about the fizzing narrative bomb or about these other, more abstract, literary properties. There are a couple of reasons why *Misery* is one of my favorite—no, scratch that, *is my favorite*—King novel. I mean, beyond the fact that the story is ferocious and, beyond that, the fact that it is, as I say, also a discourse on writing. One reason is that as a horror novel it finds its horror not in supernatural sources but in human ones. I had a grandmother who saw ghosts and specters on a regular basis, but she was always telling me that I shouldn't fear ghosts, and that it was "the living ones you have to worry about." This is what she meant.

The character of Annie Wilkes is as sphincter-flapping scary as they come. The scene in which Annie turns her Medusa's head after Paul expresses a preference for a particular kind of typing paper will freeze any writer's heart. Because King is so far inside Annie and she is so authentic as a character, you kind of—*gulp!*—agree with what she's saying about prissy authors! Ack! The humor inside the horror is just beautiful.

I can think of very few other novels that so effectively manipulate the parable—or the allegory, if that's what it is—without diminishing the narrative of the story. One of these is Ernest Hemingway's *The Old Man and the Sea*, yet another fiction partly about writing. That author, lauded early in his career, was taking some hammer from the critics before he trounced them with this extraordinary work. Stephen King at his best—and *Misery* is certainly one of his best—is on a par. Some of Stephen King's novels are a long, slow excavation and others seem to parachute in quickly, forming as they reach the ground.

I suspect *Misery* must have been one of the latter for Stephen King, probably because the content was carried around in his unconscious for a long time. Whatever the reasons for its genesis, it's easily one of the best horror novels of all time.

GRAHAM JOYCE (b. 1954) grew up in a mining village near Coventry, England. He spent several years in youth work before quitting his job for the Greek island of Lesbos to concentrate on his writing, and it was there that he wrote his first novel, *Dreamside* (1991). His second book, *Dark Sister*, won the British Fantasy Award for Best Novel of 1992, and it was followed by a return to Lesbos, at least in the setting, for *House of Lost Dreams*. Two more British Fantasy Awards came, for *Requiem* and *The Tooth Fairy*. With his 1998 novel *The Stormwatcher* came a new blending of fantasy and reality. *Indigo* netted him a fourth British Fantasy Award, while the novella *Leningrad Nights* won the French Grand Prix de L'Imaginaire. Set in Thailand, *Smoking Poppy* was followed by the World Fantasy Award-winning *The Facts of Life*, *The Limits of Enchantment*, and the collection *Partial Eclipse and Other Stories*. He has a Ph.D. in literature and teaches creative writing at Nottingham Trent University.

80 [1988]

FRANK M. ROBINSON on

The Silence of the Lambs
by THOMAS HARRIS

Thomas Harris (b. 1940) became a best-selling author with the terrorist-themed thriller Black Sunday *(1975) and the serial killer procedural* Red Dragon *(1981), which both became well-known if not-quite-smash-hit films. However,* The Silence of the Lambs—*a semi-sequel to* Red Dragon—*elevated him to the more exalted position of publishing phenomenon even before Jonathan Demme's Oscar-sweeping 1992 film, the only horror movie ever to win Best Picture, cast Jodie Foster as Clarice Starling and Anthony Hopkins as Dr. Hannibal Lecter. Because Michael Mann's* Manhunter *(1986), based on* Red Dragon, *had not performed at the box office, producer Dino De Laurentiis failed to exercise his option to make the sequel. However, he clawed back rights to Harris's follow-up* Hannibal *(1999), which reads more like a sequel to Demme's film than his earlier novel, and hired Ridley Scott to direct Hopkins and Julianne Moore (as Clarice) in the 2001 film, then had Brett Ratner remake* Manhunter *in the style of Demme (with Hopkins replacing Brian Cox) as* Red Dragon *(2002). No one has yet suggested remaking* Silence *in the style of Mann and giving the excellent Cox another shot at the role. Harris and De Laurentiis have ensured that, Bond-like, "Hannibal Lecter will return" in a prequel to be called* Behind the Mask, *with the film at least due for 2006. As played by Hopkins, Lecter became a pop culture icon—imitated by Billy Crystal at the Academy Awards and Steve Coogan in a sketch about* Silence of the Lambs: The Musical, *and evoked by Kathy Acker in her essay collection* Hannibal Lecter, My Father *(1991). Parody* *versions have been played by Ben Kingsley (*National Lampoon's Loaded Weapon 1, *1993) and Dom DeLuise (*The Silence of the Hams, *1993), while Jerry Butler takes the lead in the porno variation* Hannibal Lickter *(1992). Chet Williamson wrote about* Red Dragon *in* Horror: 100 Best Books.

THERE ARE MANY sub-genres within the horror novel category, one of the most popular of which deals with "things that go bump in the night"—the tales by H.P. Lovecraft in which eldritch horrors stalk the ghost-haunted streets of Arkham or where slimy, many-tentacled things dwell just beyond the veil.

But there is another sub-genre that is far more terrifying. Rather than dealing with the monsters without, it deals with the monsters within—those human monsters who kill one-by-one and face-to-face. And here, fiction cannot compete with reality. Pedro Alonzo Lopez, the "monster of the Andes," is credited with more than 300 kills. Gilles de Rais, an ally of Joan of Arc and later named a marshal of France, had a score of 140, mostly boys.

More recently there was Chicago's John Wayne Gacy, "Pogo the Clown," who performed at children's parties and strangled thirty-three children or adolescents. And then there's Jeffrey Dahmer, who had a taste for seventeen young men, literally.

Most of these monsters have faded from public memory, but the fictional monsters live on in song and story. Three of them are archetypes of the species: Sweeney Todd, the "demon barber of Fleet Street," Darth Vader, the most terrifying of villains immortalized in science fiction films; and Hannibal Lecter, the greatest literary—and movie—monster of them all.

Sweeney Todd was more than a character in English "penny dreadfuls." He was a real, live person and so was Margery Lovett, both of them destined to give generations of young Brits nightmares. Sweeney was immortalized in *The String of Pearls; or the Sailor's Gift* by Thomas Pecket Prest, a story later adapted for the stage. The first movie about him was a 1920s silent, *Sweeney Todd, a Romantic Comedy.* The second was the 1936 film *Sweeney Todd: The Demon Barber of Fleet Street,* which was anything but funny. Stephen Sondheim's musical about Sweeney was largely based on this film.

Darth Vader was certainly in the running as a major pop villain before George Lucas decided to humanize him, turning him into Luke Skywalker's daddy and resurrecting him as a friendly ghost at the end of the first trilogy.

And then there's "Hannibal the cannibal."

Dr. Lecter had a walk-on in Thomas Harris's first serial killer novel, *Red Dragon,* filmed as *Manhunter* with a creditable Brian Cox playing Lecter. But it was Anthony Hopkins who earned his retirement playing Lecter in *The Silence of the Lambs* and in the sequel, *Hannibal.*

Of the three books starring Lecter, it's *Silence of the Lambs* that stands out as the perfect thriller and horror novel.

The plot of *Silence* is relatively simple. Clarice, a young FBI trainee, is sent to interview Dr. Hannibal Lecter, held in a maximum security prison. The FBI would like his help in capturing "Buffalo Bill," who kidnaps young women and skins them for their pelts, which he intends to wear, reminiscent of the real-life drama that inspired Robert Bloch's *Psycho.* Lecter trades bits and pieces of information about Buffalo Bill, a former patient, for bits and pieces of information about Clarice—plus a prison cell with a view. Subplot complications set in when Buffalo Bill's latest victim turns out to be the daughter of a U.S. senator. The head of the prison then makes his own deal with the senator and Lecter, seeking to cut out the FBI and gain some glory for himself. Once out of the maximum security prison, Lecter makes a bloody bid for freedom in one of the most riveting scenes in any thriller. This is almost equaled when Clarice corners Buffalo Bill in the blacked-out, nightmarish basement of his house. Buffalo Bill is wearing night-vision goggles; Clarice has to depend on her ears to locate him.

All's well that ends well. Clarice ices the perp and rescues the fair (if slightly fleshy maiden), but it's Lecter who has the last word as he escapes to play the lead in the next novel.

Why does *Silence of the Lambs* qualify as a horror novel? And why does it stand out in our minds more than the newspaper stories about real monsters like Gacy and Dahmer? The tote board numbers of real serial killers run the danger of drowning in their own statistics. Thirty-three for Gacy and seventeen for Dahmer. The next of kin and the relatives see them, but we don't. We forget the photographs, and the stories on the tube or in the morning paper.

Who do you think ends up with the most audience recognition? Gacy and Dahmer or Hannibal Lecter? Lecter lingers in our imagination, more alive than the villains of reality.

The casualties in a war are beyond imagining. So are the serial killers of reality. We cannot comprehend them—they're nightmarish fantasy figures. But when it comes to the reality of prose, the devil is in the details and author Harris researches *everything*. The scene in the Smithsonian where Clarice is trying to locate the name and background of a moth? It's all there, exactly how it would be done—with a throwaway bit about the moth that lives on tears. The procedures followed in Lecter's maximum security prison? Lecter's psychiatric undressing of Clarice as she questions him? All perfectly researched and perfectly believable.

And Harris spares us nothing. Lecter killing guards Pembry and Boyle in his escape from maximum security? Stomach-turning—and again, perfectly believable.

If absolutely everything else in the story becomes believable, then so does the unbelievable. It's no longer fantasy, it's reality.

Is *Silence of the Lambs* a horror novel?

The editor of *Terror Tales* and *Horror Stories* a long time ago defined "terror" as what you feel when the killer is after you. "Horror" is what you feel when you watch the victim being murdered and cannot turn away.

By these lights, *The Silence of the Lambs* is one perfect horrifying novel.

FRANK M. (MALCOLM) ROBINSON (b. 1926) was born in Chicago and currently lives in San Francisco, with one of the foremost collections of pulp magazines in the world. After graduating from high school in 1943, he worked as an office boy at *Amazing Stories* before he was drafted into the navy, where he served during World War II and the Korean War. His first science fiction story, "The Maze," appeared in 1950 in *Astounding Science Fiction,* while his debut novel, *The Power* (1956), was filmed by George Pal in 1967. During the 1970s and '80s Robinson co-wrote a number of techno-thrillers with Thomas N. Scortia, such as *The Glass Inferno* (filmed as *The Towering Inferno*), *The Prometheus Crisis, The Nightmare Factor, The Gold Crew* (filmed by NBC-TV as *The Fifth Missile*), and *Blow-Out!*. As well as collaborating with John Levine on the political novel *The Great Divide* and Paul Hull on the spy thriller *Death of a Marionette,* Robinson's solo science fiction novels include *The Dark Beyond the Stars, Waiting,* and *The Donor.* In 1981 his short fiction was collected in *A Life in the Day of... and Other Stories,* while his recent non-fiction studies are *Pulp Culture: The Art of Fiction Magazines* and *Science Fiction in the 20th Century: An Illustrated History* (reprinted as part of *Art of Imagination,* along with studies by Robert Weinberg and Randy Broecker). Robinson was assistant editor at *Science Digest* (1956–59, replacing Fritz Leiber), managing editor at *Rogue* (1959–65) and *Cavalier* (1965–66), and a staff writer with *Playboy* (1969–73).

81 [1988]

MARK CHADBOURN on

Prime Evil
Edited by DOUGLAS E. WINTE

Douglas E. Winter (b. 1950) contributed an essay on Joseph Conrad's Heart of Darkness (1902) to Horror: 100 Best Books. *As the editor of this Big Name anthology, he shows where he's coming from in an epigraph that quotes (in Italian) Dario Argento's script for* Demons *(1985):* "faranno dei cimiteri le loro cattedrali e delle citta le vostre tombe" *(for the cemeteries shall be their cathedrals and the cities shall be your tombs). Winter divides his volume of "new stories by the modern masters of horror" into five sub-sections: "In the Court of the Crimson King" (Stephen King's "The Night Flier," Paul Hazel's "Having a Woman at Lunch," Dennis Etchison's "The Blood Kiss"), "Turn to Earth" (Clive Barker's "Coming to Grief," Thomas Tessier's "Food," M. John Harrison's "The Great God Pan"), "Secrets" (David Morell's "Orange is for Anguish, Blue for Insanity," Peter Straub's "The Juniper Tree"), "Spinning Tales" (Charles L. Grant's "Spinning Tales with the Dead", Thomas Ligotti's "Alice's Last Adventure," Ramsey Campbell's "Next Time You'll Know Me"), and "By Reason of Darkness" (Whitley Streiber's "The Pool," Jack Cady's "By Reason of Insanity"). "The Night Flier" became a 1997 low-budget feature with Miguel Ferrer as a tabloid reporter who stalks a vampire. "The Great God Pan" was expanded into a novel,* The Course of the Heart *(1992), which is the subject of the essay by China Miéville in this volume.*

THE 1980S WERE a strange, creepy time to be alive. Fueled by societal decay and right-wing politics, the first flowering of the cult of consumerism and "greed is good" psychotics in expensive suits, it was a decade that could have been hand-tooled for a horror resurgence. And so it turned out.

There was a desperate need for devastatingly brilliant fiction that would hold up a mirror to those real-world nightmares and show them for what they really were. Barker, King, and Straub led the pack, but there were many other authors who contributed to an unprecedented outpouring of creativity in the field of scares. And in *Prime Evil*, the 1980s—horror's last great decade—got the anthology it deserved.

"What makes great horror fiction?" Douglas E. Winter asks in his introduction, and then proceeds to give the answer in the most elegant way possible. It's not simply because *Prime Evil* contained the best of that era's crop of horror authors, nor because Winter managed to pull from them some of the most accomplished work of their career; all of the stories in this anthology are good, some are great. And two are bona fide classics that could hold their head up with any short story, genre or not.

It was because Winter also had the insight to recognize that horror sprawls across the landscape, rising here and there in different forms like the alien in John Carpenter's *The Thing*; sometimes it looks just like us, quietly spoken but with a manic look in the eye, at other times so hideously monstrous it takes the breath away.

Winter has ensured there's a story for every kind of horror fan by dividing the anthology into different sections that capture some of the core moods or styles that make up the essential horror experience. And if you look at it askance, you'll see that the whole anthology is really Winter's philosophical reflection on the genre, its hidden meanings and its importance in our lives. He sets the bar very high in what he plans to do and clears it easily.

And so, in "In the Court of the Crimson King" we find "The Night Flier," where Stephen King indulges his E.C. comics fascination with a blackly humorous tale of a vampire with his own private plane, and where, we learn that the nosferatu urinate blood. This section is about *Grand Guignol*, where no scalpel cut is spared.

"Turn to Earth" delivers subtle tales where the horror is on the fringes of the vision and is all the more chilling for it. Clive Barker notably writes against type with the moody "Coming to Grief," about a woman haunted by her past and a consuming sadness. This is the kind of horror that creeps up on you on a gray day and never leaves.

And here we find the first of the two truly great tales, M. John Harrison's "The Great God Pan," a riff on Machen's classic tale of the same name. Harrison is often described as a writer's writer with good reason. He has effortless mastery of the language, using words in a way few others can. His story is a masterpiece of hints and mood, each delicate but unsettling reflection a part of a puzzle that only by the end reveals the true horror of the situation. "The Great God Pan" is rooted in the mundane and the quiet miseries of people's lives, but terror is never more than a whisper away.

"Secrets" investigates the fringes of reality and how horror can be uncovered in any situation, defined by a truly disturbing, quietly told story by Peter Straub. "Spinning Tales" leads us into the garden of madness, with Ramsey Campbell, Charles L. Grant, and Thomas Ligotti all turning in excellent reflections on the psychological state.

The final section, "By Reason of Darkness," is very much Winter's way of summing up his dissertation. It examines why horror is so important to all of us, illustrated by Winter in a quote from Joseph Conrad: "[A] shadow darker than the shadow of the night . . . the heart of a conquering darkness."

Here we find the second of those two modern classics, Jack Cady's "By Reason of Darkness." Winter has taken Cady's title for this section because the novella perfectly captures the essence of Winter's whole argument. Cady's tale is "haunted not only by the ghosts of Korea and Vietnam, but by the specter of Cady's spiritual ancestor Joseph Conrad." Laden with symbolism filtered through quiet contemplation, it tells of an ex-soldier struggling to live with the legacy of all the real-life horrors he has seen.

Cady shows the best aspect, in my opinion, of the horror genre: that it is not escapist, but instead deals with archetypes and symbols to probe aspects of the world around us that we cannot bring ourselves to consider.

I would recommend *Prime Evil* just for the stories by Harrison and Cady, but the anthology is greater even than the sum of its contents. Much of that is down to Winter's brilliance as an editor and his desire to turn the anthology into something more than a simple showcase of '80s horror. Through his erudite introduction, he invests in it meaning and depth as well as real insight.

As Winter says, "Great horror fiction is not about shock, but emotion; it digs beneath our skin and stays with us." *Prime Evil* is an emotionally exhausting journey into the places inside us that we rarely visit. Not every tale will be to your taste, but I guarantee that by the end of the trip you will be changed.

MARK CHADBOURN (b. 1960) comes from a long line of Midlands coal miners, but after gaining an honors degree in history, he broke with family tradition to become a national newspaper and magazine journalist. Other jobs include running the independent record label Faith, managing bands, a fitter's mate at a power station, and a production line worker. After winning *Fear* magazine's Best New Author award for his first short story in 1991, he landed a publishing deal that saw his debut horror novel, *Underground,* launched a year later. Since then he has worked firmly in the field of contemporary fantasy with a string of novels that include *Nocturne, The Eternal, Testimony, Scissorman, World's End, Darkest Hour, Always Forever, The Devil in Green, The Queen of Sinister,* and *The Hounds of Avalon.* He won the British Fantasy Award in 2003 for his novella *The Fairy Feller's Master-Stroke* from PS Publishing.

82

[1989]

JAY RUSSELL on

By Bizarre Hands: Stories by Joe R. Lansdale
by **JOE R. LANSDALE**

By Bizarre Hands: Stories by Joe R. Lansdale *was originally published by California small press imprint Mark V. Ziesing in trade and slip-cased hardcover editions, with the mass-market paperback reprint coming from Avon. The collection comprises fourteen stories that Lansdale (b. 1951) published between 1982 and 1989 in magazines like* Twilight Zone *and* Hardboiled *and original fiction anthologies like Charles L. Grant's* After Midnight *(1986) and John Skipp and Craig Spector's* Book of the Dead *(1989), the originals "The Steel Valentine" and "The Fat Man and the Elephant," and an introduction by Lewis Shiner. "Hell through a Windshield" made its first appearance in the author's preferred version after* Twilight Zone *cut it for length on initial publication. "On the Far Side of the Cadillac Desert with Dead Folks" won the Bram Stoker Award and the British Fantasy Award, while "Tight Little Stitches in a Dead Man's Back" was a World Fantasy Award finalist. The stories "The Windstorm Passes" and "Boys Will Be Boys" were later incorporated into the novels* The Magic Wagon *(1987) and* The Nightrunners *(1986).*

A FEW YEARS BACK, Elmore Leonard cobbled together some rules of writing. I mention this not because I'm the biggest Elmore Leonard fan in the world—in fact, I think he's overrated—nor do I believe that there really can be any rules for writers or writing. Only suckers and wannabes who piss-away their hard-earned cash on tripe like *Writer's Digest* fall for such fancies. But Leonard—who does, I concede, know a thing or three about his craft—boils his very entertaining set of rules down to one simple idea, which I paraphrase: writers should write what readers want to read. That may not be a recipe for high art, but it is a rule for great writing.

Nobody follows this imperative better than Joe R. Lansdale, who is twice the writer Leonard is forever acclaimed to be.

By Bizarre Hands was Lansdale's first story collection, and it displays all the strengths and qualities that characterize the author's now prodigious and diverse bibliography. At the time the book appeared Lansdale had already published several novels, but while enjoyable, none seemed to achieve the intensity, focus, and depth of his astonishing short fiction. I remember thinking then that Lansdale was just one of those writers—like Harlan Ellison, perhaps—for whom the short story was seemingly invented, and whose novels would always come off as second-best. Great for devotees of the form; tough luck for the writer's mortgage. Lansdale has long since proved me wrong, of course, having since produced a body of novel-length work every bit as powerful and affecting as the finest of these stories. But I still love this collection the best of all Lansdale's work, and I think maybe it is because you can see the boiled-down essence of the full-strength writer-to-be bubbling away on every page.

At the time *By Bizarre Hands* appeared, horror was in the last bloom of its short-lived commercial boom and "splatter" was the talk of the day. Lansdale was never really a "splatterpunk" writer—was anyone?—but his unflinching writerly gaze, applied in potently equal measure to violence and character, made it possible to mistake him for someone who was just playing with grue. There is an undeniable degree of excess in some of these stories, a certain uncomfortable reveling in the details of pain (and there is still a category of horror readers for whom this remains the genre's key appeal), but even Lansdale at his most overwrought—in nasty, stripped-down exercises such as "The Pit" or "The Steel Valentine," or in an over-the-top, postapocalyptic Boschian triptych such as "Tight Little Stitches in a Dead Man's Back"—always constructs and overlays his tales with a complex humanity; his characters and situations invariably transcend the limits of even the basest of genre trappings. Though their testicles get eaten by dogs or their severed heads get stuck on poles, Lansdale's characters live in *our* heads because of who they are and not simply how they are killed. It makes the difference between being merely repulsed and being genuinely horrified.

Lansdale is one of the great voice writers of our time: he is, in fact, the anti-Grisham. There is no mistaking Lansdale's authorial voice for any other, and while I regard that as the highest praise you can pay to a writer, there are masses who run shrieking from such singularity. They want that bland, lifeless, water-left-in-a-glass-on-the-nightstand-for-three-days prose that characterizes most bestsellers. Lansdale will not give in to them, though. He takes remarkably different tacks in these stories, to be sure: from the terse, Shirley Jackson-with-a-shotgun smile exhibited in "Duck Hunt," to the elegiacally Waldropian alternate-history pitch of "Trains Not Taken," to the gently haunting (and distressing) sui generis character study "The Fat Man and the Elephant." All very different, but each unmistakably Lansdale in tone, in measure, in diction . . . in *voice*.

The collection culminates with not one, but two masterpieces. "Night They Missed the Horror Show" remains one of the great modern horror stories. No vampires or werewolves or supernatural trappings of any kind here, just the distilled horrors of human perversity. The tale is excessive, to be sure, but so true in revealing the depths of the amoral heart that the extremity of the situation is beside the point. The story works so well because it touches something deep and foul—an animalistic and instinctive hatred of any brand of *other*—that sits somewhere in all of us, waiting always to get out. It is a story you might wish you could forget, but like certain images of real life (and death) that get burned forever into your brain, it ain't going to happen.

The last story in the book, "On the Far Side of the Cadillac Desert with Dead Folks," is, impossibly, even better than its title. Written for Skipp and Spector's infamous *Book of the Dead*, it is the ultimate zombie story and exemplifies everything that is wonderful (and probably a thing or two that is flawed, but we won't harp on that here) about Lansdale's writing. It is so extreme in its violence and black-comic attitude as to render itself immune from any criticism of that tendency. It takes an already absurd premise—a world overrun by flesh-eating zombies—and says, "Okay, boys, let's go a little crazy here today." The even moderately offended won't get past the second paragraph. Well, fuck 'em, I say. And so does Joe. Every sentence in this fantabulous novella is a delight to the eye and mental ear. It is laugh-out-loud funny sixty times an hour, but no less horrific for its humor. And that is a Lansdale trademark. There are precious few writers working in any genre with his comic gifts, a talent all the more impressive for its seamless blending with blazing action, multi-dimensional characterization, and meticulous plotting. Everything Lansdale does, he does well. Goddamn the sumbitch.

Christ, now I'm trying to talk like him. Which you *always* want to do after you read a few pages of Lansdale. So I'd better stop, because I can't do it anywhere near as well as he does.

But then, no one can.

JAY RUSSELL (b. 1961) is the pseudonym of a writer born in New York, aged in Los Angeles, and currently living in London with his wife and daughter. He is the author of five novels, one short-story collection, and assorted bric-a-brac. *Brown Harvest* (a World Fantasy Award nominee for Best Novel) is a textbook guide to many of his key influences and unfortunate tendencies. Guaranteed to confuse or your money back! His most recent work is the novella *Apocalypse Now, Voyager* (Earthling Publications), the latest adventure in the fantastical/comic life of reluctant supernatural detective Marty Burns, who also stars in the novels *Celestial Dogs, Burning Bright,* and *Greed & Stuff.* Russell's other books include *Blood,* the *Twilight Zone* novelization *Memphis/The Pool Guy,* and the short-story collection *Waltzes and Whispers.* His distinctively off-center fiction also can be found in such anthologies as *The Mammoth Book of Best New Horror, The Year's Best Fantasy and Horror, Stranger, Dark Detectives: Adventures of the Supernatural Sleuths, Embraces,* Skipp and Spector's *Still Dead, Splatterpunks,* and *The King is Dead.*

83

[1989]

PETER H. CANNON on

The Grotesque
by PATRICK McGRATH

Patrick McGrath (b. 1950) melds the worlds of Mervyn Peake's Gormenghast, Vivian Stanshall's *Rawlinson End, and J. B. Priestley's* Old Dark House *in this old dark house mystery of grotesque murders, improbable names, and manipulative social climbers. The author adapted the novel into a screenplay, directed in 1995 by John-Paul Davidson; among the cast were Alan Bates as Sir Hugo; Theresa Russell as Lady Harriet; Sting as Fledge the butler; Anna Massey as Mrs. Giblet; and McGrath's wife, Maria Aitken as Lavinia Freebody. Released in the United Kingdom as* The Grotesque, *the film also has been seen under the odd titles* Grave Indiscretion *and* Gentlemen Don't Eat Poets. *The author is the stepfather of actor Jack Davenport, whose horror credits include* The Wisdom of Crocodiles *(aka* Immortality*) and* The Bunker, *and brother-in-law of born-again ex-convict Tory M.P. Jonathan Aitken, which suggests that the world of his books isn't as removed from reality as might seem likely.*

WHEN I WAS a sophomore in college, I took a course called "Eighteenth-Century Gothick Taste in England," which introduced me to such early novels of the genre as Horace Walpole's *The Castle of Otranto* and William Beckford's *Vathek*. Some years later I had the pleasure of discovering Patrick McGrath, whose first book, *Blood and Water and Other Tales,* both mocked and paid homage to the Gothic tradition. McGrath, I was amused to find, wrote as if the most recent author he had read was Edgar Allan Poe!

As impressive as the short stories were in *Blood and Water,* they only hinted at the achievement of McGrath's first novel, *The Grotesque*, a deliciously decadent, blackly humorous variation on the Golden Age English murder mystery, set vaguely in the same well-to-do world as that of Agatha Christie or Dorothy Sayers. There are few if any topical references, though we learn that the death penalty is still in force.

Sir Hugo Coal, the eccentric and ill-tempered lord of Crook Manor, has suffered "a cerebral accident" that has left him a vegetable in a wheelchair. Nonetheless, he manages to describe in retrospect—just how is never explained—a series of sinister events at Crook, centered on the disappearance of his daughter Cleo's fiancé, Sidney Giblet, whose gnawed bones eventually surface on nearby Ceck Marsh. (McGrath's choice of short names with hard "C" sounds is an inspired touch.)

An amateur paleontologist, Sir Hugo used to work in his barn on reconstructing the skeleton of a dinosaur he'd unearthed, *Phlegmosaurus carbonensis*, while in a tank in his study he kept a fat toad named Herbert, of whom he says, "I did not find him monstrous, however, nor was there anything revolting to me in the spectacle of a toad eating maggots at the dinner table." (By coincidence, I had recently read a passage in Gilbert White's eighteenth-century nature classic *The Natural History of Selbourne*, in which he describes an overgrown toad who eats maggots at the supper table—no doubt the source for this bizarre image.)

Sir Hugo suspects most everyone of nastiness, but it is Fledge, the new butler whom his pious wife, Harriet, has hired, who bears the brunt of his antipathy. Sir Hugo is certain that Fledge is attempting to seduce Harriet; at the same time, Sir Hugo fantasizes about having sex with Doris, Fledge's drunken wife. Of course, all this may be the product of a diseased mind, as Sir Hugo himself realizes: "There is something I have learned since being paralyzed, and that is that in the absence of sensory information, *the imagination always tends to the grotesque.*"

Finding out who killed Sidney Giblet, as skillfully as McGrath reveals the clues and the developments in the case, is ultimately of less interest than his memorable portrait of his unreliable narrator as well as of such minor characters as Mrs. Giblet, the victim's indomitable mother, and Sir Hugo's ten-year-old grandson, who reads Freud's *Totem and Taboo*. McGrath has the gift of selecting just the right suggestive detail. Especially memorable is Sir Hugo's dream of a Mesozoic swamp, which evokes the distant geological past as vividly as any comparable passage in H. P. Lovecraft's *At the Mountains of Madness* or "The Shadow Out of Time."

McGrath, incidentally, has been careful to keep his distance from Lovecraft and the *Weird Tales* school—indeed, from anything that smacks of commercial horror fiction of the past century or so. He and other literary authors have even gone so far as to identify themselves as practitioners of the "New Gothic." The one time I met McGrath, at a signing at the old Scribner's bookstore on Fifth Avenue in New York, he confirmed that his fiction was aimed at an *adult* sensibility.

McGrath's three subsequent novels—*Spider, Dr. Haggard's Disease,* and *Asylum*—share similar themes, but they're grimmer than *The Grotesque*, dealing realistically with abnormal psychology and sexual obsession in often recognizably modern settings. Each of them is nearly as exquisite and concise as *The Grotesque*, but because they lack the earlier novel's extravagant humor, they hold a lesser place in my affections.

PETER H. CANNON (b. 1951) was born in California, grew up mostly in Massachusetts, and lives in New York City with his wife and three children. He is the Mystery and SF/Fantasy/Horror Forecasts editor at *Publishers Weekly*. Nearly all his work, both fiction and non-fiction, is related to H. P. Lovecraft, starting with his acclaimed 1984 short novel *Pulptime*, which paired HPL with fellow *Weird Tales* writer Frank Belknap Long Jr. and an aging Sherlock Holmes. It was followed a decade later by *Scream for Jeeves: A Parody*, and both books were collected in *The Lovecraft Papers*. Cannon's other fiction has been published in two volumes of *The Early Cannon, Forever Azathoth, Episode of Pulptime,* and *The Lovecraft Chronicles*. His non-fiction work includes *The Chronology Out of Time: Dates in the Fiction of H. P. Lovecraft,* the Bram Stoker Award-nominated study *H. P. Lovecraft, Sunset Terrace Imagery in Lovecraft,* and the personal memoir *Long Memories: Recollections of Frank Belknap Long.* In 1998 Cannon edited *Lovecraft Remembered,* a collection of essays for Arkham House, and with S. T. Joshi co-edited *More Annotated H. P. Lovecraft* for Dell.

84 [1989]

DAVID MORRELL on

Carrion Comfort
by DAN SIMMONS

Dan Simmons (b. 1948) wrote an essay on John Gardner's Grendel *(1971) in* Horror: 100 Best Books, *while Edward Bryant wrote about Simmons's World Fantasy Award-winning debut novel* Song of Kali *(1985). A rare author to score equal success in horror and SF (with* Hyperion, *1989), genres rarely as Siamese-twinned as they seem, Simmons partially set his epic* Carrion Comfort *in the mythical Elm Haven, Illinois.* Summer of Night *(1991), influenced by Stephen King's* It *(1986), returns to Elm Haven in more depth, and it is the hometown of characters in* Children of the Night *(1991), a slightly more traditional vampire novel, and* Fires of Eden *(1994).*

My enthusiasm for Dan Simmons began with *Carrion Comfort* and became an addiction. He is the only author whose complete signed works I've collected. Back in 1990, however, all I knew about him was that two of his other novels, *The Song of Kali* and *Hyperion,* had terrific reputations and a ton of awards. Luckily for me, *Carrion Comfort*'s paperback publisher requested a publicity quote. I couldn't resist the editor's enthusiasm and asked to look at the hardcover.

Even as a physical object, that three-pound book was impressive. Most hardcovers measure five by seven inches or six by nine. But this was a whopping seven by ten, with a corresponding thickness, its 636 pages crammed with half a million words ("the first truly epic horror novel," the flap copy noted). The book was also handsome, with brooding illustrations by Simmons and Kathleen McNeil Sherman. But I expected no less from the publisher Dark Harvest. Horror-writer veterans know the place that Paul Mikol's specialty press occupied in the genre back then. Paul's ambition was impressive, and numerous authors (including me) were happy to be in his publications, one of which was the original *Night Visions* series.

Carrion Comfort, I learned, was originally a novella with the same name published in *Omni* magazine in 1983 (reprinted in a Simmons collection, *Prayers to Broken Stones*). The novella deals with three elderly friends, Melanie, Nina, and Willi, who can project their minds into other people and seize control of them. Once a year the group meets to play a chilling game: to show who can use surrogates to achieve the most inventive carnage (Mark Chapman's murder of John Lennon, for example). Not only do the players gain amusement from their abilities, they also suck energy from their victims and thus prolong their lives.

But on this particular evening, betrayal is the essence of the game. Soon Willi is dead, the victim of an explosion. Meanwhile, Nina uses intermediaries to stalk Melanie, leaving a trail of corpses through Charleston's Old Section. The fear and gore are palpable as Melanie, the narrator, turns from hunted to hunter and triumphs. On the final page she thinks of a nuclear submarine she once saw in the waters of Charleston's bay. She imagines how others with her power might indulge "in their own gigantic, final Feeding."

According to Simmons, the novella is his "inquiry into the psychology of absolute power corrupting absolutely." In contrast, the novel is his "exploration of the effect of such absolute power on people who refuse to be victims of it." The book begins with the novella's text and builds from it to examine the nature of charisma. The idea is that the world has numerous mind vampires, that we encounter them every day in many contexts, and that far from seeing them as threats, we enjoy the influence they exert. Politics, Hollywood, religion—these three arenas are especially rife with mind vampires, the novel argues. Demagogues and zealots control our minds to a degree we never suspect.

Carrion Comfort's disparate protagonists, brought together by violence and destiny, are a law-enforcement officer, a black woman whose father was one of Nina's victims, and a Jewish psychiatrist who survived the Nazi death camps. (The camps are one example of a massive mind-vampire Feeding.) As the trio investigates the implications of the trail of corpses that Nina and Melanie left in Charleston, it soon becomes clear that Willi faked his death, that Nina, too, might still be alive, and that a devastating psychic war is in progress. But there are other Feeders, men at the highest levels of influence who crave a larger, deadlier game in which whole countries, instead of individuals, are manipulated to achieve the greatest, most inventive carnage.

Carrion Comfort is important in the genre because it is one of the few major reinventions of the vampire concept, on a par with Jack Finney's *Invasion of the Body Snatchers*, Richard Matheson's *I Am Legend*, and Stephen King's *'Salem's Lot*. But the novel's greatness isn't due only to its innovations, as considerable as they are. Simmons manages the rare horror achievement of making his narrative convincing. He uses various forms of science to persuade us. He provides a ton of palpable details to suspend our disbelief. Charleston and other settings are described with loving vividness in sentences that have texture and conviction. The grand shifts of locale and the complex leap-frogging time scheme make the narrative feel three-dimensional. The numerous viewpoint shifts from character to character and first-person to third-person also add a sense of many dimensions. The characters are developed to such a degree that when a protagonist dies halfway through the plot, the shock of the murder reverberates through the rest of the novel, making us fear for the safety of the survivors as if they are actual people.

Carrion Comfort's highest achievement is that it makes us look at our world in a different fashion. Too often horror novels have no relevance to the reality outside their pages. But Simmons uses the concept of mind vampires as a metaphor that makes us look at charisma in a new, disturbing way. Governments, TV screens, and pulpits become enemies. Free will becomes our most precious resource. The irony is that every compelling fiction writer is a mind vampire, seizing control of readers and drawing imaginative strength from them.

DAVID MORRELL (b. 1943) is the author of *First Blood,* the award-winning novel in which Rambo was created. He holds a Ph.D. in American literature from Pennsylvania State University and was a professor in the English Department at the University of Iowa until he gave up his tenure to devote himself to a full-time writing career. "The mild-mannered professor with the bloody-minded visions," as one reviewer called him, Morrell has written numerous best-selling thrillers that include *The Brotherhood of the Rose* (the basis for a highly rated NBC-TV miniseries in 1989), *The Fifth Profession,* and *Extreme Denial* (set in Santa Fe, New Mexico, where he lives). His recent books are a collection of dark-suspense stories, *Nightscape,* and *Lessons from a Lifetime of Writing,* a discussion of what he has learned during his more than thirty years as an author. Eighteen million copies of his books are in print. His fiction has been translated into twenty-seven languages, and his short stories have appeared in many of the major horror/fantasy anthologies of the past twenty years, including the *Whispers, Shadows, Night Visions, Masters of Darkness III, The Dodd Mead Gallery of Horror, Psycho Paths, Prime Evil, Dark at Heart, MetaHorror, Revelations, 999, Redshift,* and *Flights: Extreme Visions of Fantasy.* Two of his novellas received Bram Stoker Awards from the Horror Writers Association. He has also been nominated for two other Stokers and has twice been nominated for the World Fantasy Award. Shaun Hutson wrote about Morrell's novel *The Totem* (1979) in *Horror: 100 Best Books.*

85

[1989–99]

STEPHEN R. BISSETTE on

From Hell
by ALAN MOORE and EDDIE CAMPBELL

Created for serialization in SpiderBaby Grafix & Publications' anthology comic Taboo, From Hell *originally appeared in volumes two through seven (Tundra co-published volumes five through seven) between 1989 and 1992. The serial halted in midstream, though* Taboo— *home also of the first version of Tim Lucas's* Throat Sprockets—*lasted until 1995. Tundra (and its successor Kitchen Sink Press) republished the serialized* Taboo *chapters in conjunction with Alan Moore's own Mad Love imprint between 1994 and 1998, continuing the series to its conclusion in eleven perfect-bound "prestige format" volumes. After the collapse of Kitchen Sink, Eddie Campbell rescued the completed graphic novel from legal entanglements and prepared the definitive one-*

volume collected edition in 1999 (via his self-publishing imprint Eddie Campbell Comics, in collaboration with Knockabout in the United Kingdom and Top Shelf in the United States). Though meticulously researched and rooted in actual history, its central premise addresses "theories" about the Ripper's identity and motives essentially made up by Stephen Knight, which had previously inspired the BBC-TV documentary Jack the Ripper *(1974), the Sherlock Holmes film* Murder by Decree *(1979), and the ITV miniseries* Jack the Ripper *(1988)*. From Hell *embraces Knight's selection of Ripper, but fully acknowledges in its overlapping realities that it is an arbitrary choice. Among the many, many literary and visual influences on the work are David Lynch's* The Elephant Man *(1980), Peter Ackroyd's* Hawksmoor *(1985), and Iain Sinclair's* White Chapel, Scarlet Tracings *(1988).* From Hell *was filmed by Allen and Albert Hughes in 2001, with Johnny Depp as an even more unlikely Inspector Abberline than Michael Caine but a great deal of melodramatic brio.*

The Ripper was born amid the journalistic comics illustrations of the 1888 *Police Gazette,* so it's only appropriate that the greatest Ripper novel of all time is a graphic novel. Those dismissing Alan Moore and Eddie Campbell's *From Hell* as a mere echo of revisionist Ripperologists and true-crime conspiracy theorists miss the point entirely (as did the Hughes Brothers, whose ambitious attempt to adapt the graphic novel to film was doomed once they lockstepped with the archetypal mystery/horror film template). *From Hell* is not just the story of Jack the Ripper, whoever he might have been. From its second chapter we know who the Ripper is: we meet him as a child and trace his formative experiences. For the sake of narrative convenience if nothing else, Moore and Campbell embrace Stephen Knight's conjecture of Dr. William Gull as the culprit, discarding the "whodunit?" trappings of most Ripper metafiction to address more momentous issues. It is not who, but what happens to whom and why, and how those events irrevocably shatter all in their wake, that provide the black heart of this graphic novel, breathtaking in its audacity and scope and brilliantly realized.

The conceit of *From Hell* is that Jack the Ripper was essential: the nineteenth century's most dire undercurrents made flesh, a necessary harbinger of the century to come, foreshadowing our twenty-first century. If history is written in human blood, were the sordid deaths of a quintet of prostitutes a sacrifice to something more than lust, a manifestation of some malignance vast beyond our comprehension? *From Hell* is Lovecraftian in concept, but in execution it is quite something else: ripe with blunt sexuality, redolent with Jacobean cruelties, rich with labyrinthian intricacies worthy of Nicolas Roeg's best films (one must evoke creators from other media, as there is nothing in comics quite like it, outside of Moore and Campbell's own distinctive bodies of work). With an orchestration of effect impossible outside the medium of comics, Moore and Campbell trace the ripples of the Ripper murders back and forward in time while telling their tale with absorbing immediacy, intimacy, breadth, and depth. Only in this medium could they so elegantly weave a tapestry in which the maturation of an affluent murderer, the savage deaths of five destitute women we come to care for, and the throes of a frustrated investigator are interwoven with queens and elephant men, masons and Indians, Aleister Crowley and Robert Louis Stevenson, the visions of Blake (what monstrous "ghost of the flea" did the poet and artist see?), the biological conception of Hitler himself, and all the blood and the butchers and the world wars to follow. In the bloodied alleys of Whitechapel, a truly apocalyptic finale to one century and first act of the next erupts, as seen, spoken, felt, and suffered by the lowly pawns in its thrall.

Conceived prior to the adoption of an occult path in his own personal life, completed after his active exploration of magic(k) was under way, Moore delineates a mythic perception of reality/realities, human and suprahuman, that is at once profane and divine. "I am a wave, an influence," Gull rhapsodizes during the mystical ascension that precedes his mortal descent; in genre terms, Robert Bloch's Ripper was here before, but Moore redefines Bloch's pulp metaphysics with bracing conviction (these are resonant concepts Moore explored and articulated in his subsequent performance pieces—one of which Campbell adapted into graphic novel form—and the comics series

Promethea). His erstwhile confederate Campbell more than keeps pace; he in fact kept Moore on task throughout the arduous execution of the graphic novel, which was a decade in the making.

What is most remarkable about *From Hell* is the manner in which writer and artist communicate this arcane philosophy while maintaining fidelity to a tactile sense of people, time, and place. Moore had already proved himself adept at any genre he chose to engage with (and, inevitably, expand), while Campbell was best known at the time of *From Hell*'s inception for his semiautobiographical *Alec* graphic novels. Working together, they wield Campbell's earthy pragmatism with surgical skill. This is central to *From Hell*'s impact: in a matter of panels, not pages, Campbell's deceptively casual pen-and-ink imagery and Moore's cunning dialogue dispose of a century of clichés peculiar to their chosen subject, maintaining their balance for another five-hundred-plus pages with alchemical grace. This uncanny collaborative synthesis evokes more than sketches of life embraced (and extinguished) beyond the narrow parameters of panel borders and the gutters between: time and time again, the quiet, secret-but-utterly-banal rhythms of daily existence assert themselves. Amid the rigorously researched and rendered historic details, the Masonic rituals, back-alley fucks, barroom banter, horrific murders, and glimpses of the most private of human exchanges punctuated by the most jarring glimpses of the infinite, they (and we) never lose our footing. There is no comforting exoticism in their/our immersion in London of the late 1880s, no retreat into the alien: even Gull's monstrous acts are rendered human and all too palpable. It is all of a piece, a lucid portrait of life lived and lost on its own terms.

This anchors the cosmological horrors of *From Hell*—real or imagined, it matters not a whit—in the unflinching re-creation of those caught in its eye, its grip, its terrible orbit. Moore and Campbell conclude their saga with a transcendent movement through time and space (enhanced by the lovely autobiographical coda "Dance of the Gull Catchers"), which ripples out of the pages. "Truth is," Moore writes in the coda, "this has never been about the murders, not the killer nor his victims. It's about us. About our minds, and how they dance." We join those within and beyond the panel borders and gutters—touched, one and all, by the dance of the Ripper.

STEPHEN R. (RUSSELL) BISSETTE (b. 1955) lives and works in Marlboro, Vermont, with his wife, Marjory, and son Daniel. Stephen toiled in the comic book industry for almost a quarter of a century as a cartoonist, writer, editor, and publisher. Bissette remains best known for his work on such titles as *Sojourn, Heavy Metal, Sgt. Rock,* the graphic adaptation of the Steven Spielberg film *1941* (with Rick Veitch), and DC Comics' *Saga of the Swamp Thing* (1982–87). He co-created, edited, and published ten volumes of the Eisner Award-winning horror comics anthology *Taboo* (1989–95) and earned the comics industry Inkpot Award for Superior Career Achievement in 1998, just before the market's collapse led to his retirement from the field the following year. Since 1990 Bissette has illustrated numerous limited-edition books by authors such as Neil Gaiman, Douglas E. Winter, Joe R. Lansdale, Rick Hautala, Christopher Golden, Nancy A. Collins, Joe Citro, and others, and painted the cover art for the Barrel Entertainment DVD *Last House on Dead End Street.* He co-created the character of John Constantine, played by Keanu Reeves in the 2005 film *Constantine,* and worked briefly on Mirage Studios' Teenage Mutant Ninja Turtles—the character "Tokka" that appeared in the second TMNT feature, *Secret of the Ooze,* was based on his drawings. As a writer, Bissette's work includes the 1992 Bram Stoker Award-winning novella *Aliens: Tribes* and short fiction for *Words without Pictures, Hellboy: Odd Jobs, Working for the Man,* and other titles. He wrote the movie guide *We Are Going to Eat You!: The Third World Cannibal Movies* and co-authored *Comic Book Rebels* and *The Monster Book: Buffy the Vampire Slayer.* His articles have appeared in numerous film magazines, including *Video Watchdog, Deep Red, Ecco, Fangoria,* and

Gorezone. Bissette's papers are now housed at the Henderson State University library's Special Collections in Arkadelphia, Arkansas.

86

[1991]

DAVID McGILLIVRAY on

American Psycho
by **BRET EASTON ELLIS**

Though Simon & Schuster paid a $300,000 advance for Bret Easton Ellis's third novel, the publisher—after protests from groups within and outside the company who considered the book pornographically misogynist on the strength of leaked extracts from the manuscript—refused to issue American Psycho. Vintage in the United States and Picador in the United Kingdom picked up the novel, which became enormously controversial, especially among the many readers who skim-read to get to the sexy and/or gruesome stuff. Among the many subjects Ellis writes about with apparent, though ironized, knowledge are fashion, food, music, serial killing, and the video nasty. It hardly needs saying that the title refers to the film American Gigolo and Robert Bloch's novel and Alfred Hitchcock's film Psycho. Ellis returned to horror briefly in his next novel, The Informers (1994), which features a vampire among many rootless, addicted, predatory characters. Though film versions of American Psycho were threatened from David Cronenberg and/or Brian DePalma, the eventual movie was directed by Mary Harron, who co-scripted with actress/lesbian icon Guinevere Turner. Christian Bale starred as Patrick Bateman, *the 1980s yuppie who combined "mergers and acquisitions" with "murders and assassinations." Michael Kremko had a cameo as Bateman in the unnecessary direct-to-video sequel* American Psycho II All-American Girl *(2002), which cast Mila Kunis as a copycat killer opposite an unlikely William Shatner.*

UNLESS WE IMAGINE that it is us teetering on the brink of Poe's pit or trapped in King's Overlook Hotel, horror tends not to work. By this token, Bret Easton Ellis's *American Psycho*, the most controversial novel of the early 1990s, works horribly well. Or, to be more precise, it works as horror even though it may not work on other levels.

Before the book appeared in 1991, we knew a fair amount about Ellis. He was born in 1964, and his first two published novels—*Less Than Zero* (1985) and *The Rules of Attraction* (1987)—were inspired by people he met at college on the U.S. West Coast. After he moved to New York, his third novel was once again about his own milieu, this time yuppie friends "making enormous amounts of money for doing basically nothing." In *American Psycho* they're privileged college boys obsessed with personal grooming, designer labels, sex, drugs, and the newest club, the trendiest restaurant. They're sexist, racist, and homophobic. Their tale is told by Patrick Bateman, age twenty-six, different from the others only in that he appears to lead a double life as a serial killer.

Like Ellis's earlier work, *American Psycho* is parody that would be impossible without personal knowledge. The book's most famous gimmick—Patrick's need to log the name of the designer of every piece of clothing worn by him and everyone he meets—is irritating but impressive. Ellis's knowledge of fashion icons seems unparalleled. Cleverly, it leads us to assume that Patrick's misanthropy is also Ellis's; and when the murders begin, they are described in such ferocious and fastidious detail that we believe they are also Ellis's own experiences. It is not until we close the book that the spell is broken and we come to our senses.

Bret Easton Ellis is a slippery customer who may or may not have cultivated an image to enhance his book sales. In interviews he comes across as a strange loner, capable of anything he has written about (and more). He has said that *American Psycho* is and isn't autobiographical. Indisputably, he was a precociously talented writer from an early age. *Less Than Zero,* published when he was twenty and still at college, catapulted him to the forefront of the literary brat pack of the 1980s. But his initial success was short-lived. He says that he began preparations for *American Psycho* during a period of great unhappiness.

Out of this came the bizarre notion of a link between consumerism and bloodlust. "I don't know where I made the connection," Ellis explains. "It just seemed logical that one of these guys would be driven so nuts by how status-obsessed everyone is that it would incite him into becoming a murderer." The psychology is not easy to accept; and although it came to be admired as such, *American Psycho* is not the most telling satire of everything that was wrong about the 1980s. (Ellis's targets—cocaine-fueled claptrap, body fascism, and celebrity worship—remain part of our lives in the twenty-first century.)

Ellis's talent for building inconceivable horror out of everyday metropolitan life is, however, considerable. His main influence, he says, is the cinema. Variations on the phrase "Like in a movie" are repeated throughout *American Psycho*; and when it's revealed that Patrick's sex killings have been in his drug-addled mind, we realize that everything he has imagined has been inspired by the videos he's rented. The sex is the imagery of pornography, while the murders are inspired by splatter movies (*Body Double, The Toolbox Murders,* and *The Texas Chain Saw Massacre* are among those mentioned in the text). Just to set the record straight, the impassive descriptions of the murders, which sear them into one's brain for life, were based on FBI accounts and books about real-life serial killers. "I couldn't really have made this up," says Ellis.

Whatever his other failings, Ellis can write horror that instills in the reader a mounting fear that almost borders on panic. He begins with the merest hint that *American Psycho* is not a story about small talk on the Upper West Side: after his morning ablution ritual with spearmint face scrub, Patrick is strangely fascinated by the Black & Decker Handy Knife in the kitchen. A quarter of the way through the book, he blinds a tramp on Twelfth Street, an incident that is followed by Patrick's four-page appraisal of Genesis, "the best, most exciting band to come out of England in the 1980s." This is the first use of Ellis's perverse juxtapositions, jarring in a book but commonplace in a film.

After Patrick has nailed Bethany to the floor, cut out her tongue, and fucked her twice in the mouth, we turn the pages in terrible fear for the welfare of Patrick's girlfriends, Evelyn and Courtney; of Luis, a male admirer whom Patrick has spurned; and, by implication, ourselves. As it happens, Patrick's friends are safe. He moves on instead to strangers, prostitutes, finally a nameless victim. We approach chapters headed "Killing child at zoo" and "Tries to cook and eat girl" with almost unbearable dread. There is a breathtakingly exciting chase, written in a single, Joycean sentence, but it doesn't end as we expect. When the end comes, some fourteen chapters later, it comes, as we should have expected, with Patrick's almost complete disintegration.

Able only to suggest the violence, the 2000 film of the book is more barbed in its satire of the 1980s, dwelling mockingly on nouvelle cuisine; Phil Collins; and, most memorably, mobile phones the size of house bricks. It's not a bad film, but thirty years from now it will seem as tame and prudish as Stanley Kubrick's once shocking film of *Lolita*. Then it will be time to film *American Psycho* full-strength, complete with the popped eyeball; the dismemberment; and, of course, the starving rat and the Brie. What will it say about the people we've become?

DAVID McGILLVRAY (b. 1947) was born in London. Like David Pirie, Anne Billson, and Kim Newman, he began his career reviewing exploitation movies for the British Film Institute's *Monthly Film Bulletin*. During the 1970s he scripted sleazy British films for directors Pete Walker (*House of Whipcord, Frightmare, House of Mortal Sin, Schizo*) and Norman J. Warren (*Satan's Slave, Terror*), plus ventures into the even murkier world of the British sex film—the ultimately sexless *White Cargo,* starring David Jason, *The Hot Girls* and the memorably titled *I'm Not Feeling Myself Tonight*—which eventually led to a definitive book (and television documentary) on the subject, *Doing Rude Things: The History of the British Sex Film, 1957–1981.* As an actor he can be glimpsed in most of his films—usually wearing noteworthy 1970s shirts, although he appears in clerical garb for the witch-whipping flashback in *Satan's Slave*—and also the short *Can I Come, Too?* He also wrote the Norwegian psycho intruders-vs.-mad magician movie *Turnaround* and has worked extensively on stage and television. His serial autobiography, *Spawn of Tarantula!,* appeared in three parts in Stefan Jaworzyn's *Shock Xpress* and *Shock* compilations from Titan Books.

87 [1992]

BRIAN HODGE on

Lost Souls
by POPPY Z. BRITE

Published by Delacorte Press in the United States and Penguin Books in the United Kingdom, Lost Souls—*a working definition of "not just a vampire novel"—was the debut novel of Poppy Z. Brite (b. 1967). The prologue appeared as a separate story ("A Taste of Blood and Altars") in* The Horror Show *magazine in 1988, and "The Seed of Lost Souls," the novella that grew into the novel, was published as a chapbook (illustrated by Dame Darcy) by Subterranean Press in 1999. The* Lost Souls *characters of Steve Finn and Ghost, musicians from Missing Mile, North Carolina, crop up in other Brite stories and fragments ("Angels," "Stay Awake," "America," and "How to Get Ahead in New York"), though she now claims that "after almost fifteen mostly happy years with Steve and Ghost, I am done writing about them." An interesting Web footnote can be found online (quizilla.com/users/discoranger/quizzes/): an easy-to-answer "which* Lost Souls *character are you?" questionnaire. A tenth-anniversary edition of the novel appeared in 2002 from Gauntlet Press. Poppy Z. Brite writes about Ramsey Campbell's* The Face That Must Die *(1983) elsewhere in this volume.*

IN THE LATE 1980s and early '90s, Poppy Z. Brite emerged as a writer to watch, based on a handful of short stories. But this, her debut novel, turned her into a bona fide cult figure almost overnight, guaranteeing both acclaim and jealous snarking. Such is the fate of those who emerge in full bloom, or appear to.

In the introduction to the tenth-anniversary edition of *Lost Souls*, Brite admits to regarding the novel as "juvenilia," and technically this is true. It was written when she was not long out of her teens ... but then, it almost had to be. Otherwise its depictions of adolescent and early twentysomething malaise wouldn't have near the credibility they do. Like so many debuts, *Lost Souls* is a coming-of-age novel, replete with the concerns and anxieties of passage. Yet it's still the work of an artist of uncommon maturity whose deep love of language is evident from the first paragraph and who even in her most lyrical moments remains in control of her gifts. *Lost Souls* is a book for those who don't just read, but also savor.

Central to the novel—the axis around which several characters, groups, and story threads revolve and whose destinies converge—is a fifteen-year-old runaway named Nothing, sired by one vampire and delivered by another, who took the infant far away and left him as a doorstep foundling in hopes of giving him a chance at a normal life. It doesn't work. Blood calls to blood.

Part of the novel's primal allure, although rendered in much darker and more savage tones, is the way it taps into the same fantasy at the core of the later "Harry Potter" phenomenon: the sense that where you grew up is *not* your home, and that your true family—so much more alive and vibrant—is somewhere *out there,* waiting to claim you and unlock your potential and the secrets of your past.

It's been said that a vampire novel is about as safe a route as there is to first getting published. But there was nothing safe about Brite's approach to this one. In contrast to Anne Rice's swank and long-suffering navel-gazers, *Lost Souls'* core trio—Molochai, Twig, and Zillah, Nothing's father—are brats to the bone, all hedonism, swagger, and gluttony, gorging on junk food and awash in drugs and alcohol. Blood is just one more addiction. They walk in sunlight and have none of the weaknesses of older vampires such as the ironically named Christian, who tried to carry the newborn Nothing beyond his heritage and who maintains a quietly touching dignity even as he admires this newer generation.

And on the opposing side, the musician duo of Steve and Ghost are as unlikely a pair of vampire hunters as has ever been seen. With Steve's slacker tendencies and beer-soaked self-pity over a lost girlfriend, and the asexual Ghost's empathic psyche and connection to the spirit world, they're as unsuited for normal lives as the vampires.

Brite clearly loves these characters and refuses to judge them, which allows for some intriguing dichotomies to emerge: the depiction of the vampire lifestyle is heavily romanticized, yet the characters who romanticize it, as early as the prologue, invariably meet bad ends. Nothing embraces his new family, even though they engage in the same kind of casual cruelty it's easy to imagine him suffering at the hands of jocks and other high school tormentors. Also notable—to some, notorious—is the novel's explicit portrayal of gay and bisexual characters, a rarity at the time.

Though the novel may revolve around vampires, the true horror in the world of *Lost Souls* is conformity, to be avoided at all costs. As Nothing tells himself midway through: *You've consigned yourself to a life of blood and murder, you can never rejoin the daytime world. . . . Fine. As long as I don't have to be alone again.* Even the major locales—the fictional hamlet of Missing Mile, North Carolina, and Brite's rendition of New Orleans' French Quarter—seem immeasurably far from interstate highways and their clusters of prefabricated sameness, stubbornly resistant to mass appropriation and their roots sunk deep into earth and time. It's as close as Brite comes to honoring tradition. Following in Clive Barker's still-warm footsteps, she likewise showed no interest in returning things to the status quo.

Decadent and amoral, *Lost Souls* is definitely not for traditionalists, but for those who won't be threatened by its worldview; it weaves a spell of narcotic potency.

BRIAN HODGE (b. 1960) was born and raised in the Midwest, although for the past several years he has lived in Boulder, Colorado, and works beside a window that looks out on the Front Range of the Rocky Mountains—at least when the leaves are off the trees. He sold his first two novels about three months apart when he was twenty-six years old and has written full-time ever since. Most of his fiction has fallen under the horror and crime-suspense umbrellas, including the novels *Oasis, Dark Advent, Nightlife, Deathgrip, The Darker Saints, Prototype, Wild Horses, Hellboy: On Earth As It is in Hell,* and *Mad Dogs.* He is the author of about ninety short stories and novellas, and his work has been collected in *The Convulsion Factory, Falling Idols, Lies & Ugliness,* and *The Sacred and Profane.* Despite being nominated for more than a dozen awards—Bram Stoker Award, World Fantasy Award, International Horror Guild Award, and Britain's CWA Dagger Award for crime fiction—for various novels, stories, and collections, it all amounted to a long Susan Lucci-like losing streak until 2004, when he won the IHG Award for the short story "With Acknowledgments to Sun Tzu," which originally appeared in the *The Third Alternative.* Hodge also dabbles in photography and music—the latter mostly dark, electronic stuff, that could be a soundtrack to much of what he writes. He used to feel guilty about being influenced by various movies until a few years ago, when Ray Bradbury came to town for a lecture and cheerfully proclaimed that he'd been influenced by film pretty much his entire career. If it didn't bother Bradbury up in his aerie, he thought, then it shouldn't bother him down here.

88

[1992]

CHINA MIÉVILLE on

The Course of the Heart
by M. JOHN HARRISON

The Course of the Heart *expands on "The Great God Pan" (1988), a novella that first appeared in Douglas E. Winter's anthology* Prime Evil *(see Mark Chadbourn's piece in this volume); between versions, characters change names and much else is revised. The novel is a bleak and enigmatic work by M. (Michael) John Harrison (b. 1945), one of the great writers of literary fantastic, renowned for, among others, the* Viriconium *books (collected 2000), the award-winning* Light *(2003),* Signs of Life *(1997), and the "realist" novel* Climbers *(1989). One hot night, with the help of the utterly selfish magician Yaxley, three Cambridge students carry out a ritual. The details are unclear, but the event leaves each of the three scarred by the Pleroma, a magical realm beyond our own. The ramifications of the contact shape the rest of their lives. One of the three, the unnamed narrator, becomes complicit in and tries to extricate himself from another of Yaxley's monstrous, tawdry schemes. Ultimately, Yaxley must watch his erst-*

while co-magicians, Pam Stuyvesant and Lucas Medlar, try and fail to live together in the shadow of what they have done, haunted by figures from the Pleroma. One of their strategies is the shared creation of the memoirs of a "Michael Ashman," chronicler of the "Coeur," an evasive, vaguely Mitteleuropean kingdom that acts as a conduit between the Pleroma and the everyday. The novel received a first American edition in 2004 from Night Shade Books.

THERE ARE SEVERAL different ways of reading *The Course of the Heart*. One can read it as an anti-fantasy—as, in fact, *the* antifantasy, the exemplary, *ne plus ultra* of the punitive fantastic that M. John Harrison spent years honing and that reaches its apotheosis in this astonishing, unremitting work. "So you want to escape, do you?" the book says. "You 'fantasy' readers? You want to run away to a Magical Kingdom? Well, here it is: it's merciless and terrifying and it'll get you nowhere." The book can be read, in other words, as the clichéd injunction to "grow up" transmogrified into an extraordinary lament—a *cri*, of course, *de Coeur*—by one who knows exactly why we don't want to grow up, why that's the hardest thing there is.

Or it can be read as a gloss on Gnosticism, "Vision for Beginners," written just before the Nag Hammadi corpus became the world's greatest magnet for grad students and two-bit mystic flakes. These days you can't spit without hitting someone wittering on about the Gospel according to Thomas. Particularly after the megaton catastrophe of *The Da Vinci Code*, we live in an aftermath of post-theological debris, a rubble of degraded dissidence in which we spuriously (re)construct mysticism with the finesse of Cro-Magnons, banging together ass-end scobs of doctrine and calling it Gnosticism. In an epoch of such debased faux vision, it can be hard to remember how strange and—yes, in context, insurrectionary—much of that muddle of suppressed beliefs really were.

Harrison remembers, and he lays it out. He gives us a "Pleroma," that Gnostic universe of fullness, a Real beyond the real, without the taint of middlebrow kookiness. As in religion, so in history: Harrison points out, with the ink still wet on the cheerful Templar porn of

Foucault's Pendulum, that counterhistory is, of course, bunk. In this book we see it written by terrified liars, and our fascination for the stories they construct is human but pathetic: to underline the utterly constructed nature of these comforting conspiracy theories, we even get to read different drafts of the same spurious descriptions.

That precise awareness of how to write suggests another possibility. Perhaps the book is best understood as a patchwork of literature and art. It was born out of a meditation on and updating of Arthur Machen's short masterwork "The Great God Pan," and its nods don't stop there. The book is neurotically referential. Among many others, in the comforting/threatening inventions of the dysfunctional couple, we see Albee's *Who's Afraid of Virginia Woolf?*; in the revelation of Lucas Medlar's grotesque Pleroma-sourced familiar is the coagulum of the demons of *Don't Look Now* and Sheridan Le Fanu's "Green Tea." In the unsustainable otherworld of the Coeur, that airlock between the everyday and the always, is Alfred Kubin's impossible city of Pearl. And on and on. Harrison even references Harrison: the book is populated with his signature ash and collapse, in Pam Stuyvesant's cigarette surname, in the "Ash-man" she and Lucas create to fantasize for them: who, after all, is Michael the Ash-Man but Mike John Harrison himself?

There is another, more bluff, way to think about this book, with its obsessively specific Yorkshire setting. "Something's going on in the Pleroma" the distraught Pam says early on, and is then echoed by the despicable Yaxley a few pages later: "Something's going on in the Pleroma." Or to put it another way, "There's trouble at t'mill." In the hidden heart of plenitude, there is trouble, and it is spilling into our world: the archetypal Northern England anxiety.

Harrison is a master of Northern England Gothic. Like an angry miner whose effete son's gone South, God glowers from just offstage of *The Course of the Heart*, outraged at these know-it-all kids who went to Cambridge and London and got uppity, followed a dream of better things, and ended up getting themselves in trouble. Lucas Medlar, look, a meddler. That's what comes from not knowing your place. Despite the folk radicalism of the mining community, that so-classic confrontation ("no son of mine . . .") is astoundingly conservative. Harrison, however, is not: the danger here comes not from not knowing your place in the world but from *the world itself,* a world you can forgive or rail against but that is saturated with danger. Noticing that—staring into the face of the Pleroma/abyss—might just increase the risk—the abyss might stare back—but it was always there. There's no sure way to play safe in Harrison's universe.

Our usual half-cocked security measures against the implacable numinous, in which traditional North-of-England culture excels, here offer no comfort at all, and are in fact dangerous. "Fuck your common sense," says Lucas, and he's right. Sentimentality does no better: the cheap romances a dying woman reads with good-humored condescension are nothing but the narrative of her own life, embedded with horror, the tragedy of seeking to be swept off her feet. Roses, such cozy and pretty flowers, cloy with their stench, are for our narrator the very avatar of that Pleroma that exacts from him an unbearable price. All of the monstrous angels that haunt the book, the wisps that cling to the failed numinauts, are made of the detritus of everyday culture: cheap flowers, stock monsters, the dangling lovers from a plastic-coated tarot deck.

For Harrison, escape has always been limited to what, in this book, he explicitly calls an "infolding": a crippled dialectic that stumbles at the moment of its synthesis and tips the unsuspecting dialectician onto her ass, aghast, back where she started. In recent years Harrison's fiction has softened, as he has come to forgive the world, just a bit, for being always already pregnant with a numinous that only leads back here. The fringe of that forgiveness is present in this book, in the occasional moments of peace Pam finds at the edge of death. But they are inchoate, and each is always followed by despair. There is humanity, but it is constrained by that austere vision. It is this that makes *The Course of the Heart* the greatest of Harrison's works, and a pinnacle of literate horror.

CHINA MIÉVILLE (b. 1972) was born in Norwich and moved very quickly to London. He has degrees in social anthropology and international relations, and a Ph.D. in the philosophy of international law. He has lived, worked, and studied in Britain, Egypt, Zimbabwe, and the United States. He was into more or less anything with monsters in it from as young as he can remember, and has never grown out of it. With influences that include M. John Harrison, Gene Wolfe, Dambudzo Marechera, and H. P. Lovecraft, Miéville's first novel was *King Rat* (1998), followed by the Arthur C. Clarke Award- and British Fantasy Award-winning *Perdido Street Station*, The British Fantasy Award-winning *The Scar*, and the Arthur C. Clarke Award-winning *Iron Council*. His novella *The Tain* appeared from PS Publishing with an introduction by M. John Harrison. Miéville's first non-fiction book is *Between Equal Rights* (2005).

89

[1992]

ADAM SIMON on

Flicker
by THEODORE ROSZAK

Film fan and critic Jonathan Gates has a lifelong obsession with Max Castle, a German Expressionist filmmaker (Judas Jedermann) *who came to Hollywood, made horror films* (Zombie Doctor), *and disappears. Gates's investigations of Castle thread between perhaps estab-*

lished cinematic history, like Orson Welles's abandoned film version of Heart of Darkness, *and a perhaps invented shadow of the medium. Meanwhile, albino movie brat Simon Dunkle, auteur of* American Fast Food Massacre *and* Sub Sub, *seems to be re-creating the most dangerous elements of Castle's style. Theodore Roszak (b. 1933) is the author of incisive non-fiction cultural studies like* The Making of a Counterculture: Reflections in the Technocratic Society and Its Youthful Opposition *(1969) and* The Cult of Information *(1986). He maintains that he is "not a non-fiction writer who turned to fiction, but a novelist who got diverted into non-fiction when I could not get my novels published." His first novels,* Bugs *(1981) and* Dreamwatcher *(1985), were "Gothic science fiction thrillers," acutely perceptive about territory that film and literature would endlessly mine in the subsequent twenty-five years. Since* Flicker *he has published an unusual gloss on one of the founding texts of the genre,* The Memoirs of Elizabeth Frankenstein *(1995), and the novels* Blizzard *(2001) and* The Devil and Daniel Silverman *(2003).* Flicker *has been announced as a film, scripted by Jim Uhls, to be directed by Darren Aronofsky. The band Sub Sub takes its name from one of the fictional films featured in the novel.*

MANY OF US can still remember a moment of magic and wonder in a darkened hall, transfixed by a scintillating, glowing rectangle of light that seemed bigger and brighter than our vision and that moved and breathed and spoke like a second life before our eyes. And we remember turning away from the light—trying to peer back into the impenetrable darkness to find the source of this image—and seeing only a flickering beam of hot light shooting out, a beam formed by the dust and smoke in the darkened hall, and a beam whose very source was lost in a darkness made all the darker by the light itself.

Long before there were any such things as movies, Plato imagined that this life was exactly that—an illusion of light and shadow thrown upon a wall to a group of immobilized spectators while the real world existed somewhere else, somewhere outside of this cave we call the world.

Before there were any such thing as movies... or not.

What if Lumière didn't invent movies a mere century ago? What if there were medieval, or even ancient, movies? What if the very heart of the movies was not a bit of science but a bit of magic? A bit of very black magic? What if the art of light and shadow stands not only at the very beginnings of all human knowledge, but farther back? What if the source of all we see—the vast play of light and sound all around us—is itself but a shadow play thrown by a vast and unseeable projector? What if the projectionist Himself is not who we think He is, and we are not His guests, not His children, not His lovers, but His slaves, His chattels, His food?

Then we are all in very big fucking trouble.

Flicker knows all this, and more. It is a literally wonderful book of secrets that, like all the most essential works, has no greater purpose than blowing the top of your head off and redecorating your ceiling with spattered brains and the remains of everything you thought you knew.

It is not only one of the very greatest horror novels, but also one of the greatest Hollywood novels, one of the greatest esoteric mystery novels, one of the greatest of half a dozen other genres. And a key member of my most favorite genre, what I consider to be the genre of genres: Gnostic *noir*.

Variations of Gnostic doctrines have percolated in our culture for thousands of years. Condemned by the church, by rabbinical Judaism, mainstream Islam, and most organized religions for much of history, these are truly dangerous ideas that will not die. When the great heresy was chased out of religion (and chased it was, with pitchforks, and bonfires, and all the torturous instruments of the Inquisition), the ideas fled and hid in other places: in the shadowy realms of what we now call the occult (meaning, simply, the "hidden"), and increasingly they fled into the realms of art and imagination.

They survived by hiding in plain sight among the trash and treasure of popular culture: in genre fiction and pop music and the movies. Gnosticism became in a sense "escapism": what we dimly dismiss as escapist is the very fictional means of Gnostic thought, with its indictment of this world as a dark prison house of matter and its promise of another world beyond. What is it we are "escaping" in escapism? And to where?

This, you might say, is a lot to hang on the shoulders of a poor, unprepossessing horror novel. But this is no ordinary novel written by an ordinary man. Roszak is, for my money, the real man in the high castle: a man whose non-fiction writings lie at the heart of the 1960s and '70s, from the hippie movement, to the sexual revolution, to the ecology movement: he coined the term "counterculture," explored the mythology of sex roles, and critiqued the ecological disasters of the postindustrial landscape thirty years ago, and then presciently warned of the increasing alienation of a "virtual" world before the term "virtual reality" even existed. In his later career he's turned to writing powerful, page-turning novels. And in doing so, Roszak reminds us that this is what the horror novel—and the science fiction novel, and the fantasy novel and the mystery novel—always were: carriers of dark, dangerous philosophical, theological, even cosmological ideas.

Roszak's novels, like the best genre novels, not only contain ideas but also are almost always *about* the consequences of ideas: reminders that every monster is precisely an idea made flesh and that every idea given flesh will inevitably turn out to be a monster.

Flicker reminds us that the mysterious flicker at the heart of the movies, the secret of light and darkness at the heart of the machinery of illusion, is itself a dim reflection, or a pointer and reminder, a whispered hint, about the machinery of illusion we call "reality": the sleight-of-hand-and-eye by which the dead, still frames of a movie create an illusion of movement is somehow intimately—horribly—linked to the demiurgical sleight-of-hand by which this world of dead matter all around us rises as an apparent reality.

So every film is a Frankenstein movie—stitched together from dead pieces of a dead world and animated by flashes of light. And the dark magic of the movies hints slyly that the world itself may equally be a Frankenstein monster, stitched from the rotted parts of a dead cosmos and animated by an infernal light.

ADAM SIMON (b. 1962) is a veteran of the Roger Corman B-movie film factory, where he wrote and directed *Brain Dead* (1989) and *Carnosaur* (1993), among other titles. His three award-winning plays for Tim Robbins and the Actors' Gang have been staged in Los Angeles, Chicago, New York's Public Theater, and the Edinburgh Festival. Simon has worked as a screenwriter and rewriter for Oliver Stone, John Landis, James Cameron, and Peter Guber, among many others. His screenplay written with Tim Metcalfe, *Bones*, was produced in 2001 starring Snoop Dog and Pam Grier. He's created miniseries and pilots for HBO, Showtime, USA Network, and Sony Television. He also made two award-winning television documentaries for the Independent Film Channel: *The Typewriter, the Rifle, and the Movie Camera* (1995), about maverick director Sam Fuller, and *The American Nightmare* (2000), which looked at the traumatic North American horror films of the late 1960s and early '70s. More recently Simon adapted David Mack's series of graphic novels *Kabuki* for Fox Searchlight Films. After a decade-and-a-half in Hollywood, he reports that he maintains a naïve belief in the transmutational power of pulp and an optimistic hope that he will someday produce a work that gains greater notoriety than his brief parody of himself in Robert Altman's *The Player*.

90 [1993]

PAUL DI FILIPPO on

X, Y
by MICHAEL BLULMEIN

Michael Blumlein's (b. 1948) short fiction, collected in The Brains of Rats *(1989), lays the groundwork for the areas explored in his second novel,* X, Y—*clinically described medical procedures; Cronenbergian scramblings of identity and flesh; a deep, dark, dry humor that too often goes unnoticed, and an interest in extremes of expression. Labeled "a psychosexual thriller" on the original cover,* X, Y *followed* The Movement of Mountains *(1987), but it was a decade-and-a-half before the author's next novel,* The Healer *(2005). In 2004, writer-director Vladimir Vitkin filmed* X, Y *with Jamie Harrold (of* Kingdom Hospital*) and Melissa Murphy as, respectively, Terry and Frankie. Dr. Blumlein practices and teaches medecine at the University of California at San Francisco.*

F. ANSTEY'S *VICE VERSA* (1882). Thorne Smith's *Turnabout* (1933). Disney's *Freaky Friday* (1976). The gimmick of "identity exchange," as this trope is labeled in Clute and Grant's *The Encyclopedia of Fantasy* (1997) is, more often than not, used in comedic fashion. Readers and viewers are deftly convinced by farcical misunderstandings that nothing could be more of a mischievous lark than to pop into someone else's skull for a stint, although awkward yet mirthful complications might ensue.

Such a blithe treatment of this fantastical theme is by no means exemplified by Michael Blumlein in his expertly horrific novel, which blends issues of alienation, gender roles, power games, S&M, body modification, and class into a potent draft.

Francesca "Frankie" de Leon is an alcoholic stripper. Her boyfriend, Terry, is a failed med student who now works in a bookstore. Their relationship is, if not loving, then at least mutually sustaining and supportive. Until the night Frankie becomes not herself.

While onstage, she experiences a strange seizure triggered by the piercing wail of an anomalous siren. Simultaneously, a middle-aged man at the bar near Frankie undergoes the same convulsion. When Frankie awakes the next day, she is a near-total amnesiac. No personal memories, hazy on cultural data as well. But of one thing she is convinced: she is a male trapped in a woman's body.

Naturally, Terry's reaction to this incredible assertion is disbelief and anger. He feels Frankie is playing him. But eventually he goes along with her desperate entreaties and attempts to find the corresponding male victim. The man is tracked down to a certain hospital, where he lies in a coma. Even in his presence, Frankie cannot effect any sort of retransference by sheer willpower—if indeed this insensate body even represents the original abode of her/his spirit. She resorts to voodoo via the mother of Marcus, a black friend of Terry's. But this is likewise ineffective. Terry, losing patience, finally rapes Frankie. She experiences a nervous breakdown. But when she emerges from her catatonia, she is a monster.

The subsequent downward spiral between a repentant Terry and a malicious Frankie ends very badly. But Blumlein offers a note of hope in the final sentence of the novel: "Leaning over, careful not to disturb any of the life-giving tubes, she wipes the man's brow."

Blumlein's prose in this book is a marvel of terse, clipped, yet vivid descriptiveness. The seedy milieu of the strip club where Frankie works, and the general hopeless sleaziness of the lower rungs of the economic ladder that Frankie and Terry cling to, recall the best "ashcan realism."

But as counterpoint to this acute mimesis, Blumlein offers extracts from various clinical journals. As a practicing doctor of medicine, Blumlein possesses a keen ear for those bits of arcane scientific terminology that will resonate in a literary fashion. This must be one of the few horror novels in history to come complete with scholarly endnotes.

The result of all this is to create a book with the same air of deracinated estrangement as the film of *The Man Who Fell to Earth* (1976). Like the David Bowie character in that film, Frankie is portrayed as an odd spirit summoned from the ether and uncomfortably housed in a foreign shell, wreaking havoc both on herself and those who surround her as she attempts to maneuver through a world she never made, where she is a hapless, bumbling visitor, ultimately asexual and hence unable to be fitted into any convenient niche.

Prescient for its period in its examination of such recently hot topics as gender roles, intersexuality, and the vogue for ritual scarification and body modification, this book has held up remarkably well after a decade. Blumlein is a far from voluminous writer, making his intermittent books cherished milestones along a singular career path.

One of the clinical passages early on discourses on the role of science as a substitute for religion: "Logic stands in place of spirit; methodology above faith." Blumlein argues in this book not that both science and religion must be present to ensure sanity, but that sometimes even the two combined are not a strong enough bulwark to hold back madness engendered by the sheerly accidental, gratuitous malice of the universe. It's not a comforting view, but it's certainly bracing in its assertion that even after suffering all the universe can throw at an individual, some small rock of self remains as an ultimate refuge on which to build.

> **PAUL DI FILIPPO** (b. 1954) was born in Rhode Island, where he has lived all his life. He met Deborah Newton in college, and in January 2006 they celebrate thirty years together. Di Filippo currently lives in a cramped house with seven thousand books, two cats (Penny Century and Queen Mab), and a chocolate cocker spaniel named Brownie. A prolific short-story writer, since 1977 his smart and often idiosyncratic fiction has appeared in numerous

magazines and anthologies, such as the *New York Times, Twilight Zone Magazine, The Magazine of Fantasy & Science Fiction, Night Cry, New Pathways, Amazing, SF Eye, Pulphouse, Hardware, Journal Wired, New Worlds, Interzone, SF Age, After Hours, Nova SF, Universe, The Third Alternative, Pirate Writings, Space and Time, The Edge, Fantastic Stories, Sci Fiction,* the *Year's Best Fantasy, The Year's Best SF, Mirrorshades, The Mammoth Book of Comic Fantasy III, The Mammoth Book of Future Cops, Disco 2000, Mars Probes,* and *Nanotech.* He is winner of the 1994 British SF Association Award for Best Short Story and a multiple Nebula nominee, and his short stories are collected in *The Steampunk Trilogy, Ribofunk, Destroy All Brains!,* the World Fantasy Award-nominated *Fractal Paisleys, Lost Pages* (winner of a Citation for Excellence from the Philip K. Dick Award), *Strange Trades, Little Doors, Babylon Sisters, Neutrino Drag,* and *The Emperor of Gondwanaland.* Di Filipo has collaborated on stories with Rudy Rucker, Marc Laidlaw, Don Webb, and Barry Malzberg. Di Filippo's other books include the novels *Ciphers, Would It Kill You to Smile?* and *Muskrat Courage* (both written with Michael Bishop as "Philip Lawson"), *Joe's Liver, A Mouthful of Tongues, Fuzzy Dice, Spondulix, Harp Pipe and Symphony, Plumage from Pegasus,* and the Hugo Award-, Sturgeon Award-, and World Fantasy Award-nominated *A Year in the Linear City.* He also contributed the text to *Dreamland,* a book of Todd Schorr's art.

91 [1993]

CAITLÍN R. KIERNAN on

Skin
by KATHE KOJA

Kathe Koja's third novel was originally published in hardcover by Delacorte Press under the short-lived "Abyss" horror imprint. Skin *explores the extremes of art, taking cues from many real-life creators: among the works evoked in the novel are the mechanical constructs of the Survival Research Laboratories (which self-destruct when on show like some industrial punk-aesthete's demolition derby), the performance art of dancer Marina Abramovic (whose "Rhythm 0" piece involved asking the audience to use various implements on her however they liked—one report claims "By the third hour, her clothes had been cut from her body with razor blades, her skin slashed; a loaded gun held to her head finally caused a fight between her tormentors, bringing the proceeding to an unnerving halt"), and the body modification of Steve Haworth (an artist who works on his own flesh, specializing in subdermal and transdermal implants and laser-cautery branding). Koja (b. 1960) produced four novels loosely classed as "horror"—the others are* The Cipher *(1991),* Bad Brains *(1992), and* Strange Angels *(1994)—before taking a more mainstream step with the similarly themed* Kink *(1996); her website doesn't mention any of these but covers her recent young adult work, from* Straydog *(2002) to* Talk *(2005). Her short fiction is collected in* Extremities *(1998).* Skin *was a World Fantasy Award nominee in 1994.*

IN THE EARLY 1990s I was still reading a lot of genre "horror," but I'd begun to realize that very little of it was having much effect on me one way or another. So when Dell launched its Abyss line of "cutting edge" dark fantasy in 1991, I was hopeful, encouraged by the powerful, distinctive voices of writers like Kathe Koja, the late Michael McDowell, and Poppy Z. Brite. Unfortunately, Abyss very quickly devolved into the same bland morass of shoddy, mass-produced spookhouse frights that characterized the majority of the field at that time (and now, for that matter). But, on the way to that dissolution, Abyss gave us three stunning Koja novels—*The Cipher* (1991), *Bad Brains* (1992), and *Skin* (1993). Together, these three books seemed to me a long-overdue wake-up call for the genre, if there even is such a thing as "genre," and I listened. I listened *hard*.

Skin is a complex, oblique novel obsessed with the search for transformation and transcendence. Thematically it skirts the periphery of the old-school "terror" Gothic novels, at least in one of the central characters' incessant straining toward unattainable and perhaps forbidden knowledge. Here, though, it's not Lovecraft's *Necronomicon* or the ancient secrets of a dilapidated family castle, but the possibility of knowledge that might have been lost during the ravages of the industrial revolution; knowledge that might still exist somewhere and that can perhaps be accessed via gateways, by returning to the rituals of the noble savage. On the one side stands Tess Bajac, a metal sculptor who we might take for an orphaned daughter of dead industry, content with the act of melting metal, living for that burn alone. And on the other side stands Bibi Bloss, a dancer and performance artist driven in her pursuit of something more, though she never seems to have even the faintest idea what that something more might be. These two women inhabit a world that, if we didn't know better (and maybe we don't), could be taken as postapocalyptic. All is decay and disintegration, abandonment and disorder.

Tess Bajac may be read as not merely an orphan, but also as a *ghost* of industry. She is, however, industry made pure through the simple desire to burn and reshape, industry freed of its ultimately destructive love for money. The *need* is still there, but it's at best a necessary evil, intruding into Tess's purer pursuits in the form of scanty "pickup jobs" that barely pay the rent and the electric bills. Tess is a phantom of solder and arc light who might have gone on this way forever, except that she's confronted by something strange and new, another human phantom, one who struggles to recall an age and a spirit situated deeper in history and the human psyche than mere industrialism. Bibi Bloss is the frantic violence and harried introspection of urban primitivism, seeking extremities of physical experience in the feverish hope that she might thereby gain the rebirth of spirit promised but never delivered by modernism.

It is entirely appropriate, therefore, and perhaps even critical, that this novel is written in the fractured, stuttering prose poetry of the modernists, of Joyce and Pound, Stein and Eliot. It leads us into the very heart of the ruined landscape at the edge of Eliot's wasteland, but, unlike Eliot, points no way out. *Skin* does not even offer hope that escape is a possibility. Like Tess's sculptural boxes, the fallen world contains each of us, divided from all others, and we may tear ourselves apart—spiritually, emotionally, physically—but, as with the hell of Sartre, there is no exit here. If the gates ever existed—if, indeed, the secrets of access were possessed by "primitive" man—they are lost now and may not be rediscovered. And *this* is the horror of *Skin*, that one may either accept one's place in the wasteland or one may be destroyed and destroy others in a futile attempt at escape. In the end, Bibi Bloss becomes only a murderer and a madwoman, and Tess's joy (as distinct from simple happiness) at the act of melting metals is replaced by the cannibalization of her earlier creations and the unanswered question "What will she burn when all of them are gone?"

Near the end of the novel, a journalist attending one of Bibi's performances, a delirious circus of blood and darkness, death and violated flesh, remarks, "Something here is wrong," a statement that might well stand as the book's chilling thesis. *Something here is wrong.* But is it Bibi's blind, ruthless search for transcendence or Tess's introverted contentment with her transformation of ruin?

CAITLÍN R. KIERNAN (b. 1964) was born in Ireland and lives in Atlanta with her partner, Kathryn, and her cat, Sophie. Trained as a vertebrate paleontologist, she continues her research on Cretaceous vertebrates in her spare time. Kiernan is the author of five novels: *Silk*, *Threshold*, *The Five of Cups*, *Low Red Moon*, and *Murder of Angels*. Her short fiction has been collected in four volumes: *Tales of Pain and Wonder*, *From Weird and Distant Shores*, *Wrong Things* (with Poppy Z. Brite), and *To Charles Fort, With Love*. Kiernan also scripted the comic *The Dreaming* for DC/Vertigo, along with the miniseries *The Girl Who Would Be Death* and *Bast: Eternity Game*. She is currently working on her sixth novel, *Daughter of Hounds*, and a collection of "weird erotica" titled *Frog Toes and Tentacles*.

92 [1994]

TANANARIVE DUE on

Throat Sprockets: A Novel of Erotic Obsession
by TIM LUCAS

Like From Hell, Throat Sprockets *began in a different medium as a serial in Stephen E. Bissette's* Taboo: *"Throat Sprockets" and "Transylvania, Mon Amour," illustrated by Mike Hoffman, appeared in 1987 and 1989 in issues 1 and 3, respectively, of the anthology comic. "The Disaster Area," a third chapter, was illustrated by David Lloyd but not published. Lucas (b. 1956) found time to complete the story as a novel, while editing and publishing* Video Watchdog *magazine and working on his monumental study* Mario Bava: All the Colors of the Dark. *An adman happens upon* Throat Sprockets, *a porn movie for a specialized audience, and becomes obsessed with the film, which takes over his life and subtly seems to become a dominant cultural influence. Lucas has admitted that one of his inspirations was Riccardo Freda's film* A doppia faccia/Double Face *(1969), in which Klaus Kinski is similarly struck by a stag film that directs attention to the neck of its mystery leading lady.*

> If thou and Nature can so gently part,
> The stroke of death is as a lover's pinch,
> Which hurts, and is desir'd.
>
> —William Shakespeare

Before there was *The Ring*, there was *Throat Sprockets*.

No, there's no accursed waif climbing out of a television screen in Tim Lucas's first novel—not *exactly*, anyway—but this is a story about a video that seizes the viewer and won't let go. And that was the impact Lucas's novel had on me when I read it in 1995. I was so impressed that I wrote about it in my journal: "*Throat Sprockets* utterly captivated me with its intelligence and originality," I raved.

No one familiar with Lucas's *Video Watchdog* magazine will be surprised that *Throat Sprockets* is soaked with affection for, and obsession with, the world of film. Film is to Lucas what trivia is to Sherlock Holmes, or treachery is to Iago. Cinema serves as Lucas's muse, so why not a story about a man whose life is forever shattered by the viewing of a film? Or a world ultimately sent into chaos by the film's spliced images?

And *what* a film. Lucas's title film, an art-house creation called *Throat Sprockets*, unleashes a fetish for biting women's throats—or "sprocketing," as the act is called—and propels this story of destructive erotic fascination for our Everyday Joe narrator.

"I was bowled over," says our protagonist, "by how the film communicated, in that single moment, the courage it takes (a detail glossed over by every vampire film I've ever seen) to *actually sink one's teeth into the throat of another person,* especially the throat of a loved one, to set their life's blood flowing—and I was stricken by the selfless yet gratifying surprise felt by the young woman, receiving yet giving, so vividly conveyed that I felt her participation too. It was perfect, mutual sex; a stunning reenactment of nothing less than the first bite of apple in Eden's gone garden."

Almost immediately, the film changes the way our narrator views everything from the Shopping Channel to encounters with new women and relationships. As Lucas describes an interaction with one woman: "The angle at which she stood . . . provided me with an ideal view of the mole on her throat, which rode her pulse like a pubic nipple. In idle moments I found myself wondering where this genetic heirloom had appeared on her mother, her grandmother, and even more distant relatives . . . as if I wanted to ravish not only her but her entire bloodline."

The pure kinkiness of *Throat Sprockets* is endearing enough, taking vampiristic images and transporting them into our everyday sex lives in a way that seems not only fully plausible but also downright enlightening. (Ah-*ha! Now* I get it!)

But *Throat Sprockets* also takes the time and care to create a protagonist with a real life, a real advertising job (Lucas's fictitious ad campaigns are good enough for Madison Avenue), and a horrific problem he wrestles with from the instant he first glimpses the fateful film at the Eros Theater. Lucas paints his characters' relationships with wisdom and a touch of sadness, imbuing the novel with an ironic sweetness in the face of growing depravity.

Beyond that, his novel brims with astute social commentary on everything from film to sexuality to the morality to war. With grim humor, sharp intellect, and no lack of literary calisthenics, *Throat Sprockets* is a lot of evil fun. Lucas's descriptions of swarms of minors boasting "virgin blood" descending on cars at stoplights, and a hotel that offers discreet sprocketing kits in its guest rooms, are particularly delightful.

But for all its societal observations, *Throat Sprockets* remains a profoundly individual journey for the protagonist and its reader. Too few novels actually make us *believe*, but *Throat Sprockets* accomplishes an eerie verisimilitude more writers could learn from. Lucas's bizarre world of glovers and chokers seems to exist on a plane somewhere just beneath our own, hidden only by an onion skin. The title film at the center of the novel is so well drawn that it might be sitting on the shelf of the video store right now—and by now, it's out on DVD.

And I can guarantee you that you won't shake the novel's final images of ruin out of your head anytime soon. Let's just say I'll never look at my *Complete Works of William Shakespeare* the same way again.

Nor my throat, for that matter.

Taste, anyone?

TANANARIVE DUE (b. 1966) was born and grew up in Miami. She recently moved to Southern California with her husband, novelist Steven Barnes, and their two children. Due has a B.S. in journalism from Northwestern University and an M.A. in English literature from the University of Leeds, England, where she specialized in Nigerian literature as a Rotary Foundation Scholar. Having had a healthy fascination with her own mortality for as long as she can remember, she had been writing fiction for years before producing her first novel, *The Between* (1995). Since then she has published books ranging from supernatural thrillers to a civil rights memoir, including *My Soul to Keep* (soon to be filmed), *The Black Rose* (a historical novel in conjunction with the Alex Haley Estate), the American Book Award-winning *The Living Blood*, *Freedom in the Family: A Mother-Daughter Memoir of the Fight for Civil Rights* (with Patricia Stephens Due), the International Horror Guild Award-nominated *The Good House*, and *Joplin's Ghost*. A two-time finalist for the Bram Stoker Award, Tananarive Due (pronounced "tah-nah-nah-REEVE doo") also received the New Voice in Literature Award at the Yari Yari Pamberi conference cosponsored by New York University's Institute of African-American Affairs and African Studies Program and the Organization of Women Writers of Africa. She has taught at the

Hurston-Wright Foundation's Writers' Week at Howard University, the Clarion Science Fiction and Fantasy Writers' Workshop at Michigan State University, the University of Miami, and the summer Imagination conference at Cleveland State University. She is also a former feature writer and columnist for *The Miami Herald*.

93

[1995]

SIMON R. GREEN on

The Off Season: A Victorian Sequel
by JACK CADY

Point Vestal is a small tourist town on the edge of the Pacific coast. When the first white settlers arrived, they asked the local Indians where they should settle. The Indians pointed to a place and said, "Take that. We don't want it. It is cursed." And so the town was founded. It has a long and colorful history, mostly concerned with smuggling, and has ghosts like a dog has fleas. Phantoms walk alongside the living, and everyone is cool about it. Timeslips are common, so that people from different periods are constantly bumping into one another, but no one seems to mind much—until August Starling comes back. In Victorian times he was the most evil man in Port Vestal. The man who danced with a corpse; and she wasn't even his wife. August Starling is determined to drag Port Vestal kicking and screaming into the twentieth century, and make the town a monument to death and destruction. Set against him are the traveling preacher Joel-Andrew, and the local pariah, Kune. It is a battle of wits and conspiracies, bold stratagems *and vile plots. Good against evil, faith verses corruption. And for some, death will be the kindest thing that can happen. Jack Cady (1934–2004) penned* The Off Season: A Victorian Sequel *in homage to the tall tale tradition of Mark Twain; the book should, on no account, be confused with* Off Season *(1980) by Jack Ketchum, which goes for a very different kind of horror.*

"The key to Port Vestal," said Kune, "is that all the time is happening some of the time."

Jack Cady's *The Off Season* isn't like most horror novels. To start with, it's often laugh-out-loud funny. Second, it's quirky as all hell. And third, it takes its underlying themes of faith, duty, and damnation very seriously.

So why is it funny? Suppose you were the ghost of a fair young maid who threw herself off a cliff for love, condemned to repeat this act every night, year after year? After thirty years of this you might well start to wonder if the young man was ever really worth it. Then there's the cop who beat a prisoner to death in his cell and whose screams can be heard every evening at the exact same time. After twenty years the cop and the prisoner got bored and swapped roles. After another twenty years they realized if they just rattled some chains and made all the right noises, they could just lounge around, because no one ever came down to check.

And quirky? Hell, yes. One of the town's oldest buildings, the Parsonage, has become self-aware, and taken to moving itself around town, materializing wherever it damn well feels like. The preacher Joel-Andrew has a cat called Obed, who can purr in many languages. And the story you are reading is actually being written by four of the main characters.

But what makes *The Off Season* such a powerful horror novel, and damn spooky to boot, is not just that the town is wall-to-wall ghosts. Ghosts always represent the past, and this town's past is coming back to haunt and judge it. August Starling embodies all the very worst Victorian values, and his slow, inexorable rise to power in the town comes by destroying all that those of the twentieth century held dear.

By appealing to the town's worst instincts he corrupts both individuals and groups, the political and the religious, like a Pied Piper leading his flock to damnation. For it isn't just the townspeople's lives that are at stake; he will settle for nothing less than the corruption of their souls.

Underneath the humor is a growing grim realization that this game is being played for all the marbles. Either the good guys defeat August Starling, or the town will go to hell. And it has to be said: the good guys are few and far between, and spiritually walking wounded. They have none of the fluency of Starling's honeyed words, and their main weapon, their sincerity, is often mocked or taken advantage of.

For all the humor in the book, it is first and foremost a horror novel. Senses of dread and melancholy suffuse the novel, which is fitting for a work that the author declares to be essentially Victorian in style and content, though its details are utterly modern. The slow turning of the town to darkness, to a delight in death and all its trappings, in the name of tourism, puts a chill into the heart. You come to care about all the characters in the book, the wise and the foolish, those who stand up to be counted and those who are too easily persuaded. This is a story of a town going to the Devil, and laughing all the way.

Did I mention that there are loads of ghosts in it?

SIMON R. GREEN (b. 1955) was born in the small country town of Bradford-on-Avon. He lived for three years in London and then decided that cities were best enjoyed from a safe distance. He has written more than thirty novels, including the science fiction *Deathstalker* series (*Deathstalker, Deathstalker Rebellion, Deathstalker War, Deathstalker Honour, Deathstalker Destiny, Deathstalker Legacy, Deathstalker Return, Deathstalker Coda,* and *Deathstalker Prelude*), the heroic fantasy *Hawk & Fisher* series (*Blue Moon Rising, No Haven for the Guilty, Devil Take the Hindmost, The God Killer, Vengeance for a Lonely Man, Guard Against Dishonour, Two Kings in Haven,* and

Beyond the Blue Moon), and the decidedly weird and offbeat *Nightside* series (*Something from the Nightside, Agents of Light and Darkness, Nightingale's Lament, Hex and the City, Paths Not Taken,* and *A Mother's Son*). His other novels include *Shadows Fall, Drinking Midnight Wine, Blood and Honour,* and *Down Among the Dead Men.* He also wrote the international best-selling film novelization *Robin Hood: Prince of Thieves.* He is not married. No one ever asked him.

94 [1996]

S. T. JOSHI on

The Nightmare Factory
by THOMAS LIGOTTI

First issued as a hefty trade paperback in Britain by Robinson Publishing's Raven Books genre imprint, The Nightmare Factory *is an omnibus edition of the works of Thomas Ligotti (b. 1953), assembling thirty-nine stories from his earlier collections,* Songs of a Dead Dreamer *(1989),* Grimscribe: His Lives and Works *(1991), and* Noctuary *(1994). "Teatro Grottesco and Other Tales" adds a further six stories, including the Bram Stoker Award-winning novelette "The Red Tower." Prefatory material consists of "The Consolations of Horror," an introductory essay by the author, and an original foreword by Poppy Z. Brite, who recalls first encountering Ligotti's work on a trip to San Francisco ("For me, those black-foaming gutters and back alleys [not to mention the Street of Wavering Peaks] will always be just across the bay from*

Berkeley."). *The Nightmare Factory won the Bram Stoker and British Fantasy awards for Best Collection in 1997.*

SOMETIME IN 1986, as a cocksure young critic chiefly devoted to promoting the work of H. P. Lovecraft and some of his worthier disciples, I received a review copy of a not particularly well-produced book from Silver Scarab Press called *Songs of a Dead Dreamer*, by a writer I had never heard of, Thomas Ligotti. In spite of an enthusiastic introduction by Ramsey Campbell (who, I suspected, was paying a tribute to friendship rather than to literary quality), I quickly dismissed the book as yet another of the seemingly endless array of "fan fiction" that has brought such disrepute to the field of supernatural horror. I have no idea what happened to my copy of this book—probably I gave it away to someone in a casual moment. What folly!—imagine what I could now get for this book on eBay!

It was only some years later, and chiefly through the urging of Stefan Dziemianowicz, that I was tempted to probe Ligotti's work again. I was at work on a book called *The Modern Weird Tale*, a broad survey of selected writers of supernatural fiction since Lovecraft, and was strongly advised to give Ligotti some consideration. I obtained the Robinson edition of *Songs of a Dead Dreamer* and began reading. Its first story, "The Frolic," electrified me, and I was a Ligotti devotee for life.

One of the disadvantages of being a practicing critic, in this or any other field, is that one falls into so inveterate a habit of reading analytically that the sheer pleasure of reading tends to be slighted. It does not help that, in the course of one's professional obligations, one is generally forced to read a considerable quantity of mediocre work. But Ligotti gave me the first genuine frisson—in the literal sense of the term—that I had received in years. His work made me realize why I had become a student of weird fiction to begin with—it was to experience that indescribable sensation of being *unnerved*. The purpose of supernatural fiction, I am convinced, is not to horrify or frighten as such; it is to *make one uneasy*. The very best of Lovecraft, Blackwood, Machen, Aickman, Campbell, and T. E. D. Klein have this quality; and the best of Ligotti has it, too. When reading his work, one enters a universe as distinctive and idiosyncratic as Tolkien's or Peake's, a world we half recognize as our own, but one that has been rendered insane—or, perhaps, a world whose latent insanity has finally been brought to the surface by a skilled hand.

The Nightmare Factory—an omnibus collecting Ligotti's first three story collections, *Songs of a Dead Dreamer, Grimscribe,* and *Noctuary*—must take its place among the cornerstone volumes of any library of contemporary weird fiction. Without the least violence of diction, Ligotti is capable of suggesting that the world, the universe, are awry in some hideous way that we fail to grasp only because of our deliberate blindness. His prose style can at times be as tortured and metaphor-laden as M. P. Shiel's, but it is a vital, indispensable vehicle for his conveyance of a world where nightmare has replaced reality: purely on the level of prose, no one in modern weird fiction equals or even approaches him. (At the same time, Ligotti sometimes becomes so enamored of his own gift for language that he lapses into preciosity and self-indulgence—a fault particularly on display in the prose poems that conclude *Noctuary*.)

Much of Ligotti smells of the study: he is among the most well-read writers in the history of supernatural fiction. He has frequently stated that it is the earlier, more mystical works of Lovecraft, rather than the later, more scientifically rationalized narratives, that have influenced him: hence "The Last Feast of Harlequin," although resonant of "The Shadow Over Innsmouth," in reality draws more from "The Festival." It is my contention that "Nethescurial" is an extraordinarily oblique pastiche of "The Call of Cthulhu." "The Tsalal," the capstone of *Noctuary,* draws subtly on Poe's *Narrative of Arthur Gordon Pym.* In a field such as ours, this bookishness may not be such a bad thing: Ligotti scorns the notion that weird fiction, and perhaps all fiction, is some kind of "treatment of life" (as Lovecraft himself said as he was entering his "realistic" phase): the writer is a demiurge, creating a universe that may or may not connect with the "real" world at his whim.

Perhaps the most heartening thing about Thomas Ligotti is that so unconventional a writer could have attained the kind of celebrity he has. Emerging from the small press (and retaining his devotion to it); consciously eschewing explicit gore; refusing to fill his works with "sympathetic" characters to whom the more naïve sorts of readers feel they need to identify; and, most courageous of all, declaring flatly that the "horror novel" is a virtual oxymoron to which he has no desire to devote his talents, Ligotti has nonetheless managed to achieve a status that goes well beyond a mere cult following. After writing the three volumes gathered in *The Nightmare Factory*, Ligotti appears to have experienced a period of uncertainty as to the direction he wished his literary career to take; but with *My Work is Not Yet Done* (2002), a scintillating volume whose title story is of short novel length, Ligotti has wondrously regained his focus. The title of this book may well be prophetic, and it is certain that we have not heard the last of this most unclassifiable of writers.

S. T. JOSHI (b. 1958) is a widely published critic and editor. He is the author of such critical studies as *H. P. Lovecraft: The Decline of the West*, *The Weird Tale*, *The Modern Weird Tale*, and *The Evolution of the Weird Tale*. He has edited the standard corrected editions of H. P. Lovecraft's fiction from Arkham House, and annotated editions of the author's work for Penguin and Dell, as well as *The Ancient Track: Complete Poetical Works* and *Collected Essays*. His revisionist 1996 biography, *H. P. Lovecraft: A Life*, from Necronomicon Press, won both the British Fantasy Award and the Bram Stoker Award. The founder and editor of the magazines *Lovecraft Studies* and *Studies in Weird Fiction*, Joshi has edited the critical anthologies *H. P. Lovecraft: Four Decades of Criticism* and *An Epicure in the Terrible*, compiled the standard bibliography of Lovecraft for Kent State University Press, and assembled *An H. P. Lovecraft Encyclopedia* (with David E. Schultz). He has also translated Maurice Lévy's *Lovecraft: A Study in the Fantastic*.

Along with writing the critical studies *Lord Dunsany: Master of the Anglo-Irish Imagination* and *Ramsey Campbell and Modern Horror Fiction,* he has prepared editions of the work of Arthur Machen, Algernon Blackwood, Lord Dunsany, Arthur Quiller-Couch, Donald Wandrei, and Ambrose Bierce, among others. He is co-editor (with Stefan Dziemianowicz) of *World Supernatural Literature: An Encyclopedia* from Greenwood Press, while a two-volume edition of the complete ghost stories of M. R. James is forthcoming from Penguin.

95

[1998]

ROBERTA LANNES on

A Sight for Sore Eyes
by RUTH RENDELL

Ruth Rendell (b. 1930), Baroness Rendell of Babergh, began her crime writing career with From Doon With Death *(1964), which introduced her series sleuth Inspector Wexford. She produces two distinct types of novel: the Wexford police procedurals, which are mysteries with character depth, and suspense stories in the tradition of Patricia Highsmith, which deal with psychologically twisted characters whose paths cross in ways that lead to crime and violence. Between* A Dark-Adapted Eye *(1986) and* Gallowglass *(1990), she published non-Wexford books under the pseudonym "Barbara Vine," a practice abandoned by the time she wrote the very Vine-like* A Sight for Sore Eyes. *The Wexford novels have been British television staples for many seasons, with George*

Baker in the lead, but the psycho-thrillers are more frequently filmed by European filmmakers like Claude Chabrol (La Cérémonie, 1995; from A Judgment in Stone, 1977), Pedro Almodóvar (Carne Trémula, 1987; from Live Flesh, 1986), and Claude Miller (Betty Fisher et Autres Histoires, 2001; from The Tree of Hands, 1975). A Sight for Sore Eyes was filmed in France as Inquiétudes (2003) by writer-director Gilles Bourdos, with Grégoire Colin, Julie Ordon, Brigitte Catillon, and Bérangère Bonvoisin.

A SIGHT FOR SORE EYES is a novel in several stories, told in parallel. Each story has its significance to the whole, as they gradually converge in the lives of the characters. Ruth Rendell's psychological stories are profoundly disturbing, and this novel is one of her best. Her fascination with the nature of obsession is evident in the distinctly uncomfortable relationships she draws. In the novel, Rendell makes a clear distinction between love and obsession; her characters refute the notion that love can be enduring in these characters' acts of selfishness, depravation, ignorance, denial, and dangerous compulsions. Obsession in relationships leads inevitably to horrific ends.

The first is a story of a little girl who has been scolded and sent to her room, and while there, her mother is brutally murdered. As Francine grows up, she is haunted by the experience, which strikes her mute for a long while afterward. She is taken to a psychologist, Julie, who marries Francine's widowed father. Julie becomes besieged by hysterical notions of evil waiting to destroy Francine; and by sheltering Francine from reality, she raises a child who never grows up, whose wounds develop in her the compulsion to save others.

Rendell's second story is of Teddy Grex, a beautiful young man whose childhood reads like a case study from Michael Rutter's text on *Maternal Deprivation.* Teddy is neglected, unloved, and ignored until finally, as a defense mechanism, he switches his emotions off. Teddy feels no fear, no loneliness, but neither can he empathize nor feel real love. He eventually discovers that murder can be an effective way to get what he wants.

Third, we meet Harriet, who from an early age has learned to use her beauty to make her way in the world. Bored by marriage to a wealthy, much older man, she scans the local newspapers for handymen to perform odd jobs around Orcadia Cottage (a place that figures in the past of many of the characters), including services in the bedroom. When she finds Teddy to do woodwork on her place, she invites a special kind of horror into her pathetic life.

From the outset the story conveys the brooding anticipation of a gathering storm. The groundwork is laid for the unhappiness of Teddy and Francine, whose relationship begins when Teddy sets his sights on her as the "perfect" woman. Their friendship becomes deeply unsettling by the appearance of "the worm in the bud." Fragile, naïve Francine, full of good intentions, spirals into the abyss being forged in the increasingly alien landscape of Teddy's mind. The intensely claustrophobic atmosphere of the book, and Teddy's rationalizations and justifications of his increasingly bizarre and cruel behavior, are reminiscent of John Fowles's *The Collector*, but Rendell deftly preserves Francine's innocence, even through Teddy's most monstrous excesses.

When these three plot strands finally converge, the result is harrowing and unforgettable. Rendell's bleak view of man's inhumanity is unrelenting, yet rings true. Although drawn into this cold, manipulative world unwillingly, one is compelled to read on. There is inevitability to the dire outcomes in *A Sight for Sore Eyes*. At its core, the novel is a horror story.

A Sight for Sore Eyes is not really a mystery, though it is marketed as such. We know who did what, when, and why, and if in the case of Francine's mother's murder we are left to wonder until the end, we are not surprised. There is enough tension and suspense to qualify the novel as a thriller, but thrillers lack the depth of character, the subtle threads unraveling and reweaving themselves to create a new tapestry. Only the best horror novels have the strength of fully realized characters who, whether beast or prey, we can relate to even as we flinch and wish to pull away.

It is Rendell's gift as a writer to create, out of a mystery story, a *noir* frisson, a bleak and steady downward itinerary to horrific destinations. Her ability to create an air of dread that buoys the story even in its lighter, narrative strains, is that of a true horror writer. Her characters are tragic enough that we feel a pathos toward them, yet their innocence and denial or guile and detachment from reality keep us from any sentimentality.

After all, horror is relative. Stories rife with monsters; dark, stormy nights; and victims littering a landscape with gore qualify. So do the quiet tales where something may or may not have happened to a character, when an author suggests something far worse awaits. It is the inexact essence of that which frightens or haunts, puts us ill at ease, or creeps us out. *A Sight for Sore Eyes* does all these things so well, it haunts me still.

ROBERTA LANNES (b. 1948) was born in Southern California and currently lives in Valencia with her husband, British software developer for the J. Paul Getty Trust, Mark Sealey. She was a member of a professional improvisational comedy troupe, and did stand-up comedy in a club on Sunset Boulevard before becoming a fine and digital arts teacher at Valencia High School. Lannes's father was a financial manager for the film production companies of many Hollywood actors, so she was fortunate to meet two of her favorite famous monsters, Bela Lugosi and Boris Karloff, unmasked. She began writing stories around the age of six, sharing them with some of her father's clients. The one about a cat with forty toes that ate the eyes of children horrified her godmother Barbara Stanwyck, who told her that she would grow up to be a "writer of scary stories." In 1986 Dennis Etchison discovered Lannes in his writing class at UCLA and published her first horror story, "Goodbye, Dark Love," in his acclaimed anthology *Cutting Edge*. Since then her many visceral and erotic short stories have been published in such magazines and anthologies as *Fantasy Tales, Iniquities, Pulphouse, Ténèbres, Alien Sex, Splatterpunks,* and *Splatterpunks II, The Bradbury Chronicles, Still Dead: Book of the Dead II, Dark Voices,*

Best New Horror, The Year's Best Fantasy and Horror, The Mammoth Book of Werewolves, The Mammoth Book of Frankenstein, Dark Terrors, Darkside: Horror for the Next Millennium, Love in Vein II, Lethal Kisses, The Mammoth Book of Dracula, Dark of the Night, Bal des Loups-Garous en Présence du Fantastique, White of the Moon, The Mammoth Book of Vampire Stories by Women, Taverns of the Dead, Don't Turn Out the Light, and *Dark Delicacies.* Lannes's debut short-story collection, *The Mirror of Night,* appeared from John Pelan's Silver Salamander Press in 1997.

96 [1999]

MICHAEL SHEA on

Reprisal
by MITCHELL SMITH

*Mitchell Smith (b. 1935) is a former army intelligence officer. After reputedly publishing a series of "Buckskin Westerns" under the name "Roy LeBeau" (*Rifle River, *1984,* Trigger Spring, *1985), he used his own name on a run of sharp, spare, chilly suspense thrillers in the manner of early David Morell—*Stone City *(1991),* Daydreams *(1991),* Due North *(1994),* Karma *(1996), and* Sacrifice *(1999, filmed 2000—albeit by Mark L. Lester with Michael Madsen as a direct-to-video effort).* Snowfall *(2002),* Kingdom River *(2003), and* Moonrise *(2004) are a change of direction, a science fiction/disaster trilogy set several hundred years after a change in Jupiter's orbit has brought about the onset of a global winter.*

WHEN WE FIRST meet Joanna Reed, a poet, a professor of poetry, and a deep-earth caver (i.e., a rock climber in absolute darkness), she has just lost her husband, who "fell" off his boat and drowned. Her father's death—he is burned alive in his lonely cabin—succeeds her husband's by a week or so. Both deaths are flawlessly staged as accidents, but Joanna intuitively knows they are something else.

The reader knows for sure.

The reader has been involved in both murders, has both times moved with the killer through an often graceful dance of arrangement, to modify the victim's environment *just so*, until that environment falls like a cleaver on his life.

The reader's complicity has, from the story's very outset, been commanded by Mitchell Smith's voice. His speech is supple. He requires of himself that whatever he presents, he evokes, but his narrative is so beautifully calibrated that evocation never slows its drive. He knows how to make it happen with just a flash here, a spark there . . . and he knows when to stop and *unfold* it. And the kind of horror he deploys with his voice is in a class of its own.

Violent death there is aplenty in *Reprisal*, and hair-raisingly unfolded. But the old Greeks knew that such was just the antechamber of true horror. In horror's inner sanctum, Antigone wills her burial alive in the tomb, and Oedipus tears out the eyes that have shown him who he is. Smith has the right to broach terrors of *this* magnitude because he has the heart to see them and the art to carry them. For my money, Smith writes the best prose in the game.

Let's take a taste of it. In the spirit of the *sortes Virgilianae* I've opened the book at random, confident of something luminous . . . and find I am not disappointed.

In this scene, Joanna is on the trail of whatever might really underlie her husband's apparent accident at sea. She drives across Asconsett Island to visit the people who leased her husband his boat. In making this foray, she is entering the harsher, sea-working half of the island, where live the "boat" families who have been fishing and trapping lobsters here for generations.

On arriving at the house of the Wainrights, owners of the *Bo-Peep*, which washed ashore capsized some days before her husband's body did likewise, Joanna beholds:

> There was one of Asconsett's rare trees—a molting, lean and knotty pine—in the Wainrights' wide front yard. A thick rope was attached to its largest limb, a car tire was suspended from that, and a medium-sized red dog hung from the tire. The dog seemed content to have the tire's heavy rubber in its jaws; it dangled clear of the ground, relaxed, still, and smiling. . . .
> The dog watched Joanna as she watched it. Its body, a compact cylinder of muscle, was completed by a head as massive, red, and rectangular as a brick block. The dog, its eye considering her, swung very slightly with the sea-breeze as it hung.

The Wainrights, a young man and his mother, are big, hard people, and hostile when they learn her identity. (Their boat was destroyed weeks ago, and they haven't heard from her until now.) Determined to talk to them, Joanna tries to thrust past their rejection; she opens the gate and steps into their yard. Their dog drops from the tire and trots to meet her. Neither of its owners intervenes.

> The animal was not big at all, but looked extraordinarily dense, solid with muscle, and carried a head so massive it seemed to belong to a bigger dog. Its white [fight-blinded] eye was not troubling, but the other, a light topaz to complement its coloring, had an odd expression—so though the animal hadn't growled at her, or threatened in any way, Joanna stopped and stood still. She wished the boy would call it.
> This close, she could see the dog had no ears—only trimmed stubs. A piece looked to have been bitten from its lip. . . . But it was the dog's good eye that held her still. The animal watched her, head cocked for one-eyed sight, looking up with no expression of either threat or friendliness, no sort of exchange at all. There was nothing in the topaz eye but study, and stern purpose.

His language is liquid, like glacier melt wrapping itself through rocks, over brightly colored gravels; all the shapes and textures of things, of skies and terrains and faces and desperate acts, come shining out of the flux of this limpid language.

Updike once said of Nabokov, "He writes prose the only way it should be written: ecstatically."

Mitchell Smith does just that. The kind of rendering he does can only come from the mantic trance of the writer who has left himself and let the world take his place. (I impute no impropriety to Mr. Smith, of course, and by "trance" mean a sober and decorous spiritual discipline.) No readers who really take horror as a serious genre should deny themselves the pleasure of reading, not only *Reprisal*, but *Due North*, *Daydreams*, *Stone City*, *Karma*, and *Sacrifice* as well.

Read them now! You'll thank me.

MICHAEL SHEA (b. 1946) was born in Los Angeles and now makes his home in Northern California. After discovering a battered copy of Jack Vance's *The Eyes of the Overworld* in a cheap hotel in Juneau, Alaska, he wrote a sequel to the book as a homage. Shea then wrote to Vance, asking if he would help get the sequel published and split the take. Although Vance graciously declined the offer, or to even read another author's addendum to a character he might himself wish to take up again, he did invite Shea to get the work published on his own. The result was *A Quest for Simbilis* (1974). In the years since, Shea's sword & sorcery work has retained Vance's stylistic stamp, especially his love of lexicon, but has also reflected the more horrific slant of Clark Ashton Smith's work. Shea has published more than two dozen stories and novellas, along with such books as the World Fantasy Award-winning *Nifft the Lean*, *In Yana the Touch of Undying*, *The Color Out of Time* (a sequel to H. P. Lovecraft's "The Colour Out of Space"), *Fat Face*, *The Mines of Behemoth*, *The A'rak*, and the World Fantasy Award-nominated collection *Polyphemus*. Also a finalist for the Hugo and Nebula Awards, the author is currently developing, with an Athenian collaborator, a film version of his novella *The Autopsy*.

97

[2000]

JOHN PELAN on

A Haunting Beauty
by SIR CHARLES BIRKIN

Edited and prefaced by Mike Ashley, A Haunting Beauty *collects the best psychological horror stories of Charles Lloyd Birkin (1907–86), the fifth baronet Birkin. It was published by Midnight House, a Seattle small press imprint, in an edition limited to 450 numbered copies, so if you're collecting the whole set of 200 Best Books associated with these volumes, be prepared to look long and pay mightily. Birkin worked in the 1930s for the United Kingdom publisher Philip Allan, who issued the author's first collection,* Devil's Spawn *(1936), but had him concentrate on editing (without credit) many anthologies of horror stories (*Creeps, *1932;* Shivers, *1932;* Shudders, *1932; etc). Later, Tandem published six collections, from* The Kiss of Death *(1964) to* So Pale, So Cold, So Fair *(1970), and Award managed a final title,* Spawn of Satan *(1971). Birkin's stories have not been discovered by many adapters, although his work would have fit easily into the formats of* Alfred Hitchcock Presents *or* Night Gallery. *However, Birkin's "So Pale, So Cold, So Fair" became "Meeting in Athens," a 1976 episode of the Vincent Price-presented BBC radio series* The Price of Fear. *In 2002 Midnight House published a further selection of Birkin's stories,* The Harlem Horror.

CHARLES BIRKIN PROBABLY did more than any other individual for the horror genre in England during the 1930s as an editor at publisher Philip Allan. As an author, he almost single-handedly kept the genre afloat in the United Kingdom during the 1960s. His paperbacks garnered rave reviews, and most were reprinted in the United States. With an impressive résumé like that, one would expect that an author-selected "Best of" would be a staple volume of any serious collection of modern horror, a book kept perpetually in print.

Sadly, this wasn't to be the case. It was not until 1981 that editor Mike Ashley suggested that Sir Charles assemble a collection of his best work. The final selections were made in 1983, but unfortunately the book did not see print until 2000. In this collection Birkin draws on his extensive world travels to offer the reader horror in a wide variety of guises and settings. Birkin has often been compared to Robert Bloch (unfairly, I think). In Birkin's tales the recurring theme of man's inhumanity to man is always portrayed with a clear, unflinching look into the abyss. In Bloch's work there's always an undercurrent of humor, a reminder that this is only fiction, after all, and it's all for laughs. You won't find that sort of humor here; in a nutshell, Birkin writes beautifully about the most ghastly of events, and if there's any humor at all, it's of the type favored by Ambrose Bierce.

A Haunting Beauty showcases the range of Birkin's fiction, beginning with a delicately stated ghost story so convincing in its sense of place that one can smell the sea breeze and feel the sand beneath one's feet during the reading. While Birkin is known primarily for his non-supernatural horror, this volume contains the former piece and one of the greatest treatments of the zombie theme in modern horror. All told, Birkin wrote very few overtly supernatural tales, but these are masterpieces of the form.

The most acclaimed story in the book is his chronicle of a doomed group of POWs, in "Waiting for Trains." It contains no elements of the genre; indeed, there are not only no haunts or specters, but also no real onstage violence. However, that being said, the commentary on the residual horror of war and the manner in which it can and does turn men into monsters makes it one of the great antiwar tales, ranking with Dalton Trumbo's *Johnny Got His Gun* and Walter Owen's *The Cross of Carl*. Not only does the story belong here in a retrospective volume of Birkin's tales, it also belongs with the great British stories of the twentieth century. Birkin served in World War II and wrote some of his greatest fiction based on all-too-real experiences. While this collection omits "Green Fingers" and "A Lovely Bunch of Coconuts," the presence of the classic "Waiting for Trains" more than makes up for the omission of the two more graphic tales.

"Hosanna" and "Text for Today" take on the theme of religious fanaticism or misinterpretation carried to horrifying extremes. In the hands of a lesser writer, these stories would come off as heavy-handed japes at the church; with Birkin, he turns both into powerful tales. In both stories monstrous acts are committed. In the former, a man's religious fervor becomes madness. In the latter, a literal interpretation of Scripture has horrifying consequences.

The unflinching cruelty that is a hallmark of Birkin's tales is never more elegantly stated than in "Fairy Dust," a look at *Peter Pan* through a very dark glass, and "King of the Castle." The former tale won a considerable amount of praise and was featured in the British *Argosy* as a prize winner in a crime writers' competition. "King of the Castle" explores a favorite Birkin theme, that the "monsters" are not necessarily unhuman or supernatural creatures but may be as close and familiar as our own families. This is a theme the author returned to many times in other tales, but this is perhaps the most noteworthy selection.

In "Lords of the Refuge" Birkin presents a horrific reflection of a society that has created a god in their own image, an image that happens to be rather savagely twisted and cruel. "The Terror on Tobit" is a rare sort of story for Birkin, far more reminiscent of the type of shuddery tale of horrors rising from the sea that one would expect from H. P. Lovecraft or Frank Belknap Long. Of all of his stories, "Tobit" most clearly shows the link between Birkin's famous "Creeps" series (a brilliant series of anthologies published by Philip Allan during the 1930s) and the American pulp *Weird Tales*. A short and powerful tale, "The Terror on Tobit" is a classic of its type, and had it been published in *Weird Tales* originally, it would likely have served to forever fix Birkin's name in the minds of American horror fans.

That the author chose to end his collection with "Tobit" and the titular story show that he's lost none of the editorial acumen that made the "Creeps" series so well regarded. "A Haunting Beauty" is one of his finest tales of madness; murder; and brutal, violent excess. Beautifully written by a writer's writer, it's a story with plot and resolution straight out of the Grand Guignol Theatre. It's the sort of story that the American shudder pulps aspired to, but written by an author at the height of his literary powers and, like the rest of this collection, it couches the horror in a polished prose that makes the subject matter all that much more horrific.

JOHN PELAN (b. 1957) was born and still lives in Seattle, Washington. He was inspired to become a writer at age thirteen when he discovered that Arkham House had published a book submitted by a sixteen-year-old Ramsey Campbell. Prior to launching his writing career Pelan worked as a sales trainer, mixologist, steelworker, and antiquarian bookseller. In 1986 he founded Axolotl Press and published a number of volumes by authors such as Tim Powers, Charles de Lint, Michael Shea, and James P. Blaylock. He has edited or co-edited single-author collections by Edward Lucas White, Fritz Leiber, Manly Wade Wellman, Keith Fleming, Russell Kirk, John Wyndham, Violet Hunt, Eric Frank Russell, and others. As an author, his books include three collaborative "hard core horror" novels with Edward Lee: *Goon*, *Shifters*, and *Splaterspunk*. *An Antique Vintage*, *The Tower*, *The Colour Out of Darkness*, *Breaking the Lines*, and the collection *Darkness, My Old Friend* from Ash-Tree Press. He has edited the International Horror Guild Award-winning *Darkside: Horror for the Next Millennium*, *The Last Continent: New Tales of Zothique*, *Children of Cthulhu* (with Benjamin Adams), the Bram Stoker Award-winning *The Darker Side: Generations of Horror, Shadows Over Baker Street* (with Michael Reaves), *A Walk on the Darkside, The HWA Presents: Dark Arts, The Cthulhuian Singularity, Lost on the Darkside,* and *Alone on the Darkside.* His most recent anthology project is *The Century's Best Horror,* which collected some of the best stories from 1901 to 2000 and took nearly three years to complete.

98 [2000]

JEFF VANDERMEER on

House of Leaves
by MARK Z. DANIELEWSKI

House of Leaves *presents itself as the republication of a novel first distributed via the Internet, with numerous appendices and footnotes (and footnotes to footnotes), not to mention photographic plates, sketches, academic references bogus and genuine, reproductions of messy manuscript pages, and even a comprehensive index. The actual author, Mark Z. Danielewski (b. 1966), conceals himself behind (or in front of) a series of stand-ins, from the anonymous editors who have prepared the Internet text for paper publication through Johnny Truant, a pseudonymous Los Angeles dropout who works in a tattoo parlor, and the blind old sage Zampanò, who has died and left Johnny what seems to be a novel in the form of a lengthy description of* The Navidson Record. *This is a documentary film that chronicles discoveries made in the eponymous house on Ash Tree Lane in Virginia, where an impossible corridor appears in the living room, opening into a black-walled, apparently endless subterranean labyrinth. The book has several detours into obsessive list-building that suggest that all its narrators, down to the supposedly well-balanced "editors," are liable to get stuck on mental hobbyhorses. Along with pages containing only a few words and passages written upside down or crammed into a corner, not to mention two separate color and font tricks for every use of the word "house" (or maison or haus, etc.), this gives the construction something of the feel of* The Shining *crossed with* Tristram Shandy—*the kind of reference Danielewski is happy to make himself, forestalling critical approaches by incorporating them into a constantly shifting text. Danielewski (who has a bit part in the movie* Gettysburg, 1993) *is the son of the acting teacher Tad Danielewski, lyricist for the Polish version of "Sweet Georgia Brown" heard in Mel Brooks's* To Be or Not to Be *(1983), and brother of the singer-songwriter Poe (b. Annie Decatur Danielewski), whose album* Haunted *has thematic connections with* House of Leaves. *Danieleweksi, Poe, and Mercedes Ruehl (one of Tad Danielewksi's students) collaborated on a promotional CD of musically illustrated extracts from the novel. The final section of the book has been published separately as* The Whalestoe Letters *(2000).*

A HOUSE THAT'S BIGGER on the inside than on the outside,[1] a family filmed falling apart and coming back together again, horror mixed with a love story, the love story intertwined with a metaphysical/metafictional mystery—and all of that hidden by frames within frames and doors within doors. Is *House of Leaves* a document related to a horror movie of events that never happened, or is it a record relating the events behind a documentary?[2] This is just one of the compelling questions set up by Danielewski in his ever-moving kaleidoscope of a novel.

I am so taken with *House of Leaves* not because it represents an updating of techniques first canonized by Vladimir Nabokov, Jorge Luis Borges and, later, the first post-modernists. Nor do I admire it primarily because, in its copious use of visuals, footnotes,[3] annotated texts, appendix-type material,[4] color coding, and odd typography,[5] it represents one of the first novels that could be considered a creature of the Internet.⁶

No, I love *House of Leaves* because the author deploys its myriad effects in the service of scaring you half to death and making you care about its characters. Will Navidson, award-winning photojournalist and his (sometimes estranged) wife, Karen Green, achieve a remarkable reality in Danielewski's mirror-fractured narratives.² Their struggles with life, their attempts to love each other, their efforts to deal with the horrors of their house—all of this has a raw yet sometimes delicate poignancy.

That may seem like a simple response to a novel composed of complex parts, but really, the duality of love and horror forms the heart of *House of Leaves.* To dismiss or ignore these elements in favor of focusing on the pyrotechnics of Danielewski's approach is to ignore the reason why this novel has lingered in so many readers' imaginations like some strange, dark, half-remembered song. It also ignores the reason why *House of Leaves,* already a cult novel, will someday be considered a classic horror novel.

I love *House of Leaves* for moments like this one about a Raleigh colony-era hunting expedition caught in winter blizzards, conveyed in a footnote that, when I first read it, had me shivering with the delight-in-shock that speaks to the so-called "primitive" part of the reading experience:

> *20 Janiuere, 1610*
> More fnow. Bitter cold. This is a terrible Place we have stumbled on. It has been a Week fince we haue fspied one living thing. Were it not for the ftorm we would have abandoned it. Verm was plagued by many bad Dreames last night.
>
> *22 Janiuere, 1610*
> We are dying. No food. No fhelter. Tiggs dreamt he faw all fnow about us turn Red with blood.

And then the last entry:

> 23 *Janiuere, 1610*
> Ftaires! We have found ftaires!⁷

This digression provides a miniature example of how the author has managed to channel the marvelous sense of expanding-contracting space and time that J. G. Ballard perfected in his early short fiction—almost as if Ballard had taken a sudden right turn into the horror field. Throughout *House of Leaves*, Danielewski plays with the reader's sense of scale, meshing more cerebral mind-bending with the emotional struggle at the heart of the book. In what other novel can the reader find the more disturbing elements of *The Blair Witch Project* cross-pollinated with a Kierkegaardian existential quest?

In the end, the novel achieves its greatest effect through its exploration of Karen Green and Will Navidson's wounded relationship—and through Will's obsession with discovering the mystery behind the house and Karen's willingness to risk everything to try to save him. These two elements could be lifted from the oldest of horror novels, because if you slough away the various tricks and special effects, *House of Leaves* is a tangled and knotted narrative rope leading down into a formless abyss. We care about the characters clinging to that rope and do not want to see them fall.⁸

1 Danielewski is exacting about *just how much* the house subverts reality. When the novel's protagonists move into the house, it has an extra six feet of corridor inside that should not exist. Not four feet. Not seven. Not some undisclosed amount. No, the husband actually measures it, based on the house's outside dimensions, and comes up with six feet. Somehow the precise nature of this measurement adds to the horror.
2 Danielewski sprinkles his story with quotes about this film from famous artists, filmmakers, etc., but in such a context that the novel absorbs them. Seventy years from now, even if no one knows who Dr. Joyce Brothers is, her quote will still resonate in *House of Leaves*. In a sense, the novel devours and recycles the real world whenever, through use of specific detail, it comes into contact with it.
3 It may be true that some of the novel's copious footnotes stumble through the text like wayward explorers caught in the bowels of a house bigger on the inside than the outside—sometimes a little closer to home, sometimes completely lost, and losing the reader at times, too.

4 It may be true that the additional text in the novel's coda provides lovely epistolary entertainment while not always justifying its presence in the narrative.
5 However, all of this can be forgiven as a necessary subterfuge—a kind of self-conscious camouflage that helps *House of Leaves* achieve greater depth and breadth. Sometimes a book has to be bigger on the inside so it can be bigger on the outside, too.
6 That *House of Leaves* is at least a familiar of the Internet is echoed by the story that the novel was first published in various editions on the Internet. Is this true? It doesn't matter; given the ephemeral nature of electronic publication, the rumor has a kind of mythical truth to it.
7 At the time I was in a small plane that was making a difficult landing in a thunderstorm, but nothing could tear my attention away from *House of Leaves*. Despite the sometimes maddening digressions, the novel held me as rapt as any airport thriller, making it hard for me to decide whether to read fast to find out what would happen next, or to read slow to savor the heady sense of unease. The hint of the house's influence extending into the past, conveyed through that one short footnote, created the same shudder of recognition as more visceral shocks I'd had reading more direct horror novels.
8 "But what about Johnny Truant? What about Zampanò? How can you ignore two whole layers of the novel?" you may ask. To which I reply, I haven't ignored them at all, if you examine this record closely.

JEFF VANDERMEER (b. 1968) grew up in the Fiji Islands and currently lives in Tallahassee, Florida, with his wife, Ann. He spent six months traveling around the world before returning to his native United States, and these travels have deeply influenced his fiction. He is a two-time winner of the World Fantasy Award as well as a past finalist for the Hugo Award, the Philip K. Dick Award, the International Horror Guild Award, the British Fantasy Award, the Bram Stoker Award, and the Theodore Sturgeon Memorial Award. VanderMeer is the author of several surreal/magic realist novels and short-story collections, including *City of Saints & Madmen, Veniss Underground, Shriek: An Afterword,* and *Secret Lives.* He is the recipient of an NEA-funded Florida Individual Artist Fellowship for excellence in fiction (1995–96) and a Florida Artist Enhancement Grant

(2004–2005). In 2001 *Locus Online* named him one of the ten best speculative fiction writers in the world. In addition to his writing, VanderMeer has run an award-winning publishing company for the past fifteen years and edited or co-edited several anthologies, including the critically acclaimed *Leviathan* series (with Forrest Aguirre) and *The Thackery T. Lambshead Pocket Guide to Eccentric & Discredited Diseases* (with Mark Roberts).

99 [2002]

RICHARD A. LUPOFF on

Feesters in the Lake & Other Stories
by **BOB LEMAN**

Published in a hardcover edition of just 460 copies by John Pelan and Aaron Bates's small press imprint Midnight House, Feesters in the Lake & Other Stories *collects fifteen stories—the entire output of part-time writer Bob Leman (b. 1922). All but one of the stories were reprints, originally appearing between 1977 and 1995; thirteen initially appeared in Edward L. Ferman's* Magazine of Fantasy & Science Fiction. *"How Dobbstown Was Saved," the sole original, was not newly written for the collection but rescued from Harlan Ellison's long-in-limbo* Last Dangerous Visions. *The best-known story, "Window" (1980), was nominated for a Nebula Award and was filmed by director Bill Pullman as "A View Through the Window" for the Sci-Fi Channel's series* Night Visions. *The book was edited with an introduction by*

Jim Rockhill and featured a cover illustration and frontispiece author portrait by Allen Koszowski.

UNLESS YOU'RE A deeply committed science fiction fan or a longtime reader of *The Magazine of Fantasy & Science Fiction*, the chances are that Bob Leman is a leading candidate for the title of "Finest Short-Story Writer You've Never Heard Of."

Born in 1922, Leman interrupted his education to spend more than three years in the U. S. Army, serving as an artillery officer in Europe during World War II. Receiving his discharge from the army, he returned home, earned a degree in political science, and thereafter pursued a career in the oil industry.

He was a lifelong enthusiast of fantasy literature, whether interplanetary romances, weird tales, or ghost stories. Along the line he became a member of the science fiction fan community and self-published fanzines filled for the most part with his own witty commentary.

Like many fans, Leman apparently decided that it would be amusing to emulate the professional writers whose works he admired, and he wrote a story, "Bait," which he sold to *F&SF* in 1967. There followed a ten-year hiatus, after which Leman's second story appeared in the same magazine. A total of thirteen Leman stories were published in *F&SF* between 1967 and 1988. All thirteen stories, plus "Come Where My Love Lies Dreaming" (sold to Charles L. Grant's anthology *Shadows 10*) and "How Dobbstown Was Saved," not previously published, are gathered in the present collection.

After producing a total of fifteen stories, Leman simply stopped writing for publication. He told his admirer and editor Jim Rockhill, "Whatever creative spark I had for a while just went away." It was largely through Rockhill's efforts that Leman's stories were collected, and it is to the credit of Midnight House, a specialty publisher in Seattle, Washington, that this volume, about as unpromising a commercial proposition as one could imagine, found its way into print.

The stories range across the spectrum from science fiction—of a sort—to Lovecraftian horror. They are narrated in a formal, often distant voice. Critic Charles de Lint has commented on "Leman's penchant for writing from an omnipresent point of view, but that distancing of the narrator—be it in first person or third—can make the story feel stiff." There is indeed a peculiarly archaic feel to much of Leman's writing. His stories do not offer much that is new, so much as they represent startlingly new explorations of familiar themes.

His most famous story is "Window" (1980). In it a three-dimensional opening is created between the rather grim modern world and the sunny Victorian milieu so poignantly longed for in the works of Ray Bradbury and in countless old *Twilight Zone* episodes. Leman evokes a sense of yearning in the reader with his descriptions of this lost, idealized American home:

> The house was drenched now with the light of a red sunset; it seemed to glow from within with a deep, rosy blush. But, Gilson reflected, the sunset wasn't really necessary; sentiment and the universal, unacknowledged yearning for a simple, cleaner time would lend rosiness enough. He was quite aware that the surge of longing and nostalgia he felt was nostalgia for something he had never actually experienced, that the way of life the house epitomized for him was in fact his own creation, built from patches of novels and films; nonetheless he found himself hungry for that life, yearning for that time. It was a gentle and secure time, he thought.

The story proceeds, including the expected attempt by a sympathetic protagonist to escape the real world of 1980 and reach that "simple, cleaner time." It is a perfect Bradbury/Serling setup that Leman inverts into a horrific event, leaving the reader in a state of shock. (Leman's device, incidentally, was lifted to equal effect in the film *Galaxy Quest*.)

Leman is notably honest in crediting his sources and influences. He is an unabashed Lovecraftian, making the Appalachian town of Sturkeyville and the surrounding Goster County his version of Lovecraft's decaying New England villages and their demon-haunted environs. The Lovecraft influence is clearly present in such stories as "Olida" and "The Feesters in the Lake."

The first of these is reminiscent of Lovecraft's "The Dunwich Horror," with its inbred, semihuman families and their monstrous members long hidden from the outer world. The second is a variation on Lovecraft's "The Shadow Over Innsmouth" with an infusion of William Hope Hodgson's nautical horrors. To this material Leman adds a fillip of doubt as to the very existence of the monsters.

Nor is Leman above essaying such classic themes as the vampire tale ("The Pilgrimage of Clifford M.") or the paranoid/solipsist theme ("Industrial Complex").

Another monster story, by no means Lovecraftian, is "The Time of the Worm" (1988), almost certainly the last written of Leman's stories and clearly among the most effective. A classic *conte cruel*, this one is worthy of Dean Koontz at his best—and nastiest—as Leman tempts and torments both his victims and the reader with alternating doses of hope and despair.

Leman's stories are not all of equal merit. The formal, mannered style of narration that de Lint refers to requires some adjustment by the reader. And Leman's conservative social and political attitudes, clearly manifest in many of these stories, will jar some readers.

Still, one can only wonder what gems Leman might have produced if he had produced fifty stories instead of fifteen, or if he had written a novel. If only his career in the oil business had palled and he had turned his energies, full-time, to literature. If only "whatever creative spark" Leman had, had blazed into a full-scale career instead of winking out in his middle age.

That, we will never know.

> **RICHARD A. (ALLEN) LUPOFF** (b. 1935) was born in Brooklyn, New York, and for many years has lived in Berkeley, California, with his wife, Patricia. He spent a few years in the U.S. Army in the late 1950s, never firing a shot

in anger and never having had one shot at him, neither of which he regrets. He has worked as both a print and broadcast journalist from his student days onward, and for fifty years has done a books-and-authors show on local radio station KPFA. He is novelist, short-story writer, critic, screenwriter, and anthologist, and his many books include the novels *One Million Centuries, Sandworld, Sword of the Demon, The Return of Skull-Face* (with Robert E. Howard), *Space War Blues, Circumpolar!, Lovecraft's Book, Galaxy's End, Night of the Living Gator,* and two *Buck Rogers* novelizations (under the byline "Addison E. Steele"). His short fiction has been collected in *The Ova Hamlet Papers, Before . . . 12:01 . . . and After, Claremont Tales, Claremont Tales II,* and *Quintet: The Cases of Chase and Delacroix.* Lupoff's non-fiction titles include *Edgar Rice Burroughs: Master of Adventure, Barsoom: Edgar Rice Burroughs and the Martian Vision, Writer at Large,* and *The Great American Paperback,* and he has edited *All in Color for a Dime* and *The Comic Book Book* (both with Don Thompson) and two volumes of *What If? Stories That Should Have Won the Hugo.* In 1963 he and Pat Lupoff won the Hugo Award for their fanzine *Xero,* and a 2004 compilation *The Best of Xero* was nominated for another Hugo. He is also a winner of the Edgar Rice Burroughs Lifetime Achievement Award and the Left Coast Crime Lifetime Achievement Award for mystery fiction. A short film based on his story "12:01 P.M." was an Academy Award nominee in 1990 and was expanded into a feature three years later.

100 [2003]

TIM LEBBON on

More Tomorrow & Other Stories
by **MICHAEL MARSHALL SMITH**

Published by Earthling Publications, Paul Miller's small press imprint, More Tomorrow & Other Stories *collects all the short fiction Michael Marshall Smith (b. 1965) published between 1988, when his "The Man Who Drew Cats" and "The Dark Land" both appeared, and 2003. It includes the entire contents of the U.K. collection* What You Make It *(1999) and the three-story "sampler"* Cat Stories *(2001), plus the fabulously rare* When God Lived in Kentish Town *(1998), a promotional bookstore giveaway, and the novella* The Vaccinator, *first put out (by PS Publishing) as a chapbook. The hardcover was issued in an edition of a thousand numbered copies and a twenty-six-copy traycased lettered edition. "Being Right," "Maybe Next Time," "Open Doors," and "The Munchies" are original to the collection, and "Happy Holidays!" can be read only by the purchasers of the lettered edition (and their friends, if they let them near the precious thing). The book includes an introduction ("Alias Smith & Jones") by Stephen Jones, an afterword by the author ("On Not Writing"), and a wraparound cover illustration by John Picacio.* More Tomorrow & Other Stories *shared the 2004 International Horror Guild Award for Best Collection with Glen Hirshberg's* The Two Sams. *Smith writes about Stephen King's* Pet Sematary *(1983) in this volume.*

A RTHUR MACHEN ONCE bemoaned his inability to convey vision to paper when he said, "I dreamed in fire, but I worked in clay." He was truly one of the greats, yet even he knew that the process between imagination and page can often filter some of the grandness from an idea. This is especially pertinent in the short-story form, because often a story will be a faultless whole in the writer's mind before pen touches paper.

But here's a secret: writing short stories is easy. Everyone can write short stories, and a lot of people do. Writing *good* short stories, however, is much harder; these are the ones that leave an impact through content, tone, or meaning. Again, lots of people write good short stories.

Writing a *perfect* short story . . . that's in a league of its own. It's incredibly difficult, because the perfect short story not only leaves an impact, it can change the reader's life. Very few people write perfect short stories. Michael Marshall Smith does. And not just one or two, but a whole bucketload of them, as witnessed by *More Tomorrow & Other Stories*. I'm not saying that every story in this book is utterly perfect, but most of them are close enough to matter, and this collection is surely destined to become a classic.

And Smith makes it all look so damn easy. His writing flows along in a relaxed and intimate style reminiscent of Stephen King at his best, but at the same time Smith is doing things with your perception, toying with your emotions, and you barely notice the whole effect until the end. Humor often presents itself in Smith's writing, sometimes a natural part of the story but also there on occasion to emphasize some of the revelations to come. You laugh, you cry. His prose is casually brilliant, drawing you along so bewitchingly that you forget you're actually reading. There's no awkwardness here, no stumbling about with inappropriate descriptions or fancy phrasing. You're there in Smith's world, watching or interacting with his characters, feeling what they feel and doing what they do. It's the ultimate effect that any writer aims for but few achieve.

And his stories *mean* something. His fiction is life-affirming and moving, mysterious and relevant. His stories say things about the world we live in, as opposed to telling us about the world the writer lives in, and the reader will come away feeling challenged and educated. His stories have soul.

It's difficult to pick out highlights from such an exceptional collection, but here are a few:

"Being Right" tells of a man who has let his relationship with his wife grow stale. She talks a lot, he thinks she's boring, and their affection seems to have waned. By conjuring a listening angel he hopes to be proven right . . . but what it really tells him is the reality of things. It's a simple, beautiful tale counseling against selfishness and indifference, and it will make you open your eyes.

"What You Make It," masquerades as a science fiction tale, but is in reality a story of acceptance and fulfillment. Its underlying moral is similar to that in "Being Right": be happy with what you have. It's an idea that informs many stories in this collection.

"The Dark Land," one of Smith's earliest stories (and winner of the British Fantasy Award), is a strange tale of shifting realities and overlapping perceptions. Trapped in a house, a young man is assaulted by its ghostly former occupants, and while he struggles to keep them at bay, there's something appearing in his living room. A jungle, larger than the room and wilder. And in the jungle, something growls. Chilling!

One of my all-time favorites—and further evidence, if it were needed, of Smith's talent for conjuring inspiring titles—is "Hell Hath Enlarged Herself." There's science here, and lots of technical genetic and computer stuff, and the end of the world as we know it. But at its heart this is a story of friendship and love, and the choices we make in both.

"Always" is a gorgeous story, a tale of mourning and the memories the dead leave behind. It emphasizes the importance of memories, and how they can help us hold on to people we love.

"Dying" is a scream against the environmental damage we rain so apathetically on our planet, and it twists around the assumption that because we can build airplanes and tower blocks and computers, we're superior to the creatures we share this world with. Set in a future world where there are no longer any animals, it's a parable about humankind's inflated sense of self-importance. And you'll never look at a cat the same way again.

Every story in this collection will leave the reader thinking, whether it is over the emotional content of a piece, or the twists that Smith is so adept at throwing our way. Yet even these twists carry meaning; they're not just a handy storyteller's device, they're also important to what this storyteller is trying to say.

Michael Marshall Smith has written best-selling novels that have been optioned by major film companies, but for me his triumph is still his short fiction. It'll hit you in the face and soothe your heart at the same time. Smith dreams in fire, and works with the flames of his singular and unique imagination.

TIM LEBBON (b. 1969) was born in London but has spent most of his life in South Wales. He currently lives in Goytre, Monmouthshire, with his wife and two children. His books include the novels *Face, The Nature of Balance, Mesmer, Until She Sleeps, Desolation,* and *Berserk*; the novellas *White, Naming of Parts, Changing of Faces, Exorcising Angels* (with Simon Clark), *Dead Man's Hand,* and *Pieces of Hate,* and the collections *Fears Unnamed, As the Sun Goes Down, White and Other Tales of Ruin,* and *Night Visions 11* (with Kim Newman and Lucius Shepard). Forthcoming titles include the dark fantasy novels *Dusk* and *Dawn* from Bantam Dell, the novelization *Hellboy: The New Ark* from Pocket, and further books from Leisure, Night Shade Books, Cemetery Dance, and Necessary Evil Press. Lebbon has won two British Fantasy Awards, a Bram Stoker Award, and a Tombstone Award, and has been short-listed for International Horror Guild and World Fantasy Awards. Several of his novels and novellas are currently under film option in the United States and the United Kingdom.

LISTS OF RECOMMENDED READING

Appendix I: Horror: 100 Best Books

Listed below, in chronological order and alphabetically by author per year, are the selections from the previous 1988 volume along with the name of each entry's essayist. These titles, along with the 100 included in this book, do not appear in Appendix II.

YEAR	SELECTION	ESSAYIST
c. 1592	*The Tragical History of Doctor Faustus,* Christopher Marlowe	Clive Barker
1606	*The Tragedy of Macbeth,* William Shakespeare	John Blackburn
1612	*The White Devil,* John Webster	Diana Wynne Jones
1794	*Caleb Williams,* William Godwin	Scott Bradfield
1796	*The Monk,* Matthew Gregory Lewis	Les Daniels
1814–16	*The Best Tales of Hoffman*	John Sladek
1817	*Northanger Abbey,* Jane Austen	David Pirie
1818	*Frankenstein,* Mary Wollstonecraft Shelley	Jane Yolen
1820	*Melmoth the Wanderer,* Charles Maturin	Peter Tremayne
1824	*The Confessions of a Justified Sinner,* James Hogg	Garry Kilworth
1838	*Twice-Told Tales,* Nathaniel Hawthorne	Edgar Allan Poe

LISTS OF RECOMMENDED READING

YEAR	SELECTION	ESSAYIST
	Tales of Mystery and Imagination, Edgar Allan Poe	John M. Ford
1842	*The Black Spider*, Jeremias Gotthelf	Thomas Tessier
1844–45	*The Wandering Jew*, Eugène Sue	Thomas M. Disch
1857	*The Confidence Man*, Herman Melville	Michael McDowell
1864	*Uncle Silas*, J. Sheridan Le Fanu	M. R. James
1886	*Dr. Jekyll and Mr. Hyde*, Robert Louis Stevenson	Jack Williamson
1887	*She*, H. Rider Haggard	Tim Stout
1895	*The King in Yellow*, Robert W. Chambers	H. P. Lovecraft
1896	*The Island of Dr. Moreau*, H. G. Wells	Gene Wolfe
1897	*Dracula*, Bram Stoker	Colin Wilson
1898	*The Turn of the Screw*, Henry James	R. Chetwynd-Hayes
1902	*Heart of Darkness*, Joseph Conrad	Douglas E. Winter
1903	*The Jewel of Seven Stars*, Bram Stoker	Richard Dalby
1904	*Ghost Stories of an Antiquary*, M. R. James	Geoff Ryman
1906	*The House of Souls*, Arthur Machen	T. E. D. Klein
1908	*John Silence*, Algernon Blackwood	Hilaire Belloc
	The Man Who Was Thursday, G. K. Chesterton	David Langford
	The House on the Borderland, William Hope Hodgson	Terry Pratchett
1909	*The Collected Works of Ambrose Bierce*	Milton Subotsky
1911	*Widdershins*, Oliver Onions	Mike Ashley
1912–34	*The Horror Horn*, E. F. Benson	Basil Copper
1920	*A Voyage to Arcturus*, David Lindsay	George Hay
1925	*The Trial*, Franz Kafka	Steve Rasnic Tem

LISTS OF RECOMMENDED READING

YEAR	SELECTION	ESSAYIST
1929	*Something about Eve,* James Branch Cabell	Robert E. Howard
	Medusa, E. H. Visiak	Karl Edward Wagner
1933	*The Last Bouquet,* Marjorie Bowen	Jessica Amanda Salmonson
	The Werewolf of Paris, Guy Endore	Marvin Kaye
1934	*The Cadaver of Gideon Wyck,* Alexander Laing	Robert Bloch
1937	*A Second Century of Creepy Stories,* Hugh Walpole, ed.	Hugh Lamb
1938	*The Dark Tower,* C. S. Lewis	Lionel Fanthorpe
1939	*The Outsider and Others,* H. P. Lovecraft	Donald A. Wollheim
	Johnny Got His Gun, Dalton Trumbo	Dennis Etchison
1942	*Out of Space and Time,* Clark Ashton Smith	Harlan Ellison
1943	*Conjure Wife,* Fritz Leiber	Gerald W. Page
1945	*The Lurker and the Threshold,* H. P. Lovecraft and August Derleth	Graham Masterton
	Night Has a Thousand Eyes, Cornell Woolrich	Maxim Jakubowski
1946	*Deliver Me from Eva,* Paul Bailey	Forrest J. Ackerman
	And the Darkness Falls, Boris Karloff, ed.	David G. Hartwell
1947	*The Sleeping and the Dead,* August Derleth, ed.	Peter Haining
1949	*Track of the Cat,* Walter Van Tilburg Clark	Robert R. McCammon
1952	*The Sound of His Horn,* Sarban	Suzy McKee Charnas

LISTS OF RECOMMENDED READING

YEAR	SELECTION	ESSAYIST
1954	*Lord of the Flies*, William Golding	Joe Haldeman
	I Am Legend, Richard Matheson	Richard Christian Matheson
1955	*The October Country*, Ray Bradbury	Joe R. Lansdale
1958	*Nine Horrors and a Dream*, Joseph Payne Brennan	Stephen Gallagher
1959	*Psycho*, Robert Bloch	Hugh B. Cave
	The Haunting of Hill House, Shirley Jackson	Lisa Tuttle
	Quatermass and the Pit, Nigel Kneale	Stephen Laws
	Cry Horror!, H. P. Lovecraft	Michel Parry
1964	*The Three Stigmata of Palmer Eldritch*, Philip K. Dick	Tad Williams
1965	*The Painted Bird*, Jerzy Kosinski	Jack Dann
1966	*The Crystal World*, J. G. Ballard	Craig Shaw Gardner
1968	*Sub Rosa*, Robert Aickman	Colin Greenland
1969	*The Green Man*, Kingsley Amis	Brian Aldiss
	The Compleat Werewolf, Anthony Boucher	Neil Gaiman
1971	*The Exorcist*, William Peter Blatty	F. Paul Wilson
	Grendel, John Gardner	Dan Simmons
1972	*The Sheep Look Up*, John Brunner	John Skipp
1973	*Burnt Offerings*, Robert Marasco	Stephen King
	Worse Things Waiting, Manly Wade Wellman	Frances Garfield
1975	*Deathbird Stories*, Harlan Ellison	Craig Spector
	'Salem's Lot, Stephen King	Al Sarrantonio
1977	*Murgunstrumm and Others*, Hugh B. Cave	Brian Lumley

LISTS OF RECOMMENDED READING

YEAR	SELECTION	ESSAYIST
	All Heads Turn When the Hunt Goes By, John Farris	David J. Schow
	The Shining, Stephen King	Peter Straub
	Sweetheart, Sweetheart, Bernard Taylor	Charles L. Grant
1978	*Falling Angel,* William Hjortsberg	William F. Nolan
	The Wolfen, Whitley Strieber	Charles de Lint
1979	*The Totem,* David Morrell	Shaun Hutson
	Ghost Story, Peter Straub	Peter Nicholls
1980	*The Land of Laughs,* Jonathan Carroll	Christopher Evans
	The Cellar, Richard Laymon	David Garnett
1981	*Red Dragon,* Thomas Harris	Chet Williamson
	The Keep, F. Paul Wilson	J. N. Williamson
1982	*The Dark Country,* Dennis Etchison	Samantha Lee
1983	*The Arabian Nightmare,* Robert Irwin	Brian Stableford
	The Anubis Gates, Tim Powers	John Clute
	In a Lonely Place, Karl Edward Wagner	Ramsey Campbell
1984	*The Wasp Factory,* Iain Banks	Malcolm Edwards
	Who Made Stevie Crye?, Michael Bishop	Ian Watson
	Mythago Wood, Robert Holdstock	Michael Moorcock
	The Ceremonies, T. E. D. Klein	Thomas F. Monteleone
1985	*Hawksmoor,* Peter Ackroyd	R. S. Hadji
	The Damnation Game, Clive Barker	Adrian Cole
	Song of Kali, Dan Simmons	Edward Bryant
1986	*The Pet,* Charles L. Grant	Guy N. Smith
	A Nest of Nightmares, Lisa Tuttle	Robert Holdstock
1987	*Dark Feasts,* Ramsey Campbell	Jack Sullivan
	Swan Song, Robert McCammon	Eddy C. Bertin

Appendix II: Further Reading

Inevitably, in a work like this and the earlier volume—an almost random selection of 100 titles in each—certain key books and authors have unavoidably been overlooked and forgotten. Therefore, in collaboration with our distinguished line-up of contributors from both books, we have compiled this list of further recommended titles. This should in no way be considered a comprehensive listing—to have done so would have filled the entire book—so regard this as an unabashedly arbitrary and biased guide to some of the best titles the genre has to offer, as opposed to a pantheon of classics engraved in marble and handed down to posterity. As in appendix I, the listings are in chronological order and alphabetically by author per year.

458 B.C.	*The Oresteia*, Aeschylus
1300	*Inferno*, Dante
1657	*Paradise Lost*, John Milton
1764	*The Castle of Otranto*, Horace Walpole
1776	*Ugetsu Monogatari/Tales of the Pale Moon*, Ueda Akinari
1778	*The Old English Baron*, Clara Reeve
1785	*Les 120 journées de Sodome/The 120 Days of Sodom*, the Marquis de Sade
1788	*Vathek*, William Beckford
1791	*Justine*, the Marquis de Sade
1794	*The Mysteries of Udolpho*, Anne Radcliffe
1798	*Weiland, or The Transformation: An American Tale*, Charles Brockden Brown
	Lyrical Ballads, William Wordsworth and Samuel Taylor Coleridge
	The Midnight Bell, Francis Lathom
1815	*Die Elixir des Teufels/The Devil's Elixirs*, E. T. A. Hoffman
1819	*The Vampyre*, John Polidori
1831	*Notre Dame de Paris/The Hunchback of Notre Dame*, Victor Hugo
1835	*Fairytales, Told for Children*, Hans Christian Andersen

1837	*The Narrative of A. Gordon Pym*, Edgar Allan Poe
1839	*The Phantom Ship*, Frederick Marryat
1845	*Varney the Vampire*, J. M. Rymer
1847	*Wuthering Heights*, Charlotte Brontë
1850	*Auriol, or The Elixir of Life*, W. Harrison Ainsworth
1851	*House of the Seven Gables*, Nathaniel Hawthorne
	Moby-Dick, Herman Melville
1851	*The Piazza Tales*, Herman Melville
1853	*Bartleby the Scrivener*, Herman Melville
1857	*Les Fleurs du Mal/Flowers of Evil*, Charles Beaudelaire
1860	*The Woman in White*, Wilkie Collins
1870	*The Mystery of Edwin Drood*, Charles Dickens
1872	*The Devils*, Fyodor Dostoievsky
	In a Glass Darkly, J. Sheridan Le Fanu
1880	*Strange Stories*, Erckmann-Chatrian
1883	*Contes Cruels*, Villiers de l'Isle Adam
1887	*The Diamond Lens*, Fitz-James O'Brien
1888	*The Phantom Rickshaw and Other Tales*, Rudyard Kipling
1890	*Hauntings*, Vernon Lee (Violet Paget)
1891	*Las Bas/Down There*, J. K. Huysmans
1895	*A Bid for Fortune*, Guy Boothby
1897	*The Hill of Dreams*, Arthur Machen
	The Beetle, Richard Marsh
1904	*Kwaidan*, Lafcadio Hearn
1906	*The Empty House and Other Ghost Stories*, Algernon Blackwood
1909	*The Necromancers*, R. H. Benson
1911	*Wandering Ghosts*, F. Marion Crawford
	Alraune, H. H. Ewers
1912	*The Room in the Tower and Other Stories*, E. F. Benson
	The Night Land, William Hope Hodgson
1913	*Seven Keys to Baldpate*, Earl Derr Biggers
	The Lodger, Mrs. Belloc Lowndes
	The Mystery of Dr. Fu-Manchu, Sax Rohmer
1914	*Beasts and Superbeasts*, Saki (H. H. Munro)

1914	*Dracula's Guest,* Bram Stoker
1915	*The Golem,* Gustav Meyrink
1920	*Les Mains d'Orlac/The Hands of Orlac,* Maurice Renard
1922	*The Undying Monster,* Jessie Douglas Kerruish
1923	*Madame Crowl's Ghost,* J. Sheridan Le Fanu
1925	*The Smoking Leg and Other Stories,* John Metcalfe
1926	*The Ghost Book,* Lady Cynthia Asquith, ed.
1926	*Das Schloss/The Castle,* Franz Kafka
1927	*Benighted,* J. B. Priestley
	The Cat and the Canary, John Willard
1928	*The Beast With Five Fingers,* W. F. Harvey
	Not at Night!, Herbert Asbury, ed.
1930	*As I Lay Dying,* William Faulkner
1931	*Creeps by Night* (aka *Modern Tales of Horror*), Dashiell Hammett, ed.
	The Dain Curse, Dashiell Hammett
	The Supernatural Omnibus, Montague Summers, ed.
1932–36	*Creeps,* Charles Birkin, ed.
1933	*Burn, Witch, Burn!,* A. Merritt
	A Glastonbury Romance, John Cowper Powys
	Miss Lonelyhearts, Nathaniel West
1934	*The Cat Jumps,* Elizabeth Bowen
	Seven Gothic Tales, Isak Dinesen (Karen Blixen)
1935	*The Circus of Dr. Lao,* Charles G. Finney
1936	*Metamorphosis and Other Stories,* Franz Kafka
1937	*The Devil and Daniel Webster,* Stephen Vincent Benet
	The Beast Must Die, Nicholas Blake
	The Burning Court, John Dickson Carr
1938	*Rebecca,* Daphne Du Maurier
	Hangover Square, Patrick Hamilton
1939	*Ten Little Niggers/And Then There Were None,* Agatha Christie
	Day of the Locust, Nathaniel West
1942	*The Best Short Stories of Walter De La Mare*

1942	*The Uninvited*, Dorothy McCardle
	Black Alibi, Cornell Woolrich
1943	*Donovan's Brain*, Curt Siodmak
	Malpertuis, Jean Ray
1944	*Ficciones*, Jorge Luis Borges
1945	*The Demon Lover*, Elizabeth Bowen
	Best Ghost Stories, Anne Ridler, ed.
1945	*Witch House*, Evangeline Walton
	All Hallows' Eve, Charles Williams
1946	*Fearful Pleasures*, A. E. Coppard
	Who Knocks?: Twenty Masterpieces of the Spectral for the Connoisseur, August Derleth, ed.
	The Deadly Percheron, John Franklin Bardin
	Skull Face and Others, Robert E. Howard
	The Hounds of Tindalos, Frank Belknap Long
	West India Lights, Henry S. Whitehead
1947	*This Mortal Coil*, Cynthia Asquith
	Dark Carnival, Ray Bradbury
	Dark of the Moon: Poems of Fantasy and the Macabre, August Derleth, ed.
	The Night Side: Masterpieces of the Strange & Terrible, August Derleth, ed.
	The Sleeping & the Dead: Thirty Uncanny Tales, August Derleth, ed.
	Night's Black Agents, Fritz Leiber
	Bend Sinister, Vladimir Nabokov
1948	*Devil Take the Blue-Tail Fly*, John Franklin Bardin
	The Travelling Grave, L. P. Hartley
1949	*The Screaming Mimi*, Fredric Brown
	Tomato Cain and Other Stories, Nigel Kneale
1950-54	*Tales from the Crypt*, *The Vault of Horror*, *The Haunt of Fear*, William M. Gaines, publisher
1951	*Ringstones and Other Curious Tales*, Sarban (John W. Wall)

LISTS OF RECOMMENDED READING

1952	*Night's Yawning Peal: A Ghostly Company*, August Derleth, ed.
	The Devils of Loudon, Aldous Huxley
1953	*Night of the Hunter*, Davis Grubb
	The Doll Maker and Other Tales, Sarban (John W. Wall)
1954	*Celle qui n'était plus/The Woman Who Was No More*, Pierre Boileau and Thomas Narcejac
1954	*Someone Like You*, Roald Dahl
1955	*Men Without Bones*, Gerald Kersh
	Satan in Goray, Isaac Beshvis Singer
1956	*The Shrinking Man*, Richard Matheson
1957	*Fire, Burn!*, John Dickson Carr
	Best Horror Stories, John Keir Cross, ed.
	The Cosmic Puppeteers, Philip K. Dick
1958	*Honeymoon in Hell*, Fredric Brown
	The Third Level, Jack Finney
	The Sundial, Shirley Jackson
1959	*The Naked Lunch*, William S. Burroughs
	The Manchurian Candidate, Richard Condon
	Night of the Big Heat, John Lymington
	Doctors Wear Scarlet, Simon Raven
	The Pan Book of Horror Stories, Herbert van Thal, ed.
	The Macabre Reader, Donald A. Wollheim, ed.
1960	*Corpus Earthling*, Louis Charbonneau
1961	*Nightmares and Geezenstacks*, Frederick Brown
1962	*Yours Truly, Jack the Ripper*, Robert Bloch
	A Clockwork Orange, Anthony Burgess
	Dark Mind, Dark Heart, August Derleth, ed.
	The Surly Sullen Bell, Russell Kirk
1963	*The Dark Man and Others*, Robert E. Howard
1964	*The Kiss of Death*, Charles Birkin
	Over the Edge, August Derleth, ed.
	Seconds, David Ely
	No Such Thing as a Vampire, Frederick Pickersgill, ed.

1964–72	*The Fontana Book of Great Ghost Stories,* Robert Aickman, ed.
1965	*In Cold Blood,* Truman Capote
	The Magic Man, Charles Beaumont
	Something Breathing, Stanley McNail
	Progeny of the Adder, Leslie H. Whitten
1965–77	*The Dark is Rising,* Susan Cooper
1966	*A Study in Terror/Sherlock Holmes vs. Jack the Ripper/Ellery Queen vs. Jack the Ripper,* Ellery Queen (Paul W. Fairman)
	Le Locutaire/The Tenant, Roland Topor
1967	*Not After Nightfall,* Basil Copper
	Travellers by Night, August Derleth, ed.
	Camp Concentration, Thomas M. Disch
	Trinity, Ray Russell
	The Mind Parasites, Colin Wilson
1968	*Nothing But the Night,* John Blackburn
	Dagon, Fred Chappell
	The Ring of Thoth, Sir Arthur Conan Doyle
	Dance of the Dwarfs, Geoffrey Household
1969	*The Cell: Three Tales of Horror,* David Case
1971	*Fengriffen and Other Stories,* David Case
	Dark Things, August Derleth, ed.
	The Caller of the Black, Brian Lumley
	Hell House, Richard Matheson
	The Other, Thomas Tryon
1972	*For Fear of Little Men,* John Blackburn
	First Blood, David Morrell
1973	*Crash,* J. G. Ballard
	Demons by Daylight, Ramsey Campbell
	From Evil's Pillow, Basil Copper
	Gravity's Rainbow, Thomas Pyncheon
1973–84	*The Fontana Book of Great Ghost Stories,* R. Chetwynd-Hayes, ed.
1974	*Jaws,* Peter Benchley

LISTS OF RECOMMENDED READING

1974	*The Hawkline Monster: A Gothic Western,* Richard Brautigan
	The Elemental, R. Chetwynd-Hayes
	The Burrowers Beneath, Brian Lumley
	The Black House, Paul Theroux
	Collected Ghost Stories, Mary E. Wilkins-Freeman
1975	*Cold Hand in Mine,* Robert Aickman
	The Fog, James Herbert
	Testament, David Morrell
	Nameless Places, Gerald W. Page, ed.
	The Dracula Tape, Fred Saberhagen
	The Auctioneer, Joan Samson
1976	*Eaters of the Dead,* Michael Crichton
	Dying of Fright: Masterpieces of the Macabre, Les Daniels, ed.
	Interview With a Vampire, Anne Rice
	The Children of Dynmouth, William Trevor
1977	*Echoes from the Macabre,* Daphne Du Maurier
	Night-Side, Joyce Carol Oates
	Blind Voices, Tom Reamy
	Nighthwing, Martin Cruz Smith
1978	*Half in Shadow,* Mary Elizabeth Counselman
	The Black Castle, Les Daniels
	San Diego Lightfoot Sue and Other Stories, Tom Reamy
	The House Next Door, Anne Rivere Siddons
1979	*Flowers in the Attic,* V. C. Andrews
	The Lizard's Tail, Marc Brendel
	The Face That Must Die, Ramsey Campbell
	The Specialty of the House and Other Stories, Stanley Ellin
	Kiss of the Spider Woman, Manuel Puig
	The Nightwalker, Thomas Tessier
1980	*The Shapes of Midnight,* Joseph Payne Brennan
	New Terrors, Ramsey Campbell, ed.
	The Vampire Tapestry, Suzy McKee Charnas
	The Voice of the Night, Dean R. Koontz

LISTS OF RECOMMENDED READING

1980	*Cold Moon Over Babylon*, Michael McDowell
	Shadowland, Peter Straub
	Puffball, Fay Weldon
1980–94	*The Year's Best Horror Stories*, Karl Edward Wagner, ed.
1981	*Tales from the Nightside*, Charles L. Grant
	The Elementals, Michael McDowell
	The Exorcism: A Play, Don Taylor
1982	*Psycho II*, Robert Bloch
	The Nestling, Charles L. Grant
	Different Seasons, Stephen King
	Fevre Dream, George R. R. Martin
	Blackwater, Michael McDowell
	The Book of the Beast, Robert Stallman
1983	*The Ice Maiden*, Marc Behm
	Incarnate, Ramsey Campbell
	The Name of the Rose, Umberto Eco
	The Revenants, Geoffrey Farrington
	Flying to Nowhere, John Fuller
	The Ice Monkey and Other Stories, M. John Harrison
	A Cold Blue Light, Marvin Kaye and Parke Godwin
	Slimer, Harry Adam Knight (John Brosnan, Leroy Kettle)
	Mystery Walk, Robert R. McCammon
	Claw, Jay Ramsey (Ramsey Campbell)
	Dead White, Alan Ryan
	The Collected Stories of William Sansom
	Monkey Shines, Michael Stewart
	Phantom, Thomas Tessier
	Familiar Spirit, Lisa Tuttle
1983–87	*Nighthunter*, Robert Faulcon (Robert Holdstock)
1984	*The Voice of Our Shadow*, Jonathan Carroll
	The Businessman: A Tale of Terror, Thomas M. Disch
	Red Dreams, Dennis Etchison
	Catch Your Death, John Gordon
	Domain, James Herbert
	The Ghost Light, Fritz Leiber

LISTS OF RECOMMENDED READING

1984   *The Night Train*, Thomas F. Monteleone
         Things Beyond Midnight, William F. Nolan
         Cast a Cold Eye, Alan Ryan
         Vampire Junction, S. P. Somtow (Somtow Sucharitkul)
         A Manhattan Ghost Story, T. M. Wright
1985   *Death is A Lonely Business*, Ray Bradbury
         Obsession, Ramsey Campbell
         Son of the Endless Night, John Farris
         Darklings, Ray Garton
         The Tea Party, Charles L. Grant
         Moon, James Herbert
         Dark Gods, T. E. D. Klein
         The Fungus, Harry Adam Knight (John Brosnan, Leroy Kettle)
         Angelus!, Peter Tremayne
1986   *Homunculus*, James Blaylock
         The Cormorant, Stephen Gregory
         Witchwater Country, Garry Kilworth
         Dreams of Dark and Light, Tanith Lee
         Time Out of Mind, John R. Maxim
         The Vampire Lestat, Anne Rice
         The Unconquered Country, Geoff Ryman
         Green Eyes, Lucius Shepard
         The Light at the End, John Skipp and Craig Spector
1987   *Weaveworld*, Clive Barker
         The Hungry Moon, Ramsey Campbell
         Bones of the Moon, Jonathan Carroll
         Wildwood, John Farris
         Valley of Lights, Stephen Gallagher
         The Dark Descent, David G. Hartwell, ed.
         Dark Seeker, K. W. Jeter
         Mantis, K. W. Jeter
         Misery, Stephen King
         The Wyrm, Stephen Laws
         Slob, Rex Miller

1987	*Scars & Other Distinguishing Marks,* Richard Christian Matheson
	Finishing Touches, Thomas Tessier
	Why Not You and I?, Karl Edward Wagner
	The Power, Ian Watson
1988	*Selected Stories,* Charles Beaumont
	The Selected Stories of Robert Bloch
	The Influence, Ramsey Campbell
	Sleeping in Flame, Jonathan Carroll
	Ripper! (aka *Jack the Ripper*), Gardner Dozois and Susan Casper, eds.
	The Big Nowhere, James Elroy
	For Fear of the Night, Charles L. Grant
	Immortal Blood (aka *Those Who Hunt the Night*), Barbara Hambly
	Lavondyss, Robert Holdstock
	The Nightrunners, Joe R. Lansdale
	The Troupe, Gordon Linzner
	Blood and Water and Other Tales, Patrick McGrath
	The Magnificent Gallery, Thomas F. Monteleone
	The Penguin Complete Saki
	The Kill Riff, David J. Schow
	Silver Scream, David J. Schow, ed.
	White Chappell, Scarlet Tracings, Iain Sinclair
	The Empire of Fear, Brian Stableford
	Koko, Peter Straub
	Dark Winds, Graham Watkins
1989	*Webs,* Scott Baker
	The Great and Secret Show, Clive Barker
	The History of Luminous Motion, Scott Bradfield
	Ancient Images, Ramsey Campbell
	A Child Across the Sky, Jonathan Carroll
	Goat Dance, Douglas Clegg
	Sunglasses After Dark, Nancy A. Collins

LISTS OF RECOMMENDED READING

1989
: *Blood is Not Enough,* Ellen Datlow, ed.
Geek Love, Katherine Dunn
Down River, Stephen Gallagher
The Woodwitch, Stephen Gregory
In the Land of the Dead, K. W. Jeter
The Dark Half, Stephen King
By Bizarre Hands, Joe R. Lansdale
Songs of a Dead Dreamer, Thomas Ligotti
The Grotesque, Patrick McGrath
Toady (aka *The Horror Club*), Mark Morris
Batman: Arkham Asylum, Grant Morrison and Dave McKean
The Quincunx, Charles Palliser
Seeing Red, David J. Schow
Carrion Comfort, Dan Simmons
Mystery, Peter Straub
Tales of the Cthulhu Mythos, James Turner, ed.
Unthreatened by the Morning Light, Karl Edward Wagner
Horrorstory Volume Five, Karl Edward Wagner, ed.
Antique Dust, Robert Westall

1990
: *Sex and Other Acts of the Imagination,* Cliff Burns
Midnight Sun, Ramsey Campbell
The Brains of Rats, Michael Blumlein
Rune, Christopher Fowler
Rain, Stephen Gallagher
Adventureland, Stephen Harris
Creed, James Herbert
Sweet Heart, Peter James
Phantom, Susan Kay
The Frighteners, Stephen Laws
The Hope, James Lovegrove
Mary Reilly, Valerie Martin
Good Omens, Terry Pratchett and Neil Gaiman
The Shaft, David J. Schow
Moon Dance, S. P. Somtow (Somtow Sucharitkul)

1990
: *The Werewolves of London,* Brian Stableford
Houses Without Doors, Peter Straub
Rapture, Thomas Tessier
Horrorstory Volume Four, Karl Edward Wagner, ed.

1991
: *Alma Cogan,* Gordon Burn
Saint Peter's Wolf, Michael Cadnum
The Count of Eleven, Ramsey Campbell
Outside the Dog Museum, Jonathan Carroll
The M.D.: A Horror Story, Thomas M. Disch
The Boat House, Stephen Gallagher
The Fetch, Robert Holdstock
Twilight, Peter James
Dreamside, Graham Joyce
The Cipher, Kathe Koja
Batman: Captured by the Engines, Joe R. Lansdale
Grimscribe: His Life and Works, Thomas Ligotti
Darklands, Nicholas Royle, ed.
Summer of Night, Dan Simmons
Downriver, Iain Sinclair
The Bridge, John Skipp and Craig Spector
Ringu/Ring, Koji Suzuki
Secret Strangers, Thomas Tessier
Horrorstory Volume Three, Karl Edward Wagner, ed.
Dirty Weekend, Helen Zahavi

1992
: *Whispers in the Dark,* Jonathan Aycliffe
Meeting Evil, Thomas Berger
Dead Girls, Richard Calder
Ghostwright, Jonathan Carroll
MetaHorror, Dennis Etchison, ed.
Foundations of Fear, David G. Hartwell, ed.
Bedlam, Harry Adam Knight (John Brosnan, Leroy Kettle)
Marvel Masterworks Volume 23: Doctor Strange, Stan Lee and Steve Ditko
Sineater, Elizabeth Massie

1993
: *Alone With the Horrors,* Ramsey Campbell

LISTS OF RECOMMENDED READING

1993
The Long Lost, Ramsey Campbell
Shadowman, Dennis Etchison
Under the Crust, Terry Lamsley
Created By, Richard Christian Matheson
El club Dumas/The Dumas Club, Arturo Pérez-Reverte
Crybbe (aka *Curfew*), Phil Rickman
The Golden, Lucius Shepard
The Throat, Peter Straub
Demons and Shadows, Robert Westall
Random Acts of Senseless Violence, Jack Womack

1994
Brittle Innings, Michael Bishop
The Early Fears, Robert Bloch
What's Wrong With America, Scott Bradfield
From the Teeth of Angels, Jonathan Carroll
What a Carve Up, Jonathan Coe
The Priest, Thomas M. Disch
Spanky, Christopher Fowler
Shadows Fall, Simon R. Green
The Great Divorce, Valerie Martin
Hellboy: Seed of Destruction, Mike Mignola and
    John Byrne
Radon Daughters, Iain Sinclair
Shades of Darkness, Robert Westall

1995
Dan Leno and the Limehouse Golem, Peter Ackroyd
Father of Frankenstein, Christopher Bram
The One Safe Place, Ramsey Campbell
Burning Your Bridges, Angela Carter
Death Stalks the Night, Hugh B. Cave
The Blood Countess, Andrei Codrescu
California Gothic, Dennis Etchison
Psychoville, Christopher Fowler
The Vampyre/Lord of the Dead, Tom Holland
*Wicked: The Life and Times of the Wicked Witch
    of the West*, Gregory Maguire
The Prestige, Christopher Priest

1995	*The Memoirs of Elizabeth Frankenstein*, Theodore Roszak
1996	*Stiff Lips*, Anne Billson
	The House on Nazareth Hill (aka *Nazareth Hill*), Ramsey Campbell
	Brand New Cherry Flavor, Todd Grimson
	The Tooth Fairy, Graham Joyce
	The 37th Mandala, Marc Laidlaw
	Conference With the Dead, Terry Lamsley
	The Nightmare Factory, Thomas Ligotti
	The World on Blood, Jonathan Nasaw
	Fight Club, Chuck Palahniuk
	Ghosting, John Preston
	Celestial Dogs, Jay Russell
	The Pavilion of Frozen Women, S. P. Somtow
	The Hunger and Ecstasy of Vampires, Brian Stableford
	The Hellfire Club, Peter Straub
	The Pillow Friend, Lisa Tuttle
1996–2001	*Preacher*, Garth Ennis and Steve Dillon
1997	*The Church of Dead Girls*, Stephen Dobyns
	100 Fiendish Little Frightmares, Dziemianowicz, Weinberg, Greenberg, eds.
	Disturbia, Christopher Fowler
	Furnace, Muriel Gray
	Signs of Life, M. John Harrison
	Midnight Never Comes, Barbara and Christopher Roden, eds.
	The Matter of the Heart, Nicholas Royle
	Darker Angels, S. P. Somtow
	Best Ghost and Horror Stories, Bram Stoker; Dalby, Dziemianowicz and Joshi, eds.
	Fog Heart, Thomas Tessier
	Revelations (aka *Millennium*), Douglas E. Winter, ed.
1998	*Ghosts and Grisly Things*, Ramsey Campbell
	The Boss in the Wall: A Treatise on the House Devil, Avram Davidson

LISTS OF RECOMMENDED READING

1998   *The Savage Tales of Solomon Kane*, Robert E. Howard
Silk, Caitlín R. Kiernan
A Coven of Vampires: The Collected Vampire Stories of Brian Lumley, Brian Lumley
King Rat, China Miéville

1999   *A Closed Book*, Gilbert Adair
The Collected Strange Stories of Robert Aickman
Brotherly Love and Other Tales of Faith and Knowledge, David Case
The Night Wind Howls: Complete Supernatural Stories, Frederick Cowles
Satan Wants Me, Robert Irwin
White, Tim Lebbon
The Unburied, Charles Palliser
999 New Stories of Horror and Suspense, Al Sarrantonio, ed.
What You Make It, Michael Marshall Smith
Mr. X, Peter Straub

2000   *We've Been Waiting for You*, John Burke; Nicholas Royle, ed.
The Amazing Adventures of Kavalier and Clay, Michael Chabon
Taps and Sighs, Peter Crowther, ed.
Beluthahatchie and Other Stories, Andy Duncan
The Death Artist, Dennis Etchison
The Mammoth Book of Haunted House Stories, Peter Haining, ed.
Tales of Pain and Wonder, Caitlín R. Kiernan
Dark Matters, Terry Lamsley
High Cotton: Selected Stories of Joe R. Lansdale
As the Sun Goes Down, Tim Lebbon
Naming of Parts, Tim Lebbon
Dystopia, Richard Christian Matheson
Perdido Street Station, China Miéville
The Director's Cut, Nicholas Royle

LISTS OF RECOMMENDED READING

2000   *Magic Terror: Seven Tales*, Peter Straub
               City Fishing, Steve Rasnic Tem
2000–02   *The Selected Stories of Manly Wade Wellman*;
                 John Pelan, ed.
2000–2001 *Planetary*, Warren Ellis and John Cassaday
               The Deadman Collection, Neal Adams, Bob Haney,
                 Jack Miller, Arnold Drake, Robert Kanigher,
                 Dennis O'Neil, Carmine Infantino, and George Tuska
               From the Dust Returned: A Family Remembrance,
                 Ray Bradbury
               The Pact of the Fathers, Ramsey Campbell
               Meddling With Ghosts: Stories in the Tradition of
                 M. R. James, Ramsey Campbell, ed.
               The Wooden Sea, Jonathan Carroll
               The Alchemist's Apprentice, Jeremy Dronfield
               Talking in the Dark: Selected Stories, Dennis Etchison
               American Gods, Neil Gaiman
               Carter Beats the Devil, Glen David Gold
               Once . . . , James Herbert
               A Pleasing Terror: The Complete Supernatural Writings of
                 M. R. James
               The Black Gondolier and Other Stories, Fritz Leiber;
                 John Pelan, and Steve Savile, eds.
               Stranger Things Happen, Kelly Link
               The Whisperer and Other Voices, Brian Lumley
               The Scar, China Miéville
               Phantoms of Venice, David Sutton, ed.
               City of Saints and Madmen: The Book of Ambergris,
                 Jeff VanderMeer
2002   *Ancient Sorceries and Other Weird Stories*,
                 Algernon Blackwood
               The Darkest Part of the Woods, Ramsey Campbell
               The Deadly Space Between, Patricia Duncker
               Coraline, Neil Gaiman
               The Snowman's Children, Glen Hirshberg

LISTS OF RECOMMENDED READING

2002
The House on the Borderland and Other Novels, William Hope Hodgson
Great Tales of Terror, S. T. Joshi, ed.
The Facts of Life, Graham Joyce
From Weird and Distant Shores, Caitlín R. Kiernan
Smoke Ghost & Other Apparitions, Fritz Leiber; John Pelan, and Steve Savile, eds.
Beneath the Moors and Darker Places, Brian Lumley
The Straw Men, Michael Marshall (Smith)
Nightmare at 20,000 Feet, Richard Matheson
Black Gods and Scarlet Dreams, C. L. Moore
Lullaby, Chuck Palahniuk
Ghosts & Other Lovers, Lisa Tuttle
Gods in Darkness: The Complete Novels of Kane, Karl Edward Wagner

2003
Bradbury Stories: 100 of His Most Celebrated Tales, Ray Bradbury
Told by the Dead, Ramsey Campbell
The Dark: New Ghost Stories, Ellen Datlow, ed.
Kissing Carrion, Gemma Files
Full Dark House, Christopher Fowler
The Two Sams: Ghost Stories, Glen Hirshberg
The Collected Fiction of William Hope Hodgson: The Boats of the "Glen Carrig" and Other Nautical Adventures, William Hope Hodgson; Jeremy Lassen, ed.
The Rising, Brian Keene
Beneath the Ground, Joel Lane, ed.
Devil in the White City: Murder, Magic, and Madness at the Fair That Changed America, Erik Larson
White and Other Tales of Ruin, Tim Lebbon
Dark Universe, William F. Nolan
The Lamplighter, Anthony O'Neill
The Idol of the Flies and Other Stories, Jane Rice
The White Hands and Other Weird Tales, Mark Samuels
Lost Boy Lost Girl, Peter Straub

2003	*Midnight Sun: The Complete Stories of Kane,* Karl Edward Wagner
2004	*The Overnight,* Ramsey Campbell
	Nocturnes, John Connolly
	Elvisland, John Farris
	Out of His Mind, Stephen Gallagher
	Mortal Love, Elizabeth Hand
	The Collected Fiction of William Hope Hodgson: The House on the Borderland and Other Mysterious Places, William Hope Hodgson; Jeremy Lassen, ed.
	White Devils, Paul McAuley
	Acquainted With the Night, Barbara and Christopher Roden, eds.
	The Banquet of the Lords of Night & Other Stories, Liz Williams
2005	*Taverns of the Dead,* Kealan Patrick Burke, ed.
	Secret Stories, Ramsey Campbell
	Fine Cuts, Dennis Etchison
	The Collected Fiction of William Hope Hodgson: The Ghost Pirates and Other Revenants of the Seas, William Hope Hodgson; Jeremy Lassen, ed.
	The Limits of Enchantment, Graham Joyce
	The Lost District, Joel Lane
	Tales, H. P. Lovecraft; Peter Straub, ed.
	The Book of Renfield: A Gospel of Dracula, Tim Lucas
	Creepers, David Morrell
	Haunted, Chuck Palahniuk
	Zombie Jam, David J. Schow
	The Mysteries, Lisa Tuttle

SELECTED WEBLIOGRAPHY

Stephen Jones: www.herebedragons.co.uk/jones
Kim Newman: www.johnnyalucard.com

Stephen Baxter: www.cix.co.uk/~sjbradshaw/baxterium
Steve Bissette: www.hollywoodcomics.com/bissette.html
Doug Bradley: www.dougbradley.co.uk
Chaz Brenchley: www.chazbrenchley.co.uk
Poppy Z. Brite: www.poppyzbrite.com
Mark Chadbourn: www.markchadbourn.net
Simon Clark: www.bbr-online.com/nailed
Storm Constantine: www.gothland.wox.org/bast
Peter Crowther: www.pspublishing.co.uk
Ellen Datlow: www.datlow.com
David Stuart Davies: www.sherlock-holmes.com/featur2.htm
Terry Dowling: www.tabula-rasa.info/MirrorDanse/TerryDowling.html
David Drake: www.david-drake.com
Tananarive Due: www.tananarivedue.com
Andy Duncan: www.angelfire.com/al/andyduncan
Les Edwards: www.lesedwards.com
P. N. Elrod: www.vampwriter.com
John Farris: home.earthlink.net/~blackleatherrequired/home.html
Christopher Fowler: www.christopherfowler.co.uk
Sir Christopher Frayling: www.bbc.co.uk/radio4/factual/
   desertislanddiscs 20031101.shtml
Gary Gianni: www.garygianni.com
Christopher Golden: www.christophergolden.com
Ed Gorman: www.edgorman.com
Muriel Gray: www.realmofphoenix.com/fan_listings/murielgray.html
Simon R. Green: www.bluemoonrising.nl

SELECTED WEBLIOGRAPHY

Elizabeth Hand: www.elizabethhand.com
Rick Hautala: www.rickhautala.com
Glen Hirshberg: www.glenhirshberg.com
Nancy Holder: www.nancyholder.com/
Robert Irwin: www.spongobongo.com/no9963.htm
K. W. Jeter: www.oivas.com/kwj
Gwyneth Jones: homepage.ntlworld.com/gwynethann
Graham Joyce: www.grahamjoyce.net
Roz Kaveney: glamourousrags.dymphna.net
Caitlín R. Kiernan: www.caitlin-r-kiernan.com
Nancy Kilpatrick: www.sff.net/people/nancyk
Allen Koszowski: www.allenk.com
Jay Lake: www.jlake.com
Terry Lamsley: www.oozingbrain.com/lamsley/index.html
Joel Lane: www.pulp.net/fiction/biogs/lane-joel.html
Roberta Lannes: www.sff.net/people/RLannes
Tim Lebbon: www.timlebbon.net
Tanith Lee: www.daughterofthenight.com
D. F. Lewis: www.nemonymous.com
Thomas Ligotti: www.ligotti.net/nightmare
Kelly Link: www.kellylink.net
Jean-Marc Lofficier: www.lofficier.com
Tim Lucas: www.videowatchdog.com/home/home.html
Richard A. Lupoff: fanac.org/timebinders/lupoff.html
Ian R. MacLeod: www.ianrmacleod.freeserve.co.uk
Elizabeth Massie: www.elizabethmassie.com
Paul McAuley: www.omegacom.demon.co.uk
China Miéville: runagate-rampant.netfirms.com
David Morrell: www.davidmorrell.net
Yvonne Navarro: www.yvonnenavarro.com
Norman Partridge: www.nightshadebooks.com/spotlightpartridge.html
John Pelan: www.darksidepress.com/pelan.html
Tony Richards: www.richardsreality.com
Barbara and Christopher Roden: www.ash-tree.bc.ca/ashtreecurrent.html
Nicholas Royle: www.sinfield.org/nicholasroyle

SELECTED WEBLIOGRAPHY

Jay Russell: www.sff.net/people/JRussell
Darrell Schweitzer: www.sfwa.org/members/schweitzer
Michael Shea: www.michaelsheaauthor.com
Lucius Shepard: www.lucius-shepard.com
Robert Silverberg: www.majipoor.com
David J. Skal: www.monstershow.net
Michael Marshall Smith: www.michaelmarshallsmith.com
Michael Swanwick: www.michaelswanwick.com
Tony Timpone: www.fangoria.com
Jeff VanderMeer: www.jeffvandermeer.com
Stephen Volk: www.bfi.org.uk/videocat/more/ghostwatch/volk.html
Howard Waldrop: www.sff.net/people/Waldrop
Robert W. Weinberg: www.robertweinberg.net
Gahan Wilson: www.lowbrowartworld.com/gahan_wilson.html
Jack Womack: www.euro.net/mark-space/bioJackWomack.html
Chelsea Quinn Yarbro: www.mindspring.com/~ebowden/Yarbro/yarbro_homepage.htm

Clive Barker, The Books of Blood: www.clivebarker.com
Robert Bloch, The Opener of the Way: mgpfeff.home.sprynet.com/bloch.html
The Collected Stories of Elizabeth Bowen: www.usna.edu/EnglishDept/ilv/bowen.htm
Paul Bowles, Pages from Cold Point: www.lib.udel.edu/ud/spec/exhibits/bowles/index.htm
Ray Bradbury, Something Wicked This Way Comes: www.raybradbury.com
Poppy Z. Brite, Lost Souls: www.poppyzbrite.com
Charlotte Brontë, Jane Eyre: www.literature.org/authors/bronte-charlotte/jane-eyre
Jack Cady, The Off Season: www.nightshadebooks.com/spotlightcady.html
Ramsey Campbell, The Face That Must Die: www.ramseycampbell.com
Albert Camus, The Stranger: www.bookrags.com/notes/str
Angela Carter, The Bloody Chamber: www.kirjasto.sci.fi/acarter.htm
John Christopher, A Wrinkle in the Skin: www.emptyworld.info/author_john_christopher.html

SELECTED WEBLIOGRAPHY

Mark Z. Danielewski, House of Leaves: www.geocities.com/run_rom_run/houseofleaves.html
August Derleth, Sleep No More: waldeneast.fsnet.co.uk/adpcontents.htm
Charles Dickens, A Christmas Carol: www.stormfax.com/dickens.htm
Sir Arthur Conan Doyle, The Hound of the Baskervilles: www.online-literature.com/doyle/baskervilles
Bret Easton Ellis, American Psycho: www.geocities.com/Athens/Forum/8506
Jack Finney, The Body Snatchers: members.aol.com/leahj/finney.htm
Bruno Fischer, House of Flesh: www.stopyourekillingme.com/Bruno-Fischer.html
John Fowles, The Collector: www.fowlesbooks.com/index.htm
Alan Garner, The Weirdstone of Brisingamen: members.ozemail.com.au/~xenophon/index.html
Patricia Geary, Strange Toys: www.geary.com/Patricia_Geary_Science_Fiction_Writer
George Gissing, New Grub Street: www.gutenberg.org/etext/1709
Charles L. Grant, Tales From the Nightside: charlesgrant.novelhost.net
Thomas Harris, The Silence of the Lambs: www.randomhouse.com/features/thomasharris/home.html
Sadegh Hedayat, The Blind Owl: www.geocities.com/Paris/Tower/2943
Patricia Highsmith, The Talented Mr. Ripley: www.mysterynet.com/books/testimony/ripley.shtml
Susan Hill, The Woman in Black: www.susan-hill.com
William Hope Hodgson, The Boats of the "Glen Carrig": www.gutenberg.org/etext/10542
William Hope Hodgson, Carnacki the Ghost-Finder: www.gutenberg.org/etext/10832
Shirley Jackson, We Have Always Lived at the Castle: www.underthesun.cc/Classics/Jackson
Stephen King, Misery: www.stephenking.com/index_flash.php
Stephen King, Pet Sematary: www.stephenking.com/index_flash.php
Nigel Kneale, Year of the Sex Olympics: www.nigelkneale.cwc.net
Kathe Koja, Skin: www.kathekoja.com

SELECTED WEBLIOGRAPHY

Joe R. Lansdale, By Bizarre Hands: www.joerlansdale.com
Fritz Leiber, Our Lady of Darkness: www.lankhmar.demon.co.uk
Bob Leman, Feesters of the Lake: www.darksidepress.com/lemanfeesters.html
Gaston Leroux, Phantom of the Opera: www.literatureproject.com/phantom-opera
Ira Levin, Rosemary's Baby: www.intercoursewiththedead.com/levcrit.htm
Thomas Ligotti, Nightmare Factory: www.ligotti.net/nightmare
H. P. Lovecraft, The Case of Charles Dexter Ward: www.hplovecraft.com
Tim Lucas, Throat Sprockets: www.videowatchdog.com/home/home.html
Arthur Machen, Tales of Horror and the Supernatural: www.machensoc.demon.co.uk
Richard Matheson, A Stir of Echoes: home.earthlink.net/~sitman
Robert McCammon, They Thirst: www.robertmccammon.com
Cormac McCarthy, Outer Dark: www.cormacmccarthy.com
Ian McEwan, The Cement Garden: www.ianmcewan.com
Alan Moore and Eddie Campbell, From Hell: www.alanmoorefansite.com
George Orwell, Nineteen Eighty-Four: www.ucsolutions.com/nef/index2.htm
Mervyn Peake, Gormenghast: ladygroan.tripod.com
Count Jan Potocki, Manuscript Found in Saragossa: www.forteantimes.com/articles/140_potocki.shtml
Alexander Pushkin, The Queen of Spades: www.kirjasto.sci.fi/puskin.htm
Ruth Rendell, A Sight for Sore Eyes: www.inejacet.nl/RuthRendellenglish/start.html
Jeff Rice, The Night Stalker: www.geocities.com/laxaria/kolchak.html
Sax Rohmer, The Trail of Fu Manchu: www.njedge.net/~knapp/FuFrames.htm
Robert Silverberg, The Book of Skulls: www.majipoor.com
Dan Simmons, Carrion Comfort: www.dansimmons.com
Clark Ashton Smith, Lost Worlds: www.oceanstar.com/cas
Michael Marshall Smith, More Tomorrow & Other Stories: www.michaelmarshallsmith.com
Stephen Sondheim, Sweeney Todd: www.sondheim.com/shows/sweeney_todd
Pierre Souvestre and Marcel Allain, Fantomas: www.fantomas-lives.com
Theodore Sturgeon, Some of Your Blood: www.physics.emory.edu/~weeks/misc/sturgeon.html
Jim Thompson, The Killer Inside Me: www.kirjasto.sci.fi/jthompso.htm

SELECTED WEBLIOGRAPHY

Thomas Tryon, Harvest Home: www.canadiancontent.net/en/jd/
    go?Url=http://summertryon.tripod.com
Karl Edward Wagner, Darkness Weaves with Many Shades:
    www.dodgenet.com/~moonblossom/kane.htm
H. Russell Wakefield, They Return at Evening: www.litgothic.com/Authors/
    wakefield.html
Manly Wade Wellman, Who Fears the Devil?:
    www.manlywadewellman.com
H. G. Wells, War of the Worlds: www.calibra.eclipse.co.uk/eve/index.htm
Dennis Wheatley, The Devil Rides Out: www.denniswheatley.info
Oscar Wilde, The Picture of Dorian Gray: www.educanet.ch/home/bac3m3/
    autre/DorianGray.htm
Gene Wolfe, Peace: www.urth.org/~gac/Wolfe
John Wyndham, The Midwich Cuckoos: www.liv.ac.uk/~asawyer/wyndham.html

ABOUT THE EDITORS

STEPHEN JONES (b. 1953) shares his name with the protagonist of the H. P. Lovecraft-Hazel Heald collaboration "The Horror in the Museum"—a story set in London, just across the River Thames from where he was born. He is the winner of three World Fantasy Awards, three Horror Writers Association Bram Stoker Awards, and three International Horror Guild Awards, as well as being a sixteen-time recipient of the British Fantasy Award and a Hugo Award nominee. A former television producer/director and genre movie publicist and consultant (the first three *Hellraiser* movies, etc.), he has published more than eighty books, including *Horror: 100 Best Books* (with Kim Newman), *Creepshows: The Illustrated Stephen King Movie Guide, The Essential Monster Movie Guide, The Illustrated Vampire Movie Guide, James Herbert: By Horror Haunted, Clive Barker's A-Z of Horror, Clive Barker's Shadows in Eden, Clive Barker's The Nightbreed Chronicles, Hellraiser Chronicles, Now We Are Sick* (with Neil Gaiman), *Shadows Over Innsmouth, Weird Shadows Over Innsmouth, Dark Detectives, Dancing With the Dark, Dark of the Night, White of the Moon, Keep Out the Night, By Moonlight Only, Don't Turn Out the Light,* the *Dark Terrors* series (with David A. Sutton), and numerous titles in the popular *Mammoth* series, including sixteen volumes of the annual *Mammoth Book of Best New Horror* series. Jones also has compiled short-story collections by Karl Edward Wagner, R. Chetwynd-Hayes, Robert E. Howard, Clark Ashton Smith, Leigh Brackett, and Rudyard Kipling. He was a Guest of Honor at the 2002 World Fantasy Convention in Minneapolis, and at the 2004 World Horror Convention in Phoenix.

ABOUT THE EDITORS

KIM NEWMAN (b. 1959) was born in Brixton, London. A novelist, critic, and broadcaster, he has worked extensively in the theater, radio, and television. His novels include *The Night Mayor, Bad Dreams, Jago, Anno Dracula, The Quorum, The Bloody Red Baron, Back in the U.S.A.* (with Eugene Byrne), *Dracula Cha Cha Cha* (aka *Judgment of Tears: Anno Dracula 1959*), *Life's Lottery, Doctor Who: Time and Relative,* and *An English Ghost Story*. His short stories are collected in *The Original Dr. Shade and Other Stories, Famous Monsters, Seven Stars, Unforgivable Stories, Where the Bodies Are Buried, Dead Travel Fast,* and *The Man From the Diogenes Club*. Under the name "Jack Yeovil" he has also written a number of titles in the *Warhammer* and *Dark Future* series from Games Workshop, plus the original novel *Orgy of the Blood Parasites*. A winner of the Bram Stoker Award, the British Science Fiction Award, the British Fantasy Award, the Children of the Night Award, the Fiction Award of the Lord Ruthven Assembly, and two International Horror Guild Awards, his non-fiction books include *Ghastly Beyond Belief: The Science Fiction and Fantasy Book of Quotations* (with Neil Gaiman), *Horror: 100 Best Books* (with Stephen Jones), *Nightmare Movies: A Critical History of the Horror Film Since 1968, Wild West Movies, The BFI Companion to Horror, Millennium Movies, BFI Film Classics: Cat People,* and *TV Classics: Doctor Who*. With Paul McAuley he edited the anthology *In Dreams,* and he has scripted television and radio documentaries. He is a consulting editor at *Empire* and *Sight & Sound* magazines. Newman's story "Week Woman" was made as an episode of the Canadian TV series *The Hunger* in 1999, and he wrote and directed the short-short film *Missing Girl* in 2001. He was a Guest of Honor at the 2006 World Horror Convention in San Francisco.

INDEX TO THE BOOKS, AUTHORS, AND CONTRIBUTORS

T HE TITLES OF the 100 books featured in this volume are italicized; the authors and editors are indicated by a bold page number, and contributors' notes are shown as an italicized page number.

Allain, Marcel, 50–54
American Psycho, 354–57
Asquith, Lady Cynthia, 149–52
Atkins, Peter, 189–93
Barker, Clive, 306–10
Baxter, Stephen, 231–34
Beaumont, Charles, 161–65
Billson, Anne, 141–45
Birkin, Sir Charles, 397–400
Bischoff, David, 136–140
Bissette, Stephen R., 349–54
Blackburn, John, 173–77
Blind Owl, The, 166–68
Bloch, Robert, 108–12
Blood Sport, 243–45
Bloody Chamber and Other Stories, The, 269–73
Blumlein, Michael, 371–73
Boats of the "Glen Carrig," The, 43–46
Body Snatchers, The, 153–56
Book of Skulls, The, 231–34
Bounds, Sydney J., 64–68
Bowen, Elizabeth, 278–81
Bowles, Paul, 224–27
Bradley, Doug, 14–19
Bradbury, Ray, 200–203
Brenchley, Chaz, 69–73

Brite, Poppy Z., 294–97, 358–61
Broecker, Randy, 121–25
Brontë, Charlotte, 14–19
Burke, John, 286–290
By Bizarre Hands: Stories by Joe R. Lansdale, 338–341
Cady, Jack, 382–84
Campbell, Eddie, 349–53
Campbell, Ramsey, 294–96
Camus, Albert, 86–89
Cannon, Peter H., 342–45
Carnacki the Ghost-Finder, 117–20
Carrion Comfort, 345–48
Carter, Angela, 269–73
Case Against Satan, The, 197–99
Case of Charles Dexter Ward, The, 55–59
Cement Garden, The, 260–63
Chadbourn, Mark, 334–37
Christmas Carol, A, 9–13
Christopher, John, 212–14
Clark, Simon, 212–15
Clive Barker's Books of Blood Volumes One, Two, and Three, 306–9
Collected Stories of Elizabeth Bowen, The, 278–81
Collector, The, 204–7

INDEX

Collier, John, 141–44
Collins, Nancy A., 145–48
Constantine, Storm, 95–99
Course of the Heart, The, 362–65
Creep, Shadow!, 64–67
Crowther, Peter, 200–204
Danielewski, Mark Z., 401–405
Dark Descent, The, 321–24
Dark Forces: New Stories of Suspense and Supernatural Horror, 282–85
Darker Than You Think, 121–24
Darkness Weaves Many Shades, 264–68
Datlow, Ellen, 219–23
Davies, David Stuart, 298–301
Derleth, August, 90–93
Devil Rides Out, The, 73–76
Di Filippo, Paul, 371–74
Dickens, Charles, 9–13
Dowling, Terry, 185–89
Doyle, Sir Arthur Conan, 39–42
Drake, David, 253–57
Due, Tananarive, 378–82
Duncan, Andy, 153–57
Dziemianowicz, Stefan, 99–103
Edge of Running Water, The, 82–85
Edwards, Les, 34–39
Ellis, Bret Easton, 354–57
Elrod, P. N., 239–42
Face That Must Die, The, 294–96
Fancies and Goodnights, 141–44
Fantômas, 50–54
Fantôme de L'Opéra, Le, 47–49
Farris, John, 228–31
Feesters in the Lake & Other Stories, 406–9
Finishing Touches, 314–17
Finney, Jack, 153–56
Fischer, Bruno, 136–39
Fletcher, Jo, 264–69

Flicker, 366–70
Fowler, Christopher, 113–17
Fowles, John, 204–7
Fraser, Phyllis, 104–7
Frayling, Sir Christopher, 269–73
From Hell, 349–53
Garner, Alan, 181–84
Geary, Patricia, 317–20
Gianni, Gary, 117–21
Gissing, George, 24–28
Golden, Christopher, 282–86
Gordon, John, 157–60
Gorman, Ed, 178–81
Gormenghast, 113–16
Grant, Charles L., 286–89
Gray, Muriel, 181–84
Great Tales of Terror and the Supernatural, 104–7
Green, Simon R., 382–85
Grotesque, The, 342–44
Hand, Elizabeth, 9–14
Harris, Thomas, 329–32
Harrison, M. John, 362–66
Hartwell, David G., 321–24
Harvest Home, 235–37
Haunted Omnibus, The, 78–81
Haunting Beauty, A, 397–400
Hautala, Rick, 43–46
Hedayat, Sadegh, 166–68
Higham, Charles, 185–88
Highsmith, Patricia, 157–60
Hill, Susan, 298–300
Hirshberg, Glen, 208–11
Hodge, Brian, 358–62
Hodgson, William Hope, 43–46, 117–20
Holder, Nancy, 215–19
Hound of the Baskervilles, The, 39–42
House of Flesh, 136–39
House of Leaves, 401–5

Hunger and Other Stories, The, 161–65
Irwin, Robert, 166–68
Jackson, Shirley, 193–95
Jane Eyre, 14–18
Jeter, K. W., 24–29
Jones, Gwyneth, 104–8
Jones, Robert F., 243–45
Joshi, S. T., 385–89
Joyce, Graham, 325–28
Jumbee and Other Uncanny Tales, 99–102
Kaveney, Roz, 250–53
Kiernan, Caitlín R., 375–78
Killer Inside Me, The, 145–48
Kilpatrick, Nancy, 310–14
King, Stephen, 301–5, 325–28
Kneale, Nigel, 253–56
Koja, Kathe, 375–77
Koszowski, Allen, 321–24
Laidlaw, Marc, 257–60
Laing, Alexander, 78–81
Lake, Jay, 20–23
Lamsley, Terry, 224–28
Lane, Joel, 108–12
Lansdale, Joe R., 338–41
Lannes, Roberta, 389–93
Lebbon, Tim, 411–14
Lee, Tanith, 125–30
Leiber, Fritz, 257–60
Leman, Bob, 406–9
Leroux, Gaston, 47–49
L'Étranger, 86–89
Levin, Ira, 215–18
Lewis, D. F., 278–81
Ligotti, Thomas, 274–78, 385–88
Link, Kelly, 317–21
Lofficier, Jean-Marc, 47–50
Lofficier, Randy, 47–50
Lost Souls, 358–61
Lost Worlds, 95–98
Lovecraft, H. P., 55–59
Lucas, Tim, 50–54, 378–81
Lupoff, Richard A., 406–10
Machen, Arthur, 125–29
MacLeod, Ian, 204–7
Manuscript Found in Sargossa, The, 20–23
Marlowe, Derek, 246–49
Massie, Elizabeth, 235–38
Matheson, Richard, 178–80
McAuley, Paul, 260–64
McCammon, Robert R., 290–93
McCarthy, Cormac, 228–30
McCauley, Kirby, 282–85
McEwan, Ian, 260–63
McGillivray, David, 354–58
McGrath, Patrick, 342–44
Merritt, A., 64–67
Midwich Cuckoos, The, 169–72
Miéville, China, 362–6
Misery, 325–28
Moore, Alan, 349–53
More Tomorrow & Other Stories, 411–14
Morrell, David, 345–49
Morris, Mark, 169–73
Navarro, Yvonne, 290–93
New Grub Street, 24–28
Night Stalker, The, 239–42
Nightmare Factory, The, 385–88
Nightshade, 246–49
Nineteen Eighty-Four, 130–34
Off Season, A Victorian Sequel, The, 382–84
Opener of the Way, The, 108–12
Orwell, George, 130–34
Our Lady of Darkness, 257–60
Outer Dark, 228–30
Pages from Cold Point, 224–27
Partridge, Norman, 166–68

INDEX

Peace, 250–52
Peake, Mervyn, 113–16
Pelan, John, 397–401
Perfume: The Story of a Murderer, 310–14
Pet Sematary, 301–5
Phantom of the Opera, The, 47–49
Picture of Dorian Gray, The, 29–33
Pikovaia Dama, 5–9
Playboy *Book of Horror and the Supernatural, The*, 219–22
Potocki, Jan, Count, 20–22
Prime Evil, 334–37
Pushkin, Aleksandr, 5–9
Queen of Spades, 5–9
Rekopiz Znaleziony w Saragossi, 20–22
Rendell, Ruth, 389–92
Reprisal, 393–96
Revenger's Tragedy, The, 1–4
Rice, Jeff, 239–42
Richards, Tony, 39–43
Robinson, Frank M., 329–33
Roden, Barbara, 60–64
Roden, Christopher, 60–64
Rohmer, Sax, 69–72
Rosemary's Baby, 215–18
Roszak, Theodore, 366–70
Royle, Nicholas, 246–50
Russell, Jay, 338–41
Russell, Ray, 197–99
Scent of New-Mown Hay, A, 173–77
Schweitzer, Darrell, 197–200
Shea, Michael, 393–97
Sheehan, Bill, 314–17
Shepard, Lucius, 130–35
Sight for Sore Eyes, A, 389–92
Silence of the Lambs, The, 329–32
Silverberg, Robert, 1–5, 231–34
Simmons, Dan, 345–48

Simon, Adam, 366–70
Skal, David J., 29–34
Skin, 375–77
Sleep No More: Twenty Masterpeices of Horror for the Connoisseur, 90–93
Sloane, William, 82–85
Smith, Clark Ashton, 95–98
Smith, Michael Marshall, 301–5, 411–14
Smith, Mitchell, 393–96
Some of Your Blood, 189–92
Something Wicked This Way Comes, 200–203
Sondheim, Stephen, 274–77
Souvestre, Pierre, 50–54
Staig, Laurence, 149–53
Stir of Echoes, A, 178–80
Strange Toys, 317–20
Stranger, The, 86–89
Sturgeon, Theodore, 189–92
Süskind, Patrick, 310–13
Sutton, David A., 90–94
Swanwick, Michael, 243–46
Sweeney Todd, 274–77
Talented Mr. Ripley, The, 157–60
Tales from the Nightside, 286–89
Tales of Horror and the Supernatural, 125–29
Tales of Terror, 185–88
Tessier, Thomas, 314–17
They Return at Evening, 60–63
They Thirst, 290–93
Third Ghost Book, The, 149–52
Thompson, Jim, 145–48
Throat Sprockets: A Novel of Erotic Obsession, 378–81
Timpone, Anthony, 306–10
Tourneur, Cyril, 1–4
Trail of Fu Manchu, The, 69–72

Tryon, Thomas, 235–38
VanderMeer, Jeff, 401–6
Volk, Stephen, 73–77
Wagner, Karl Edward, 264–68
Wakefield, H. R., 60–64
Waldrop, Howard, 173–77
War of the Worlds, The, 34–38
We Have Always Lived in the Castle, 193–95
Weinberg, Robert, 82–86
Weirdstone of Brinsingamen, The, 181–84
Wellman, Manly Wade, 208–11
Wells, H. G., 34–39
Wheatley, Dennis, 73–76
Wheeler, Hugh, 274–77
Whitehead, Henry S., 99–102
Who Fears the Devil?, 208–11
Wicking, Christopher, 55–59
Wilde, Oscar, 29–33
Williamson, Jack, 121–124
Wilson, Gahan, 78–82
Winter, Douglas, 334–37
Wise, Herbert A., 104–7
Wolfe, Gene, 250–52
Womack, Jack, 193–96
Woman in Black, The, 298–300
Wright, T. M., 86–90
Wrinkle in the Skin, A, 212–14
Wyndham, John, 169–72
X, Y, 371–73
Yarbro, Chelsea Quinn, 5–9
Year of the Sex Olympics: 3 TV Plays, The, 253–57

ACKNOWLEDGMENTS

OUR THANKS TO Peter Straub, Nate Knaebel, Claiborne Hancock, Dorothy Lumley, Stefan R. Dziemianowicz, Mike Willmoth, Ellen Datlow, Hank Wagner, Paul McAuley, John Pelan, Sue and Del Howison, Lucy Ramsey, Mark Kermode, Barbara and Christopher Roden, Gill Plummer, Mandy Slater, Sara Broecker, Gordon Van Gelder, Tina Rath, and Philip Harbottle for their help and support. Unlike the first volume, most of this book was put together using the Internet (which didn't exist back in 1988!). However, among the reference works most consulted were *Who's Who in Horror and Fantasy Fiction* by Mike Ashley, *The Penguin Encyclopedia of Horror and the Supernatural* edited by Jack Sullivan and *Locus* edited by Charles N. Brown. Once again, we'd also like to thank all our contributors for their hard work and enthusiasm, acknowledge those we approached who turned us down with a polite response, and trust that those who couldn't even be bothered to reply are now feeling suitably chastised—especially those writers whose work is featured in this book.

Foreword copyright © Peter Straub 2005; *The Revenger's Tragedy*/Tourneur copyright © AGBERG, Ltd. 2005; *Pikovaia Dama/The Queen of Spades*/Pushkin copyright © Chelsea Quinn Yarbro 2005; *A Christmas Carol*/Dickens copyright © Elizabeth Hand 2005; *Jane Eyre*/Brontë copyright © Doug Bradley 2005; *Rekopiz Znaleziony w Sargossie/The Manuscript Found in Sargossa*/Potocki copyright © Joseph E. Lake, Jr. 2005; *New Grub Street*/Gissing copyright © K. W. Jeter 2005; *The Picture of Dorian Gray*/Wilde copyright © David J. Skal 2005; *The War of the Worlds*/Wells copyright © Les Edwards 2005; *The Hound of the Baskervilles*/Doyle copyright © A. G. Richards 2005; *The Boats of the "Glen Carrig"*/Hodgson copyright © Rick

ACKNOWLEDGMENTS

Hautala 2005; *Le Fantôme de L'Opéra/The Phantom of the Opera*/Leroux copyright © Jean-Marc Lofficier and Randy Lofficier 2005; *Fantômas*/Souvestre-Allain copyright © Tim Lucas 2005; *The Case of Charles Dexter Ward*/Lovecraft copyright © Christopher Wicking 2005; *They Return at Evening*/Wakefield copyright © Barbara Roden and Christopher Roden 2005; *Creep, Shadow!*/Merritt copyright © Sydney J. Bounds 2005; *The Trail of Fu Manchu*/Rohmer copyright © Chaz Brenchley 2005; *The Devil Rides Out*/Wheatley copyright © Stephen Volk 2005; *The Haunted Omnibus*/Laing copyright © Gahan Wilson 2005; *The Edge of Running Water*/Sloane copyright © Robert Weinberg 2005; *L'Étranger/The Stranger*/Camus copyright © T. M. Wright 2005; *Sleep No More: Twenty Masterpieces of Horror for the Connoisseur*/Derleth copyright © David A. Sutton 2005; *Lost Worlds*/Smith copyright © Storm Constantine 2005; *Jumbee and Other Uncanny Tales*/Whitehead copyright © Stefan Dziemianowicz 2005; *Great Tales of Terror and the Supernatural*/Wise-Fraser copyright © Gwyneth Jones 2005; *The Opener of the Way*/Bloch copyright © Joel Lane 2005; *Gormenghast*/Peake copyright © Christopher Fowler 2005; *Carnacki the Ghost-Finder*/Hodgson copyright © Gary Gianni 2005; *Darker Than You Think*/Williamson copyright © Randy Broecker 2005; *Tales of Horror and the Supernatural*/Machen copyright © Tanith Lee 2005; *Nineteen Eighty-Four*/Orwell copyright © Lucius Shepard 2005; *House of Flesh*/Fischer copyright © David Bischoff 2005; *Fancies and Goodnights*/Collier copyright © Anne Billson 2005; *The Killer Inside Me*/Thompson copyright © Nancy A. Collins 2005; *The Third Ghost Book*/Asquith copyright © Laurence Staig 2005; *The Body Snatchers*/Finney copyright © Andy Duncan 2005; *The Talented Mr. Ripley*/Highsmith copyright © John Gordon 2005; *The Hunger and Other Stories*/Beaumont copyright © Norman Partridge 2005; *The Blind Owl*/Hedayat copyright © Robert Irwin 2005; *The Midwich Cuckoos*/Wyndham copyright © Mark Morris 2005; *A Scent of New-Mown Hay*/Blackburn copyright © Howard Waldrop 2005; *A Stir of Echoes*/Matheson copyright © Ed Gorman 2005; *The Weirdstone of Brinsingamen*/Garner copyright © Muriel Gray 2005; *Tales of Terror*/Higham copyright © Terry Dowling 2005;

ACKNOWLEDGMENTS

Some of Your Blood/Sturgeon copyright © Peter Atkins 2005; *We Have Always Lived in the Castle*/Jackson copyright © Jack Womack 2005; *The Case Against Satan*/Russell copyright © Darrell Schweitzer 2005; *Something Wicked This Way Comes*/Bradbury copyright © Peter Crowther 2005; *The Collector*/Fowles copyright © Ian MacLeod 2005; *Who Fears the Devil?*/Wellman copyright © Glen Hirshberg 2005; *A Wrinkle in the Skin*/Christopher copyright © Simon Clark 2005; *Rosemary's Baby*/Levin copyright © Nancy Holder 2005; *The Playboy Book of Horror and the Supernatural*/Playboy copyright © Ellen Datlow 2005; *Pages from Cold Point*/Bowles copyright © Terry Lamsley 2005; *Outer Dark*/McCarthy copyright © John Farris 2005; *The Book of Skulls*/Silverberg copyright © Stephen Baxter 2005; *Harvest Home*/Tryon copyright © Elizabeth Massie 2005; *The Night Stalker*/Rice copyright © P. N. Elrod 2005; *Blood Sport*/Jones copyright © Michael Swanwick 2005; *Nightshade*/Marlowe copyright © Nicholas Royle 2005; *Peace*/Wolfe copyright © Roz Kaveney 2005; *The Year of the Sex Olympics: 3 TV Plays*/Kneale copyright © David Drake 2005; *Our Lady of Darkness*/Leiber copyright © Marc Laidlaw 2005; *The Cement Garden*/McEwan copyright © Paul McAuley 2005; *Darkness Weaves With Many Shades*/Wagner copyright © Jo Fletcher 2005; *The Bloody Chamber and other Stories*/Carter copyright © Christopher Frayling 2005; *Sweeney Todd*/Sondheim-Wheeler copyright © Thomas Ligotti 2005; *The Collected Stories of Elizabeth Bowen*/Bowen copyright © D. F. Lewis 2005; *Dark Forces: New Stories of Suspense and Supernatural Horror*/McCauley copyright © Christopher Golden 2005; *Tales from the Nightside*/Grant copyright © John Burke 2005; *Thery Thirst*/McCammon copyright © Yvonne Navarro 2005; *The Face That Must Die*/Campbell copyright © Poppy Z. Brite 2005; *The Woman in Black*/Hill copyright © David Stuart Davies 2005; *Pet Semetary*/King copyright © Michael Marshall Smith 2005; *Clive Barker's Books of Blood Volumes One, Two, and Three*/Barker copyright © Anthony Timpone 2005; *Perfume: The Story of a Murderer*/Süskind copyright © Nancy Kilpatrick 2005; *Finishing Touches*/Tessier copyright © Bill Sheehan 2005; *Strange Toys*/Geary copyright © Kelly Link 2005; *The Dark Descent*/Hartwell copyright © Allen Koszowski 2005; *Misery*/

ACKNOWLEDGMENTS

King copyright © Graham Joyce 2005; *The Silence of the Lambs*/Harris copyright © Frank M. Robinson 2005; *Prime Evil*/Winter copyright © Mark Chadbourn 2005; *By Bizarre Hands: Stories by Joe R. Lansdale*/Lansdale copyright © Jay Russell 2005; *The Grotesque*/McGrath copyright © Peter H. Cannon 2005; *Carrion Comfort*/Simmons copyright © David Morrell 2005; *From Hell*/Moore-Campbell copyright © Stephen R. Bissette 2005; *American Psycho*/Ellis copyright © David McGillivray 2005; *Lost Souls*/Brite copyright © Brian Hodge 2005; *The Course of the Heart*/Harrison copyright © China Miéville 2005; *Flicker*/Roszak copyright © Adam Simon 2005; *X, Y*/Blumlein copyright © Paul Di Filippo 2005; *Skin*/Koja copyright © Caitlín R. Kiernan 2005; *Throat Sprockets: A Novel of Erotic Obsession*/Lucas copyright © Tananarive Due 2005; *The Off Season: A Victorian Sequel*/Cady copyright © Simon R. Green 2005; *The Nightmare Factory*/Ligotti copyright © S. T. Joshi 2005; *A Sight for Sore Eyes*/Rendell copyright © Roberta Lannes 2005; *Reprisal*/Smith copyright © Michael Shea 2005; *A Haunting Beauty*/Birkin copyright © John Pelan 2005; *House of Leaves*/Danielewski copyright © Jeff VanderMeer 2005; *Feesters in the Lake & Other Stories*/Leman copyright © Richard A. Lupoff 2005; *More Tomorrow & Other Stories*/Smith copyright © Tim Lebbon 2005. All other material copyright © Stephen Jones and Kim Newman 2005.